Storms of

Retribution

Talon Series

Book 8

His coat of arms

Storms of Retribution

by

James Boschert

www.penmorepress.com

Storms of Retribution by James Boschert

ISBN-13: 978-1-946409-70-6(Paperback)
ISBN :13: 978-1-946409-71-3 (e-book)

BISAC Subject Headings:
FIC014000 FICTION / Historical
FIC032000 FICTION / War & Military
FIC031020FICTION / Thrillers / Historical

Senior Editor: Chris Wozney
Editing: Danielle Boschert
The Book Cover Whisperer: Christine Horner : *ProfessionalBookCoverDesign.com*

Address all correspondence to:

Penmore Press LLC
920 N Javelina Pl
Tucson AZ 85748
USA

Dedication

It was my soul mate, Danielle, who reminded me of a
dear friend who left us long before his time.
This book is dedicated to

Buddy Height

Though wounded in body and mind
he treated all men with courtesy and kindness

Acknowledgements

My sincere thanks to Danielle Boschert, Christine Horner, Midori and Chris Wozny for their efforts and help with this manuscript.

And to my sources:

Dungeon Fire and Sword by John J. Robinson
Deus Lo Volte by Evan S. Connel
The Crusades Through Arab Eyes by Amin Maaloof
A Short History of Byzantium by John Norwich
Civilization in The Middle Ages byNorman Cantor
Byzantium by Judith Herrin
The Assassin Legends by Farhad Daftary
Castles of the Assassins by Peter Willey
Who's Who in the Middle Ages by John Fines
The Dream of The Poem by Peter Cole

Wikipedia
Google

Names of Characters:
Storms of Retribution

Talon's Family and Followers
Talon de Gilles
Rav'an—Wife of Talon
Reza—Lifetime companion to Talon and family
Max Bauersdorf—onetime Sergeant in Templars; companion
Rostam de Gilles—Son of Talon and Rav'an
Jannat—Wife of Reza
Theodora—Physician from Constantinople
Damian—Son of Theodora
Georgios—Agent Shipping

Talon's Men
Yosef—Long time Persian companion
Dar'an—Long time companion and Assassin
Junayd—Talon's man, Assassin
Khuzaymah—Talon's man, Assassin
Maymun—Talon's man, Assassin
Nasuh—Talon's man, Assassin
Palladius—Sergeant of the Guards
Psellos—Greek Priest
Dimitri—Spymaster in Famagusta
Boethius Eirenikos—Merchant in Cyprus (Spy)
Irene—Young daughter of Boethius
Henry—Captain of Falcon
Guy—Captain of ship
Brant—Saxon Warrior
Dewi—Welsh Archer
Caradog—Welsh Archer

Arab Forces
Salah Ed Din—Leader of Arab army
Usama ibn Munquid—Brother of Salah Ed Din
Al-Malik al-Adil Sayf ad-Din Abu-Bakr Ahmed ibn Najm ad-Din Ayyub—Brother of Salah Ed Din.

Najm ad-Din Ayyub—Father of Al Malik
Al-Aziz Uthman (Egypt)
Al-Afdal (Syria)
Al-Adil I—Younger Brother of Salah Ed Din
General Muzaffar ad Din-Gökburi

Arab Pirates
Ibn al-Bannā Makhid—Leader of corsairs, cousin to Sultans Al-Adil and Salah Ed Din
Abul-Zinad—Makhid's cousin

Rashid Ed Din—Master Assassin in Lebanon, known as the School Teacher

Kingdom of Jerusalem
Baldwin IV—King of Jerusalem. Leper (Died 1185)
Baldwin V—Nephew of Baldwin VI (Died 1186)
Sibylla—Sister to King Baldwin IV
Guy de Lusignan—Husband to Sibylla (King in 1187)
Raymond de Tripoli—Count of Tripoli
Odo de St Armand—Grand Master Templars 1171-1180
Arnold de Torroja—Grand Master Templars 1181-84
Gerard de Rideford—Marshal of Jerusalem,
        Next Grand Master in 1185-1187
Roger de Moulins—Master of the Hospitaliers
Gerard Jobert—Master of the Hospitaliers 1172-77
Balian of Ibelin—Lord, and friend of Raymond de Tripoli
Count Conrad de Montferrat—Defender of Tyre
Reginald Grenier—Lord of Sidon, married to Agnes of Courtenay (third husband)
Joscius (also Josce or Josias)—Archbishop of Tyre
Reynald of Châtillon—Pirate and marauder who caused the battle of Hattin
Sir Guy de Veres—Talon's mentor, killed in the battle for Jacob's Ford
Sir Matthew d'Aix—Knight to Tripoli
Brother Martin—Monk in Acre who saved Talon's family

Names Byzantium
Emperor Isaac Angelos

Manuel I Komnenos—3rd Komnenos Emperor of Byzantium
Andronikos Komnenos—Murdered Emperor
Theodore Kastamonites—Uncle to Angelos
Porphyrogennetos—One born to the purple
Pantoleon/Exazenos—Former Executioner

Family Kalothesos:—Family Name
Damianus— Senator executed by Andronikos
Alexios—Son of Damianus and brother to Theodora

Palace of Emperor Komnenos
Isaac Komnenos—Brother to Manuel I, King of Cyprus
Tamura—Chief Concubine for Isaac
Martina—Slavegirl to Tamura
Siranos—Eunuch to Tamura
Diocles—Chief Minister and advisor
Julian—Village elder
John—Village leader
Zenos—Gatherer of Information
Himerius—Greek agent in Beirut
Aeneas Sanna—Palace Secretary
Aquila—Bodyguard for Aeneas
Macrobius—Bodyguard for Aeneas
Marcianus—Captain of the ship that brings Aeneas to Cyprus

Greetings
As-Salaam-Alaikum, the Arabic greeting meaning "Peace be unto you" was the standard salutation among members of the Nation of Islam. The greeting was routinely deployed whenever and wherever Muslims gathered and interacted, whether socially or within worship and other contexts. *Wa-Alaikum-Salaam*, meaning "And unto you peace," was the standard response.

Insha'Allah—"As God wills" or "If God wills"

Map of The Middle East and Cyprus - 12th Century.

Prelude

The King is Dead. Long Live the King.

How comes the Day o'ercast? The Flaming Sun
Darkn'd at Noon, as if his Course were run?
He never rose more proud, more glad, more gay,
Ne'er courted Daphne with a brighter Ray!
And now in Clouds he wraps his Head,
As if not Daphne, but himself were dead!
                                        —Anne Killigrew

It was towards the end of summer, August of the Year of Our Lord 1186, when in the late hours of the night the young King of Jerusalem, Baldwin V of Montferrat, also known as *Baudouinet,* died. Sickly since birth, he had been King for only three years. He was just a boy of eleven when his time came, in the austere, candle-lit chamber within the darkened Templar citadel that dominated the western side of the city of Acre.

Gathered around his bed were not only his two physicians and the priests but most of his immediate family, as well as others who had a keen interest in the future of the Kingdom of Jerusalem. Raymond, the Count of Tripoli and Regent of the Kingdom—up until this point—grimaced in disgust. He stood with his back to the narrow window, firmly shuttered to keep out the clean night air, and regarded the people clustered about the deathbed.

He had wanted to bring his own physician, a man infinitely more skilled than the two Leeches currently leaning over the bed. But his man came from Egypt, and the shrill objections of the boy's mother and the priests had put a stop to that. He glanced at the men who called themselves physicians. Filthy hands, dirt ingrained under their fingernails, their clothes stiff with grime and other people's blood. They had probably hastened the boy's death with their willful ignorance.

Arrayed around the walls of the stark chamber were several Knights of the Temple: dark, bearded, silent guardians clad in chain mail with black crosses sewn onto their surcoats. Some wore their white cloaks despite the stifling warmth of the room, which rendered them ghost-like in the gloom. The Count held a kerchief over his nose. The rank smell of unwashed bodies (the Templars never bathed) in the stuffy room already thick with women's perfume and incense gave him a headache.

The boy's mother, Princess Sibylla, and his aunt the Countess Isabella were in attendance, surrounded by their ladies in waiting and important nobles of the kingdom, present to witness the somber event. The weak draft seeping in through the shuttered windows caused the candle flames to sway and to cast ghostly shadows that swept across the grim, bearded faces of the men and the pale faces of the women in the further reaches of the chamber. The light gleamed on chain mail half covered by dark cloaks and hoods; it glittered on the gold and jewels around slim female necks, and produced a sheen on expensive silk dresses.

The gleam of candlelight in the watchful men's eyes as they observed the activity around the bed reminded Raymond of wolves waiting in the shadows. But who was their prey, now that their young King Baldwin V, nephew of King Baldwin IV, who had been known as the Leper King, had passed away?

William of Montferrat, the boy's grandfather, and Lord Joscelin of Edessa were also present, kneeling with their hands clasped in prayer and their bearded faces tilted heavenwards. The Patriarch, Eraclius of Caesarea, overladen with rich robes of the church, had administered the last rights. He now knelt as near to the two nobles and as far away from Raymond as possible in the crowded room. He and his attendant priests were now chanting prayers for the departed.

Something brushed by Raymond's head, and as he jerked away he realized it had been a bat. For a brief, absurd moment he wondered if the soul of the boy was within the creature and trying to escape the confines of the death chamber. He shook his head and crossed himself. Raymond was not deeply religious, but he was as superstitious as the next man, and wondered cynically what the Bishop might think of that!

Standing nearby was another man whom Raymond detested. Lord Guy de Lusignan, a mere knight from Poitou, now the husband of Sibylla, had gained rank which the Count felt the man had no right to enjoy. Raymond deemed him an adventurer who had seduced Sibylla, little more; but the man was accumulating power at an alarming rate and bore watching. He was standing close to the kneeling Sibylla, scratching his neck and picking his nose. His disrespect for the dead bordered on treason, but this was not the time or place to deal with this upstart. Later, Raymond promised himself, there would be a reckoning.

The Count heaved a deep sigh quietly as the women began to go through the ritual of wailing and symbolically tearing their hair in grief. Their cries and wails all but drowned out the high-pitched chanting of the priests. The ladies-in-waiting measured their own demonstrations of grief by the behavior of the two noblewomen. He doubted that anyone really pulled their hair out, even if the tears were copious. Sibylla didn't possess enough to part with, so her vanity would prevent too much damage.

Isabella behaved in a somewhat more dignified manner. The child, after all, had not been hers, but the throne to the kingdom might be—if her champion Raymond had anything to do with it.

Observing the restless and fidgeting gathering, the Count of Tripoli gave some thought to what might come next.

As the body could not be suitably preserved for any length of time in late summer, it would have to be taken immediately to Jerusalem for burial in the Church of the Holy Sepulcher, alongside his uncle Baldwin IV. The boy had, after all, been a king. Raymond assumed that the boy's grandfather, William of Montferrat, would take responsibility for the transportation of the body and the funeral. He, meanwhile, had other things to arrange.

Unless he could keep control of the situation, the succession could spiral out of his hands, which to his mind would be a disaster for the kingdom and all its subjects. There were two men who could contribute to that condition. Raynald de Châtillon and Gérard de Rideford. Both were his implacable enemies.

*****

In a region known as *Oultrejordan,* just to the south and east of the Dead Sea, is a massive castle called Kerak. It sprawls along the walls of a steep cliff edge, and its immense glacis alone would daunt any would-be conqueror. This castle currently belonged to Lord Raynald de Châtillon. It dominated the southern approaches to the Dead Sea and overlooked the caravan routes used by the Arab and Egyptian merchants on their way north to Damascus and the domains of the powerful new leader, the Arab Sultan, Salah Ed Din.

The Lord Raynald was eating with his wife in his quarters when there was a loud banging on the chamber door.

"Enter!" Raynald roared, wiping grease from his bearded mouth. His lank, greying hair hung loose, and some of it was dragged across his beard as he did so. Raynald was not one to fuss over his appearance. He had, after all, been a prisoner of the Saracens for years, and they had not provided him with a mirror.

The door opened and a young soldier poked his head through the opening.

"Well, what is it? Speak up, man!" Raynald called out, fixing the unfortunate youth with his fierce glare. "Why am I being interrupted in the middle of my meal?"

"Sire, er, Sire, Sir Gandar sent me," the boy stammered. "He, he said that you wanted to know immediately if there was a caravan in sight."

"He did, did he?" Raynald snorted and tossed a chicken bone to a couple of shaggy hounds which had been watching his every move with the meat. They jumped on it almost before it landed on the filthy wooden floor and began a snarling fight.

"Shut up!" Raynald shouted and kicked at the hounds, making one yelp as his boot connected. The hounds scampered out of range with their tails between their legs.

"How close is the caravan?" he demanded.

"Two leagues, perhaps a little more, Lord," the soldier replied.

"Get out!" Raynald grunted. The man vanished, leaving the door open for his leader to follow through. Raynald seized a side of roasted fowl, glanced at his wife and smirked. "This might be the one!" He chuckled, took a swig of his wine, and got up from the table. He slammed the door on his wife, who turned away with a grimace of disgust.

Raynald was still chewing when he emerged onto the eastern battlements of the castle and joined the men gathered there. They were a rough crowd, clad in a mixture of chain hauberks that had seen better days, sporting an assortment of surcoats denoting former lords to whom they had once owed allegiance. There were even the surcoats of

Templars to be seen among the scarred group of cutthroats. However, they parted ranks respectfully enough as their lord lumbered towards them.

"So, what have you seen?" he demanded. He leaned over the parapet and peered eastwards.

"Yonder, Lord." Gandar, an old retainer and warrior of Raynald's, pointed south towards a low dust cloud.

"Someone had sharp eyes," Raynald commented through a full mouth, and he tossed the remains of the fowl over the edge of the walls. He could just make out a cloud of dust quite some distance away, but little else in the shimmering heat of the day. Although it was late autumn, the heat remained in this region until well into November.

"It's quite a large caravan from what we can make of it, Lord," Gandar told him, shading his eyes from the glare.

Raynald nodded. The dust cloud attested to a sizable caravan making its way along the road, more of a well-worn track, two leagues to the east of his castle. He stared ruminatively at the dust, then smacked his hand down on the wall.

"Tell the men to get mounted up," he said. "We are taking them."

The men let out whoops of glee and rushed off to see to their mounts. He himself sauntered down to the courtyard and joined them at his leisure. The caravan would be the usual lumbering camel train and could not run away from his fast horses.

When all were ready he lead his eager horsemen out of the castle gates at a trot.

The people in the caravan were not prepared for an attack. The truce that had been agreed between the Christian Count Raymond de Tripoli and the Lord Sultan Salah Ed Din in 1185 was still in effect. A few soldiers walked or rode alongside the long train of camels to defend them from skirmishes with the Bedouin, who respected no one and certainly not truces. With the Christians, however, the merchants assumed they would abide by the terms and allow them free passage unharmed across the *Oultrejordan*.

They were tragically mistaken. When the Egyptian guards noticed horsemen galloping towards the caravan they did not immediately take alarm. Only when they saw the raised weapons and the hard faces did they sound a belated warning. There was immediate panic. The warning, however, came far too late, and the armed footmen could do little but form a protective line facing the danger, knowing full well how inadequate would be their defense. They screamed invectives at their cowardly mounted companions who wheeled their horses and fled the scene leaving their own cloud of dust behind.

Raynald and his men, seeing how thinly manned the caravan was, fanned out to engage them in a line abreast and charged full on into the Egyptian soldiers, running them down. The screaming and terrified foot soldiers could do little against the ferocious attack of the horsemen, who roared jubilant battle cries as they thrust their spears into the luckless men. The horsemen then drew their swords and went after those who had survived the charge, cutting them down without mercy. In the dust and turmoil of the initial attack some of the Egyptians even knelt on the ground, begging for mercy.

"No quarter!" shouted Raynald. "Kill the armed men! We'll take the rest prisoner for slaves."

His men obliged him, dismounting and striding up to their victims, then either beheading them or running them through with their swords. The screams and groans of those wounded but still alive filled the dust-laden air, along with the shouts of glee as Raynald's men saw what a huge prize they had won.

Raynald, intoxicated by the stench of fear and blood, rode up to the terrified merchants, who fell to their knees along with the drovers. He was filled with the bloodlust now and chopped at the outstretched arms of a merchant in expensive clothing who had had the temerity to beg for mercy. The man fell back with a scream, clutching at the stump of his severed arm. Raynald laughed as he tried to estimate his gain. This was a rich haul indeed!

There must have been nearly fifty camels, all heavily laden with goods, but something else had caught his eye. There were women in the very center of the caravan, perched on several of the camels which were still held by terrified and cowering drovers, who did their best to calm the frightened creatures and prevent them from tipping their human cargoes into the sand. The women's screams became shrieks of terror and outrage when Raynald signaled his men to haul them off the camels.

The rapine began. Amid the wreckage of the skirmish, with a pall of dust hanging over all, with the dead lying everywhere and the prisoners looking on in horror, the men of Kerak took the women, oblivious to their wails and pleading. Raynald was sitting on his horse, laughing, when two of his men brought a heavily veiled figure towards him that struggled and fought against them.

One slapped the struggling figure across the face, which loosened her veil; the soldier tore the rest of the expensive cloth away. As it fell, Raynald could see that they were holding a woman of exceptional beauty. Slight and of olive complexion, she was about twenty-four years of age. The two men stopped in front of Raynald, and one said, "Found her on one of the camels near the center of the caravan, Lord. Could be important. She was attended by some servants. We killed them, and here she is!" He gave a raucous laugh. The men were clearly excited by their find and the prospect of a great ransom, but Raynald grunted and dismounted, his eyes fixed on the woman before him.

"I'll take her. She's mine."

"But—" the man didn't get to continue. Raynald backhanded him with a mailed fist across the face. With a startled shout the man staggered back, spitting out a tooth and wiping blood off his dirty beard. He released his hold on the woman and instinctively reached for his sword. The woman began to thrash at the other man with her free arm but could not break free. She let out a whimper, not of fear but of outrage.

"I said she's mine!" Raynald bellowed. Although his eyes were locked onto the struggling woman, he still held his bloody sword ready. He seized her by the other arm. "Get hold of some of the others. There are plenty to go around. Go!"

The men slunk off without a word to join their celebrating comrades, and the plundering continued.

Raynald dragged the struggling, screaming woman towards some low bushes, leaving his men and his horse behind. There was only one witness who was not captured nor badly wounded, who made his escape into the desert. He would take the dread tale north to Damascus, arriving at the palace of the Sultan, Lord Salah Ed Din, two weeks later.

———————

Chapter 1

The Messenger

The messenger runs, not carrying the news of victory,
or defeat; the messenger, unresting, has always been
running, the wind before and behind him,
across the turning back of earth.
                                    —*Eleanor Wilner*

On the island of Cyprus, on a bright spring afternoon that was warm and almost cloudless, three young men were diving in the deep waters of the harbor entrance, looking for octopods to tease. While they were diving, splashing and shouting exuberantly to one another, they were being observed by the villagers working with the day's catch on the piers. Several young women were also watching their activities with interest. Their eyes took in the bronzed lithe bodies of the youths who themselves, aware of being observed, fooled about, showing off their swimming prowess to the giggling maidens. It was not often that the youths from the castle came to the harbor to enjoy the water.

Rostam was thoroughly engrossed with one octopus in the deep water, which had managed to squeeze itself into a small fissure and would not be persuaded to come out for any reason. The boy dived repeatedly, trying to coax the shy creature out from its lair. Finally, running out of air and patience, he released the morsel of sardine he had been tempting it with and kicked himself back up through the crystal clear water to join his waiting companions, leaving a trail of air bubbles behind him.

The moment Rostam left for the surface the creature detached itself from its refuge, seized the piece of fish, then jetted itself further along the rocky bottom. It insinuated itself into the depths of another crevasse, where it assumed the mottled color of the rocks around it, rendering it almost invisible to the casual searcher.

Rostam swam towards the two boys perched half-naked on the rocks on the east side of the channel. It was one of those rare times when Rostam and his older companion Junayd had been allowed to do what they wanted instead of training under the sharp eye of Rostam's uncle, Reza. Andreas, a younger Greek boy from the village was exclaiming and pointing towards the distant castle perched high on the mountains to the south.

"What is happening?" Rostam asked, taking deep breaths as he clambered over slippery rocks, then out of the water to join them. The former calm of the harbor front changed abruptly, replaced by a great deal of activity as men poured out of the small barracks and the eating houses and began to run towards a galley that was moored against the quayside some fifty paces away.

"There is a signal from the castle, Rostam. They must have noticed a ship coming this way."

Rostam glanced quickly towards the castle and noticed the trail of smoke left by one of the signal rockets that his father used to alert the harbor folk to possible danger from marauders, or any strange vessel. He felt a rush of excitement.

"Come on, we've got to get to the ship before Captain Guy leaves us behind!" he exclaimed.

The boys seized their clothes, bows and other weapons, then leapt from rock to rock to the stone quayside and ran pell-mell to join the sailors who were themselves rushing to join their ship. Captain Guy was short with anyone who dallied. They ignored the villagers, who had their own concerns. There were very few to be seen, now that the alarm had sounded.

"Ah, there you are, Rostam," Captain Guy shouted as he caught sight of the boys racing towards him. "Hurry or I'll leave you behind!"

His men were already casting off, and the rowers were standing ready at the oars, while others began to push the boat away from the quayside with long poles.

"You can't leave me behind, Captain Guy, I am your navigator!" Rostam laughed at his nautical mentor.

"Humph! I am sure I am not too old to steer a ship out of this harbor without your help, you young whelp!" the captain called back affectionately.

"Can I come with you?" Andreas panted, as they raced towards the ship. He was younger than even Rostam, but he was almost as tall and was very strong. Junayd called back, "Only if Captain Guy says yes."

Guy, a huge, burly man with a shaggy greying beard, grinned; the young men were eager as hounds to get to some kind of action. It had been quiet for months now. "Get on board! You too, Andreas, but don't get underfoot or I'll throw you back into the sea!"

Andreas laughed excitedly. This was the first time he had been allowed to join Rostam and Junayd on such an adventure. The youths tossed their clothes and other weapons onto the moving deck, but held onto their bows as they leapt with athletic agility onto the galley to land easily on the deck.

"Best arm yourselves, just in case. We don't know who it is," Guy called down from the afterdeck as the youths collected their battle gear and ran below. Guy turned his attention back to his ship and the maneuvers necessary to sail the sleek galley out to intercept the visitors. Listening to the bellowed orders on the deck above, Rostam and Junayd hurriedly donned mailed shirts and leather trews.

"Here, wear this!" Rostam thrust a breast plate and a thick leather jerkin at Andreas. "You'll need your bow. Come on!"

Not wanting to miss anything, they grabbed their bows, quivers and swords, then piled back into the busy waist of the galley to rush up the steps and join Guy on the steering deck. There was indeed a visitor, in the form of a large ship about three leagues northeast of their port. Guy watched the vessel with close attention as it came towards them.

"Rostam, Junayd, you two go forward and make sure those idiots don't do anything stupid with the Scorpions," he ordered. "Andreas, you stay here with me." He was referring to the two enormous bow-like devices that Lord Talon and his close companion Lord Reza had installed in their ships. While the weapons had proven to be lethal against enemies, not many of the men who served Talon knew how to use them, nor had the nerve to do so.

Leaving Andreas hopping about with excitement on the steering deck under Guy's care, Rostam and Junayd ran forward, dodging the busy crew members and other obstructions. Within minutes they had not only assumed command of the two frightening weapons but had readied them for an encounter. Rostam called over to the men hovering around.

"We need some oiled coverings, hurry! The sea is sending spray all over us." He worried that the Chinese powder, compacted into a tube along with its fuse, might get damp. The men hurried off, glad to be away from these menacing weapons that they knew little about.

The two eager youths peered forward. They could now see the intruder was a cumbersome ship of the Latin kind.

"I don't know how those things stay afloat, let alone sail anywhere," Junayd said in a disparaging tone. Their own sleek galley cut through the water like a knife. The Latin vessel, under all sail, lumbered directly towards their own ship. It dipped and rolled in the comparatively calm seas whereas the sleek galley rolled only slightly by comparison. The strange vessel was apparently on a course towards their harbor, but that would not be unless Captain Guy allowed it passage.

Within a very short space of time the other ship was close enough to hail. It shortened sail to bring it closer and Captain Guy called over, "What ship, and what is your business?"

"We sail with the seal of Count Raymond of Tripoli! Who are you and why are you in our way?"

"You must present proof before I allow you passage to our harbor. Orders of Lord Talon de Gilles!" Guy roared back.

Rostam and Junayd could observe the ensuing conference on at the afterdeck of the other ship. Several men in chain mail and wearing dark cloaks stared back at them.

"I wonder who they are?" Junayd said.

"They look very like Christian soldiers. See, some of them bear the Christian cross on their tunics," Rostam observed. "However, I am not taking any chances. They are all armed to the teeth and helmeted. Make sure your bow is ready."

"I am sure I could take down any one of them at this range, especially that big fellow," Junayd remarked, indicating a very large blonde haired man standing amongst the others on the strange deck, as he reached for his weapon. The intruding ship was now only about a hundred paces away, rising and falling in the waters. They had lowered their mainsail.

"I want proof as to who you are!" Captain Guy called out again. He cut an imposing figure, braced comfortably on the deck, rocking with the movement of his ship. A soldier who had an air of command about him stepped over to the rail of the other ship. He took off his helmet to show greying hair that was bound at the back of his head.

"I am Sir Matthew D'Aix; I am a vassal of the Count Raymond of Tripoli. I bear letters for Lord Talon de Gilles." He waved what looked like a roll of parchment in the air. "It is urgent and imperative that I speak to Lord Talon," the knight shouted.

Guy, who appeared to be pondering the words, glanced along the deck to where Rostam was standing. Finally he nodded assent, but then he called over. "Take up station in front of us. Anchor in the middle of the harbor; I shall be watching," he warned.

Rostam grinned. Guy knew what one of the Scorpions in the bows could do. One false move and Rostam would be ordered to light the fuse and release the spear that would inflict a mortal wound on the other ship.

They turned about while the other ship began the two-league passage towards the harbor. The men on the other vessel took Captain Guy at his word and sailed their cumbersome ship directly towards the harbor. There was no sign of any threatening behavior on their decks, but the men on Guy's ship stayed alert. This was a well-practiced operation for them.

Within an hour the visiting ship was anchored in the calm waters of the harbor and its passengers were standing on the stonework of the quayside. Captain Guy took Rostam, Junayd and Andreas along with him to halt in front of the small group of newcomers. They looked askance at him and his three attendees, as though they had expected a more elaborate reception.

Rostam, lithe and dark from hours in the sun, and his very Arab-looking companion Junayd, were not exactly the kind of people they had expected to greet them. However, Captain Guy was, so it was to him that the leader addressed himself. He was a large, well-built man, clearly a warrior, but no longer young. The scars and lines on his weathered face were indicators of time long spent in the sun and dust of the

Kingdom of Jerusalem. His chain hood was settled around his shoulders and he did not wear his helmet, although the two men accompanying him did so. The coat of arms sewn onto his tunic just above the red cross was unfamiliar to Rostam, even though his father and his father's old friend and retainer, Max, had schooled him in the elements of heraldry. It resembled a crude image of a mounted knight holding up a banner.

The knight in question still held the parchment in his mailed hand. It was clear that this was a well secured missive, with a red wax seal and ribbons tying the roll together.

"I am Sir Matthew. To whom am I talking?" he asked in a gruff tone, although he was civil enough.

Guy stepped forward. "Captain Guy, and this"—he gestured for Rostam to come forward—"is Lord Rostam de Gilles. The son of Lord Talon."

Sir Matthew gave Rostam a surprised look, followed by a more penetrating stare from his blue eyes. He saw before him a youth of about sixteen who stood straight and tall, wearing a fine-linked chain hauberk that had seen better days. The youth was burnt dark brown but had light-colored hair, bleached by sun and salt, and in disarray from his swimming. The youth stared back directly, without any indication of apprehension, with curious hazel eyes.

Sir Matthew gave a perfunctory bow and asked, "Sir, is your father here that I might discharge my duty and give him a message from the Count of Tripoli?"

Rostam half turned and pointed to the distant castle perched high on the top of the mountain behind them. "I shall take you to him, Sir," he said in slightly accented French. "We can provide horses for you and your men."

Sir Matthew stared into the distance towards the castle. "Ah," he murmured. "The rumors are true. Lord Raymond said that he lives on a peak." He turned back to Rostam. "We must hurry, as there is little time to lose."

"Lord Rostam will escort you, Sir Matthew. I must remain here with my ship." Guy informed him. "Andreas, you stay with me, boy."

Within a few minutes the boys had obtained horses from the village stables and they were riding out, watched by the curious inhabitants who did not often have visitors to their harbor, other than the ships belonging to Lord Talon himself.

During their journey, Sir Matthew's keen eye had time to observe the land on either side of the road. The crops were planted and growing well, cows grazed in grass paddocks, and off to his left he noticed water ditches and vineyards, with people working along the rows. He remarked the drains alongside the road and noted that they were in fact small irrigation canals carrying clear rushing water. They seemed to be well maintained. On the slopes of the mountain there were extensive olive groves. The people working in the fields appeared to be cheerful and, more importantly, well fed. This was in stark contrast to the peasants who lived on the lands of the Kingdom of Jerusalem these days, even in the area of Tripoli from whence he had just come.

Some of the people even waved to the young man with hazel eyes, who waved back or responded with calls in what Sir Matthew guessed must be Greek. He himself only spoke French, although he had tried to learn some Arabic. His master, Lord Raymond of Tripoli, had insisted.

He noticed that the two youths who accompanied him and his men carried their weapons with an ease that suggested long familiarity. He wondered if they'd had any occasion to put them to hard use. The one named Rostam seemed consumed with curiosity, yet he was polite and spoke only when asked a question. Sir Matthew had not a few to ask.

"Your peasants appear to be contented, Lord Rostam," he commented at last.

Rostam laughed. "They should be, Sir. Father invests enough in their well-being. He is always telling me that it is important to have contented people working for you."

They rode past some wagons drawn by oxen, then passed some women carrying large baskets of olives. It was not lost on Sir Matthew that some smiled prettily at the two young men.

Finally they crested the ridge, and Sir Matthew could gaze up at the formidable walls of the castle belonging to Lord Talon de Gilles. Rumor had it that the knight had stolen this fortification from right under the nose of the so-called 'Emperor' Isaac Komnenos of Cyprus. Every attempt to reclaim it had failed, so that now Sir Talon was a lord in his own right, and firmly established. Sir Matthew resolved to ask some questions about that when the opportunity presented itself.

They rode along the southern flank of the castle for some distance, with the formidable walls towering over them and a steep drop on their right, as they made for the twin towers which dominated the gateway. Sir Matthew nodded his head with growing respect. This was not an easy target for a siege, he decided, and the sentries staring silently down at him looked alert.

They rode at a walk through the opened gates, the horses' hooves clattering on the paving stones, then drew rein where a small group of men and a couple of hounds waited for them, just inside the bailey.

Grooms ran forward to hold the horses, and men-at-arms closed the gates with a crash. A tall, well-built man wearing what appeared to be eastern clothing and a loose turban stepped forward. Rostam hastened to dismount and said, "Father, this is Sir Matthew D'Aix from Lord Tripoli. He is bringing news and a letter." Then, remembering his manners, he added, "Sir Matthew, may I present my father, Lord Talon de Gilles."

Sir Matthew bowed respectfully to the man, who dipped his head. "You are very welcome to my house, Sir Matthew." His hand strayed to the head of one of the hounds, which was pushing its nose affectionately against his leg. Matthew noted the scarred features of the man and his proud but watchful bearing. Matthew noted that there were streaks of grey in his beard and on his temples. The Count had re-counted several tales about Lord Talon, some of which were quite sinister.

"This man has traveled to the end of the earth and has amassed much knowledge. Some even call him a wizard. He is not a man to be trifled with, Matthew. Many have tried and all have paid a heavy price. But speak forthrightly to him and I am sure he will be your friend," the Count had admonished him before they parted.

"Lord Talon de Gilles," Matthew's tone was formal and initially a little nervous, "I, er, I bring an urgent message to you from my Lord Raymond of Tripoli." He drew out the rolled parchment from the folds of his cloak and presented it to Talon, who took it and looked it over. He recognized the seal as that of Tripoli.

"I bid you welcome," he said. "You have traveled far to deliver this, and the voyage, I know, is not a simple under-taking. Allow my Sergeant-at-Arms to lead your men to where they can partake of refreshment." Talon indicated the three men who had come with Matthew. "They will be well taken care of; he has been in my service since I gained the castle and is a trusted man."

"Palladius, please see to our guests," he murmured in Greek to a burly man-at-arms standing nearby, who nodded. "Yes, Lord." He bowed to Talon and lead the three men to-wards the doorway that led to the inner castle grounds. Palladius had joined Talon on the day he gained possession of the castle, preferring to serve Talon than his former cruel master.

Talon turned so that he could indicate his other companions with his gesture. "Sir Matthew, I wish to present my comrades-in-arms of many years, Lord Reza and Sir Max Bauersdorf."

Sir Matthew bowed to the two men, one of whom was a slight, swarthy man dressed in similar clothing to that of Talon's; he also wore a loose turban. His dark eyes remained disconcertingly steadily on his. Matthew felt that he was being assessed very thoroughly. However the smile he gave Matthew was friendly enough. "You are welcome, Sir Matthew," Reza's white teeth gleamed under his short beard. There were a few thin streaks of grey in his beard also.

The other man, Max, clearly a Frank and thinner than his more muscular companions, had made some concessions to the loose robes of eastern clothing but did not wear a turban. Instead he wore a blue felt cap over his white hair, the color of the cap matched by piercing blue eyes set in a stern, deeply lined face. Max's smile was also friendly enough as he gave a bow in return.

Sir Matthew had heard of Sir Max before, something to do with once being a Templar Sergeant, and later being held prisoner in the Temple dungeon in Acre. He had mysteriously vanished one night, about the same time as the huge fire that nearly burned down a large portion of the city. Lord Talon was rumored to have been involved somehow.

"We bid you welcome, Sir Matthew." Max said in his guttural French. "We are eager to hear news of the Holy Land."

"Come, Sir," Talon indicated the way. "We are all as eager as Max to hear news, but you have indicated this message is urgent. We will hear the news later as we eat in the hall, but meanwhile you and I will go and talk in my study."

Talon turned and led the way across the wide space of the bailey, past what Matthew was surprised to see, an actual trebuchet! A man-at-arms threw open another solid door and saluted Talon respectfully. The doorway opened onto a

wide and busy courtyard, dominated by a keep which towered over the castle grounds.

Talon continued to lead the way up some stone steps
through a large doorway into the huge hall. Servants ducked
their heads and maids curtsied with polite smiles as they
passed. Leaving his companions on the first floor, Talon carried on up some more circular stone steps to open a small,
thick, iron-studded door which led into a cluttered but well-
lit room at the top of the square tower. He smiled. "We are
finally here, Sir Matthew. Would you like some wine? I can
even provide you with some tea."

The knight nodded his head mutely. "Er... wine, thank
you, Sir." Everything he had seen on their way to this room
had given him an impression of considerable wealth, but also
there was a clean, orderly atmosphere about the building
which impressed him; few Castilians bothered with cleanli-
ness in his world. This particular room was, in contrast to the
rest of what he had observed, anything but tidy. He sat down
in the chair opposite Talon, who made himself comfortable
and then broke the seal of the letter.

While Talon was thus engaged, a servant silently poured
some wine and handed Matthew a silver goblet which he
gratefully accepted. The visitor sipped the red wine and
stared about him with wide-eyed interest at the collection of
beautiful leather-bound manuscripts, the rolls of paper and
parchment lying about on the desk and on shelves that
reached to the roof of exposed beams. Sir Matthew, like most
of his warrior class, could not read, but he had a grudging
admiration for anyone who could. To him, there did not
seem to be any kind of order in the room; indeed some rolls
lay on the carpets in complete disarray. There were large
maps of the region pinned casually to fine tapestries, and a
few banners hung from the roof collecting cobwebs and dust.
The man absorbed in reading the message appeared to be

just as much at ease within a library as he was in command
of the castle.

*****

Talon ignored the curious knight and focused on reading
the parchment. As he read he tried to keep the concern from
his face. If the words written by Count Raymond of Tripoli
were to be believed, then the situation in the Kingdom of
Jerusalem was dire. Despite his loose network of informants,
Talon did not have anyone left in Acre to keep him fully
aware of the activities going on in the Kingdom; a fact that
had made him uneasy. The Jews with whom he had done
much in the way of business had departed the city over a year
ago, almost en masse, due to the depredations of the avari-
cious Lord Gérard de Rideford and his followers, including
the Bishop of Acre.

Talon had not been able to find anyone reliable enough
who could keep him informed since then. Hence he had
heard of the death of the young King Baldwin V belatedly,
and then very little of the intense political turmoil that had
followed when the quarreling royals had left Acre for
Jerusalem.

According to Tripoli, the two factions who had emerged
after the death of the boy-king Baldwin V were still locked in
a vicious power play. On the one side were Raymond and the
Countess Isabella, Balian Ibelin, and several other nobles.
The other camp consisted of the boy's mother Sibylla, sister
of Baldwin IV, the Leper King; her lover, now husband, Guy
de Lusignan; Gérard de Rideford, the Master of the Templar
Order; and Raynald de Châtillon. Talon had known that
Sibylla had married against her brother's wishes the knight
Sir Guy, upon which he had become Lord of Gaza. A huge
jump for anyone, let alone a mere adventurer knight!

On inheriting the throne after her son Baldwin V died, Sibylla had tricked everyone during the coronation by accepting the crown as the rightful queen but then immediately passing the crown to her newly wed husband, Guy de Lusignan, who had then crowned himself King of Jerusalem! It had been a hasty ceremony, not attended by many of the nobility. Lord Raymond had not been present. There had been bad blood between them ever since.

As if that were not worrisome enough, the fragile peace that had been painstakingly negotiated by Baldwin IV and Lord Raymond with Salah Ed Din, the Sultan and leader of the Arab neighbors to the Kingdom, had been broken once more by Lord Raynald de Châtillon. This time the Sultan had had enough and was mustering a huge army with the intent to invade the Kingdom of Jerusalem and punish the Christians once and for all. Raymond of Tripoli was calling upon his many disparate allies and liegemen, including Talon, to come to his aid.

Talon glanced at Sir Matthew, who was looking around his cluttered study with wide-eyed curiosity, and noticed his eyes lingering on a trophy depicting a lion and a dragon battling for the game of polo.

"I'll tell you about that some time," he told the knight, then turned his attention back to the letter, ignoring the sounds of activity down in the courtyard: grooms calling to one another or flirting with the maids, geese squawking, a peacock screaming, horses snorting and stamping impatiently, or being walked on the stones. One of the hounds which had accompanied them to the chamber yawned loudly. He continued to read:

> *It is with great reluctance that I call upon you for help in these dark times. While I have not forgotten your pledge of loyalty to me those many years ago, out of our friendship, which I value greatly, I do not*

call upon that pledge. Instead I simply beg for your help. You and I are among a very few in the Kingdom who have met the Sultan and know him as a man of honor. I am deeply concerned that unless we can renegotiate a truce, then disaster will follow and our entire kingdom will be thrown into peril. With God's help we might be able to avert a war which we could not win, and return to some form of peace. Should we be successful, then there must be a reckoning with Châtillon. He must never be allowed to commit such crimes again. I ask that you come as soon as is possible for I think time is short, perhaps perilously so. Sir Matthew is one of my most loyal aides and you may trust him implicitly. He will bring you to me in Tyre.
"

The letter was signed with Lord Raymond's flourish, the wax stamped with a seal depicting a mounted knight bearing a banner encircled by the legend *Raymondus Comus Tripoli Sigil,* confirming the authenticity of the document.

Talon looked up from the parchment and fixed his gaze upon the visitor. "You are aware of the contents of this document and are here to take me to him?" he asked.

Sir Matthew nodded. "I am instructed to provide you, and any men you wish to bring with you, transport to Tyre, Lord," he responded.

Talon gave him a wry smile. "Not to Acre then?" he queried.

Matthew shook his head and grinned back. "No, Lord, not to Acre. I fear your reputation would precede you and men would all waiting be for you on the quayside with unpleasant anticipation."

Matthew was referring to the time when Talon had set fire to his own house in Acre, after he had been charged with witchcraft and all his property confiscated by the Church. The diversion had enabled him to escape with his people on two of his ships, but the fire had spread to burn down a whole section of the city. The authorities would not be forgiving.

Talon glanced back down at the missive and re-read it in the silence that followed. Finally he looked up. "I shall give you my answer in the morning, Sir Matthew. In the meantime, my servants will provide you with every comfort we can. You will have to excuse me while I consult with my people, as this is not an easy decision to make and there seems to be little time."

Sir Matthew made to speak, but then appeared to rethink what he was about to say and simply nodded. "Very well, Lord. I shall await your answer with the morning."

"You will eat with us this evening and we shall talk some more. My family is eager to hear your news, good or bad," Talon told him as they both stood up. Talon ushered the knight out of the room and nodded to the man standing outside. "See Sir Matthew to his quarters."

The man, one of Reza's Companions, bowed and led the knight away.

———————————

Chapter 2

Corsairs

O'er the glad waters of the dark blue sea,
Our thoughts as boundless, and our souls as free,
Far as the breeze can bear, the billows foam,
Survey our empire and behold our home!
These are our realms, no limits to their sway—
Our flag the scepter all who meet obey.
                                    —Lord Byron

Talon sat motionless for a long time after the knight had departed for his guest quarters. His attention was drawn to the small noises coming up to his tower from below. They were the sounds of people living and working in a peaceful time. He could hear the sound of laughter mingled with the other normal sounds of a castle going about its evening tasks. He was content, notwithstanding there was always danger lurking somewhere, but danger was at present outside the boundaries of his lands. He had done much to ensure this, and his reward had been loyalty and hard work from the inhabitants of the two villages and the castle. For the first time in his life he was not looking over his shoulder for danger, but now? Without notice the outside world and its chaos had reached into his calm life with a clawed hand to drag him away from all that he held precious.

He put his head in his hands and shook it from side to side, feeling a deep sense of foreboding. When would the world learn to live in peace? Tossing the letter aside with a frown of anger he got up and walked over to the window. He leaned on the stone sill to stare out over his lands to the north. Talon was still staring out of his window towards the tiny harbor in the distance where two ships idled at anchor, when there came a discreet knock on the door.

"Come!" he called.

Reza and Max, his two closest friends, entered with Rostam right behind them.

"We have come," stated Max, his grizzled old Templar friend, "to hear what news would bring a knight belonging to Count Raymond of Tripoli to our shores."

"I have brought some of our best wine along to help with your memory... just in case you forgot what he wanted," said Reza, Talon's friend from the time when they had been trained as young assassins. He grinned and flourished a dark bottle of their own pressed wine.

Both Max and Reza were quick, however, to sense his mood. "Not so good eh, Talon?" Reza commented, cocking an eyebrow at his friend.

Talon sighed, then gave a rueful chuckle.

"No, it is not good news, my friends. Rostam, you are to go and ask your mother, your aunt Jannat, and Theodora to come to the Solarium to meet with us there. There are important matters to discuss and I want them to be present."

Rostam rushed off while the three men looked at one another. "Is it such bad news, Talon?" asked Max, eyeing him from under his bushy, grey-flecked brows.

"I fear so, Max." Talon responded. "Come along, we cannot keep the women waiting; they are always so busy. I will explain everything I know."

They found the women already seated when they reached the Solarium, a wide, airy room with large windows that opened out onto the north side of the castle with a view of the bay. Rav'an, Talon's wife, and Jannat had transformed a bleak stone chamber into a homey place with carpets strewn about the wood floor and many large cushions piled against the walls where people could make themselves comfortable. The austere walls had been hung with tapestries from Sicily and with lighter carpets and khilims from Syria to keep the chill from the walls during the winter months. Today it was early April and the weather was quite warm, so the shutters were thrown open to allow a cool breeze from the sea to waft into the room, tugging gently at the light material of the drapes. Placed on the low table in the middle of the room were polished copper bowls containing fruit and nuts. There were even some baklava squares on a plate, which Rostam was eyeing hopefully.

Talon liked what the women had done to the chamber. It was their family room, which served as a council chamber when occasion demanded. At present only the adults were gathered; the infants were being overseen by the nurses who cared for them. The three ladies looked up from a low-toned conversation as the men entered. Rav'an, his beautiful Rav'an, seemed to sense something ominous, for her huge grey eyes went wide with concern. She spoke, even before he had taken his place on a cushion, pushing aside a lock of her jet black hair that had strayed across the smooth pale oval of her face.

"Who is this unusual visitor, Talon?"

"Yes, who is he and where did he come from, Talon?" chimed in Jannat, Reza's young and beautiful wife, mother of his newborn son. She sounded just as concerned. Talon remained silent as he settled himself, still holding the parchment letter in his hand. The third woman, Theodora, their close friend and physician, who had come to them from Constantinople, having fled the depredations of the former Emperor, looked askance. Her presence always brought an aura of calm; now her warm smile returned when she saw Max, who slowly lowered himself onto a cushion next to her. Talon could see that Max was feeling his age. The time he had spent in a cold and dank Templar prison had not been good for his health. There was an attachment between Theo, as she was known, and Max, that had been growing for some time now.

"What does he want, Father?" Rostam added his question to that of his mother's, seating himself next to her. She reached out to touch him on the shoulder in a gesture of affection.

"Well, now that we are all here I do have something to tell you, and yes, it is very important." Talon paused.

"Talon, my Prince, stop giving us all that look of yours and tell us!" Jannat said with her usual impatience. Reza, who had already opened the bottle of wine, looked up, pretending hurt and said, "I thought I was your only Prince, my Princess! We must all have something to drink. This might get him to open up and tell us more." He handed the ruby red wine around in silver cups.

"We should really be drinking tea!" Rav'an admonished Reza, who chuckled. "Not when he has something important to tell us, Princess," he retorted.

Talon savored the liquid, rolling it about on his tongue and allowing it to slip down his throat, drawing out the moment. It really was quite a good wine, he decided. "It is improving, Brother," he commented.

He noticed the narrowing of Rav'an's eyes. A tapping foot would follow. She knew him only too well, so he decided it was time.

"His name is Sir Matthew, and he is sent by the Count of Tripoli, who has called upon me to honor a commitment I made a long time ago to serve him should he be in need."

He looked around at the startled faces in front of him. "It was a very long time ago, and since then we have become friends rather than Lord and lowly Knight, and he has made an appeal which I will have difficulty refusing."

"This should be interesting!" Theodora, who had remained silent up till now, stated.

"I was under the impression that you were all outlaws from the Kingdom of Jerusalem." She cast a questioning look at Max, who nodded in the affirmative but said, "Yes, Theo, that is true, but the Count of Tripoli is very much his own master, and while he owes a certain allegiance to the crown of Jerusalem there appears to have been a rift between him and the palace. Talon, you need to explain," he concluded.

"Talon, what are you telling us? That this knight is here to take you to Tripoli?" demanded Rav'an. She sounded worried. "Tell me this is not so."

"No, to Tyre, but yes, unfortunately, that is the case, my Love. According to Sir Matthew, Raynald de Châtillon ambushed one caravan too many and the truce between the Sultan Salah Ed Din and the King of Jerusalem is now in fragments. As a result, Salah Ed Din is marshaling a large army in readiness to invade."

"So what has this got to do with you, us, or anyone here on Cyprus?" Reza demanded.

"Count Raymond would not have written to me asking for help had he not considered this situation to be very dire, Brother," Talon responded.

"I still don't understand what it could possibly have to do with you, Talon. You are outlawed over there and would probably be thrown in prison should you show up anywhere near that ugly crowd. Furthermore, Châtillon would happily cut your throat while you were in prison," Max said with some feeling. "He will not have forgotten how you bested him that time when he tried to ambush your men."

"The Count has provided me with a letter, a guarantee of safe conduct, but that isn't really the point." Talon took a deep breath and tugged at his short beard. "He is calling for help. He knows that I and my people," he glanced at Reza, "are familiar with the lay of the land, unlike almost anyone at the royal palace other than himself, and he wants to avert an invasion."

"Are they then so powerless to defend their own lands?" Theodora asked. Her tone was mildly sarcastic. Her full lips were compressed and her hazel eyes narrowed as she questioned Talon. He recognized the expression that she normally wore when interrogating a patient.

Talon nodded and pursed his lips. "It is very likely that they are conceited enough to think otherwise, but the Count knows differently. There are only a few men like him who speak Arabic and understand that the survival of the Kingdom depends more upon diplomacy at this stage than force of arms."

"Can he not negotiate a peace on his own? Is he not well known by Salah Ed Din and even respected?" Max put in.

"They have had their interactions, and it is true, Max, that he and Sir Guy de Veres, when he was alive, could make an impression on the Sultan. There is one other, Lord Sidon, but he avoids getting involved and keeps to himself. Raymond is in need of support. He has few allies in the Palace, other than perhaps Count Ibelin Balian, whom I once met."

"How then is Count Raymond able to represent the palace if he has so few friends? Will others respect a truce, even if he can succeed?" Theodora asked. He shot her an appreciative glance.

"You have a good point, Theo. I am not sure. The Count is from the older generation of Crusaders who, having carved out their lands, came to appreciate the civilization that they encountered. He was imprisoned by the Arabs for nearly ten years but harbors no apparent grudge. Unfortunately, most of the new arrivals in the palace are hopeless zealots and consider him to be more of an ally of the Sultan than the Christians which is utter nonsense. But that very understanding between them could enable Raymond to avert an invasion. He sees that he has to try."

"So this is another one of those moments when you have to *honor* a commitment, Talon?" Rav'an said, her tone a trifle bitter.

"I remember the last time we had to follow this '*honor*' thing of his," Reza said with a wry grin. "It got us into all sorts of trouble." He snorted. "What do you owe those people, Talon? Nothing, from what I can tell. They stole everything you had in Acre and would have burned you at the stake had they been able to catch you. It makes no sense, Brother!"

"But a call for help does, Brother. I might remind all of you that had it not been for the Count I might have ridden up to the gates of Acre and found myself arrested before I had even known they were waiting for me!" Talon retorted. "I, we, owe him for that at least. Peace is vital. Not least to our trade and our longer-lasting safety. Should an invasion of the Kingdom succeed, then Cyprus could also become a target, and you all know how long this idiot 'Emperor' of ours would last against a determined Arab invasion. If I can in any small way assist the Count in achieving peace, then it is worth the effort. Reza and I know the Sultan to be a man of integrity and honor. Perhaps we can make a difference and help to change his mind?"

Reza subsided. He nodded reluctantly. "On the other hand, he might throw us both in prison if we venture near him. You for stealing a ship and me for stealing his peace of mind one dark night for the sake of a letter."

Talon and Max chuckled at the memory; it broke the tension that had been building in the room. They had both been on that ship when it fled down the Nile and out into the

Mediterranean Sea, closely followed by war ships intent upon capturing them and re-enslaving them.

"I loved what *you* did, Uncle!" Rostam chortled, referring to the incident when Reza and his men penetrated the tower where Salah Ed Din slept, and demanded a letter from him. "I will do the same one day! I shall break into a well guarded chamber and place a knife on a pillow, the way you and Father have."

"Rostam, you will stop this idiotic nonsense at once!" exclaimed Rav'an, sounding exasperated. "What are these ideas you two are putting into his head?" She glowered at them, then at a not so contrite Rostam. Reza winked at the boy. "Don't let your skills go to your head, boy," he admonished Rostam with a grin.

"You are not to encourage him either, Reza!" Jannat chided her husband, but it was said with affection.

"I suspect that we might get a hearing with the Sultan if the Count of Tripoli is with us and we have a safe conduct pass." Talon told his family

"But who will you take with you, Talon?" Rav'an asked the question on everyone's mind. "You cannot go alone."

"I cannot leave without anyone to protect the village and the castle," Talon said. "Reza, I ask that you stay. If Isaac gets wind of my departure he might try something that would imperil our families."

While Reza was silent, as though thinking of a reason to object, Max spoke up. "Then I should go with you," he said. Theodora gave him a horrified look but said nothing, biting her lip. Talon smiled at his old friend.

"I need someone here to keep Reza in check; you know how impetuous he can be, Max!"

Reza pretended to be mortally offended and said, "You see how I am treated!" Then he looked more sober. "I really should come with you, Talon. We both know the Sultan, and I can help, I am sure of it."

Talon reconsidered, then nodded slowly. "Perhaps you are right, Reza. The two of us can manage this and be back before anyone notices our absence in Famagusta. Max, you must stay. Your knowledge and experience will keep Palladius and his men on their toes." He had not failed to notice Theodora's reaction to Max's statement. "I want to make sure that this place is well looked after."

"Can I come too, Father?"

Talon smiled at his son. "Not this time, my boy. But the time will come before too long."

Rostam looked very glum. "You are doing very well with the other trainees, Rostam. Stay with it and your time will come," Reza assured the boy.

"You will, however, accompany us on the sea voyage to Tyre, as Guy wants to keep your navigation skills sharp," Talon told the surprised and delighted boy. Rav'an rolled her eyes in defeat.

"Hurry down to the harbor and tell Captain Guy what is happening. Don't forget to swear him to secrecy. We cannot leave before Henry gets back, but he is due any day now. I don't want to leave the harbor unprotected without a ship remaining in the port when we leave."

"So there we have it. Reza and I will be going, but it will be in Guy's ship. I do not want to be dependent upon any ship but one of our own. Where is Henry, by the way, Famagusta or Paphos?" He was referring to the second of their ships.

"He is in Famagusta at present, Father. We had a pigeon in today, remember? Things are going well with the sale of our oil and figs in the market there. Dimitri said that even people in Antalya on the mainland want to buy our produce!" Rostam chirped up.

"Very good, Rostam. Auntie Jannat, I entrust our pigeon communications with Boethius and Dimitri in Famagusta to you. Please keep Max and Rav'an informed, and don't forget to reply to Diocles should he send a message next week. It is important that he feels secure."

Boethius and Dimitri were Talon's spies in Paphos and Famagusta respectively, while Diocles was the Chief Minister of the Palace in Famagusta, where the Emperor lived. He was also one of Talon's most important informants.

"He is a very useful man to have on our side. Perhaps another case of wine could find its way to the palace too?" Reza chimed in. Talon chuckled his agreement.

The Emperor had, according to the Chief Minister, developed a taste for the wine from Kantara but didn't know its origin. Had he done so it might have gone badly for the minister. Isaac had been humiliated too often by Talon and his people to endure a nightly reminder in his cups. Talon turned his head and glanced out of the window. The sun had set, leaving a reddish glow in the sky.

"We have a guest to entertain tonight, and I shall give him my answer tomorrow," Talon stated. There is much to do before I go. We should take Yosef and Dar'an with us, Reza. What do you think?"

"I will take Junayd as well. All three are competent." This was a big compliment from an instructor as exacting as Reza.

"Then we must keep all this between just the family for now. I don't want word of any of this to get to the Emperor by any means," Talon told them.

The evening meal was a quiet affair. Despite the fact that they had a guest from the Kingdom of Jerusalem, which was very rare, there was a pall hanging over the meal. Those in the family who knew of the situation were quiet and thoughtful, yet still eager to hear more from the knight, who was willing enough to tell them what he knew.

Talon and Max drew Sir Matthew out and as he relaxed in the friendly atmosphere in the noisy hall, he told them that he had come to Palestine with a contingent from Languedoc via the bay of Aigues Mortes and had been attached to the Count of Tripoli ever since. He was a veteran of several of the battles that had taken place in Talon's absence and during Max's incarceration after the disaster at Jacob's Ford in 1179. Since then there had been skirmishes and periods of tentative, short-lived peace. While he didn't speak the Arabic well, he appeared to share the Count's respect for the cultures that moved about in the country. Talon spoke to him in French, as did Max, who was eager for news of the Templars despite the fact that they had abandoned him.

The tables were laden with food that Matthew had not enjoyed for a long time, not even at the Count's table. There were huge loaves of bread, big cheeses, bowls of olives in oil, roasted fowl, and baked fish covered in capers and herbs. The fish roe paste was plentiful, and bowls of steaming baked mussels and oysters were handed around by the servants to lords, ladies and attendants alike. The knight and his men leaned over their bowls and devoured a mouthwatering mutton stew, with the meat floating around in a soup of gravy, garlic and olives. The course bread soaked up the gravy with the wine to help wash it all down.

Talon and his family observed the common practice of being seated at a high table while the attendants, men-at-arms, huntsmen and their families were seated on benches along the center of the hall. The conversation, shouts of laughter and titters of amusement at some joke or other generally lent a happy atmosphere to the meal that Sir Matthew had not enjoyed for many years. He could barely take his eyes off the vision who was the Lady Rav'an.

"You have a very plentiful table and your people seem contented, Mistress," he stammered in a clumsy compliment to Rav'an, who nodded back, pleased.

46

"We have settled here into our new home and our people are contented," she responded, but he noted there was a tinge of reserve. Her husband was about to leave for the Kingdom. Even Sir Matthew, who was not a sensitive man, recognized that Lady Rav'an did not welcome the fact that her husband was to leave for the confused world of warring factions on the mainland.

"My Lady, I apologize for bringing this ill news, but your husband is very respected by my lord the Count. I am sure his presence will be valuable, and God willing it will not be for very long."

"I pray that it will be so. It seems that every time we find a degree of peace somewhere, the outside world intrudes yet again," Rav'an stated. "But I am not being a good hostess. Tell me how it is with the people from your lands." She smiled at him, and Sir Matthew felt encouraged to continue.

"There are shortages everywhere now in Tripoli, my Lady," he continued. "The coastal cities, like Tyre, Acre and Tripoli, are supplied from the sea, but lands further inland now lie untilled because of the fear of Arab raiders from the North. They come and plunder wherever they can. They take slaves, and people are afraid. Bad news travels fast, so people are migrating to the cities, which cannot feed them well."

Talon was thoughtful. Raynald de Châtillon was a fanatic who had spent time in Arab prisons, eventually coming home a pauper. He had hardly done badly since, having gained possession of a rich wife who owned the castle of Kerak down in the south. His persistent attacks on caravans, however, were causing ripples of pain all across the Kingdom as the Arabs retaliated.

Talon pointed out a man to Matthew, one seated further down the long tables with some of the villagers who had been invited to the feast. Although the large, crowded hall was full of dancing shadows thrown against the walls from the flickering candles, in the light of the oil lamps his features were clear enough to be seen. His nose had been cut off and his lips mutilated. It had turned his face into something from a nightmare.

"See that man over there? He is a priest."

Matthew stared. "My God! He is so ugly!" He noticed the priest's garb. "One of those Byzantine heretics? Was he born like that?" he asked with a smirk.

"No, Sir Matthew," replied Talon, and his tone was hard. "This island was once paid an unwelcome visit by Châtillon. Among his other crimes, he sought out and mutilated every Byzantine priest he could lay hands on. I am told that Psellos was formerly a handsome young man. Despite this great sin perpetrated against him, Psellos is a good and kindly priest, and his flock love him. We have all come to value him."

Sir Matthew looked shocked. "I, I, er, I didn't know," he said, sounding chastened.

"No; you could not have known, Sir Matthew, but this is what is hurting your cause so much in the Kingdom. The new men who come out, full of thunder, bluster and zeal, do not realize how much damage they do by ignoring the realities in the land. They see diplomacy with the Arabs as a weakness. Châtillon is worse. He is a cruel, greedy, violent and ignorant fool, and he is very dangerous to the Christian cause."

There was an uncomfortable silence after that, but Rav'an came to the rescue with some sweetmeats. "Try these small cakes and those pastries, Sir Matthew. I am sure you will like them." She smiled at the chastened knight.

He took a bite of one and his features creased into a smile of pure contentment. "My Lady, it tastes as though it came from heaven!" he exclaimed and shut his eyes while he munched on the delicious pastries. "Then heaven is a kitchen and you'd better have another before my son takes them all, Sir Matthew," she told him while offering the plate again before Rostam could reach for it.

That night, as Talon lay with Rav'an in his arms, he held her close. Her hair, jet black and lustrous, fell across his chest.

"You are worried, I can tell," she murmured, as she gently stroked his scars. He could feel her breath on his chest.

"I cannot lie to you, my Love," he responded. "I hear little to indicate there will be a lasting peace. However, I am certain that the Sultan does not want war and I am sure that we will be able to persuade him to hold off for a while longer."

"A while longer? You mean it cannot last?"

"No, my Rav'an, it cannot last. Not as long as he, Salah Ed Din, wants Jerusalem as his legacy and the Latins ignore the fact that he has an unlimited supply of men, arms and food. while they have to beg for men and supplies from reluctant kings in far off countries."

"Come back to me safe. That is all I ask of you, my Prince. Do not tarry there any longer than you have to," she told him. There was a plea in her tone.

"I shall, God willing. I shall."

The next day was full of preparation and bustle. Talon had his family put it about that he was merely going to see one of his merchant friends. This would allay any suspicion that he was departing for any length of time. Neither he nor Reza thought they would be gone more than two to three weeks at the outside.

That same morning a ship was sighted heading for the harbor. Talon stood with Max, Reza, Sir Matthew, and one of Matthew's servants on the top of the tower and watched the scene play out at the distant harbor entrance. They had already warned Guy and Rostam, who had spent the night on board, that a ship approached, using a signal rocket. The flash and ferocious hissing, along with the long flame and sparks as the projectile was launched with a loud whooshing sound, had caused Sir Matthew to flinch and his servant to fall to his knees with fear.

"God save us!" the servant had cried out involuntarily, raising his arms to protect himself. Matthew, seeing that the others were not in the least bit fazed by the noise and fire, recovered his wits enough to gather his tattered courage around him, cross himself and then to snarl at his servant, who was still groveling on the floor, moaning with fright.

"Pull yourself together, man, and get off your knees! You are disgracing me!" All the same he stared in awe and wonder as the rocket soared high into the sky, leaving a dark trail of smoke behind. He crossed himself again surreptitiously, muttered a prayer, then hurried over to join the others, who were nonchalantly leaning against the northern parapet, watching the effect of the rocket upon the people in the distant harbor. They had seen almost instant activity, and before very long Guy's ship nosed out of the harbor to intercept the newcomer.

"That has to be Henry's ship." Max stated. "I recognize it, and he is flying your colors, Talon." It was clearly Talon's second captain and his ship. Within a short while both vessels returned to port alongside each other.

"That was pretty quick of Guy," Reza remarked. "They get further out each time, which is good, as it gives them room to maneuver."

Talon was sure that Rostam's sharp eyes had hastened Guy's departure from the port.

"So this was what we saw from our ship when we came towards your port!" Matthew said. There was awe in his voice. "God help me, but I have never seen such a thing!" He was looking at Talon and his companions with something akin to fear as well as respect.

"If any ship got past one of our captains, there are other ways to deal with them once they try to land inside the port," Max told him, watching Matthew's reaction with amusement. "I, too, used to think this was a fearsome thing to behold. Now I know what makes it happen and I am not so frightened of it," He waved his hand at Talon and Reza. "They learned all this in China; do you know where that country is? Matthew shook his head. "Is it where magicians live? Do they teach magic there?"

"No, it is not magic, but it certainly looks like terrible magic when delivered the right way," Talon told him. He went on to briefly tell Matthew about an ambush he and Reza had prepared for Châtillon on their way to Jerusalem a year ago.

"He does not like me one little bit, nor I he," Talon told the bemused knight.

Finally all was ready for Talon and Reza to depart. They said their goodbyes in the Solarium where there was some privacy. Everyone was aware of the uncertainty, none more so than Rav'an, who held their small daughter, Fariba, in her arms when Talon kissed her and the baby goodbye. She handed him their daughter. Fariba opened her eyes and grizzled up at him. "So that you remember her and us," Rav'an told him.

"How could I not!" he whispered. "Look after the little one for me. God protect you, my Rav'an," he told her, and they embraced. There were tears in her eyes as she nodded and murmured, "Come back to me, Talon. Soon!"

Reza and Jannat were embracing in the other part of the chamber. Then the two men left together. Theodora met them in the hall below and called out, "Be safe. God protect you!" They waved as they left the hall and joined the mounted assembly in the courtyard.

Their journey to the harbor was short and they arrived unannounced. The villagers were not surprised by the sight of their Lord and Reza with their men. Both were well known for their abrupt departures and unobtrusive returns. Nevertheless, they gathered to get a glimpse of their Lord and master, who had improved their lives measurably since his arrival over a year ago.

The little port bustled with men and women working on the catch from that morning. Men were cleaning and preparing their fishing boats for the next day, repairing nets and stacking baskets and lobster cages. Women were standing at long tables gutting the fish and salting some. The offal was tossed into the harbor water to be squabbled over by the excited and screaming seagulls and other birds looking for a free meal. The seagulls wheeled and screeched at the humans below, and the stink of drying fish on long racks pervaded the port. The feral cats in the vicinity were gathered there waiting eagerly to snatch a morsel that might come their way. Some would even jump onto the tables only to be shoved off again by the humans carrying out the work. The fishing off the coast provided more than enough for the village and the castle that protected it. A portion of the catch would make its way up to the castle later that day.

Talon enjoyed the smells and sounds of the small harbor. His harbor now, and his people, where the work on two substantial towers on either side of the entrance was almost completed. They would have a couple of deadly Scorpion bows mounted on each tower eventually. Arab pirates were becoming more bold now that summer was almost here. The Emperor was unable or unwilling to do much about them on the south coast, let alone the remote north side. Talon, however, had no intention of letting pirates plunder his land and did what he could to prevent them. A palisade was half built around the port which would eventually be followed by a stone wall. He sighed inwardly. Everything took time, and there was never enough of that commodity.

Sir Matthew was rowed out to his ship while Talon and Reza handed off their horses to waiting grooms and then walked with their men to the ship that Guy captained. Talon had already informed Matthew that he would be taking his own ship.

"It's not that I do not trust you, Sir Matthew. It is simply that I wish to sail with my people on this particular journey. Besides, I will need a ship to bring me home!" Matthew had reluctantly nodded his head, then stalked off to the boat waiting to take him to his own vessel.

Talon met Henry, his other captain, on the quayside. "How did it go, Henry?" he asked, after he had extricated himself from the bear-hug greeting Henry had administered. "Very well, Talon!" Henry boomed. "Dimitri sends his greetings and he is happy. I think there is a woman somewhere in his life now. His men are of good morale and all seems quiet at the palace... for the time being. I actually got a glimpse of the Lady Tamura this time around. Damn good looking girl, I have to say." He leered. "Wouldn't mind a tumble with her m'self!"

Talon smiled back affectionately at his old friend. "Don't even think it, Henry, you might be heard by all the wrong people. In any case, you are now on guard duty here in the port. Reza and I are on our way to Tyre. No time to explain, but I want you to talk to Max, who is in charge and will explain. Have a rest, and we will be seeing you back here, perhaps in a couple of weeks. No one outside of Max and the ladies is to know where we have gone."

Henry looked his surprise but nodded, then replied, "Very well, Talon, I understand. I'll certainly talk to Max. Besides, I have some bolts of cloth for their Ladyships which they asked me to purchase, and some baskets of Trudos mountain herbs for the Lady Theodora. We will keep on the alert down here, have no fear, nor concerns. God speed both of you." He embraced them in turn, then stood back to watch them stride down the small quay towards Captain Guy's ship.

Talon and Reza were armored in their fine chain hauberks, not the clumsily made hauberks the Latins such as Sir Matthew wore, but fine steel links that could be worn without too much discomfort. Matthew had looked over their hauberks with undisguised envy and had even asked Talon where they had obtained them.

"You can purchase these in Damascus, but ours came from those who had no further use for them," was the laconic response.

Junayd carried their bows, which he lovingly tended. They, of course, carried the Japanese swords which had been presented to them when they had left Guan Zu in China, several years ago. Neither man would be parted from these magnificent weapons. The remainder of their equipment was brought on board by their men, all known to Rostam and Captain Guy, who greeted each man by name.

"Take it all below to the Lord Talon's cabin," Guy told them. "Otherwise it will get in the way." Yosef and Dar'an, accompanied by Junayd, lugged the bulky shields, weapons and bags below.

Rostam was hopping about with ill-contained excitement as his father and uncle boarded the ship. Talon smiled at him, amused at the eagerness of his son, and then glanced at Guy. "We can leave now, Captain, whenever you are ready. Um... do we have a navigator on board? I don't see one."

Guy grinned. "Oh, cruel, Sir! You know full well we do. Furthermore, you know very well that it is your son," he admonished his leader. "As soon as we are clear of the harbor we are all at his mercy, Lord help us!"

In fact Guy had developed a healthy respect for Rostam's skill as a navigator and rarely let an opportunity pass whereby he allowed the boy to test his skills.

Talon smiled at Rostam. "Very well then, we will leave it to you. Let us see what you can do. We sail all day and all night. See if you can get us there in less than three days!"

He looked over at the visiting ship and swore under his breath. "Damn, Sir Matthew was supposed to leave harbor behind us. It seems he is already on the move. We need to get past him and lead the way, Guy. That lumbering old tub needs to be guided home I suspect."

He stayed on deck and watched as his captain shouted orders to his crew and then set all sails to overtake the vessel carrying Sir Matthew.

They cleared the entrance of the harbor where the work on the towers appeared to be proceeding well. The workers paused to watch the two ships slide by, and many waved. Talon lifted his hand in reply, then turned and stared back at the castle in the receding distance.

"Captain Guy!" he exclaimed. "Look!" His tone was urgent as he pointed to the castle on the peak.

Guys whirled right about and stared. A bright light, followed by a thin dark line of smoke, had streaked into the sky above the castle.

"A signal, but what for?" he exclaimed.

"It has to be a ship!" Talon replied. "They would not send up a rocket otherwise! Rostam, do you see anything ahead?" Talon called.

"No Father, nothing. Wait!" He leaped up onto the transom, shielding his eyes from the sun. "Yes, I do see something ahead. A sail?" Agile as a monkey he scampered up the shrouds till he was half way up the mast. "It is a ship, Father. Not one but two... perhaps even three!" The boy was pointing now. "Father, Uncle Reza, I see three ships ahead of the visiting vessel. They are coming this way!" he squeaked, his voice breaking in his excitement.

"Thank God someone had the good sense to send up the rocket," Talon murmured to Reza, who had come to stand next to him. "Now we are forewarned."

Reza nodded grimly. "Now we're in trouble! I will get our men ready," he said, and began to leave.

"You and Rostam are in charge of the Scorpions, Brother." Talon told him. Reza raised his arm in acknowledgment and ran off to collect their men. Talon stared forward towards the oncoming sails, which were beginning to emerge over the horizon. This was an inauspicious start to a journey.

Guy was roaring at the crew to tighten sail. "Come on, you lazy blobs of fat!" he roared. "I want to see if you are real sailors! Put your backs into it. Oars out!"

The men scampered to obey. Within a few minutes of frantic activity, shouted orders, and the stamp of running feet on the deck, the long oars were pushed out and the men braced to their labor. In a flurry of foam the ship surged forward.

Talon glanced back at the harbor, now a quarter league behind them, and was relieved to see that Henry's ship was already making its way out of the harbor to follow them.

––––––––––––––––

Chapter 3

Intervention

No dread of death—if with us die our foes—
Save that it seems even duller than repose:
Come when it will—we snatch the life of life—
When lost—what wrecks it—by disease or strife?
Let him who crawls enamored of decay,
Cling to his couch, and sicken years away;
Heave his thick breath; and shake his palsied head;
Ours—the fresh turf, and not the feverish bed.
　　　　　　　　　　　　　　　　—Lord Byron

By the time Guy's ship had almost caught up with Sir Matthew the crew of that ship had become aware of strangers bearing down on them from the north. The ship's captain brought Sir Matthew's attention to the following vessels, then ordered his men to slacken off sail.

"Those could be pirates ahead, Sir," his captain said, looking worried. "We cannot fight them on our own. We should wait for Lord Talon to come up. See, there is another of his ships leaving harbor. There must be cause for concern if both his ships are chasing after us."

Sir Matthew stared back towards the port where he could see the second of Talon's ships pulling out of the harbor entrance with all sails set. It, too, had its oars out and seemed to be in a tearing rush.

"How did they know?" he began to ask, but then he noticed the traces of smoke in the sky above the castle. "Of course!" he said. "Arm yourselves, men!" he called out.

He and his attendants hurriedly went below to prepare for battle, while the forward progress of the ship was slowed to allow Talon's ship to catch up with them. The approaching vessel's oars were rising and falling in a rapid but regular rhythm, foaming the sea on either side. Its bow tossed spray high into the air as it raced through the choppy sea to catch up with the Latin ship, which was now wallowing in the swell, waiting for them. By the time Guy's ship surged past Matthew's vessel, the strange sails were only a league away, Talon called across the water to Sir Matthew.

"They could be pirates! We have had news of them on the other side of the island before. Stay close behind us in line and be ready for a fight!" he shouted.

Matthew raised his hand in acknowledgment, Talon then called over to Guy, "Put us a hundred paces ahead of them, Guy."

"Yes, Lord," Guy responded. During emergencies he liked to address Talon, as "Lord". It served to show his own men who was in charge.

"Pull, you motherless mob! We are going to have a fight!" he roared out to his panting but grinning men; they pulled and cheered. The sails were hauled taut and their slim boat surged forward. Talon glanced behind him. Henry's ship was catching up fast; before long it would be taking up station behind Matthew's vessel, so that they could protect the more vulnerable ship should the intruders prove to be hostile and decide to attack.

Talon glanced forward and saw that Reza had already taken his post with Rostam in the bows next to the Scorpions, and the oilcloth covers had been dragged off the deadly machines. The enormous, oversized bows squatted on either side of the bowsprit. While these were Scorpions, huge bows, which were not uncommon in this day and age, the ones mounted on Talon's ships had an added sting, a tube of Chinese powder with a fuse which could be ignited just before the spear was launched. The spear would strike the side of an enemy ship and then the tube would explode, causing much damage and even fires on the target vessel. He turned and stared back at Henry's ship. It, too, carried Scorpions, and the men who manned them were competent, although he would not put them in the same class as Reza. They could inflict much damage at close range, should the need arise.

He felt a nudge at his elbow and turned to find Junayd standing nearby, holding his helmet and a small shield. "You should prepare, Lord," he said, holding them out respectfully. Dar'an arrived to thrust his bow into his hand. "I have arrows here, Lord," he told Talon.

"Thank you, Junayd. I shall be fine, Dar'an. Leave the arrows with Junayd. Go forward and support Reza and Rostam. I don't want any accidents." Dar'an, he knew, could handle the Chinese powder safely and effectively better than anyone including Reza.

Dar'an grinned and disappeared off the command deck. Yosef stayed with Talon and Junayd. Both men held their bows ready. Even Guy had been persuaded to don a breast plate, a helmet, and to carry a light shield. Larger shields had been hooked to the side of the ship near to the steersmen to offer nominal protection against arrows, which would surely fly if there was danger ahead.

It seemed there would be, as keen eyes up near the top of the mainmast called back that the visitors were definitely not Latin and very likely to be Arabs, which could only spell trouble. Talon strode forward to join Reza, who was standing with Rostam on the head-rail, holding onto a stay while he tried to assess the approaching ships. Spray from the bow wave occasionally flew over the rail, wetting them.

"Make sure that the Scorpions are protected from the spray and the slow match is kept alive." Reza called back to the seamen crouched over the deadly weapons. "I do not want any hitches when it is time."

"What do you want to do, Talon?" Reza inquired. "They don't look friendly to me."

Talon jumped up on the rail the better to see. He could now make out figures on the foredeck of the leading vessel, which had turned towards their own ships. They were turbaned, and there were many of them. He could just make out the glint of blades, and that decided him."

"They are not friendly, and we cannot let them get past us, Brother," he growled. It was the second time that Arab prates had prowled past his port in the last few months. This time they appeared to mean business.

"We will let them come close, and then we will loose our Scorpions," he said. "I will go back to Guy and leave it to you to prepare the weapons, Brother. Look after the boy." He slapped Rostam on the shoulder, jumped down and strode back along the deck to where Guy was standing waiting for his orders.

"Prepare for a fight, Guy. They are pirates," he told his captain briefly. "We cannot allow any of them to gain entry to the port."

"You heard the Lord Talon!" Guy bellowed to the eager men on deck, who had hauled in their oars and were now arming themselves with swords and spears, and donning chain hauberks. Talon had cleaned out the armories in Paphos to provide his men with suitable armor. They roared back and waved their weapons in the air.

Bowmen arranged themselves along the sides and stood on the higher command deck near Yosef. Dar'an, the man who knew all about throwing explosive devices, returned from the bows and, along with two assistants, climbed into the small platform near the top of the mainmast. They carried some long, narrow, wooden devices which they treated with great care.

"Get the men out of sight. Just leave the sailors in view. Let's bring them in close enough for Reza," Talon said. Guy bellowed an order and the armed men, including the archers, crouched down under the cover of the high sides of the ship.

Talon stared back at Sir Matthew's ship following them. It was not a lean galley like his but a rounder, larger ship of the kind the Latins built, clumsy in any wind other than one directly behind. It would have been almost defenseless against the pirates had they encountered it alone. Now, however, it was firmly established between Guy's ship and Henry's. Talon mentally shrugged. They were as prepared as they would ever be, and it now depended upon the intentions of the Arabs and what kind of weapons they possessed.

The Arab ships were lean, fast vessels with two masts carrying huge lateen sails, making them highly maneuverable and able to sail very close to the wind. Now that they were closer he could see men crowding the sides of the lead ship. He realized he would have to strike first or be overwhelmed.

Talon thought about the situation. It would not serve to just cripple one and drive the others off. They might come back while he was in Tyre.

"I want to try to destroy all three, Guy," he said to his captain, who nodded.

"I agree, Lord," the big man rumbled. "They are a menace now and in the future."

"Let's see what our Scorpions can do. We've practiced often enough," Talon said to Junayd and Yosef.

"Hold your course, Guy. That will bring them to us, but be prepared for any one of them that decides to go for the lamb in our midst."

Talon realized that his own ships were not quite as fast as those of the pirates, which cut through the water like deadly sharks about to strike at a slower prey. No galleys these; they reminded him of the long, sleek boats that he had seen in Oman and the Red Sea. So now the Arabs of Syria or Egypt were becoming good at building ships of the same design, he surmised. He, however, had range and surprise on his side, which he fervently hoped would be enough.

He began to feel the old familiar rush of excitement and a tightening in the pit of his stomach that came with the beginning of a fight. Taking a couple of deep breaths he felt his heart settle. His responsibility was to protect the ships in his care, he reminded himself, and to drive the enemy away, killing them if possible.

Guy held their vessel on an intercept course, and the Arabs appeared to be happy to oblige. Their lead ship was now only five hundred paces away with the men crowding its decks waving their weapons threateningly in the air. As the ships approached one another, the shouts and insults coming from the Arab ship nearest them became clearer as they promised all manner of horrible things they intended to do once they had taken the ship.

Talon took an arrow and placed it on the string of his bow. His men who had bows followed his lead, and then they waited. The distance shrank to two hundred paces, and now they could distinguish brightly dressed and armed men on the command deck. Several wore polished armor and gold pointed helmets with plumes attached. Talon decided that these men would be his targets, and murmured to Junayd and Yosef that they too should take them down if they could.

Still they waited, and the tension grew as the distance went down very rapidly from two hundred to sixty yards. Arrows began to fly. One whispered past Talon's head, while several embedded themselves with heavy thuds in the rails and one of the shields protecting the steersmen. Just as Talon was beginning to wonder why Reza had not loosed the Scorpion, he saw a small plume of smoke in the bows, followed by a loud twang, and the huge arrow shot away from his ship. The speed of the rod was phenomenal. Leaving a thin trail of dark smoke behind it, the arrow made a shallow arc across the narrowing gap between the ships and hammered into the side of the enemy ship, burying itself with a loud thud deep into the wood below the railing in its very middle. Moments later there was a loud explosion, the blast of which shook their own ship. The side of the Arab ship was blasted into a welter of splinters and shrouded in a small cloud of dirty yellow smoke. Reza had aimed at the area where most of the men had been standing, and the result was devastating.

"Again, again!" Talon muttered. "We need to sink them! Arrows!" he called out, and drew his own bow, which creaked slightly under the strain. Resting the fingers holding the string just below the corner of his cheekbone and right ear, he took careful aim at one of the more decorative men on the enemy command deck, who appeared disoriented by the explosion.

His arrow flew across the water and struck his target just below the man's helmet. It went deep and knocked the pirate onto his back. He struggled feebly while his men crouched over him ineffectively, then the body convulsed and was still. Other men on that deck fell to the arrows of Yosef and Junayd, while a hail of arrows fell onto the survivors of the first explosion. Panicked men fled from their steering deck, now a target for all the archers on Talon's ship.

During this time Reza had prepared another of his devilish devices. He looked back at Talon and waved. Talon waved back, gesturing at him to hurry. He had seen the second ship sailing rapidly past the first, making for Sir Matthew's vessel. If they attacked and boarded, it could be all over for Matthew and his men. They would be slaughtered.

"Shoot!" Talon called.

Reza crouched over his Scorpion, made a small adjustment, then waved Rostam and the other men back. Another twang of the great string, the Scorpion snapped and shuddered, and its spear-like arrow, a smoking wrapped bundle secured to its shaft, sped the short distance to the pirate ship. There was pandemonium on the vessel, so no one was prepared for the second arrow, which struck the ship just above the water line towards the stern.

The second explosion rocked the entire vessel, which seemed to shiver from one end to the other. When the yellow smoke cleared, the men on Talon's ship could see a black and splintered hole, as wide as a man's outstretched arms, where the arrow had struck. The crew of Guy's ship cheered wildly. Salt water was already pouring into the crippled vessel. A fire had started on the main deck where the first arrow had struck, which the pirates were desperately trying to put out, but Talon and his archers were shooting them down every time they came close to the fire. The flames reached the pitch-covered rigging, after which there was no stopping it. Fire raced up the tar-covered stays and caught the mainsail, which blossomed into a beacon of flame, and then the other sail also caught fire. The ship transformed into an inferno.

Pirates began to leap overboard. Many were dragged down by their heavy armor. Those who could swim called out for help, but Talon's men watched them in stony silence.

"Do we pick them up, Lord?" Guy asked.

Talon shook his head. "No," he growled. "They can swim to land, if they are able. We have another problem to deal with over there." He pointed to the second of the Arab ships, which was closing with Matthew's. "Turn us, and be quick about it, Guy," he ordered. "We might already be too late."

He could see Henry's vessel turning towards the third pirate vessel. Something dark sped from the bows of Henry's ship, and even at that distance he could hear the thud of the strike on the pirate vessel. It had been aimed high, however, and merely demolished part of the after deck. The subsequent explosion vented much of its force into the sky, but several small fires broke out on the deck. Talon was impressed by the speed at which the Arab ship spun about, put on all sail and fled the scene. They had witnessed the rapid destruction of their companion ship and clearly wanted no more of this kind of treatment. Henry tried to send another arrow after the fleeing ship, but it vanished into the choppy waves with a splash. The pirate ship raced away, putting as much distance between their ships as possible.

Disappointed, Talon turned his attention back to the nearer conflict. He was disturbed to see that the second Arab ship had closed the distance between itself and Sir Matthew's. Arrows were flying, and they were merely a dozen or so paces away from boarding. The captain of that ship, undeterred by the destruction of its companion, was recklessly determined to take a prize, or at the very least avenge its lost companion by destroying Matthew's ship.

"Guy, get us on Matthew's port side. Hurry! This one is determined to seize his ship! We do not have time to go around. Do you see what I mean?" Talon called out to his captain.

"I do, Lord." Guy shouted instructions, and his crew dropped their weapons and raced to their oars, pushing them out of the sides of the ship as fast as they could. In a flurry of foam the oars bit into the water the ship wheeled around, heeling over alarmingly, and then they were racing back to help Sir Matthew. Guy was already yelling at the men to trim the sails to catch every bit of wind. Out of the corner of his eye, Talon could see that Henry was making haste to close with the pirate vessel from the other side.

"How many did we lose?" he asked Junayd, as they sped towards the two ships, now about to become locked in mortal combat. "Only one, Lord. He stuck his silly head up and caught one in the eye. Some people never learn," he added with a grimace.

"Hmm, not bad odds for an entire shipload of pirates. I wish Henry had managed to disable that other one." Not only might the pirates return to harry his harbor, they might tell other Arab pirates what had befallen, warning them, which would cost his captains the element of surprise in future battles.

He and his men watched with growing impatience as the scene ahead of them unfolded. Reza and Rostam, both fully armed, had rushed to join Talon and Guy on the steering deck. They were still two hundred paces away when the pirate ship closed with an audible, splintering crash against Sir Matthew's ship, and then pirates began to swarm aboard. Talon and his men could hear yells and screams as battle was joined. The struggling mob of fighting men swayed back and forth across the deck of the Latin ship.

Talon wondered at the boldness of the attack. Surely the pirate captain had seen what happened to the two other ships. The prudent thing to do would have been to make a swift departure and wait for another chance, but this man seemed to put recklessness ahead of caution.

Staring hard at the pandemonium reigning on the deck of the Latin ship, Talon could see that the boarders were not having it all their own way. Sir Matthew, with roars of encouragement to his own men, battered the shrieking boarders back with pike, spear and sword. Talon saw a shield wall forming, which the pirates were having trouble overcoming. It was a nearly impenetrable barrier of overlapping shields, behind which knights and attendants crouched and stabbed at their enemies. It formed the only coherent defense the ship appeared to offer, but it was enough to allow Talon's ship to arrive just in time.

Talon and Reza were standing together, ready to jump onto the other ship, when Talon noticed Rostam nearby. The boy was clearly eager to come with them. "Stay here, Rostam!" Talon shouted at his son. "Junayd, make sure he doesn't come with us!" He didn't have time to see whether Junayd heard him because just then the ships ground together with a shattering crash, sandwiching Matthew's ship between Talon's and the pirate ship, and it was time to leap.

Both he and Reza landed on a deck full of yelling, cursing and screaming men trying to hack and stab each other to death. It was already slippery from blood, and men groaned and wept on the deck where they lay. The metallic stink of blood and the stench of opened guts and loosed bowels enveloped the boarders, making some gag.

Talon easily tapped a thrust spear blade aside and stabbed upwards. The spearman fell away with a cry, but another leapt forward with his sword high and shield held close. Without pausing, Talon swept his sword in a short arc and nearly severed the man's bare leg. The pirate's scream of agony was cut off as Reza stabbed him in the throat. That was when Talon became aware of a high-pitched yelling going on to his left. He looked in that direction and saw Rostam waving his sword at a big, hairy man with a huge axe in his hand, which he was brandishing in preparation to demolish the boy, who appeared to be quite unafraid.

Both Talon and Reza reacted. They came at the man from two directions, and with their speed and razor-sharp blades finished him off. As the huge man flopped to the deck, bleeding form several mortal wounds, Talon shouted over the noise, "Stay close to your uncle!" Then he plowed on, with Yosef and Dar'an close by him, into the mass of shouting men. He brushed past Sir Matthew, who called out hoarsely, "Thank you, Lord," before he, too, waded back into the mass of struggling men, cutting and hacking at anyone who got in his way.

Talon's blood was racing and his eyes were everywhere as he parried and stabbed at opponents in front and to the sides, boring into their ranks, closely followed by the yelling men behind him. Talon forgot about everything but living and killing during these frantic moments, the all too familiar fire of battle driving him on. Reza led a charge of screaming men to crash into the flank of the gang of plunderers who had not realized their peril in time.

Rostam, realizing he could not keep up, hesitated, but Reza stepped in front of him with a shout, "Stay close to me, Rostam. Don't get left behind!" Rostam searched for his father, but Talon was in the middle of a group of yelling men, clearing a path for himself with his flashing blade.

Just as he was about to take on a man with scimitar and shield, Reza slipped on the bloody deck. He went down on one knee and was almost on all fours. The pirate, seeing his opportunity, gave a yell of triumph and drew his weapon back to slash down onto Reza's back. With a scream of his own, Rostam rushed in and drove his own sword into the exposed gap of the pirate's neck. His sword went in deep, and the blow was fatal. The shocked man gaped at the boy; then, choking on his own blood, fell to his knees alongside Reza, who gave an exclamation of surprise as he leapt to his feet.

The pirate was a dead weight when he slumped to the deck, and Rostam, wide-eyed, had to wrestle his sword free from the corpse. Seeing the boy's shock, Reza seized him by the shoulder and gripped him hard.

"Glad you don't always obey your father, lad," he shouted. "You saved my life! Come on, stay close." He led the way for his yelling men. Their small charge at the flank of the mob broke the will of the pirates. Those who could fled back to their ship, and once aboard they tried to pole their boat away. Too late. Henry's ship appeared on their seaward side, blocking off any escape. His ship thumped against their side, sending a shudder through both vessels, and then his howling and shrieking men were pouring over the other side of the pirate ship and the slaughter began. Swords flashed and spears stabbed as the roaring, shouting men took on the re-maining pirates. Reza led a rush of eager men across the pi-rate ship to join Henry.

The pirates, knowing they would get no quarter, sold their lives dearly, and Talon's men suffered for it; but it was only a matter of time before they were overwhelmed. One man in particular, wearing expensive armor and a gold-in-laid helmet and shield, fought like a tiger. He was cutting and stabbing with deadly effect, which drew Talon and Reza towards him.

"He has done a lot of damage!" Talon panted as he sur-veyed the carnage.

"Give him to me, Brother!" Reza called over the din.

Talon nodded. "Try not to kill him, Brother." Then he no-ticed Rostam hovering behind Reza. "Get behind me!" he snapped. The boy hastened to obey.

Reza darted forward, elbowing men aside and in one case cutting away the sword of another by the simple means of cutting off his hand with a flick of his blade. That man died from another's spear thrust. It was only a moment before Reza stood before his chosen opponent who drew back after cutting down one of Henry's men with breathtaking ease.

His black hair was drawn back in a ponytail that extended from under his helmet, and the large gold rings in his ear-lobes bounced as he moved. His black eyes glared balefully at the slim, dark figure who suddenly appeared before him.

"So you want to die, do you?" he shouted at Reza. "I am here to oblige. Your turn to go to hell!"

He leapt forward with his shield held across his lower body and his heavy sword swinging more like a club than a sharp weapon. A thin stream of blood flew off the blade as it swept sideways in towards the motionless figure of Reza. But then there was a clink of steel on steel and Reza was gone from where he had been. He danced out of the way and nicked the sword arm of the pirate, making the man wince.

Reza's blade had cut through the expensive chain links as though they were mere cloth.

The pirate stepped back hurriedly and glared at Reza as though reassessing him. He flicked a look at the wound on his upper arm; blood was welling up, staining his armor. He shook his head and charged, swinging his sword left and right, holding his shield forward like a battering ram. Once again his target was gone from where it had been, and there was another cut on his upper arm. This time it was deeper, and the pirate could feel the pain. His sword arm wavered and dropped for just an instant. But that was enough for Reza. He slipped in and his sword blade prodded the pirate's throat, drawing blood.

"You may surrender now and live," Reza invited the man, who coughed as Reza's blade pushed harder, causing more blood to flow. "Or you can die. Drop the sword and the shield!" Reza ordered sharply.

The pirate hesitated, but another prod from Reza and he reluctantly complied. He had no sooner done so than Talon's men rushed forward, snatched up his weapon, then bound him. He submitted with resignation, only wincing as his wounded arm was pulled behind him.

Reza wiped his own blade clean on a rag, displaying the unique waved effect on the surface of the long, slim blade, then slid it into its sheath.

"I think we have won the day, Brother," he called.

The only people left standing on the bloody pirate deck were Talon, his companions and their wildly cheering crews. A small space was cleared around Talon and Reza by the jubilant men. Everyone was spattered with blood, and many were wounded. Neither Talon or Reza were hurt, but both were soaked with other men's blood.

"Where is that boy?" Talon roared, looking for Rostam, suddenly panicked with worry.

"It's all right, Brother. He is right here with me." Reza laughed at the concern in Talon's voice. Talon visibly relaxed, then was about to bellow angrily at his son when Reza cocked his head at his friend and shook his head.

"He did well, Brother. He saved my life. He is a true warrior." He reached behind him and pulled the boy forward. Rostam still held his sword, which was bloody. Reza tousled his hair. "The boy is his father's son!" Reza shouted at the happy men with a laugh. They cheered again, and Talon gave his son a quizzical look, tinged with respect. "If Uncle Reza said so then it was so," he told the boy. "I am proud of you."

Rostam looked as though he were going to burst with pride.

Junayd slipped up to Talon and went on one knee. "I could not stop him, Lord. He was too quick. I kept near him, though. He is like..."

"His father! Ha ha!" Reza finished for him.

Talon had been ready to chastise Junayd; his face was grim, but then he decided to let it go. Smiling down at the contrite Junayd he said, "He is certainly that, Junayd; you must watch him more carefully." Everyone let out their breath with relief. Talon was known for being a hard taskmaster, no less so with his son and his closest aides.

As the crew set to work to clean up, Sir Matthew came and stood before him. His rent hauberk and battered shield were testimony to the intense fight on his own ship. He grinned and ducked his head. "My thanks for your timely arrival, Lord Talon. Your men are formidable fighters."

"Are you wounded, Sir Matthew?" Talon asked with concern.

"I? No, but I have men who are injured, and I am worried because I have no one who can dress their wounds and prevent infection. We had not expected to encounter pirates."

"At this end of the sea you *always* expect pirates, Sir. We have seen these ships before." Talon searched the horizon. "I just wish we had been able to destroy the third one."

Henry and his men were rounding up the very few pirates still on their feet and binding their arms. The dead were being piled into a corner, while the mortally wounded were being dispatched by crewmen using knives to cut their throats.

"We have a physician from Byzantium, one of the very best, at the castle. Your men can go back to port with Captain Henry here, and he will make sure they are sent up for treatment. He will be hanging the surviving pirates."

Matthew looked alarmed. "A Greek? A *woman?*" He sounded uncomfortable.

"You seem not to know this, but the Byzantine and the Arab physicians are among the finest in the world. I would never allow myself to be placed in the ignorant hands of a Latin 'Bleeder'," Talon told him with some asperity. "Believe me, she will save many lives which the Latins would lose through neglect, ignorance, or sheer stupidity. But it is your choice. Let me know as soon as you can." He turned away just in time to hear a shout behind him.

He turned and noticed some of the crewmen dragging a boy almost the same age as Rostam towards him. The boy was dressed in expensive clothing and wore a breast plate like the man Reza had bested. He was bare-headed, and it was easy to see his resemblance to the formidable pirate in the younger, pale and frightened face.

"Bring the other prisoner to me," Talon ordered his men, who shoved the pirate in front of him, none too gently. They forced him down onto his knees alongside the boy. His helmet was gone, presumably booty for one of the crew, Talon surmised. His long black hair was now loose and fell about his face. He was still defiant and spat on the deck. "My cousin will be back with more ships to avenge me, you will see. Do what you will!"

"Do we see a likeness there, Reza?" Talon asked.

"I'd say so. Father and son, perhaps?" They were speaking Farsi at this point, so no one except Rostam and Yosef could understand them, but it seemed the adult prisoner understood. "You speak Farsi?" he demanded in surprise.

"Shut up, you!" one of his guards slapped his wounded arm, making him wince but not cry out, although it must have been painful.

Talon raised his hand to deter further punishment, but then responded in Arabic. "Yes, we do, but that is not your native language, is it?" he said.

"No, I am Syrian," the man said. He stared back at his captors with a proud expression.

"Pirates are usually hung no matter where they come from," Reza told him, his tone ominous.

"You may hang me; I do not care." He looked at the boy, who stared tearfully back at him. "I ask only that you spare the boy." There was an edge of pleading in the proud man's voice.

"First things first. Who are you, and what are you doing here?"

"My name is Makhid and I am a cousin of Sultan Al-Adil. We can provide ransom."

Talon looked startled, as did Reza. "If you are related to Sultan al-Malik al-Adil Sayf ad-Din Abu-Bakr," Talon gave the name all its syllables, "then you are also related to Sultan Salah Ed Din, for they are brothers," he stated. He was watching very carefully for a response and was not disappointed. Makhid had not anticipated that Talon would know of Salah Ed Din. Few Crusaders knew any of the leaders of the Arab coalition.

So it was Makhid's turn to look surprised. He ducked his head clumsily. "Yes, we are related on my mother's side."

"What were you doing here? Were you coming to raid?" Talon demanded.

Makhid hesitated. Reza gestured for the boy's captors to bring him forward and drew his knife, which he placed alongside the boy's neck. "Answer the Lord Talon, or you will have no son."

Makhid stiffened. "I have heard of you... Lord Talon. And you," he turned and half bowed, "must be Reza, known as the Ghost! I ask again that you spare my son if you will not spare me."

Reza looked pleased, but Talon frowned and said, "Answer the question. What were you doing here?"

"We... we came to raid, yes," Makhid said reluctantly. "But it would appear to have been a bad idea."

"I would have to agree with that," Reza said, and pushed the boy roughly back into the unkind hands of the crewmen.

Makhid raised his head. "Tell me, Lord. Did anyone survive from the first ship that you sank with your devilish devices? That was not Greek Fire I saw strike his ship."

"Not that I can tell," Talon responded, and glanced towards the distant coastline three leagues away. "Not unless they can swim like fish."

In his mind's eye he could see the splendidly dressed man he had killed lying on the deck of the sinking boat.

Makhid sighed and looked down at the deck. "It was commanded by my brother. I shall mourn him."

"You knew the risks of raiding. I doubt that you would have given a thought for mercy had your raid been successful," Talon retorted. "Junayd, Yosef. Search him carefully and then take him below. Guard him well."

"Your son is my hostage," Talon told Makhid. "If he misbehaves, he will be hung out of hand by my people. Equally if you misbehave he will be hung. If and when a ransom is offered for you, you have my word that he will be released. That is my word."

Makhid struggled to his feet and bowed his head. "It is God's will. I accept your terms, Lord." He turned his head to stare at his son. "Remember to honor my word, which I give to Lord Talon. You are not to try and escape. I know of this man Reza; he will find you no matter what. I shall, God willing, live and be able to receive you when my freedom is granted. God is great. Go with God."

The boy was in tears, but he nodded and dropped his head. "I shall obey you, my Father, and the Lord Talon."

Makhid was led away to Talon's ship.

Henry had been hovering about, unable to understand everything that was being said but just enough. He said formally, "What are your wishes, Lord Talon?"

"You arrived just in time, Henry!" Talon complimented his friend. "It will be your task to take the wounded back to the castle, where our physician will, I am sure, be eager to put her skills to work. He..." he pointed to the boy, "goes with you as a hostage. He is to be treated well but not allowed to escape, and one of Reza's men is to be in attendance upon the boy at all times. Do you follow, Henry?" Talon spoke French to his captain, who replied in the same language, "Yes, I do, Lord Talon. It shall be as you order."

Henry turned away and began to shout commands to his willing crew.

"Oh, by the way, Henry!" Talon called.

"Yes, Lord?"

"Remember to take any treasure that is found on this ship back with you." They both laughed. On a grimmer note he said, "Don't forget to hang the remainder of the pirates, when you get to port, Henry."

Henry nodded somberly. "Yes, Lord. And the ship itself?"

"Take it with you. Repair what is necessary."

Henry grinned with delight. "I shall take care of everything, Lord. Now we have our third ship again!"

"Send news to the castle as soon as you arrive, Henry. They will have seen this fight from up there and be very concerned. Relieve their worries and tell them we are all in good health."

Talon turned his attention back to his own people. Sir Matthew was busy supervising the transfer of his nervous wounded to Henry's ship, while others were put to work cleaning up. There were four ships alongside one another, three of which now belonged to Talon. He surveyed the abundance of vessels with satisfaction. It crossed his mind that he might even have a navigator for the captured vessel, but that would have to be discussed it with Henry and Guy.

Sir Matthew, once he could see that his wounded were in good hands, approached Talon. "You must tell me about that pirate, Lord," he said with a wry smile. "I did not understand a word, but I suspect that you were negotiating. I would have simply hung him."

"Yes, I dare say you would," Talon responded. "But you see, understanding the way people think in this part of he world is a good thing. A prisoner of this rank can be useful. He will be ransomed, and his son is now a hostage for his good behavior. Also, his cousin might be deterred from raiding my lands, once he learns that two of his blood are out prisoners."

"He is a noble?" Matthew said with surprise.

"More noble than you or I," was the laconic response. "His own people probably consider him to be a raider. All of Christianity is fair game to them."

Matthew shook his head. "It seems I have much to learn."

Talon merely nodded. "Your captain should prepare to make sail. I am about to leave. This time, stay behind me and you will be safe. Take your dead back with you if you insist, otherwise you should bury them at sea. Throw any of the dead pirates overboard. They belong in the sea." Even as he spoke there were splashes as the dead pirates, and there were many of them, were tossed overboard.

"Safe sailing, Sir Matthew," he told the knight, but then he paused. "Sir Matthew!"

"Lord?"

"I noticed an interesting maneuver while you were defending your ship. The last time I saw it at work was during the battle of Myriokephalon. The Varangian Guard formed a shield wall, and it was highly effective. It seems you know how to do this?"

"Not I, Lord. I'm a horseman. It was that fellow over there." Matthew grinned and pointed out a huge man with gold torcs on his arms and blond braids hanging down his back, who was helping toss the limp bodies of dead pirates overboard. He had an axe thrust into his belt next to his sword, and his shield was slung over his back by a strap.

"He is a warrior who joined the Count's service and now works for me."

Talon stared. "A Norman?"

"No. A Saxon, and his French is horrible!"

Talon snorted a laugh and looked around for his brother and son. Rostam waved impatiently from Talon's ship.

"What is his name?"

"Brandt. I do not know its meaning."

"Hmm," Talon said. "We will talk more in Tyre."

Standing on the battlements of the castle, Rav'an, Jannat and Max, along with Palladius and several men, had seen the arrival of the distant ships and the ensuing engagement. They watched in a fever of apprehension as the pirates attacked. When the messenger's ship was boarded, Jannat squeezed Rav'an by the hand till it hurt as she gazed with anguish at the conflict, knowing as she did that Reza would put himself in the thick of the fighting. At last the ships parted, two returning to port while two others began to sail away towards the horizon. Rav'an put an arm across her sister's shoulders. "I think it is all right, my Jannat. Look, the ships with our men are sailing away. Had the battle gone badly they would surely be coming home."

"Palladius, send men to the harbor for news of what happened out there. I must know as soon as possible," Rav'an ordered, never taking her eyes off the ships.

Palladius saluted. "At once, my Lady. I shall go myself. if Sir Max will allow it."

"Of course. As speedily as you can, Sergeant. The survivors may need assistance," Max told him.

"It becomes clear to me that we are now solely responsible for the safety of our people, Max. We must prepare for whatever might come our way while Talon and Reza are away," Rav'an said slowly.

The old Templar sergeant nodded. His features were somber. "We will make ready, my Lady."

———————————

Chapter 4

Aeneas Sanna

What is the price of Experience? Do men buy it for a
* song?*
Or wisdom for a dance in the street? No, it is bought
* with the price*
Of all that a man hath, his house, his wife, his children.
Wisdom is sold in the desolate market where none come
* to buy,*
And in the wither'd field where the farmer plows for
* bread in vain.*

—William Blake

Aeneas Sanna hurried along the busy road between the
Palace of the Porphyrogennetos and the Royal Palace of
Blachernae, the center of the Byzantine Empire and to all in-
tents and purposes his home.

The street vendors of Constantinople were cluttering the
streets with their makeshift stalls and the accompanying
rubbish. He was forced to watch where he put his sandaled
feet. Dog and donkey feces, interspersed with the larger
lumps of camel dung, sullied the paving stones, along with
rinds and trash tossed aside by careless buyers. He wrinkled
his nose at the noisome fumes emanating from the drains
alongside the highway.

Aeneas liked to assume the attire of a man of means; he
had aspirations to become eventually a member of the upper

class. His attire almost, but not quite, resembled that of a senator. His tunic was white, and he wore something akin to a toga. Anyone not familiar with the details of the garb might indeed mistake him for one of that august club.

He was careful, however, not to dress too obviously. To be caught dressing above his station could lead to reprimands—even dismissal. His title as the Undersecretary for the Treasury of the Palace of Porphyrogennetos, a satisfying and lengthy title, gained him some respect and modest earnings, although he still had a way to go before he could put his name forward as a senator. He would need property for that. He was employed because he had a very good head for figures, and the treasury desperately needed a numerically imaginative staff these days.

After the destruction wrought by the late Andronikos Komnenos, who had been killed by an angry mob and hung by his heels from the very gates of Blachernae palace, the empire had struggled to recover financially. His department was taking the brunt of the new Emperor's frustration.

His department chief had sent a terse message, ordering him to appear for an audience with the Emperor. Aeneas thought he knew the reason why. He had spent the last year hunting for clues to the disappearance of the gold that had vanished during the coup, and had excitedly reported to his chief that he might now know its whereabouts, or at least its destination.

After painstaking research and much questioning of people, both willing and unwilling, for months on end, several clues had surfaced which had led him to a villa perched on the Second hill of the city of Constantinople where a family called Kalothesos had once resided. He had gone to the villa on his own and found it in very sorry condition and all but deserted, except for a man who called himself Alexios Kalothesos, who claimed to be the son of the former famous senator, Damianus Kalothesos.

At first skeptical, Aeneas had eventually concluded that, while the man was prematurely aged and infirm, dressed in threadbare clothing while existing on an estate that must be worth hundreds of thousands of dinars, he might well be whom he claimed to be. There was a companion of sorts with him, and two scruffy, surly servants who were barely civil towards the visitor.

Alexios, however, if that was who it was, had been polite. He had offered some vinegary wine, with apologies, and had made his guest as welcome as his means allowed. The servants made themselves scarce. Aeneas was reluctant to explain the purpose of his visit, but finally, after some sparring, he had opened up enough to explain that he was trying to follow the trail of one Exazenos, who had disappeared just before the city mob had captured the Emperor and butchered him.

The reaction from Alexios surprised him. It was one of shock and rage. "Yes, he was here! Damn him and all his family to hell!" the thin, worn out man shouted.

"Stephan!" he called out. "There is someone here who wants to know about Exazenos." He practically spat the name. The man Stephan appeared like a djinn. "Who is asking?" he demanded, his tone truculent.

"Yes, exactly who are you?" Alexios spoke a little more aggressively. Aeneas decided that these two scarecrows and their sullen servants were perhaps dangerous, and as he had come alone he decided candor might be the better strategy.

"My name is Aeneas; I am the Undersecretary of the Treasury. The *Royal* Treasury," he added pompously for emphasis. "It is known that the vaults of the palace were plundered, in fact the entire palace was plundered, but it is a matter of record that the vaults were almost empty when the mob arrived to steal whatever they could. A huge amount of gold was removed by this man Exazenos. He actually signed for it!" He stopped and shook his head at the sheer effrontery of the act.

The two men listening were shaking their heads, dry amusement written all over their emaciated and deeply lined features. "What is so funny?" Aeneas demanded, somewhat testily. They looked like vagabonds squatting in this formerly beautiful estate. Who were they to mock him?

"Well, *Mister Undersecretary,* we know where it went after leaving the palace," Alexios stated with conviction. "It was here!"

"Here?" Aeneas almost gobbled with surprise, but also satisfaction. He had been right after all, despite the skepticism of his boss. The two men went on to describe their escape during the chaos of the revolution and their subsequent arrival at the villa, only to discover the place swarming with mercenaries. "You do know who Exazenos really is?" Stephan asked.

Exasperated by the question, Aeneas responded. "Everyone knows who he is! He is a monster who tortured and killed for the Emperor. His name struck fear into all who heard it."

"His real name was Pantoleon. Does that ring any bells?" Alexios demanded.

Aeneas thought for a moment, then it dawned on him. "You don't mean... *the* Pantoleon? The famous charioteer? But he died at the Battle of Myriokephalon! Everyone knows that," he scoffed.

Stephan and Alexios shook their heads with bitter laughs. "Oh no, he didn't," Stephan said. "He came back, but as the monster Exazenos. Alexios heard it from his own lips, curse that demon deep into hell. He tortured both of us! When the palace fell he came here. He must have brought the gold with him prior to leaving the city."

"So you think he took the gold and fled the city?" Aeneas asked, to be sure that he heard correctly.

"When we arrived, after being released from prison, his men chased us off. The next day we came back with reinforcements to have it out with them, but they had gone, disappeared into thin air!" Alexios waved his thin arms in the air, his bearded face animated.

"There was evidence that transport had been used. One wagon had been left behind because it had broken a wheel. The old man who was our gateman mentioned that several wagons, heavily guarded and drawn by oxen, had left in the dead of night. They went downhill towards the port. At the time no one paid him any attention; probably thought he was senile. He died a few months ago, but he was sure. Pantoleon, Exazenos, however you want to call him, was here all right. He chose his moment. When everyone was preoccupied at the palace, he and his men vanished."

"How could he have left with so much cargo?" Aeneas demanded, his tone skeptical. "Gold is heavy stuff, and there was a lot of it! He could never have left via the city gates. The mob was there at every portal, making sure no one escaped, least of all the rich merchants. They were checking everyone's property for precisely this kind of thing. He could not have made it past them!"

"He left by sea! There could have been no other way!" Alexios stated firmly.

"Do you have any idea as to where he might have gone?"

"Not really. Remember, the Franks were about to beat down the doors of the City. The Arabs would have welcomed him, confiscated the gold and tossed him back to us to execute just for their amusement. The Lord William of Sicily has no love for any of us, so his Normans would have killed him for much the same reason. There are not many places he could have gone, when you think about it. I doubt it would have been the Kingdom of Jerusalem. He would have stood out there like a sore thumb. Those Latins are a miserable lot. Perhaps Syria, or one of the islands? I don't know."

Aeneas had left it at that. He had taken his leave of the two gaunt vagabonds and gone home with his mind in turmoil. Where could this Exazenos, as he had been known, or Pantoleon as he was originally, have gone? A wagon train of gold is not so easy to hide. Sooner or later someone would have observed something. He was sure of it.

Days later, the next clue had appeared when a servant announced there was a boy at the palace gates who wanted to see him. The boy had a piece of paper that he would give to no one except Aeneas, despite being chased off by the guards on several occasions. Aeneas had finally gone out to see what the urchin wanted. All the boy did was to ask his name, thrust a piece of paper into his hand, and vanish into the crowded street. Peering after the boy, Aeneas unfolded the scrap of paper. Then he read the note.

It read: *We know where it went. Alexios.*

Aeneas wasted no time. He took a two-man litter to the villa and left the sweating men at the gates, telling them to wait for him. They were glad to rest, as he was not a lightweight. He hastened along the driveway towards the villa. It was mid morning on a bright April day, and despite his haste he could not fail to notice how well laid out the estate had once been.

Stephan let him in with a sardonic grimace. "Didn't take you long, did it?" he remarked. "Come on, they are in the living area."

A stranger who appeared to be a merchant was seated opposite Alexios by the empty fireplace. He was clearly in better health than the other two, and much better clad. Everything about the house had a look of neglect, but Aeneas didn't pay much attention to his surroundings now, he was too eager for the news. His gaze was on the stranger, who looked up, then stood to meet him. Alexios didn't stir from his chair. He looked emotionally drained.

"Secretary Aeneas, meet Merchant Giorgios, a well traveled man," he said in his crisp, upper-class accent. "Tell him what you know, Giorgios." Alexios took a swig of wine, as though to settle his emotions. Something of importance had passed between this merchant and Alexios, but Aeneas didn't think it was only about Pantoleon.

"I have just come back from Rhodes and several other islands, Master Secretary," Giorgios informed Aeneas, who looked his enquiry with wide eyes as though to say. "Well, get on with it, man!" Giorgios swallowed nervously.

"I came here not knowing the Master Alexios was alive and was shocked to find him here. We all thought he had died in... in the dungeons."

Aeneas fought to control his impatience. "What has this got to do with my mission?"

"The man everyone called Exazenos was in Cyprus, Lord."

Aeneas gaped. "Cyprus?" His mind began to race. Who ruled Cyprus these days? In these chaotic times it could be almost anyone.

"How... how long ago was this?" he demanded.

"A few months ago."

"Is he still there?"

"No, Lord, he vanished several months before I arrived."

Aeneas exclaimed and looked about him with frustration. The trail had gone cold again.

Giorgios held up his hand. "There is something odd about the whole thing, Lord."

"What is it?" Aeneas snapped.

"Rumor has it that almost to the day Exazenos vanished, the Emperor, Isaac Komnenos, came into a lot of money, rather suddenly. He did not have very much before. Everyone hates him because he visits cities like Larnaca and robs the merchants blind. Rumors are everywhere about how he came by that wealth. There was also a great deal of excitement in Paphos around that time, from what I heard."

"So the trail might not be cold just yet?" Aeneas asked.

"There are many rumors. Some say that the Lord Talon might have had something to do with there disappearance of Exazenos. But no one knows for sure."

"Who is Lord Talon?"

"Hmm... one really interesting person. You don't want to get on his wrong side," Alexios commented with a short bark of laughter. He took another swig of the execrable wine and grimaced. "God, I wish Father were still here to make something drinkable," he complained.

"We will tell you what we know," Stephan said to Aeneas.

The day after the encounter at the villa, as he walked into his chief's office, Aeneas considered what he would say, but he was given little chance to go into any detail.

"Where have you been? We can't keep His Majesty waiting!"

His chief hastily led him along the long corridors, past tall, blond-haired, stoic Varangian guards posted at most doorways, until they arrived at one of the audience rooms. This one was a smaller chamber, and very private. There was only the one door, and no windows. Evidently the Emperor Isaac Angelos wanted to keep this visit quiet. He had inherited the empire through violence that he himself had not instigated, only to find a treasury that was virtually empty, and it was causing him some serious headaches. When the two secretaries were ushered in and had gone through the ceremonies of obeisance, he indicated that they should stand.

He was a man of medium height, with a well trimmed beard; for this audience he had not worn the customary high crown, merely a silk hat without a rim, its bright flowery pattern exactly matching the long silk robe he wore.

"I have been informed by the Chief Secretary of the Treasury that you have something to tell us, Master Undersecretary." The Emperor addressed Aeneas directly, who ducked his head, glanced at his chief, and then said, "Your Majesty, I am honored to be here. After several months of intensive investigation I have found where the man called Exazenos went after the rev... after the, er, death of, um, your predecessor, Sire," he stammered.

Isaac Angelos threw a glance at the Chief Secretary. "This is good news, isn't it?" He frowned, as though not sure whether it were or not. "Where did the foul traitor go?"

"Er... to Cyprus, Sire. At least that is where the trail leads thus far," Aeneas stated. "But our sources tell me that he has disappeared under very strange circumstances. There are rumors that quantities of gold found their way into the coffers of the pretender Isaac Komnenos, Sire." He stopped at that point and waited.

The Emperor's eyes widened, and for a long moment he stared hard at the two men in front of him. His dark brown eyes were tired, but now they expressed anger.

"I could send a fleet and an army to take back that which is mine, and not just the gold. The whole island of Cyprus," he murmured. "That filthy traitor Isaac was in league with William of Sicily."

"My Liege," one of three attending people in the room spoke up. Aeneas recognized Theodore Kastamonites, the Emperor's maternal uncle. He had somehow managed to survive the brutal reign of Andronikos.

"Yes, Theodore, what is it?" Angelos demanded, without taking his eyes off the two secretaries before him, who were beginning to feel very uncomfortable.

"Perhaps verification would be prudent first, my Liege?" came the reply. "We could send people to find out precisely where the gold might be at present, and search for the traitor while they are at it. That way we will be sure of what we seek, and can then take the appropriate measures."

The Emperor looked thoughtful. "Ye...es," he said slowly. "The covert way, you mean? I agree with you, Uncle. Sensible advice, as always." He looked directly at Aeneas and said, "You have done well." Then, "Whom should we send, Uncle?" he asked.

Theodore indicated Aeneas. "This man has found out more than our other investigators. Perhaps he should go to Cyprus and put his skills to work. He did bring us to this point, my Liege."

"Very well. I shall leave you to take care of the details. Uncle, Secretary," the Emperor said with a hint of a nod, and turned away; the audience was at an end.

"Yes, Your Majesty." Aeneas and his boss bowed very deeply and shuffled out of the room backwards.

As they tramped along the labyrinth of corridors past empty offices and stony-faced Varangian Guardsmen, the Chief Secretary grumbled under his breath.

"I don't know why *you* should go. His Majesty has been looking for an excuse to invade Cyprus and take it back into the empire for some time. Why not now? He has good reason."

"Invade Cyprus? Whatever for?" Aeneas asked.

"Have you not been paying attention?" his chief snapped. "The treasury started low and now it is empty. People are groaning from the taxes we have had to impose. He has to finance the perpetual skirmishes with Bulgaria! Cyprus would be a ripe plum for the empire to regain."

Aeneas said nothing. His father had died during one of those 'skirmishes' while serving in the army under Manuel Komnenos, the predecessor to Andronikos. He had been a low level officer, but had had the foresight to send his son to school instead of allowing him to join the army. Aeneas was very glad of it. He had enjoyed school and had excelled in mathematics, which was one of the reasons he had ended up in the treasury.

Although he was apprehensive at the prospect of going to Cyprus and the potential dangers there, he was excited too. He fully intended to find the gold and get as much of it back to the Emperor as he could. Success would mean fame and hopefully fortune, perhaps even the realization of his life's ambition.

Then, he thought to himself, as he listened with only half an ear to his chief's ramblings, *I shall have your job, and I'll be well on my way to becoming a senator. I hate you, you pompous, incompetent ass. If I am sufficiently rewarded, I will at last be able to afford land!* Having land was the biggest hurdle to becoming a member of that august body. As these thoughts were churning through his mind, it suddenly occurred to him that there might be a property he could lay his hands on. The villa that belonged to the vagabond Alexios Kalothesos! A tiny idea began to form inside his busy mind. He turned his head to his chief. "I'm sorry, Chief Treasurer, I didn't hear that last part?"

"I said," his chief responded rather testily, "that you can't go on your own. You will have to have an escort of some kind. I shall talk to Lord Theodore Kastamonites and see how he wants to play this."

Lord Theodore Kastamonites ordered Aeneas to appear before him with his chief three days later.

"You will be given the status of a Junior Ambassador for the purposes of this visit. Papers will be drawn up to that effect," he informed Aeneas. "You sail in one of our naval vessels, which will add to your status. I have several men I want to go with you."

He gestured, and two villainous looking individuals stepped forward. They leered at Aeneas, whose heart sank at the sight of them. Both looked like hard cases, and dangerous. He immediately put them down as mercenaries, or worse.

"These are your body guards, Macrobius and Aquila, who are experienced at what they do and will be reliable protectors," Kastamonites stated firmly to the appalled secretary. "They will accompany you from the time you take ship. The ship leaves at dawn tomorrow."

Both secretaries bowed low and prepared to leave. Aeneas felt slightly ill. Being hustled off, in the company of ruffians, had not been part of his plan at all. He had wanted to go as a merchant who would be virtually invisible to any government officials in Cyprus. Alexios's agent might have helped him in that regard.

"One more thing," Kastamonites said. "The fleet will be just three months behind you, which means you have a limited time to find the gold. I don't want hoards of soldiers ransacking a palace and stealing that which should be back here in our national treasury. So be quick about it, and find a way to secure the gold before the fleet arrives. You can trust these men. They work for me." There was emphasis on the last sentence.

The voyage to Cyprus was uncomfortable and tense. Aeneas tried hard to ingratiate himself with Macrobius and Aquila, but they maintained a reserve that he could not penetrate. He became increasingly aware that they held him in contempt, which he found humiliating. He could feel their eyes boring into his back when he turned away, and once overheard Aquila say, "Look at 'im. We're nursemaids to an abacus-slider! What was the Prince thinking?"

Aeneas's entire head and face became bright red with mortification.

Eventually, he turned the tables on them by suggesting that they read a letter he had written. His pretext for the test was that he wanted their opinion before he sent it back to the City. He was pretty sure that neither of the former mercenaries could read. Aquila took the thick paper, covered with Aeneas's scrawl, and held it upside down pretending to read it, while Macrobius looked sour at being tested thus. It didn't improve their relationship, but now Aeneas knew he could best them in at least one dimension.

His two minders spent a considerable amount of time during the long and uneventful voyage competing with one another by throwing knives at a wooden panel tied to the base of the mast. They were very good at this. Even hardened sailors were appreciative of their skills; but Aeneas grew sick of hearing the thud of knives hammering home into the panel, which became pitted and shredded from the impact of their heavy-bladed knives. The captain, a grizzled old hand who had seen much in his life, muttered sourly to Aeneas that the two thugs had better not use their skills on his crew, or there would be trouble.

They pulled into Rhodes to fill up the water casks and to take on fresh vegetables, live chickens and goats for the long crossing to Cyprus. Aeneas, who had been sea-sick for much of the voyage and had kept to his cabin, was persuaded by Marcianus, the captain, to take a turn around the quayside to refresh himself. His two minders insisted upon following him no matter where he went.

Before they even made it to the main street Aeneas had been accosted by a dozen beggars, and not long after by several young women, one of whom who called out to him, "Want a quick one, Senator?" Another came up to him with a leer on her painted face and tugged insistently on his toga.

He kept on walking, pretending not to notice her; but Aquila gestured to the woman, and then vanished for a good half-hour. Aeneas didn't notice his absence; he was goggling at the huge pillars and ruined temples that dominated the skyline of the city. It was not long before one of the eager tourist guides, who were seated on a low wall looking like a line of hungry vultures, spotted him, and there arose a clamor for the attention of this senatorial-looking visitor to the island. Before he knew it, and to the sardonic amusement of his bodyguard, he was being shown around the temple of Apollo at the Acropolis, then taken to see the gigantic plinth where the colossus of Rhodes had once stood.

"Some say it fell into the sea, but others say that the Arabs stole it, curse them to hell. No one has a clue where they took it," the guide informed him with an unctuous smile while rubbing his hands together. "That is why there is, well... not much to see any more, ha ha!" he added, waving his fingers about. Nevertheless, Aeneas was delighted with his tour and, feeling very superior, he tipped the man far more than he should have.

Then it was back to the ship and they were sailing out past the plinth with its gigantic missing statue and past the massive fortifications of the citadel. Off to the south he could see the shipbuilding yards in the distance, which he had been told were the most modern in the whole of the Inner Sea.

A week later, Aeneas noticed that Aquila was looking more morose than usual and very hangdog.

"What's the matter with him?" he asked Macrobius. He noted with some relief that the practice with the knives had fallen off sharply since Rhodes.

"He got the pox," Macrobius answered shortly. "Them poxy bints in Rhodes is what did it. Claims it's like pissing broken glass. Silly beggar, I told 'im not to do it. I'm surprised it hasn't dropped off!"

Aeneas grimaced in disgust. "We'll find a physician for him in Famagusta," he suggested. "Meanwhile, keep him away from me. I don't want to get what he's got." He sighed. Home with his mother seemed a long way off, and here he was with two thugs, one of whom was diseased. It didn't bode well for the rest of the trip.

It took ten more days to reach the port of Famagusta, because they ran into one of those sudden storms which appear out of nowhere in the Mediterranean in springtime. It was a harrowing experience for Aeneas, leading him to conclude that sailors were madmen and the sea was to be avoided at all costs in the future. By the time they arrived, Aeneas had lost a fifth of his original weight, and he had had quite enough of the sea, of sailors, and the ships they sailed in.

It was with profound relief that he set foot in the city where, he knew in his bones, the gold he sought was to be found. The very first place he visited was a church. One dominated the center of the jumbled mass of narrow streets and alleyways. There he gave thanks to God for his deliverance.

Chapter 5

Tamura

Oh youth! Go with reckless faith
and trust the flattering voice,
Which whispers, "Take thy fill till death.
Indulge thyself and then rejoice."
                                    —Minstrel

"You appear to be very tense, my Lady," Siranos remarked to his mistress. They were in the Lady Tamura's chambers within the palace, which was situated in the city of Famagusta. He massaged her back while she lay naked on the long table. "You could say that, Siri," she responded. "Work your magic on me, and perhaps I will be able to relax a little." Siranos went to work with practiced hands and cunning fingers all over her oil-covered body.

Soon Tamura gasped, and then began to writhe with pleasure, "Oh, yes!" she groaned. "My God, what would I do without you, my Siri! Ah, down a bit... yes, yes, there!" she exclaimed, and sped off on the crest of a huge wave which left her gasping for breath.

Siranos allowed her time to recover, then came back to the bed bringing fresh hot towels and a robe. She would want to bathe now. He guided her to the bath and helped her to step into the warm water. Although it was very relaxing, she was in a pensive mood. She had surrendered herself to the pleasure of his hands, but now she was back in the reality of the present, and it worried her.

"What am I to do with that awful man?" she complained to her slave, as he gently bathed her with a sponge. She was referring to the self-proclaimed Emperor of Cyprus, Isaac Komnenos, who owned both of them. Tamura was a concubine, while Siranos was a eunuch and slave. Ordinarily, concubines were little more than slaves themselves, but with her instincts for survival and with much cunning and skill in the bed of the Emperor, Tamura had risen in status to become almost a queen. And yet not quite, and that, among other things, was worrying her. Isaac's ever-changing moods contributed to a sense of insecurity that pervaded the corridors of the palace.

Despite all her skill, which was by now considerable, lately her best efforts had failed to arouse enough interest for Isaac to perform adequately, neither with herself nor with other girls who had been provided. She was in charge of this department and took it very seriously. Because her Emperor was willful, unpredictable, erratic—and more and more impotent—her own frustration was mounting. She had never derived much pleasure from his not infrequent attentions, but this sudden lack was making life difficult. She turned to Siranos to fulfill her sexual needs.

"He comes in wanting to do something, but by the time we get to the bed he has lost it! It's like a wilted sea cucumber," she complained to the attentive slave. "I am at my wits' end trying to get him going again. I don't know what else to do!" she almost wailed.

Siranos moved the warm sponge over her neck and shoulders to ease the tension. Tamura was a very beautiful woman. Still a girl really, only seventeen, but wise beyond her years, well used to dealing with the petty jealousies of the palace harem. Other women and their slaves trod warily around her, and woe betide anyone who crossed her or felt inclined to disobey her. She was in a privileged position with regard to the favors of the Emperor, but with that came the dangers of high position. The distance to fall was ever greater, and this was what bothered his lady.

"I am at a loss to suggest anything at present. You have tried several of the standard aphrodisiacs, lettuce and so on."

"If I have to share another bowl of lettuce with him I shall start bleating like a goat," she snapped. "It seems to do very little for him in that area. I am amazed that he managed to father a daughter!"

Siranos gave a depreciative snort. "She is but a slip of a girl from what I hear, and is well out of the way in Kyrenia."

"That would be the final straw if she were to come back here," Tamura muttered. If she is even a little like her father she would be unbearable, and so would life be."

Siranos decided to do some research into the status of the daughter, and to find out if the people in castle on the hill might be able to help with the other problem; but for the time being it behooved him to change the subject. "Did you hear about the embassy that has just arrived, my Lady?"

Tamura looked up from her glum contemplation of the soapy bath waters and pushed aside a stray strand of dark blonde hair from her damp forehead. "No, I have not. When did these people arrive, and why wasn't I told before?" She sounded aggrieved and ready to snap at him.

"You were, er, closeted with His Majesty, my Lady," he responded tactfully. "This is the first chance I have had to tell you. The embassy only arrived in the port a few hours ago. They sent a messenger to the palace; the Chief Minister is making arrangements for an audience with the Emperor at his convenience."

Tamura wondered when that might be. The Emperor had left her room in a bad temper, which boded ill for anyone who crossed his path, even an embassy if he felt spiteful enough.

*****

A day later at a prearranged time, Siranos made his cautious way out of the palace to meet the Greek man who was his contact with the mysterious castle on the mountain north of Famagusta. These days, no one seemed interested in his comings and goings, but from force of habit he approached the side door of a disreputable wine shop surreptitiously and, after a glance behind him, slipped into the gloomy room. He searched for a bulky man and saw him seated in a dark corner, nursing a mug of wine.

The young eunuch slid onto the empty bench opposite the Greek, who barely acknowledged him, and looked around. Dimitri never showed up without an escort but, try as he might, Siranos could never spot the minders, which amused Dimitri.

Dimitri scrutinized his guest. Siranos seemed nervous, but that was normal. He'd had one nasty encounter in the past, and truly, every time he came to meet with Dimitri he took his life in his hands. Dimitri had advised the boy to be cautious on every occasion. "You only have to be discovered once, and then it is all over," he had told him.

"Is all well at the palace?" Dimitri asked in a low tone.

Siranos nodded his head. "You know we have a visitor?" he asked.

"We saw a new ship in the port. It looks very smart, so we think it is from Constantinople. That's rare enough these days," Dimitri remarked, his tone dry.

"I have been told that it is an emissary from the Emperor himself, but I don't know what he is here for."

"We will find out eventually," Dimitri responded. "How is your beautiful mistress?" he inquired politely, and waved to the serving girl to bring him some wine. She came over and sloshed some into his cup.

"Um, she is well, but...." Siranos hesitated.

"Spit it out, man," Dimitri said, raising his drink to his lips.

Siranos leaned across the table and spoke in a very low voice. Dimitri had to lean forward to hear.

"She is frustrated because the Emperor can't get it up!" Siranos crooked his left forefinger up and down to illustrate the problem.

Dimitri had just taken a gulp. He choked, his eyes bulged, his broad face turned puce. He could barely contain his laughter. Siranos looked as though he worried the older man might be having a heart attack.

"What did you just say?" Dimitri spat the sour wine back into his cup.

"I said," Siranos repeated, casting a furtive look around the half-full inn, "that her master is having trouble getting it up."

Dimitri leaned back in his chair, wiped his mouth with the back of his hand, and stared. "What in hell's name has this got to do with me? Why tell me?"

"Because she is desperate! She wonders if your people could help?" Siranos pleaded.

"I'm here to collect information, not report nonsense!" Dimitri protested.

"It isn't nonsense! It's very serious! When he can't get it up he becomes violent, and more unstable. His moods are erratic, always have been, but it's getting worse as the problem persists. I... she is afraid, and very worried."

"Doesn't she know how to deal with him? For the good Lord's sake, I don't have answers for this kind of shit!" Dimitri snapped, raising his voice, but then became guarded once more. He shook his head with an incredulous expression on his face.

"You don't understand," Siranos whispered, his tone urgent. "This could jeopardize her survival. The man is unhinged and could turn on her like a rabid dog unless she can keep him... well... satisfied. And before you ask, yes, she has brought in younger and younger girls. There has to be a limit to that," he finished in a disgusted tone.

Dimitri nodded his head slowly. "You are right about that." The perversions and depredations of Isaac were widely talked about. "So what do you want me to do?" he asked, with heavy reluctance.

"Those people up at that castle. Do you think they might be able to suggest something?"

Dimitri could think of many things the people on the mountain could do to rectify a situation, but helping the Emperor get his member up and keep it up was not one of the solutions that came to mind.

He shook his head. "I doubt it very much, but I suppose I can at least ask," he said, sounding doubtful. They discussed a few other items of court gossip, then Siranos slipped away. He didn't notice Dimitri signal one of his men to follow to see to it that he got safety back to the palace.

That night Dimitri held his head in his hands and tried to compose a note. Three drinks of Arak later, he began to write. The messages had to be very short, but informative. With the dawn, grumpy and tired, he rolled the tiny piece of paper up and slipped it into a copper tube, which he attached to the leg of a pigeon. "I shall never live this one down!" he muttered. Holding the bird high, he released it into the air. With a rapid flutter of wings it took off, circled once, then took off in a straight line for the mountains to the north. Dimitri shook his head. This was going to be embarrassing.

*****

Later that same morning, at the castle of Kantara, Jannat went up for her usual inspection of the pigeons and to check for any new arrivals. One pigeon was perched on the sill of the stone window as though waiting for her. The iridescent green and grey colors of its breast gleamed in the sunlight. The bird calmly allowed her to take it in her cupped hands and to gently remove the missive, after which she brought it in among the others to feed and rest.

Unrolling the tiny slip of paper she began to read. Her eyes widened with surprise, then she bent almost double and her squeal brought others running up to the tower.

Rav'an was the first to arrive. "Jannat, what is it, dear?" she demanded, when she found Jannat still doubled over. "Are you hurt?" Her voice betrayed her concern. Jannat handed the note off to Rav'an and wiped tears from her eyes.

"Sister, please tell me that I am mistaken," she begged.

Rav'an read the note aloud. *"King floppy, Queen needs help. Medication needed urgently. Advise. D."*

"No!" she said with a disbelieving look. She re-read the note and checked the initial. It was from Dimitri, sure enough. "It's not a practical joke, is it?" she queried, but then shook her head. Dimitri would not do that; it could backfire dangerously.

"We need to take this to Theo, and not pass it along to anyone else, at least not until we fully understand the meaning."

"I think the meaning is clear enough, don't you, Sister?" Jannat smirked. She sobered. "With Reza and Talon gone, we are on our own in this matter. I doubt if they could help anyway. What about Max?"

"Max would not have a clue as to what to do about this," Rav'an retorted. "This would be too embarrassing for him. He is Max, after all. We have to get together with Theo and figure it out. Come on."

They bustled into Theo's chambers to find her engaged in grinding herbs in a stone pestle and mortar. She looked up with a smile of welcome. "What are you two smirking about?" she asked.

Rav'an thrust the paper towards her. "It just came in from Famagusta, Theo. What do you make of it?"

Theo wiped her fingers on a cloth, took the paper and glanced at it. She frowned, then her mouth twitched with amusement. "Is this some kind of joke?" she demanded.

"I, we don't think so, Theo. It arrived this morning from Dimitri," Jannat told her.

"Hmm. If this is as serious as I think it is, we have to try to find a solution. Is the Queen that girl Tamura?" Theo inquired.

Rav'an nodded. "If she really is in difficulties we owe it to her to help, don't we? It's a question of, um, experience and sisterly support... isn't it?" She said with an arch look at her friends, who both began to laugh.

The bewildered servants, the wounded patients in the chambers nearby, and other occupants of the castle heard the animated but muffled voices of the three ladies, interspersed with shrieks of laughter, from the closed doors of the physician's chambers for well over an hour. The servants shrugged, smiled at one another, and agreed that the women were at last enjoying their time free of their men.

*****

Diocles, Chief Minister to Isaac Komnenos, was worried. Who was this newcomer who professed to be a Junior Ambassador for the Emperor of Byzantium? The title itself was insulting enough. A full ambassador would have been more diplomatic. On the other hand, Isaac had supported William the Norman, King of Sicily, in his abortive attempt to wrest the empire from Angelos, during and immediately after the gruesome killing of Andronikos the butcher. It was common knowledge that Isaac had held hopes of being appointed emperor by William. Diocles had felt that Isaac was being not only premature but delusional. But then, the Emperor rarely listened to good advice. He had sided with William, and now here was an official visitor from Constantinople. He came talking of peace and unity, but in Diocles' experience, what a politician said and what he intended were very rarely one and the same.

Diocles sighed. The Emperor had just come back from a flying visit to Larnaca and Limassol, where he had heard complaints from the merchants about high taxes and the depredations of pirates, who were becoming ever more bold.

As usual, Isaac had barely listened, not even when the new commander of his forces added his voice to the growing lament. The pirates were well coordinated, and they probably had spies on land for they were masters of surprise: attacking at night, burning, kidnapping people for the clamoring slave markets, and plundering whatever they could.

Instead, Isaac had demanded that they lend him money on credit against his legendary store of gold. No one believed the Emperor would keep his word. He seldom told the truth; he issued absurd edicts that no one, least of all the eunuchs who swarmed the palace, knew what to do with; and he forced merchants to lend money to him on promises to pay them back with gold. He never did pay anything back. Diocles was one of the few people who knew that in reality there was gold hidden in the cellars of the palace at Famagusta. He thought it was very immoral of the Emperor to keep borrowing coin while reneging on his promises.

Now he was having to organize at very short notice an audience with this odd-looking fellow from Constantinople, who oozed good will and smiled far too often, demanding an audience. Diocles hoped that the man had brought letters; if he had not, he might find himself in the dungeons for being a fraud. Diocles instinctively disliked the man, who called himself Aeneas Sanna. What kind of a name was that? A family name that alluded to hay!

The ship had actually arrived the previous day, but the passengers had been forced to remain on board until the Emperor and Diocles returned to the city. Diocles decided that he would put the stranger up in the house abandoned by Pantoleon, the monster who had formerly occupied the place with his mercenaries. A fitting accommodation, he thought to himself, as he climbed the steps to the women's quarters to talk to Tamura.

She welcomed him into her rooms and offered a little of the very drinkable wine that Diocles shared with her, though he remained mysterious about its origin. She smiled a welcome and seated herself. At her command the slaves Martina and Siranos brought some tiny refreshments—she knew Diocles had a sweet tooth—and, following a hand gesture from Tamura, disappeared into another room. Diocles was quite sure they had their ears glued to the curtain, but he didn't mind.

Here he could let his guard down, just a little, for a while, and share some gossip with Tamura, who as always wanted to hear his perspective while providing her own.

"So how is the Chief Minister, and what is the news?" she enquired with a pretty smile, showing good teeth.

He smiled back with his hand just in front of his mouth. He knew his teeth were in very poor shape. He had very little to be vain about. He was balding, his ears were sprouting hair like a rabbit, and his beard was straggly; but somehow she made him feel younger, so he enjoyed coming to see her. It wasn't as though they didn't see one another about the palace and in the extensive gardens, but here, somehow, he always felt as though she was on his side.

"The Emperor heard the usual complaints, my Lady. The merchants, and now even the garrison commanders, are concerned about the pirates who infest the coast."

She sighed. "They are dangerous. I long to go to Paphos for the baths, but I am afraid of the coastal road."

Diocles agreed with her. "It would be best to wait until something has been done about them, my Lady." He had no idea what the Emperor might do, however. When pressed by his commanders, Isaac had snarled at them, which meant that he didn't have a plan, and the subject had been dropped.

"Did he, did he... *enjoy* himself while in Larnaca?" she queried.

Knowing exactly what she was talking about, Diocles sent her a sympathetic glance.

"Well... I think he *tried*, my Lady, but... it didn't go well." He recalled the crying girl who had been chosen for the Emperor being hustled out of his tent late that night and told to go home by the unpleasant guards. Clutching her clothing about her she had run off into the night, wailing. Her family might not even accept her back, which meant that yet another innocent would be condemned to the streets, to end up in a mean and dirty brothel or starve to death. He shook his head and looked with respect at Tamura, who had so nearly suffered the same fate but had somehow managed to beguile this fickle and spiteful man into making her the senior lady in the palace.

She gave a sigh of her own, then sent him an odd look. "I have asked for help," she stated.

"What kind of help?" he asked, curious.

"You know that he has this problem, and because of that he gets angry, and makes things worse. For everyone. I have asked for help from someone I know in the city."

Diocles was intrigued. It had been a very long time since he had been able to do anything in bed with anyone, either boys or girls.

"I wonder what might be going on in the castle?" she asked rhetorically.

He smiled. The question always came up during these visits. Each of them knew that the other had some kind of contact with people of that enigmatic place on the mountain.

"I was going to ask if you could be at the audience tomorrow, my Lady," he asked to change the subject.

"You know I would be delighted, Chief Minister. Now tell me all you know about this mysterious visitor. Is he from the City?" she asked, referring to Constantinople, which was known far and wide by that name, especially in the provinces, none of which could boast of having a city even a fraction of the size.

*****

Aeneas prepared himself for the audience with care. His robes were of good patterned silk, as was the matching rimless hat lined with fur. He wiped his face and bald head, which had beaded with sweat for the second time within an hour. Despite the sweltering heat of the crowded city of Famagusta, he felt that to be anything less than perfectly dressed for even this pseudo -emperor would be considered a slight, and he wanted to start off on the right foot. He called his servant to come and brush some imaginary motes of dust off his shoulders, but because he was nervous he slapped the man's hand aside and shouted for Aquila.

The bodyguard slouched into the room and leaned against the wall. "What is it... Sir?" he rasped, in his dry-as-a-desert voice.

Aeneas bridled. "I want you to be a good deal more presentable than that!" he exclaimed irritably. "You look like a common sailor. We are going to see the Emperor of Cyprus! And where is that lout Macrobius? He should be here by now!"

Macrobius, the other thug who had been foisted upon Aeneas for his 'protection', had been sent to the ship to collect the rest of the baggage Aeneas had brought with him.

"He's on his way back. The laborers in this town don't know their left from their right. They have dropped things all over the place, and God alone knows what they might have stolen," Aquila remarked.

Aeneas threw him a shocked look. "You mean they have plundered our baggage?" he asked, his tone incredulous. "Are they not slaves to be flogged to death for such behavior?"

"Hmm, no. These are what are called 'Freemen'. They work the docks, and I suspect they steal whatever they can from whomsoever they can. If I caught one of them I'd kill him on the spot, but... I haven't yet!" Aquila took out a knife and cleaned his fingernails.

Little did he know how right he was. Dimitri had infiltrated the ranks of the labor force in the harbor and now his men controlled most of the activity. Talon had been very pleased to hear of this initiative, as it meant that no ship came or went without Dimitri knowing exactly who was on it and why. He also kept the looting to a minimum, because it would not do to gain a reputation for plundering. Word got around fast among the merchants that the Freemen of the docks of Famagusta were more reliable than most. Unfortunately, the Emperor's taxes were exorbitant. In this case, Dimitri had wanted to know as much as he could about the new arrivals; so Maymun and Khuzaymah, his two best henchmen, had done some careful searching among the boxes and cases that came off the ship.

Aeneas arrived at the palace right on time and walked up the steps to the entrance, where he was greeted by a minion of Diocles, who had instructions to humiliate him if at all possible. In this manner the Chief Minister could find out a little more about the temper of his visitor. People who are nervous and tense tend to betray their real feelings, he knew, so the servant who approached Aeneas looked down his elongated nose to ask, "What might your business be here?"

Aeneas was taken aback. "I am here to see the Emperor, and you should be more respectful!" he spluttered, adjusting his hat and sweating all the more.

The servant gave him an unctuous smile and pretended to consult a list, slowly running his finger down the margin. "Name?"

"Aeneas Sanna, Ambassador from the Emperor of Byzantium!" he almost shouted.

The servant frowned at him as though to say, "No need to shout, I'm only doing my duty."

"Hmm, don't see you here, Sir. Was it for today? The Emperor is very busy."

Aeneas nearly burst a blood vessel. "Yes!" he shouted this time, his face and bald head going puce. "I was summoned by your Chief of something or other and here I am!" Who *was* this little functionary to question him? "The *Emperor* of this copper pot little island?" he gobbled to himself.

The minion consulted his list again, looking aggrieved, "There is no need to be rude, Sir. Hum, hum, hummmm. Oh, here it is! Yes, of course, you are on right this minute." The servant feigned surprise. "We'll have to hurry. Please follow me." He spun about and led the way briskly into the gloomy interior of the palace, ignoring the murderous looks he received from both Aeneas, who had to trot to keep up, and his accompanying thugs.

"You and you alone must present yourself with your papers to the Emperor," the haughty servant explained when they had entered the audience room. The room was filled with spectators, as the arrival of an emissary from the City was cause for great curiosity. The throne seemed like a league away along a narrow, reddish carpet that looked dirty and moth-eaten.

"You must approach on hands and knees, Sir, until you arrive at the base of the steps leading to the throne, and then you must bow low and await the kindness of His Majesty," the servant intoned.

Aeneas stared at the carpet and the rows of people on either side of it with horror. Never in his life had he been forced to do anything of the sort, although he had heard that this had once been common practice in Constantinople itself.

Giving a great inward sigh, he signaled his men to wait for him and dropped to his knees. "God help me, but this had better be worth it!" he muttered to himself as he began the long journey along the carpet towards the throne, clutching the rolls of paper which announced his rank. The crawl along the worn and dirty carpet, listening to the provincial Greek of the Cypriot nobles and their tittering wives, cemented Aeneas's determination to tear this place apart and leave with the gold that he was charged with finding. His disdain for the crowd was now matched by his rage at the humiliation he was experiencing.

At last he arrived at the steps in front of the throne and paused. He dropped his head to the carpet and waited.

After a few moments the Emperor spoke. "We are pleased to greet an embassy from Constantinople. You may rise."

Aeneas nearly got to his feet, but an old man standing next to the throne gestured sharply for him to remain kneeling. He sat back on his heels and raised the documents for someone to take. The old man obliged, opened the sealed rolls, and laid them in front of Isaac, who pretended to read them.

"We ask, what brings an embassy to our shores?"

This public talk was a mere prelude to the interview which Aeneas prayed might follow. This audience was to impress, and, he feared, entertain the crowd present. Well, he could send a message of his own to the lickspittles of this up-start tyrant. "Your Majesty, I bring news of Constantinople and greetings from his Majesty Isaac Angelos, Emperor of all of Byzantium, who wishes you good health and happiness."

There was a pause while Isaac Komnenos looked at him from slightly bulging, dark brown eyes as though assessing him. It was not a friendly look. But then the Emperor nod-ded. "We will talk later. Chief Minister, arrange it."

The old man retrieved the papers and bowed. "At once, Your Majesty."

Aeneas, still on his knees, had time to look around. He noticed some hard-looking men in an assortment of armor who stood behind the throne. Then his glance landed on a very beautiful woman seated on a smaller throne to the King's left. His eyes widened. She was stunning, and quite a lot younger than the Emperor. She regarded him with a dis-interested look and he dropped his eyes. It was time to pay attention to what the Emperor might say next.

In fact the audience was over. The Emperor rose to his feet, and the entire room full of people bowed very low as he swept away in a rustle of stiff silk robes and a strong whiff of perfume. The beautiful woman also rose and followed the Emperor out through the passage behind the throne.

The moment Isaac left, the room erupted with shouts as people who had wanted an audience realized that for yet an-other day they were to be denied. For this they blamed the Chief Minister, at whom they waved their petitions and shouted angrily for attention. Meanwhile, a minion touched Aeneas on the sleeve and beckoned him to follow.

They arrived at a closed doorway where a rough-looking guard scrutinized them before opening it and allowing them passage. Aeneas was nothing if not a man who attended to detail. He'd already noticed the whole palace was in a de-plorable state of maintenance, from the stained and dirty carpets to the cobwebs in the corners of what had once been brightly gilded ceilings. He was therefore not too surprised to find this room in only slightly better condition. The Emperor Isaac Komnenos was standing this time, with several people nearby. One of them was the beautiful woman, who stared at Aeneas as though he had just crept out of a hole.

A very bulky man stood to the Emperor's right and scowled, and there was the Chief Minister again. Aeneas bowed before the Emperor as low as he possibly could, and then waited in that position.

"We have decided to talk privately with you, *Junior* Ambassador Aeneas," Isaac said in an imperious manner. "We find it interesting that after much time we finally have a *junior* ambassador at our doors from the City at our doors! What could possibly have brought this occasion about?" His tone was dripping sarcasm, and Aeneas winced inwardly. However, he steeled himself and looked up.

"Sire, I have come on behalf of the Emperor of Byzantium on a mission to establish an embassy here in Cyprus and to promote relations between our two countries. There have been, as you may know, er... disturbances, but now that matters have calmed, His Majesty thought it important to send an embassy to renew our friendship."

Isaac looked skeptical. "Is that all?" He fidgeted with the tassel on his sash, looking uncertain.

"Indeed it is, Sire. It has been far too long since the Emperor and Your Majesty have had communications, and he felt strongly that we should amend that situation. Hence my presence here."

Chapter 6

Zenos

Trained to another use,
We march with colors furled,
Only concerned when Death breaks loose
On a front of half a world.
Only for General Death
The Yellow Flag may fly,
While we take post beneath—
That is the place for a spy.

                                    —*Rudyard Kipling*

After Aeneas had departed for the villa that Diocles had assigned him, the group remained in the chamber to discuss the situation. Isaac's newly appointed Chief Gatherer of Information, a man named Zenos, was being careful about how he responded, while Tamura wore a pensive look.

"Well, what do you think?" Isaac asked testily.

"I think he is a spy, Sire," Diocles said without preamble. Tamura nodded emphatically in agreement. "He has been sent here to find out what happened to that satanic Pantoleon," she murmured to the Emperor.

"Do they think we are so stupid as to accept this man at face value, Sire?" Zenos demanded. His tone was sharp. "Do you want me to arrest him, Sire?" Zenos was a stocky man of twenty-five years who already had a bald patch forming on the top of his head. His round, well tended, bearded face and

111

small, dark eyes set in fleshy features did not present a very friendly aspect. He enjoyed dressing expensively and wore jewels on his fingers, which indicated that he was not a man who had to use his hands for a living.

"Give him a little time to stew, your Majesty," Diocles suggested. "There is something going on here that we should think about."

"Like what?" Isaac, who understood nothing of subtleties, demanded an explanation of his advisers.

"I think the lady Tamura is correct, that he is here to find out what become of Pantoleon. But he may be here for another reason as well. Is it not possible that he searches for the gold stolen from the treasury in Constantinople? We all know there were rumors that Pantoleon—"

"The Chief Minister might be right, Sire," Zenos said agreeably, although he hated to agree with the minister on anything, believing the man to be too old for the job that he himself aspired to.

"If this man is a spy, which we all suspect him to be, then we could give him some rope and see what he gets up to. I have seen his 'bodyguards'." Zenos made a distasteful grimace. "As villainous a pair of back-alley thugs as I have ever come across."

Diocles and Tamura nodded, although both had seen worse men before: those whom Pantoleon had brought over from the mainland with him.

"His documents are impeccable, Your Highness. I have examined them carefully," Diocles stated. "I do believe the Emperor sent him, but to what end we don't know yet."

"There is something ominous about that... smiling face that I simply do not trust, my Lord!" Tamura stated with conviction. She had nearly said "bald head", but all the men in the room were in similar condition, if only to a lesser degree.

"Put watchers on his house, and that ship of his," Isaac told them. "If I am not mistaken it is a Royal ship? In which case, confine the officers and crew to the vessel. They are not allowed to come ashore."

"I have already done that, Your Majesty," Zenos stated, with a smug look at Diocles.

"Good. Then keep me informed." Isaac stood up and, accompanied by his servants, left the chamber, the group bowing to his retreating back.

Zenos straightened up, "Lady Tamura, where does your slave go every couple of days?" he asked her.

He didn't fail to see the flicker of alarm at the back of her eyes, swiftly brought under control.

"He goes to the markets and to merchants to obtain herbs, medicine and cloth... among other things. Why do you ask?" she responded casually.

Zenos nodded as though that was sufficient. "You do understand, my Lady, that the security of the Emperor, as well as all of our people in the palace, is my principal concern." His spy, someone whom he had brought into the palace with his appointment, often returned frustrated and bewildered after attempting to follow Siranos.

"He leaves the palace, Lord, and then vanishes," the man had exclaimed. "I cannot find him until," he snapped his fingers for emphasis, "there he is, wandering about the corridors of the palace on some errand for his mistress. Very strange!"

Tamura threw a look at Diocles, who was staring at the ceiling as though contemplating its shabbiness. He rolled his eyes back at her and looked away.

She took a deep breath. "If you really must know, he is very careful when he is outside the palace. You might not remember the chaos of our existence when that monster Exazenos was here, but no one was secure, and our people were being waylaid in the very streets, just outside the walls of the palace!" Her tone was sharper now.

Diocles nodded in agreement. "It has calmed down of late, but all our slaves and eunuchs have to be careful out there. Famagusta is a dangerous port, with all sorts of bad people looking for an opportunity to harm an innocent servant. He has had two very narrow escapes thus far. I'm not too surprised to hear that he is being very careful, Zenos."

Zenos, who was new to the position and had no real allies inside the palace, nodded his reluctant acceptance of the information. He decided, however, to keep a closer eye on both these none too forthcoming people who appeared to wield power of a very subtle kind with the Emperor.

*****

Zenos went away to deal with the matter of placing spies all around the villa, an action that gave someone else in the city a feeling of *déjà vu*. Dimitri, Talon's primary spy, was also concerned about the arrival of a splendid galley that was undoubtedly a royal vessel, and the bald man who dressed somewhat like a senator who had just had an audience with the Emperor. Now his concern sharpened, for the behavior of the new Chief Gatherer of Information was all too familiar.

Diocles had rolled his eyes in exasperation when Zenos was selected to fill the post left vacant by the man known as Exazenos, but tried to maintain a civil relationship with him. Tamura had been scathing about the man's appearance and his background, but her dislike for the newcomer had only made the Emperor dig his heels in and insist that he stay.

Zenos himself was ambitious, and saw the role of Chief Information Gatherer as a mere stepping stone to the position held by the aging Diocles. He wanted to achieve something that would elevate him to that post so badly he could taste it. He extended the scope of his duties to spy on his fa-

ther's merchant acquaintances, and indeed on his own father, to discover what coin they had hidden away from the
tax collectors. Knowing what to look for, his collectors very
effectively found ways of extracting more coin to keep the
treasury from going completely empty. But these activities
were boring to someone with as much ambition as he.

He did not have the stomach for the savage torture that
had been a hallmark of his predecessor, although he believed
that the threat and judicious use of torture could effectively
elicit information. There was one puzzle, however, that no
information gathering could shed light on, and that was the
castle on the mountain over looking the city from the North,
where the man known as Lord Talon lived with his sinister
band of followers.

Ever since he had arrived to take up his duties, whenever
he brought up the subject of Kantara and who lived there,
people would look around them nervously and make excuses
to hurry away, making the sign to ward off evil. Even the
Emperor had looked uncomfortable when he had casually
mentioned it one day, and had abruptly changed the subject.
A thorn in the side of the Emperor, Zenos had decided. Perhaps it was time to go and have a chat with Diocles, who, despite being old and far past his prime, was without doubt the
one person in the palace who knew what was going on...
everywhere.

Two days later, after making enquiries, Zenos found the
old man in the northeastern tower, which had a dove-cote.
The pleasant sound of crooning birds came to Zenos as he
mounted the stone steps leading up to the tiny room, which
enclosed the cages and about ten pigeons. Diocles was holding a pigeon as Zenos arrived at the top of the steps. There
was something guilty about his expression when he noticed
the visitor. He hurriedly placed the pigeon into a cage and
stood back.

"Ah, Chief Gatherer, how nice to see you again," Diocles said, wiping his hands on his work robe. Had he placed something in his pocket at the same time? Zenos decided to let it go, for the moment, and smiled up at the old man.

"Yes; do you have a little time? I wanted to ask you about that castle on the mountain, the one inhabited by that Lord Talon fellow."

"What about it, Zenos? You know the story. He stole it, the Emperor tried to take it back and we failed, and now it sits up there minding its own business," Diocles stated in a brusque manner without looking at him. "We should go down to the gardens and talk, as we are disturbing the birds," he added.

Once they were in the extensive gardens, Diocles made a point of admiring the flowers and shrubs. Zenos, who had little interest in flowers, pressed his point.

"So he does not pay any taxes, there are no hostages, and we leave him alone?" he enquired, frowning at the leopard cage. The two fierce animals were lolling in the shade, their slitted yellow eyes watching the two men, the only people in the garden at this time.

"That is not exactly true," Diocles stated with some emphasis. "Every year, a chest of gold for the Emperor is delivered to the gates of the city, but we never know who delivers it. We do know, however, from where it comes." He pointed in the general direction of the castle. "So the Emperor has decided it is well enough to leave him alone. I agree with that sentiment, by the way." This last was delivered almost as a warning.

Zenos thought that this explanation left a lot to be desired, but like all the others Diocles did not want to pursue the discussion. Zenos left it at that and went off, thinking hard.

Days passed, and his spies watched the villa. The newcomer, Aeneas, seldom went out, but when he did he was accompanied by a couple of tough-looking men, so people cleared a path for him and he was left very much alone. He did little other than peer at the wares in the market, and on no less than three occasions he went to the grand service at the church. It seemed to be a very normal behavior for a first time visitor to the country.

Zenos was not very experienced in the subtleties of spy work; the kind of ideas that flowed around in his head were related to kidnapping, arrest and torture, but he was a quick learner. He knew that to do anything precipitous would merely anger the Emperor, who was currently absorbed with his woman, Tamura. So he tried to figure out how to worm some information out of the Ambassador in another way. Perhaps if he poked the bee hive with a stick something might fly out?

Some very interesting news had arrived from Beirut the other day by ship; a messenger had come to see Zenos as soon as it had docked. The main news was that Salah Ed Din was once again on the move with an enormous army, this time making straight for the Latin Kingdom. Apparently, one of the arrogant Latins had ignored the treaty and ambushed a caravan, despoiling and raping, and a female relative of Salah Ed Din, or certainly someone dear to the Sultan, had disappeared. Zenos's spy told him this, shaking his head in wonder at the stupidity of the Latins. If Zenos had learned one thing in Beirut, it was that Salah Ed Din was almost worshiped by his subjects, and now his people would be coming from far and wide, flocking to the Sultan's banner to teach the Latins a lesson they richly deserved and would never forget.

While that news did not directly affect his interests here in Cyprus, he had also heard that the man called Talon de Gilles had recently landed in Tyre and had met with the Count of Tripoli, then they had gone off to mediate with the angry Sultan. He had sent his messenger back to Beirut to find out more. Now it registered that Talon had left the region, hence the castle. Zenos smiled. His informants on the island, and he had many, had told him that there had been some kind of sea battle, with much fire and noise off the north coast, not far from the port that belonged to the castle.

The question was, would this man Talon be returning soon, or would he be long away? Zenos would know more when his messenger returned. Talon's absence might prove a golden opportunity. If he could somehow succeed in taking back the castle and destroying those people on the mountain, he was sure the Emperor would reward him with anything he might want. The first person to be removed from the palace would be that self-satisfied old man, Diocles. Zenos rubbed his hands together in a gesture he usually made when he was pleased with an idea. But his first order of business must be this 'Ambassador'. What could be done to make him open up about the real reason for his presence on the island?

It turned out to be easier than he expected. He simply decided to pay Aeneas a visit. He was announced by one of the thuggish attendants, and Aeneas rose from his chair to greet him.

"What can I do for such a distinguished visitor?" he enquired politely.

They both ducked their heads and observed one another, seeing perhaps a likeness.

"I am here to pass along the Emperor's good wishes, and to ask if there is anything that we can do to make your visit more pleasant," Zenos informed him.

"I am certainly very interested in exploring the island and becoming more acquainted with your population," Aeneas began.

I can well imagine that! You are a spy for the Emperor of Byzantium, so you want to look around, Zenos thought to himself, but out loud he said, "You will understand, I trust, that the Emperor would prefer it if you stayed within the city for the time being. There is not a good feeling about the Empire since the last ruler, Andronikos...." He trailed off delicately. "We were all in great fear of him. His reputation went far beyond the borders of his empire. Besides, we had an unpleasant experience with a man who came from the City soon after Andronikos was... removed."

"Oh, yes! I know of him." Aeneas tried to sound disarming. "Well, who didn't?" He spread his arms. "He simply vanished, and no one knew where he had gone! He would have had to face trial for his crimes, of course," Aeneas finished. "Pantoleon, or Exazenos, as he was also called. He did come here, then? We wondered where he disappeared to."

It was now clear to Zenos that the Ambassador knew more than had previously been guessed, but what else did he know?

"Yes, he did. Briefly, very briefly, he was close to the Emperor, but then he disappeared... and no one knows quite how, or even why." Zenos spread his hands.

Aeneas, who had listened very carefully to what Alexios in the City had told him about Talon, hazarded a guess. "Could it be that he and this knight Talon came into conflict?"

There was that name again! Zenos contained his surprise and shrugged dismissively. "I don't know, but of one thing I am sure: that Talon fellow is a traitor, and one fine day we will have a settling of scores."

Aeneas's ears perked up at this. "Please explain what you mean?" he asked. Perhaps something might come of this conversation after all. He had become a little desperate at his forced inactivity. This assignment was a golden opportunity to impress his emperor, and the lack of progress bothered him. He didn't have much time; the looming invasion would be under way in a couple of months.

"Has no one told you of the castle on the mountain over to the north?" Zenos asked, waving his hand in that direction. By this time a servant had brought wine and food for them, and Zenos, who enjoyed eating, got started on the smoked fish, olives, and bread.

While he munched, he told Aeneas what he knew about the castle on the hill and its occupants. Aeneas, who was nothing if not an abacus slider, stopped him at one point. "You say he delivers a chest of gold from time to time?" he asked.

"That is what the Chief Minister told me. It doesn't change the fact that he stole the castle and we need to take it back... one day," he added darkly.

"Is it in coin?" Aeneas asked, his interest quickening.

"No, that is a little bit of a puzzle. It is in gold bars," Zenos told him with a snort of derision. "Our taxes are usually in small coin; no one has any bars! Why do you ask?"

Aeneas looked as though he could barely breathe. "Have you actually seen any of this... these gold bars?" he asked in a weak tone.

Zenos frowned. "No, as a matter of fact I have not. Why the interest?" he asked again, staring at Aeneas, who looked as though he was on the edge of a heart attack. "Is something the matter?"

"No, no, it's nothing. I must have swallowed something that disagreed with me," Aeneas gasped, reaching for a cup. He took a long swig. Then he tried to change the subject. "Please do have some more wine. I have to say, the back olives on this island are terrific!" he oozed. "As for the first figs of the season, they are so moist and taste divine! And perhaps you could help me. I would very much like to meet again with the Emperor, whenever that might be possible.

"Why is that necessary? The Emperor is a very busy person. Is it important?"

Aeneas appeared to be trying to come to some decision. He said in his most persuasive manner, "Can I trust you? I mean really trust you?"

Zenos was intrigued; his mind went on alert. "Of course! Anything you say will be held in the strictest confidence." Even to his own ears he didn't sound very convincing.

"Then you should check the bars and see what is marked on them."

Zenos stared at him. "So the gold is what this is all about... you are here as a spy!" He pretended to sound very angry at this point. "You need to know that I am the Chief Information Gatherer for His Majesty Isaac Komnenos"—he raised his voice to make the pompous point—"and I can have you arrested on what I have just heard alone."

Aeneas looked aghast. "But I am an Ambassador to the Emperor! That is the truth!" he protested.

Zenos picked out an olive and popped it into his mouth. "Not the whole truth, if I am not mistaken," he said through his chewing, then spat the pit out onto the table. It was a very rude gesture, which was not lost on Aeneas, who wondered if he should call for help. He was sure that his two henchmen could deal with this man in an instant, but what then? How would he explain the disappearance of a senior court official who had come to visit, with a detail of attendants waiting outside?

"You should tell me what you can, or I shall put you in prison," Zenos said in a threatening manner.

"Perhaps *you* should hear what I have to say," Aeneas countered. He realized that he had broken a golden rule for even the most amateurish of spies by confiding in someone like Zenos. It caused him to break out into a sweat. His worst fears were coming to pass, but he hung onto the shreds of his nerves and attempted to keep his voice low and normal, even though his heart was pounding with fear. He knew he wasn't cut out to play this kind of game, but now he was here, and unless he wanted to die in a prison he must somehow enlist this man. Perhaps greed would serve? He wanted to keep the knowledge of the impending invasion as a last resort.

Zenos nodded. "Very well, try me."

"I am here because of the gold that disappeared from the treasury in the City," Aeneas said, watching for a reaction. Zenos didn't disappoint him; he sat forward and looked shocked.

"Are you... are you telling me that the gold we are getting from this Talon fellow is the gold from your treasury?" he whispered.

"It is very possible. Didn't anyone tell you that Pantoleon emptied the treasury before he disappeared? How it managed to find its way to that castle on the hill is anyone's guess. That is, if it is indeed the same gold. We—you need to check up on that. I can show you how it is marked, and you could verify it."

Zenos leaned back, looking very thoughtful. After a long pause he said, "First steps first. I shall verify the markings. I have the authority to do that." He paused. "Then we talk, you and I." His tone was ominous, as was his expression.

"Yes, we should talk," Aeneas retorted. "I will tell you then what else I know about Pantoleon."

Zenos wondered impulsively whether he should just arrest the man then and there and extract that remaining piece of information from him in the dungeons, but then that would mean the senior advisers and the Emperor himself would be party to the news. So instead he simply glowered at Aeneas and said, "Very well. We will meet again to discuss this, and I shall know by then from where the gold originated."

Aeneas sketched an image of the markings he might find on the gold bars for him, and they took their leave of one another, eyes locked and distrust written all over their faces, rather like two hyenas backing off a kill but with the promise they would be back. If Zenos could have worn a snarl and bared his teeth he would have. Aeneas just looked apprehensive.

*****

Dimitri was informed of the visit by his men who were scattered around the villa. Khuzaymah, one of Dimitri's best hoods, reported.

"It's just like old times at the villa, but this time there are not as many guards, and the two that I have seen are half-wits," he informed Dimitri. "But who is this Zenos, and where does he come from?"

"Well, his father is a moderately wealthy merchant who has been sucking up to the Emperor ever since Isaac got here. Every time Isaac picks his teeth he is picking that man's nose!" Dimitri said contemptuously.

"The new Chief of Information is not a complete cipher." he continued thoughtfully. "I heard from Boethius Eirenikos of Paphos"—another of Talon's spies—"some interesting things about the man. As a merchant, he has extensive contacts along the eastern seaboard, from the great City itself all the way past Armenia, Beirut, Tripoli, Tyre, and on down to Jaffa. They have informed him that Zenos is a native of Larnaca and spent much of his youth in Beirut acting as an assistant agent for his father's business there. He got a reputation as a big spender and a man who indulged his tastes without much care. We should keep a close eye on him."

Both Dimitri and Boethius knew that Beirut enjoyed a flourishing illicit trade with Damascus. It was a city teaming with out-of-work mercenaries of all stripes rubbing shoulders with spies who served the interests of anyone who was willing to pay them in gold. This included pirates and the notorious *Batinis,* the Assassins who lived deep in the Lebanese mountains. Life was very cheap in Beirut, for there was no strong man to keep the peace. Hence it was with some trepidation that Dimitri and Boethius viewed Zenos in the position of Chief of Information. Isaac had simply returned from one of his trips to Larnaca with Zenos in tow and informed everyone of the new appointment.

*****

Glancing back at the villa, Zenos began to formulate a plan. He hastened to the palace and was admitted by the armed guards, after which he scurried down the steps to the labyrinth of corridors below ground. Walking down the steps to the cellars was not the most pleasant experience. The corridors were gloomy, some led to dungeons, others to storerooms like the treasury, and still others led to dead ends. They were for the most part unlit since the departure of Pantoleon, who had kept torches everywhere. There was an unpleasant smell of damp, but also something else that had permeated the walls. Zenos shivered. It was the taint of terror and residual stink of blood and feces. The horrendous stories that had percolated out of these dark chambers had spread far and wide. He knew of them, and felt cold.

He steeled his nerves as he approached the doors which led to the treasury. There he demanded entrance to the rooms where the loot of Isaac's empire was kept. The guard was respectful and permitted him passage into the inner sanctum of the treasury.

Zenos took an already lit torch from a sconce outside the chambers and walked down a short corridor to another locked room. He had the sentry open the door, then told him to go back to his post. Alone, he entered the dark space and looked around.

The room was not large but it seemed so, because the open chests, sacks and barrels of silver or copper coins did not in any way fill it. A trio of small, closed chests against the wall caught his eye. He raised the torch on high and strode over. Each small chest bore a seal similar to the image on the sketch Aeneas had given him. He tested one; there was no lock on the latch and it opened readily enough. He placed the torch in an iron sconce on the wall and returned to the chest. Lifting its lid, he gave an involuntary gasp.

Inside, lying packed close together, were bars of metal; he had heard of but never before seen gold in this form. He was immediately drawn to their dull glitter. By his estimate they numbered somewhere between twenty-five and thirty bars, each one a full hand's span long, two fat fingers wide and a knuckle deep, with rounded ends. They had all been cast from the same kind of mold. Zenos stared for a long time at the open chest, then reached down and opened the other. It, too, was almost full of gleaming bars. His heart began to pound rapidly. For anyone other than an emperor, who was supposed to spend it on his people, this represented a massive fortune! But then he remembered the words of the Ambassador. Almost the entire treasury of the Byzantine empire had been emptied out by the man Pantoleon. Zenos could barely imagine how many chests that must have been. They were clearly not all here. Just three chests!

He bent down to examine the stamps on the top bars. The sketch was very accurate: the twin heads of the eagle were clearly marked on each bar, followed by a stamp that denoted weight. He lifted one of the heavy bars out of the chest. Its feel was unlike any other metal he had handled before. Involuntarily his hand gripped it. He stroked the bar with trembling fingers, which tingled with pleasure. On impulse he slipped the gold bar into his sash. One for a keepsake to hold. Why not? he thought. No one was going to challenge him for being down here. They would not know if just one was missing. He repositioned the remaining bars to even out their spacing.

He realized that he could not tarry for long; the sentries would become inquisitive and come looking if he didn't leave soon. Closing the chests, he took up the torch again and backed out of the chamber, shutting the door behind him.

His mind in a fevered dream of imagined riches transported from Constantinople to this island, he exited the dungeons and made for his chambers. There he placed his newfound wealth in the back of a cupboard and sat down to think.

His hands were shaking and his breath was short. The big question now was, if these were the tribute that man Talon paid to the Emperor, how many other chests were to be found up in that castle? Zenos was sure it was a fortune beyond imagining! The gold was without any doubt the property of the Empire of Byzantium; however, he was beginning to formulate some ideas of his own about its disposal.

*****

It was midmorning when Diocles knocked gently on the door to Tamura's apartment. After a brief pause it was opened by her eunuch Siranos, who, upon seeing Diocles, immediately bowed very low. "My... my Lord! Er, her ladyship is still abed, my Lord," Siranos stuttered weakly.

"Who is it?" Tamura called from the bed.

"My Lady, it is the Chief Minister," Siranos called back.

"Ah, my Lord Chief Minister, do come in," Tamura replied, sitting up in the bed. "Siranos, go find Martina and tell her to bring some wine for the Minister, at once!" she commanded.

Siranos vanished, and Diocles walked into the room almost gingerly. He felt he had cause to be wary. The stories that emanated from this chamber were tales of bloodshed, poisonings and other bizarre occurrences, which the rumor-mongering and very bored inhabitants of the palace, women, eunuchs and even the lethargic guards, shared in whispers.

After bowing ceremoniously, Diocles began. "Dear Lady, I have come to discuss our new ambassador with you."

Tamura's eyes widened with surprise, but she quickly regained her composure and smiled at him. "I am very honored to be of what assistance I can. Please make yourself comfortable." she motioned him to a fabric-covered stool nearby.

Diocles had just seated himself when the maid slipped into the room, carrying a tray of silver cups brimming with wine. He took one and silently regarded Tamura for a few minutes. The wine, he knew, originated from Lord Talon's vineyard. Diocles had seen no reason why he should not share some of the wine with this very beautiful young lady, whom he regarded with real respect. She had, after all, managed to see off several Chief Information Gatherers, although the details were not clear as to how. He was almost sure that she had some kind of contact with the people on the mountain. He suspected Siranos, who was as slippery as an eel, might be her messenger; no one had yet been able to find out where he went during his infrequent forays to the city.

She was aware of the scrutiny, but smiled at him in a friendly manner. "You are always a welcome visitor, Chief Minister," she said.

"Please, my Lady, call me Diocles. We are not on ceremony here," he replied.

"Very well, Diocles, what do you want to discuss regarding the Ambassador?"

"I think that we have both decided that he is not to be trusted, and that his role is probably a front for something else," Diocles said in a low tone. She nodded emphatic agreement. "Yes, a sly one, that's for sure."

"There appears to be another angle to ponder," Diocles said, sipping his wine slowly and watching her over the rim of his cup.

"What would that be?" she asked, her eyes questioning.

"My, er, my people noticed that our new Chief Information Gatherer went to the ambassador's house yesterday and spent some time there." Diocles put a hand up to forestall the exclamation on Tamura's lips.

"It is not a crime to do so, as he is well within his rights to investigate newcomers to this city, this kingdom, including 'Ambassadors'. But... when he came back, he went below the palace and visited the treasury."

"Why would he do that?" she asked, sounding puzzled and intrigued at the same time.

Diocles sipped his wine and paused before speaking again. "I asked myself the same question, my Lady. Do you remember the chest of gold that Exazenos brought to the Emperor that very first day?" he asked her.

"I certainly do!" Tamura remembered only too well that remarkable day when Pantoleon crawled all the way along the carpet of humility while his two minions dragged a small chest along behind him. She remembered also the exclamations from the watching nobles and merchants as the chest was opened, and the more restrained shock and surprise of the Emperor himself. "I think the gasp of awe was heard all the way to Paphos!" she retorted. "What has that got to do with...?" Her expressive eyes opened wide as it dawned on her.

"The ambassador is here to find out about the gold?"

Diocles nodded, his eyes squinting thoughtfully. "It is very possible. For some time now I have known that the gold was stamped with the mark of the Empire. It wasn't hard to figure out that Exazenos might have stolen it, and indeed the rumors coming from the City tended to strengthen that theory. But the second and third chest definitely came from the man on the mountain. Talon!" he said with emphasis.

"So soon after the disappearance of that dreadful man, too." Diocles was pensive. "A couple of chests of gold is one thing, but if there were more... much more, that is another matter altogether."

"Where could it be, if there is indeed more?" Tamura asked, sounding skeptical. "You have just implied that there isn't much of it here in the palace, just three chests? Does that mean.... No! Lord Talon has the rest?" She put a hand to her mouth, her eyes wide. "Oh my good God!"

Diocles nodded the affirmative. "It is just possible that those two, Zenos and the Ambassador, put two and two together and came up with the same answer," he responded. "Or they are about to do so. Lord Talon needs to be warned."

But neither volunteered the information that they had a direct line to the man on the mountain; they looked at one another with an awareness that they were now perhaps allies in this affair.

Diocles looked very pensive, as though he wanted to say something else but was hesitant. Tamura, observing his expression, asked him, "You have something on your mind, Lord Diocles. What is it?"

"I was just wondering... no, perhaps not. It is too dangerous." He sighed.

"What *do* you mean?" she demanded, her curiosity piqued.

"This Ambassador might be more likely to impart information to a woman than a man. We need to be able to incriminate him with his own words somehow," Diocles said slowly. He raised his hand. "Of course I don't mean you, my Lady."

By now thoroughly intrigued, Tamura pressed him. The old man took a swig of the wine and pretended to be reluctant to go on but finally said, "He appears to be shy. Most visitors, male visitors you understand, would have visited a house of... er...."

Tamura laughed. "A whorehouse, Minister?" she asked.

"Um, yes, but there has been no indication of that kind of behavior, not as yet anyway," Diocles said. "So I wondered if he might just open up to someone of the fairer sex if it could be arranged... very discreetly," he finished. Tamura laughed again. It was a pretty sound.

"Ha ha! A woman who just happened to encounter him in the street, perhaps?" Tamura leaned forward and patted the back of his hand. "You leave it with me and I shall see what can be arranged," she told him.

"I urge you to use the utmost discretion, my Lady," Diocles cautioned her; then he retired to his rooms, well satisfied with his mission. Tamura was still naive enough to be maneuvered. However, he warned himself, she was not to underestimated. He was fairly sure that she'd had murdered at least two people who'd crossed her, including a previous Gatherer of Information. That made her someone to be wary of.

———————

Chapter 7

Palace Games

Wild nights—Wild nights!
Were I with thee
Wild nights should be
Our luxury!
—Emily Dickinson

Zenos didn't waste any time after his visit to the treasury. He took an escort, as the streets were no longer safe for a lone man dressed in palace garb, and arrived at the gates of the ambassador's villa late in the afternoon, where he demanded entrance. He more or less stormed into the main living chamber, where he found Aeneas eating supper.

Overcoming his initial fearful reaction to the manner of Zenos's entrance, Aeneas played the diplomat and beckoned his visitor to the table. "Join me, Chief Information Gatherer, I am once again enjoying the food of this country." He waved his hand over the table, strewn with chicken bones and other detritus. "I have never tasted such figs in my whole life!" he exclaimed enthusiastically.

Zenos was not in the mood for niceties, so he ignored the comments and the food and addressed Aeneas sarcastically.

"So, Mister Ambassador. You are here to further the relations between our countries?" His loud voice brought one of

Aeneas's dangerous-looking men, who had been hovering nearby, to the entrance.

"Is everything all right, Master?" he inquired.

Aeneas looked a little pale but kept his calm and waved the man off. "It's all right, Macrobius; we are just talking," he said. The man nodded and withdrew, but remained near the door. Zenos shot him an irritated glance.

"As I said earlier," Aeneas said calmly enough, although he had stopped eating. "I am here for another reason. I am here for the *stolen* gold."

"I could arrest you here and now as a spy and lock you up in one of our dungeons," Zenos hissed.

"Yes, you could do that, but sooner or later the word would get out, and then what? The Emperor is very interested in this matter; if I do not return, he has other people who would hear about my incarceration. Imprisoning an official envoy, even such a humble one as myself, is a mark of contempt for the Emperor who sent him. That would annoy Emperor Isaac Angelos, possibly even provoke him into contemplating, shall we say, punitive actions? Even a small naval fleet would overpower your puny little forces, and pop! The whole island is back in the fold and *you* are a guest in one of *his* dungeons. I don't recommend that approach, but..."

Zenos was silent for a long moment. Taken aback by this unexpected show of teeth, he was forced to rethink his plan. He had thought to simply get rid of the one man who could impede his scheme, but now it didn't look so simple.

As though reading his mind, Aeneas said in a very low voice, "There are other ways to do this, but only if we put our heads together—and trust one another."

"I'm listening," Zenos growled.

"Firstly, I take it that you have identified the bars and they do belong to the Emperor?"

"Yes. They match the sketch."

"How many chests were there in the treasury?"

"Just three small, compact chests, and one of them was half empty!"

Aeneas shut his eyes and shook his head from side to side, wearing an expression of pained understanding. Taking a clean napkin from the table, he wiped the perspiration off his bald pate, then turned to look directly at Zenos. "You have probably figured out that the rest of the gold is somewhere else?"

"They are certainly not in the palace, I can assure you of that," was the retort.

"So it is back to the theory that the chests might have come from this Talon fellow, at least one of them, anyway?"

Zenos hesitated.

"Trust... remember?" Aeneas prompted him.

"I think it just possible that the rest of the gold is up in that castle on the mountain," Zenos conceded, his tone grudging. "Unless, of course, Exazenos absconded with the rest when he disappeared, in which case we will never find where it is. He vanished so completely that people are still talking about it.

Aeneas sighed. "Let's assume that at least some of it is on that mountain. Any ideas as to how we can recover it? I assume you have a plan?"

Zenos glared at him, not liking his high-handed manner. "Yes, perhaps, but it is going to be very difficult and will involve a lot of people. None of whom must ever know the real purpose. Least of all the Emperor or his senior advisor."

Aeneas wanted to laugh. With these words Zenos had committed treason. And from what he knew about Isaac, the mere whiff of disloyalty could mean a horrible death for Zenos. They, therefore, had each other gripped by the short and curlies; and neither was going to let go before the other. Now they were committed.

He took a swig of the awful wine that his servants had bought in the market, shook his head and muttered, "There must be something better than this piss water!" He looked up and said, "Then we must hurry up and make a plan."

"What is the hurry?" Zenos asked suspiciously. "That castle has withstood one siege, it's almost impregnable. We won't get in easily, I can tell you. I ask you again, what is the hurry?"

Aeneas looked disconcerted. "No reason, but, well... before anyone finds out what we are doing."

"You are holding something back from me," Zenos snarled. "Tell me what it is, or I will take you to the dungeons and beat it out of you! To hell with everything else!"

Aeneas knew he had blundered. He thought for a long moment, then decided that it might be as well to inform Zenos of the pending invasion.

"As... as I told you, the Emperor has taken a keen interest in this island since the Normans tried to... tried to take the City. He knows that your king was on the side of William, so he ...." Aeneas stopped and wiped the perspiration off his bald head.

"So he what?" Zenos snapped, by now thoroughly alarmed.

"He is going to invade!" Aeneas blurted out.

"You treacherous rat! You snake!" Zenos exclaimed, jumping up from the table and clenching his hands as if he wished they were gripping knives to use on Aeneas.

"All this time you knew what was going to happen!"

"No! No!" Aeneas said shakily. "I know he is *considering* it. I don't know if he is *going* to," he lied.

Zenos didn't believe him. "You do know! When," he asked, his tone dripping sarcasm, "is this visit to take place?

By God and all the saints!" He swept plates off the table with a crash. "I should have you killed for this!"

"Then they *will* come after you," Aeneas said shakily. "The Emperor has a long reach, and don't forget it was he who sent me to find the gold. This I have partially accomplished, but unless we move quickly none of it will come our way." He was appealing to the basic greed of his comrade in crime, and he could see the feverish workings of Zenos's mind in his face as he considered his options. "We can take *some* for ourselves and say that this Talon fellow either hid it off the island or spent it. No one will be able to dispute that, especially if they get back *most* of the gold."

It took a huge effort for Zenos to calm down enough to speak. "I will have to travel to Beirut," he stated. "I know people there who might be able to help."

"Remember that there will be huge rewards for those who do recover the treasure, Zenos. I may call you Zenos? Please call me Aeneas. All these titles get in the way of things, don't you think?" Aeneas gave Zenos a weak smile. It crossed his mind to send a message to the Emperor to report progress, but decided that might jeopardize his own plans.

*****

Zenos left for Beirut a few days later, having informed the Emperor and anyone else who cared to listen that he was going to Paphos to investigate a murder. He did intend to drop by Paphos on his way back, to examine the castle and find out what he could about the mysterious sea battle that had taken place just prior to the disappearance of the fiend Exazenos. He had a license to go almost where he pleased in the interests of his job description, so no one commented.

No one, that is, except Diocles, who was concerned about the second visit paid to the Ambassador enough to tell Tamura about it.

They still maintained some of the initial reserve each had with the other, but this was fast being replaced with a sense of their mutual need for survival. They both realized that if they worked together they could perhaps maintain the status quo, which, while not perfect, was considerably better than the chaos which might ensue should there be any skullduggery on the part of the Chief Information Gatherer and the Ambassador. Their second meeting was brief, but there was an urgency to it because of the activities and mysterious departure of Zenos.

Instinctively Tamura was a curious girl, and she knew how powerful were her assets; but how to use them to winkle information from this prim newcomer while Zenos was away?

"Siranos! Where are you? You lazy thing!" she called one day. He came running from the back rooms, replying, "You called, Mistress?"

"Does the Ambassador ever visit the city?" she enquired. "I mean, does he stay cooped up in that villa all day, or does he look around the city at all?"

Siranos thought about that, then brightened. "He goes to the church on a regular basis, at least twice a week. He also takes walks along the harbor wall in the evenings, when there are fewer people about."

"Which days are those?"

"This morning would be one of those days for the church, Mistress."

"I am going to the service this morning, and you are coming with me," she ordered. Come along! Martina? Where *is* that girl when I need her?"

Thus it was that Aeneas, a moderately pious man who believed in being seen showing respect to his Maker, was standing in the church, listening to the seemingly endless litany chanted by deacon, when he became aware of the presence of a woman on the other side of the nave. She was observing him with apparent interest.

Later, he wondered whether it was the perfume wafting his way or simply the fact that a beautiful woman appeared to be taking an interest in him that captured his attention. Being quite unused to any woman paying him any attention, his own curiosity was piqued and he stared at her, wondering where he might have seen her before. The heavy veil that hid her face moved and revealed a delicate jawline and full lips. With a start he recognized the Lady Tamura from the palace! He felt an abrupt quickening of his senses. He looked around to see if there were any bodyguards lurking in the shadows, but could find none. The only person with the woman was a young girl, also veiled, but clearly a servant.

In the City such a meeting could never have occurred, but here in this hayseed town that had the gall to call itself a city it was evidently permitted for the young queen to go to a service without very many guards in attendance. Out of the corner of his eye he could see only two slouching against the pillars by the entrance. Her attendant even stepped aside into one of the aisles and initiated a murmured conversation with another man, leaving her mistress alone. Aeneas barely heard the next part of the service; his attention was surreptitiously fixed on the woman across the nave.

The service finally came to an end and the woman turned away to leave, but then she did something so unexpected that Aeneas's mouth fell open. She gestured to him to attend her as she walked out of the building. Aeneas might have been a counting-man with little imagination, but he also fancied himself an opportunist. Motioning his own two men to keep back, he scurried out of the building into the bright sunlight to catch up with the Lady Tamura, who was moving slowly in the general direction of the palace. She appeared to notice him approaching and waved her guards off. It was market day, and she lingered by some of the cloth stalls, fingering the expensive silks, but did not buy any. He came up behind her and her attendant, cleared his suddenly dry throat and asked, "Did you need to talk to me, My Lady?"

"I understand that you are on your own here in our country, Ambassador?" she enquired with an arched brow.

"Ye, yes, my Lady. I was sent alone."

*****

Siranos met Aeneas by the garden doors of the palace and led him to Tamura's quarters. Before they crossed the gardens, the eunuch thrust a mask and a floppy hat into Aeneas's hands and told him to put them on. Siranos knew every passage and every room in the building, so it was easy enough to smuggle a cloaked, masked man into the harem using the excuse that he was one of the mimes sent to entertain the women.

They passed noisy musicians and bustling servants and eunuchs, who were too busily engaged upon catering to the bored wives of the Emperor to notice the newcomer, and slipped on up the stairs to the women's bed chambers. To Aeneas's surprise no one seemed to notice him or Siranos as they made their way along some crowded corridors and then some quieter ones, which eventually led to a stout wooden door.

Siranos knocked gently on the door, and at a muffled command it was opened to show Aeneas a candlelit room that was sumptuously decorated. Silk curtains were drawn across the open windows, and Persian rugs overlaid the multi-colored tiles on the floor. A pleasant scent of lavender, mingled with a very subtle scent of frankincense, permeated the room. Tamura herself glided across the floor to greet him with an outstretched hand, which felt deliciously cool to his own fevered touch. He tried to emulate the queen in politeness; he did, after all, come from the Blachernae Palace, and bent over her hand to brush it with his lips.

She smiled coquettishly, then waved him over to some huge cushions, indicating that he should seat himself. When Tamura clapped her hands, a maid hurried into the room bearing a tray laden with sweetmeats and silver goblets. Wine was poured, then the maid vanished back behind the curtains at the other end of the room.

Aeneas was still somewhat bewildered by the situation, but he was also excited by the presence of the lovely lady and full of hopeful anticipation as to what might happen next. She lowered herself onto a cushion across from him, took up one of the silver goblets and brought it to her lips, all the while looking at him over the rim.

Aeneas felt himself stir. Despite the cool room a bead of sweat appeared on his brow. He sipped his own wine and found it to be very good, as fine as any he had tasted in Constantinople. His surprise must have shown on his face for she smiled and said, "The wine is from this island, Master Ambassador. I hope you like it."

He nodded, wanting to gargle the deep red liquid, it felt so good on his tongue. He restrained himself and replied, "It is excellent, my Lady. You are fortunate to have wine of this quality. I wonder if I might find some of it to take back with me. Where is it grown?"

She smiled again. "I am unsure as to exactly where it is grown, but it is from the north side of the mountains nearby, I believe." She waved her hand vaguely towards the region of Kantara.

Aeneas frowned and said, "Is that not near where this man called Talon lives? I have heard much about him."

Tamura took a sharp little breath. "Yes, indeed it is. It is rumored that he is fabulously wealthy, but he is also considered dangerous and reputed to be a wizard."

She didn't fail to notice the gleam of interest in the Ambassador's eyes as he took another sip of his wine.

"Fabulously wealthy, my Lady?"

"Oh, that is only a rumor, and rumors are everywhere on a small island like this, but the general opinion is that this man, who came from nowhere, is very rich indeed, especially since—" She stopped abruptly and placed her cup down on the silver tray. "But I must not say too much, as it is only gossip... mere hearsay."

"I, for one, would be very interested in hearing *any* gossip of this kind," replied Aeneas, displaying uneven teeth in what he hoped was an encouraging smile. More beads of sweat had appeared on his shiny pate, which he wiped off apologetically with a cotton cloth. "I am sorry, my Lady. It is a little warm in here."

Tamura almost laughed out loud; that cunning Diocles had been right. She poured her guest another full cup of wine, which he took up and almost immediately drank down. She watched him carefully and with some satisfaction. This man was here about the gold! Nothing to do with diplomacy, just as Diocles had surmised, and his bulbous nose was sniffing for information of any kind that might lead to it. She looked at his heavy linen toga and its wrap, which were more suited to a wet winter in Rome than the hot climate of Famagusta, and said sweetly, "Alas, even though the shutters are open there is no breeze today, Ambassador. However, please do feel free to take off your outer wrap. You must be suffocating in all that clothing."

Aeneas didn't think; he took off the thick linen wrap, which left him in his gold-trimmed tunic with his arms bare. He leaned back on the huge, comfortable cushions and swallowed more wine. That felt a lot better.

Tamura decided to ask a few questions of her own. "What have you heard on the street for yourself, Ambassador?" she cooed.

"Please, my Lady, call me Aeneas; it is a great deal less official. But yes, I have heard things too." He leaned forward in a more conspiratorial manner, and his eyes strayed from her face down her exposed neck to lock onto the swelling of her breasts, which strained against the thin fabric of her bodice.

Being very familiar with this form of male stare she ignored it and focused in on extracting more information.

"So you think that this man, the one on the mountain, might be in possession of..." she stopped and her eyes prompted him.

Aeneas's eyes crawled off her breasts back up to her face. His own was flushed from the effects of the wine, and he slurred in a very low voice, "Gold, my Lady." He touched the side of his nose with a forefinger.

Tamura pretended she didn't understand. "Well of course he will have gold; he is reputed to be very rich."

He waved his hand in the air. "No, no, no, my Lady. *Gold!*" he emphasized. "the gold bars from the City."

"What are you talking about, Aeneas? Gold from the city of Constantinople?"

"Yes, yes... it was stolen by Pantoleon the charioteer and brought here to Cyprus!" Aeneas was about to say more when there was a loud banging on the outer door and a shout. Tamura paled and looked terrified,

"Oh, God help me! Its the Emperor!" she whispered. "You must leave, at once!" She sounded desperate.

Isaac called from behind the door. "I am coming in this minute, my honey-drop! Make ready!" This was followed by a cackle of laughter. Siranus appeared with an ashen face, wringing his hands. "What will we do, my Lady?" He gave a low wail of terror. "We are dead!"

Tamura wasted no time. "You," she snapped to Aeneas. "Get under there," she pointed to the large canopy-covered bed, the silks of which came down to the floor. "Now!" she hissed. Aeneas scrambled off the cushions and hurriedly paddled on hands and knees to the bed, then crawled underneath.

Tamura reached for the silver cup he had just used. It was empty, so she tossed it behind the curtains near the window, where it landed with a light clinking sound. She stood up and waved to Siranos to open the door, as the Emperor was sounding impatient. The door crashed open and Isaac charged inside to stop in the middle of the chamber, his feet braced wide. He was alone, which reassured Tamura somewhat. All the same she shrank from Isaac, who was obviously very excited about something.

"My Lord! My King! I, I have been waiting for you. Where have you been?" she stammered.

"You have, have you?" Isaac bellowed. "Good, because by God I am ready!"

"Ready for what, my Lord?" she asked in a tremulous voice.

"Ready! Ready for us!" he grabbed himself by the crotch and cackled. That powder your man-thing gave me several hours ago has worked its magic! Get on the bed, woman, and be quick about it. Ha ha!"

Tamura tried to protest, "My Lord, should I not come to your quarters? Would it not be proper if I accompanied you there and we can then..?"

"No, no! Now! I want you now, my beauty." He grunted as he wrestled with his waistcoat, which he finally tore off, ripping some of its gold buttons off in the process. "Help me with this!" he commanded the cringing Siranos, "and then get out of my sight!"

Tamura pretended to be delighted. "Oh, my Lord! It worked!" she squealed with excitement.

While Siranos began helping the impatient Emperor out of his clothes, Tamura, her eyes wide with acting out the part, eased herself gingerly onto the bed.

"Oh, yesss! Look at this!" Isaac pointed to himself. "Now get undressed, my Princess. I want you ready for me!" Isaac yelled, as he hopped about the floor with one leg still in his under-draws.

The subsequent copulation was noisy, the more so as Tamura joined in with exaggerated enthusiasm while at the same time she frantically signaled Siranos to get the Ambassador out of the chamber. She glimpsed Aeneas's wide backside disappearing into the other room as he fled on hands and knees, to be hauled without ceremony out of sight by Siranos and the almost hysterical Martina. When the curtains had finally stopped moving she turned her attention fully to her king and set about making his visit as memorable as she knew how.

Their yells and cries filled the corridors. The other women who heard wept with frustration, the stoical sentries grinned to one another, and the eunuchs in the vicinity eyed one another with satisfaction. There would be a return to relative tranquility in the palace, for a little while longer at least.

Eventually a note found its way to Dimitri, which was then sent on by pigeon to Jannat. It read, *"All is well in the palace."*

Chapter 8

The Count of Tripoli

Is greatness endowed by the flick of a sword?
You look just the same to me.
Is taking up arms in the name of our lord
really enough to be free?
                                            —*Joe Hill*

Two ships negotiated the channel between the rocks and
the walls of the city and then nosed into the inner harbor of
Tyre past the twin guardian towers. Talon, standing on the
afterdeck, had a chance to scrutinize the city. It was a well-
fortified town with tall, solid looking walls, which to his criti-
cal mind would be hard to take because of several singular
factors. The main characteristic of the city was that it could
only be approached by land across a long, narrow causeway.

He began to see why it was such an important entry port
for the Kingdom of Jerusalem. While Acre was closer to the
Holy City of Jerusalem, Tyre was clearly more defensible. He
gazed up at the solid, weather-streaked walls of the port city,
stained dark with salt and seaweed, as the crew rowed the
ship past and then between the tiny, rocky islands that ran to
the north and south. He noted the way the fortifications went
straight up at a sharp angle from the coastal rocks of the
main island, providing no space to land for would-be invaders from the sea. He also observed the numerous, well-
armed sentries who lined the walls to watch their arrival.

The city roofs and towers looked very picturesque with the long, colorful banners snapping in the wind. The colors of the Count of Tripoli were intermixed with the cross of Jerusalem and with the colors of the other nobility who were currently within the city.

"I wonder why there are so many men on the walls," he said to Reza, who shook his head.

"More than the usual number, I'd say. The city looks as though it is preparing for trouble," he responded. "I suspect we are about to find out." He pointed to a gathering on the quayside of men and horses. "They seem to be expecting us, Talon."

Guy ambled over to join them as their ship led the way into the inner harbor. "They say that the causeway over there joining the city and the shore was built by Alexander." He pointed with a gnarled finger. "It is even called the Alexander Causeway," he added.

Talon stared at the causeway stretching off towards land until the buildings and towers obstructed his view. Guy had to direct his attention to docking their vessel.

There was a long space cleared along the quayside for the two ships; there a small group of dismounted horsemen waited. As the ship came alongside the quay, one amongst them stepped forward and shouted across the water, "Where is Sir Matthew?"

"He is in the ship behind us," Guy called back.

"Who, then, are you?"

"This is Lord Talon de Gilles," Guy responded.

"Ah. Welcome, Lord Talon. I am Sir Bertram de Villiers. I am here to escort you and your party to the Count, who is waiting in the keep."

In a very short space of time the two ships were docked and tied off. Before he left the ship, Talon called his son over to join him, Reza, and the captain. "I want you to stay here until such time as we know what the Count wants," he told them. "Do not leave the ship, Rostam. This time I am very serious. I want Guy to be able to leave at a moment's notice. Do you understand?" Rostam ducked his head. "Yes, Father. I shall remain on board with Guy."

"Good. Then we will go with these men and find out what is going on," Talon said. "Until I know more, the prisoner stays in chains; and Junayd, I want you to stay with Rostam."

Junayd nodded. "As you wish, Lord."

Talon and Reza walked down the gangplank to join Sir Matthew, who was already talking to Sir Bertram and his men. He gestured towards Talon as they approached the horsemen.

"Sir Bertram, I have the honor to present Lord Talon de Gilles," he stated formally.

All the men present bowed respectfully. "So this is what happens when you are a Lord, eh?" Reza muttered into his ear, speaking Farsi.

Restraining a grin, Talon presented Reza. "I bring with me Lord Reza of Kantara, one of my most trusted companions," he stated, trying to keep his face straight.

Immediately everyone bowed again. Some even doffed hats.

"Only a Lord, eh?" Reza murmured. "But it's nice to have this lot of Christians bowing and scraping to us, isn't it?"

"Don't push your luck, Brother," Talon muttered out of the corner of his mouth.

Horses were led forward, and they all mounted, including Yosef and Dar'an, who accompanied the two men.

It was only a short ride to the palace where Count Raymond had ensconced himself and his considerable retinue. They clattered over the cobbles and under an arch which had a portcullis and openings for defense. Talon by now could recognize when a city or castle was well built, and he approved of Tyre.

Alert sentries had informed the Count of their arrival, and he was standing on the steps to the main entrance of the palace waiting to greet them. He was slightly built but a strong looking man nonetheless; not tall, and darker than most Franks. His hair was bleached to a dark straw color by the sun, and there were deep lines on either side of his eyes from squinting into the unforgiving sunlight of Palestine virtually all his life. These same lines were deepened by the smile he bestowed on Talon.

He lifted his arms in greeting from the top of the steps. "At last I see you again, Sir Talon. Or is it *Lord* Talon now?" he called out with a chuckle. His hazel eyes appeared to be genuinely pleased to see Talon. Although most of his retainers dressed as most Christians did in uncomfortable woolen clothes and crudely sewn hauberks, he wore light cotton robes, as would any Arab prince. With his slim, dark form and slightly hooked nose he could easily pass for one. Talon noted pronounced streaks of grey in his beard; the duke was now forty-seven years of age, but to Talon he appeared older and careworn. However, his smile of greeting was very welcoming.

Talon dismounted and walked up the steps to kneel in front of the Count. "They call me Lord these days, my Lord Tripoli, but as you can see I came at your request."

Raymond laughed. "God help me but I am glad to see you, my friend!"

He seized Talon by the hands, hauled him to his feet and embraced him. "I have prayed that you would come, and here you are. Thank you," he murmured into Talon's ear. "You must call me Raymond. It would be good."

Talon embraced him back with feeling. It was good to know he had a friend in the Count, but he shook his head. "I shall still call you Lord, because that is fitting, Sir." He turned and indicated Reza with his left hand, speaking Arabic. "Lord Raymond, I wish to present to you my companion of many years; indeed, he is my brother. He is known as Master Reza to our own people."

The Count smiled and waved Reza to his feet, then embraced him too. "I know of you, Lord Reza. Rumor is true, then. You do exist, and are a companion to my friend Talon here. You are known far and wide as The Ghost, did you know that?"

"I recently discovered that fact, Lord," Reza responded, his dark features wreathed in a grin.

"Ha! I heard the epithet came from the palace of none other than the Sultan. I doubt he is pleased to hear it bandied about!" The Count laughed. "I am keen to hear how this name came about.

"But I digress," the Count continued. "You must be tired from your long journey. Come, my attendants will take care of you and your servants." He glanced appraisingly at Yosef and Dar'an, who were standing behind Reza and Talon. "I see you have men who appear to be real warriors, Talon," he remarked.

"Reza trained them as only he could, Lord," Talon responded. "These two men have traveled the world with us and we would not be parted."

"I see," the Count said. "We must talk as soon as you are settled, Talon. There are urgent matters to discuss."

They walked into the gloomy halls, which were stark and functional, appearing all the darker because of the contrast with the bright sunshine outside. Talon was already missing the sunlit garden and Solarium of his home.

"I shall meet with you within an hour," the Count said, as they parted ways.

As servants guided them towards their accommodations, Talon sensed tension in the air. They passed retainers, knights and men-at-arms who would turn and stare at them, and their looks were wary, even hostile.

He began to wonder why, then realized neither he nor Reza, and especially not his retainers, were dressed anything like the people all around them. They no doubt resembled the hated and feared Saracen, for they all wore loose-fitting coats and the typical pointed helmets and fine chain armor to be seen on their enemies. It gave him pause for thought.

"These people think we have arrived from the Saracen camp and are upset," he commented to Reza, once they were ushered into their chambers.

Talon glanced around at the stark, gray stone walls and narrow windows, feeling claustrophobic. It felt more as though they had just entered some kind of prison than guest quarters.

"I felt that too, Brother," Reza remarked. He shook his head. "Almost all of them wear woolen clothes! In this heat that is insane. The Count, however, wears much the same as we do."

"That is because he was born here, a *pullani*, and grew up in this country; he feels as though he belongs. Why would he *not* wear the right kind of clothes? It is hot enough in summer even with these light garments we wear."

"His Arabic is almost without accent, Lord," Yosef said hoarsely. His voice box had never completely recovered from being slashed when they were in China. "You told me that few speak Arabic here in this Christian country."

"Very few, Yosef. It is remarkable how resistant the majority are to learning anything from this place. For your own safety, you and Dar'an should be careful. I don't like what I am seeing here. Everyone is on edge."

The Count of Tripoli, being a *pullani*, had obviously insisted upon having his creature comforts made available, not only to himself but to his guests. Talon and Reza could therefore partake of baths and light refreshments before they presented themselves to the Count in his chambers, which were well appointed and spacious, with larger windows.

Raymond greeted them, then noted Talon's gaze wandering over the beautiful frescoes on the walls and the ceiling.

"Those are from the time of the Greeks, who preceded even the Arabs, Talon," he commented, and came to stand next to Talon and gaze up at the figures on the walls. "The Arab zealots have done much damage by simply neglecting these exquisite scenes. We Christians lack the ability to emulate them, let alone repair them, so they are gradually disappearing. I mourn the loss of these treasures. In his neglect of the refinements of life man is a foolish creature." He turned away with a shake of his head and gestured for Talon and Reza to be seated nearby at the high table.

"We can talk while we eat," he stated. "I have brought my own fruit to the table from my gardens in Tripoli. These barbarians think that meat and bread are the only forms of nourishment. The Templars are the worst of all," he grimaced. "You would know about that, wouldn't you, Talon?"

Talon gave him a rueful smile as he seated himself and took up a peach from a large bowl of ripe fruit. "I was only subjected to that diet for a short while, Lord. The corned beef never varied, and the only relief was bread or stew, yet they thought they were privileged. Sir Guy rescued me and obtained permission for me to live outside the Temple while in Jerusalem. God protect his soul."

"He was a very good man who recognized in you a person who could replace him, Talon," the Count stated with conviction. "He spoke much of you after you disappeared into the East. Is that where you met Lord Reza, here?"

Reza smiled. He had helped himself to fruit and while contemplating the velvety peach in hand said, "No, Lord. Talon and I go back to the time when we were boys, being trained by the *Rafiki*."

The Count's eyes widened. "Now the rumors make sense. Is it true, then, what they say?'

Reza laughed. "Perhaps, Lord, but one must not say too much." He glanced at Talon and added, "But Lord Raymond, you must tell us why you called upon my Brother and why we are here in Tyre."

Talon breathed a small sigh of relief. He didn't want to dwell upon their background, rather on what the future held.

The Count nodded his head. "You are right, Reza. Time is pressing, and I do not believe we have much of it. I shall bring you up to date as best I can."

He took a sip of wine and seemed to collect his thoughts. "Since the death of the King, and I am referring to Baldwin IV, two factions have grown up in this land."

He paused, then began again.

"For some time now, Princess Sibylla's mother, Agnes, the former Countess of Jaffa and now the Countess of Courtenay, has been at the core of the palace intrigues. She is an ambitious meddler who wished to see her daughter on the throne. Years ago, Guy de Lusignan, that contemptible adventurer, managed to seduce the Princess, who went and married him despite strong opposition from the King. When the King died, his young nephew Baldwin V came to the throne. This you know already. However, what you perhaps do not know is what has transpired since the boy died in Acre."

"I know little of these matters," Talon said.

The Count sighed. "I was appointed Regent during the young King's reign, but he didn't live beyond his minority. According to an agreement drawn up with King Baldwin IV, we were supposed to wait for a decision from King Henry of England and the Pope as to who was entitled to the crown should the boy die early, which was not unexpected. But that didn't happen.

"Count Jocelyn of Edessa and the Marquis William were supposed to escort the young King's body to Jerusalem for burial in the Church of the Holy Sepulcher. I went to Nablus to call upon the *Haute Cour* members to discuss events. Many of them supported Isabella, whom I believe is the rightful heir. Certainly the more competent."

Talon detected a huge frustration emanating from Raymond and suspected that the man in front of him had actually possessed larger ambitions than he was letting out.

The Count continued. "Sibylla is nothing if not cunning and manipulative, just like that witch mother of hers. Sibylla and her mother, aided and abetted by that snake Châtillon and his imbecilic partner Gérard de Rideford, managed to steal the crown. She had herself crowned Queen by the Bishop, tricking everyone into thinking that she was eager to play the role of ruler of this country. This was hard to dispute, for the Pope himself had finally declared that she was the rightful heir. What astonished everyone was that as soon as she was crowned she immediately declared for Guy, her husband, and had him crowned King."

The Count gave a bleak smile. "Those of us in Nablus were taken completely by surprise, as were most of the nobles in Jerusalem. Then, to add insult to injury, Châtillon told the world at large that she was '*the most evident and rightful heir of the kingdom.*' Both he and De Rideford have curried favor since with that despicable man, and his useless wife has been side-lined by Rideford. It is he, Rideford, who is whispering into Guy's ear. The King"—Raymond almost spat the word—"is incapable of making his own decisions, and it is Rideford and Châtillon who are pulling the strings. He is a mere puppet!" The Count was up and pacing back and forth now, clearly agitated.

"Well, then came the news that Châtillon had ambushed a caravan on its way to Damascus. He slaughtered all of the guards and enslaved the merchants. Nothing too surprising about that. He has been attacking caravans ever since he was granted the castle of Kerak through his marriage." Raymond clenched his fists and all but shook them in the air. "But this time it was infinitely more serious. This time he did something heinous. He personally raped a woman who is rumored to be related to Salah Ed Din!"

Talon and Reza gasped. "Lord protect us!" Talon whispered.

"Salah Ed Din is, I assume, incensed by this?" Reza managed to ask. He looked dazed.

"To put it mildly, yes. He has declared war," Raymond said. "When this became known in Jerusalem, King Guy agreed that Châtillon had overstepped all bounds and should be punished." Raymond snorted with disgust. "But Guy has *no* backbone. And he owes his throne to that God-damned... pirate." Raymond shrugged in disgust. "So nothing happened!"

"Nothing?" Reza blurted out, looking incredulous. Talon was equally appalled.

"No! Nothing!" The Count almost shouted the words and glared at them. "It is despicable what was done, and just as deplorable that no punishment was meted out to that criminal! Châtillon should have been imprisoned at the very least and had his castle confiscated. Better yet, he should be handed over to Salah Ed Din." Raymond ground out the words between clenched teeth.

"Is Salah Ed Din going to invade, Lord?" asked Reza.

"I suspect so," Raymond answered, and turned aside to cough. It was a deep, hacking cough that made Talon and Reza look at one another in alarm.

Raymond wiped his lips and continued. "I have a treaty with him that is still in place, as does the Count of Edessa, but both treaties as fragile as glass now, and might easily be shattered."

"Why are we here, Lord?" Reza asked directly.

"I am going to the Sultan to plead for restraint and to see if we cannot salvage a peace, or at least a truce from this disaster. I will need support, and people like yourselves who are knowledgeable of the Arab ways and can gauge the mood. There are so few of us who know with whom we are dealing! May I depend upon you for your help?" he asked. This sounded like a plea.

Talon spoke up. "You may, Lord, but by the sound of it this is no easy thing we commit to."

"God help us, but I know that, Talon. Curse Châtillon to hell and damnation!" he snarled.

"He *is* the curse, Lord. He was quite prepared to murder my own people and take all our lives when we passed through his lands in the south a year ago. He has no honor, nor any moral code. God protect us all from this kind of pirate, for we are all branded with the same iron as far as the Arabs are concerned," Talon stated.

"We are beset by zealots who ignore the reality on the ground and think that, because they are faithful to our God, they are immune to the wrath of our neighbors and can behave like savages." Raymond paused. "You understand what I mean, Talon. You too were born here! We are the *pullani!* We want to preserve the Crusader states, and this means living with our neighbors in peace; we have been proved right time and again. Yet they consider us to be no better than peasants and are contemptuous of us. They never listen and never learn. They think diplomacy is a cowardly way to behave." He sounded resigned. "My lands and my people will suffer if we are not successful. I must try to save us all from this stupidity."

*****

Talon and Reza set off with the Count and a small retinue for Damascus the following day, just as the first streaks of dawn were showing in the east. This time Talon took Yosef and Junayd with him, leaving Dar'an in charge of the ship with Guy and Rostam in Tyre.

"We will be able to reach Damascus by this evening if we keep moving at a brisk pace," Raymond said. With them were Sir Matthew and the Saxon who called himself Brandt. The Count made sure that his banner and a large white flag were displayed, to make clear that they were on a diplomatic mission.

It was being reported through various sources that the Sultan was recruiting from all the tribes in Syria and around the region of nearby Mesopotamia. This included people from as far afield as the Arab gulf, and even some of the Persian lands further to the east. The summer was not yet far advanced, allowing tribesmen and land owners to join the army without having to worry about their crops and animals until late in the season. This might mean that a host was being assembled hastily to be used before or during July and August.

Their route took them over a central ridge of low mountains directly to their east, then they skirted a higher range which rose off their north where there were perched castles belonging to the Templars. The Count did not tarry. The keepers of these manned forts made no effort to communicate with the column of riders heading eastward towards Damascus. While they rode, the Count plied them with questions as to their past, and in particular about their visit to China some years before.

Sometimes he coughed, which concerned Talon. "Are you well, Lord?" he asked at one time. The Count irritably shook his head. "Dust! It gets to my chest from time to time."

Talon didn't pursue the question but cast a look at Reza, who shrugged.

As they progressed eastward, the fertile lands on the outskirts of Tyre had given way to flat desert for some time. After they traversed the mountains they began to see evidence of more cultivation, palm trees and wells, followed by clusters of walled villages.

"We have left our Crusader lands and are not far from Damascus now," the Count remarked. It was late afternoon with the sun low on the western horizon before the familiar pale walls of the city finally appeared.

Talon had always been somewhat in awe of Damascus. It had been, after all, the very center of the Umayyad Caliphate, then the center of the empire carved out by Nur Ed Din, and now it was the undisputed capital of the Sultan, Salah Ed Din.

Leagues before they saw the city they had noticed scouts on the low hills, mounted on camels and fast horses, who had ridden ahead to alert the city and the Sultan as to their presence. Now a large contingent of horsemen with the green banners of Islam rode towards them, throwing up a cloud of dust behind them.

In the distance they could see the white walls of Damascus, but between them and the city was a vast military encampment. To Talon it seemed to move like an ants' nest above ground. A haze of dust hovered over the camp, but there was no mistaking the enormous numbers of cavalry and the woven black tents of semi-permanent tribal camps that had been set up within the confines of the army. Here was the menace that Raymond feared, and with good reason from what Talon could see.

"It was like this the last time I came to visit the Sultan," Reza muttered out of the corner of his mouth to Talon. "Perhaps I should have done the deed. Rashid would have thanked me." He was referring to the man known far and wide as the School Teacher, the Master of the Lebanese *Batinistas* or Assassins, as they were known by the Franks.

"You could have, but I doubt if that man would thank anyone. It's too late now," Talon replied, awestruck by the size of the multitude arrayed in front of them. The last time he had seen such a large body of men had been just before the Battle of Montgisard those ten long years ago. Then Talon had been part of the minuscule army of Baldwin IV and of the Templars who had led the charge to break the back of the Sultan's army. He had little doubt that the Sultan would not fall into such a trap again, which made the sheer numbers here appear even more ominous.

The Count ordered his group to halt, and then they waited for the horsemen to approach. The lead man was young, clad in the finest chain mail, with gold filigree worked into his spiked helmet and a red horse's mane attached to the topmost part. His followers were dressed in like manner. They were all mounted on magnificent Arab horses that strutted and danced, foam dripping from their bits. The Prince's animal's whole being just begged to fly into a wild gallop; no doubt its pedigree came from the finest breeds to be found in Yemen. The young man held his mount easily in check with the confidence of a superb rider. His attendants were older, harder-looking warriors who were watchful and protective.

Talon and Reza could feel tension in the air, but the young man smiled and said, "*As-Salaam-Alaikum*, Lord Raymond of Tripoli. Peace be with you. We are honored by your visit."

Raymond smiled at the young man and responded in like tongue, "*Wa-Alaikum-Salaam*, Prince Al-Afdal, son of Salah Ed Din, Sultan of all Syria and Egypt! I trust to God that I find you well?"

"I am well, Lord Raymond. I, too, trust to God that you are in good health?"

"Well enough, Prince. I bring with me two trusted companions who also speak the Arab tongue. Lord Talon de Gilles and Lord Reza de Kantara."

The prince gave a start, as did one of the riders with him. "I greet you in peace, Lords," the surprised prince said, once he had regained his composure. "Our city Damascus awaits your arrival. The Sultan, May God always be with him, is looking forward to greeting you in the palace."

The young prince maneuvered his steed alongside Raymond and they rode towards the city, which took less than an hour, by which time it was early evening, but the call to prayers had not yet sounded. The cavalcade was impatient to gain entry to the city and palace so they could leave the Count and his entourage and attend to their prayers. The prince informed the Count that the audience would take place the next day.

Not long after, they were shown to well-appointed apartments overlooking a wide garden and orchards of orange trees. The scent of flowering jasmine wafted on the evening air that filtered into the cool rooms. Talon and Reza shared a chamber with their two men, while the Count and his men were given other rooms nearby. The Count had pointed out that his two companions would prefer this arrangement, and the prince, after a word with his servants, had smiled and said, "We shall see you tomorrow, Lords. We will send an escort to bring you to His Highness the Sultan. In the meantime, please avail yourselves of our hospitality." He left them as the first call to prayers was resonating throughout the city.

They dismissed the obsequious servants almost as soon as the tea and sweetmeats had been brought. "They are sure to be spies, and the less they hear, and see, the better," Reza said to Talon, after he had seen the reluctant servants out of the door. "It has been some time now since I've heard that sound," he said of the call of the muezzins that emanated from the minarets around the city. He checked out the comfortable bed in his alcove by testing it with his palm. "Hmm, soft enough," he said, and smiled at Talon, who was also listening.

"Perhaps we should be saying our prayers too, Brother," Talon remarked. He was gazing at the quiet gardens below their balcony, enjoying the scent of roses and sipping a tiny cup of hot tea. "We might well need God's help before very long."

Then he changed the subject. "I wonder if there are any openings onto the streets from the orchard?"

"Do you mean to spy on the city, Brother?" Reza asked quietly, as he came to stand next to Talon.

"One of our number should, but not you nor me this time. They would notice our absence; and besides, we might be called upon by the Count. Did you notice the reaction of the prince when the Count mentioned our names?"

Reza nodded. "It struck a spark. So we should be careful."

"Yes. I was thinking of Yosef or Junayd. What do you think?"

"Either or both. They are now equally good," Reza told him. They were talking in very low tones. Scenting intrigue, the other two men had joined them.

"Both I think," Talon decided. He turned to Yosef and Junayd, who looked as eager as hounds before a hunt. "Now remember, all I want to hear is the talk on the streets. Nothing else. I do not want any trouble that will endanger our mission, do you understand?"

His two killers nodded their assent, then began to make preparations to leave. Meanwhile, Talon and Reza availed themselves of the baths provided at the end of the corridor, soaking in the heated pool as they talked about the Count's health and the prospects of success.

"I suspect he is not well," Reza said quietly. They were being careful about what they said outside their own apartments.

"No, he is not," Talon replied, "but he has access to good physicians. I wonder why he has not been to see one?"

Chapter 9

Salah Ed Din

O Lord of the Highest, search the depths of our hearts
And reveal all the foolishness of our own ways.
Show us the senselessness and arrogance in us
And may our hearts be broken before you.
                              —Yehoshua Shim'onai

Talon and Reza indulged themselves with the steam baths and a meal of roasted lamb with peppers and rice, and cucumber finely sliced and turned in yogurt. Slices of melon and ripe figs completed the meal on a sweet note.

While they were luxuriating in these comforts, Yosef and Junayd slipped over the balcony and down into the garden, where they disappeared from view. Talon knew they had been placed on the second floor to prevent anyone from doing just what his men had accomplished, but that kind of obstacle presented little problem to his people.

The two Companions, as Reza euphemistically called his men, made their way with extreme caution across the garden to arrive at the small gate without being seen by anyone and very quietly let themselves out onto a back alley. From here it was simple enough to shuffle down the alleyway, to slip past some beggars and into the evening crowd.

Families had emerged onto the tree lined streets to enjoy the relative cool of the evening, men and veiled women, some of them carrying babies or dragging their young along with them. The *Chai Khane*, the tea houses, were already open and full of Damascene citizens making jokes and scornful comments about the gawping newcomers wandering their streets. Street vendors, aware of profits to be had, began to open their stands to light charcoal or wood fires.

Smoke from the many fires drifted in light haze up into the trees, giving them an ethereal look in the evening light. Candles and lanterns were lit, and many candle lanterns were strung from the branches of the trees lining the streets, which gave the area a festive air. The aroma of cooked chicken, mutton and goat's meat rose from the fires, making the two men's mouths water. They had not yet eaten.

All around them were not only families but large numbers of men, either formally dressed as soldiers or carrying weapons and dressed in the garb of the various tribes who had come to join the cause. Some of these men were Bedouin straight from the dry deserts of Mesopotamia and were agog at the sights and sounds of the great city of Damascus. There were even ragged tribesmen from Yemen who wore their Khanjar knives tucked into their sashes like a badge of honor. They stared back with black eyes at any man who looked at them, as if to say they would challenge him if he stared too long.

Junayd and Yosef both felt at home in this setting, but although they had covered the lower part of their faces they were also acutely aware that should one of the palace servants be about and recognize them it might be disastrous. They therefore set out to determine what might be of use to Talon and Reza and return as quickly as possible.

They arrived at a stall enveloped with smoke; the owner, a burly man with a badly trimmed beard, was fanning the charcoal flames to broil some meat of an indeterminate nature. He was not in the best of moods, perhaps because his fire was slow to heat up, and he barely acknowledged them.

They stopped here because there were no other people nearby at present, and they wanted to ask questions.

"*Salaam*. How is business?" Junayd asked politely.

"What's it to you two? Where are you from? No one comes from this city any more, its full of inquisitive people like you," was the less than courteous reply.

"Persia," Yosef said.

"That's a long way away," the stall owner acknowledged. He was going to fat, and his arms were very hairy all the way up to his shoulders. He peered through the haze of smoke at the strangers and saw two very lean, wiry looking men. Their steady, unwavering gaze was just a little unnerving. He modified his tone somewhat. "Well, at least you don't look like most of those sand rats, who wander about the place with their mouths open catching flies."

"We have just arrived. We performed our duty to God and now we are hungry," Junayd stated.

"I think I can accommodate you in that regard. What would you like to eat? I have chicken and rabbit and some lamb, but that's expensive. The likes of you might not be able to afford it."

"Try us."

"Very well. The lamb, which is very fresh, is going to cost you four *fals*," he said, looking sly.

Yosef snorted with disgust "Where do you think we just came from?" he sneered. "Here, take two and be glad that we don't report you, but I'll give you a *dirham* if you can tell me some gossip."

It was a dangerous question to ask, but the stall owner's small eyes brightened in his puffy face as he looked at the coins Yosef was rattling in his hand. He held up the silver *dirham* between a finger and his thumb and it glinted in the lamplight.

"The Sultan has just receive a delegation from the Frans. The man they call Tripoli is here to beg for peace," he said, reaching out for the coin. "Not much chance of that, I can tell you!"

Yosef withheld the coin and asked, "Who is this Tripoli and what does he do here?"

The man fanned the fire more and placed the small slabs of lamb to cook. The fat on the edges of the meat sizzled and darkened.

"Don't burn the meat!" Junayd admonished him. "I like it just singed on either side."

"So now you are a cook and telling me my job?" the man demanded with a sour look, but he used tongs to turn the meat, because Yosef waved the coin again and he subsided.

"He is a noble, and he is very knowledgeable of our ways. But he is far too late. Rumor is that his Excellency is so angry this time that no matter what the Frans noble pledges or promises, the Sultan, may God bless his presence, will invade. He has had enough of their false promises."

"How many men do we have for the task?"

"As many as the sands of the beaches! Tens of thousands, and more horses than we can keep, which is why the Sultan's son is about to march. He needs to feed them somewhere else. There is no more grazing left about the city, and the great lake down south is the perfect place!" The man chuckled and held out his hand, into which Yosef placed the coin.

The lamb was done, so the stall owner wrapped the meat in two rolls of *nan* and handed them over. He was staring at them more intently now, as though regretting what he had told them.

"Thank you and God bless you. Peace," Junayd said as he turned away.

As they walked off munching on the rolls, Yosef glanced back and noticed that several armed men were talking to the stall owner. He was pointing in their direction.

"It's time we disappeared. He is ratting on us to a patrol," he told Junayd.

"Come on; we will take a small alley and then pop over a wall and find another. That should lose that bunch. They don't look very bright," Junayd said as they walked on.

They decided that they should return to the palace before there was more interest in them, and before long they were back in the chambers occupied by Talon and Reza, where they finished off their food.

"I kept some of the cucumbers and yogurt, which I know you love, Yosef," Reza told him. Yosef grinned his thanks, then he and Junayd finished off every scrap of food on the table, after which they described what they had seen.

"At least we know the mood on the street," Talon commented, when he heard their report.

"The Count will want to know where he stands when we meet up with the Sultan in the morning, so this is useful." He stopped, as there was a pounding on their door.

Yosef went to open it and found one of the senior officials standing outside with several guards. "I wish to speak to Lord Talon," he stated without preamble.

Yosef stepped aside and allowed him in, but stood in the way of the other men. "These are the chambers of my Lord Talon, who is a guest of the Sultan. You do not come in." He was joined by Junayd and even Reza, and the three menacing men stared down the soldiers, who backed off in silence.

The secretary sidled into the chamber where he was met by Talon, who breezily asked him his business. The secretary seemed to be rethinking what he was about to say. Finally, in a politer voice, he said, "I simply wished to inform your Lordship that there have been reports of spies in the city. We wish to make you aware that the streets are very dangerous. They are full of soldiers, so you should not go out there. We also have reports that there are dangerous individuals who might wish you and your people harm."

Talon snorted and waved to the balcony. "Have you seen the drop to the ground? Anyone who wanted to get into our chambers would have to be a monkey to get in here. No, I feel perfectly safe, thank you very much."

*****

Early the next morning Talon and Reza, with their two companions, visited the Count to discuss the up coming negotiations.

The Count greeted them looking tired, but he appeared cheerful enough. Talon told him that his men had gleaned information from the street the night before.

"Do you mean that you sent your men out of the palace to roam the streets last night?" The Count's tone was incredulous and he looked surprised.

"I have always found it useful to have information which is not provided by my host," Talon remarked. "Word on the street is that the cavalry has to move very soon, as they cannot feed all the animals around the city. Lake Tiberius is on people's lips, Lord. That is deep in your lands and would be an infringement of the treaty as far as I can tell. Were you aware of this?"

Raymond shook his head. "No. So they are preparing to send cavalry south as soon as this month?" He sounded dismayed. "This tells me the Sultan is determined to move his army into an unassailable position. We must be careful as to how we approach this."

They were greeted at the entrance of the Count's apartments by an armed guard who had been waiting for them.

Their leader, a grizzled scarred soldier snapped to attention and addressed the Count respectfully.

"My Lord, my instructions are to escort you to the audience chamber. Please to follow me."

"They look as smart as grasshoppers," Reza remarked, as they fell into step behind the soldier, to be followed by his small contingent. The guards were indeed very well dressed, their chain mail burnished to a bright silver. The helmets were polished and their spearheads gleamed. Each man sported a huge mustache and short beard, but the most spectacular mustache belonged to the veteran who led them. This man led the way to the conference chambers with a strutting pace. Somehow the Sultan had instilled a sense of pride in their bearing, for his personal guard at least, Talon reflected. How well the tribal people would fight still remained to be seen.

Raymond was quiet and thoughtful as they crossed the wide, flagstoned courtyard past several fountains. Talon and Reza looked around, taking note of the well-kept stables and the soldiers who manned the parapet. No loose mercenaries here; the Sultan liked to keep his army in good order, their weapons bright and their accoutrements clean and polished. Every man wore a tightly wound turban of the same patterned cloth and carried a long lance. Colorful banners bearing Salah Ed Din's emblem, a single-headed eagle facing to its right with a shield on its chest colored red, white and black, streamed out in the light breeze above the roofs and towers. One huge flag with the crescent and the scimitar sewn in white on a bright green background dominated the courtyard.

"He has a good, solid personal guard by the look of it," Reza murmured to Talon, as they approached the steps leading up to the main palace. They were met by a finely dressed man sporting a huge turban who introduced himself as the Chamberlain. He smiled politely and asked them to leave their weapons with some guards by the main door. Neither Talon nor Reza gave any indication that they possessed other small but deadly knives hidden on their persons. He also indicated that only the Count, Reza and Talon were to follow. Matthew, Brandt, the other men of the Count's escort, Yosef and Junayd were to remain at the doors.

They were treated with the greatest of courtesy and respect as they moved towards the main doorway of the audience chamber. Talon saw expensive and opulent furnishings ton display everywhere. There was great wealth accumulated here in Damascus. Some of it had been left behind when the Abbasid dynasty of Caliphs removed to Baghdad, but the Sultan had also improved upon much and made the palace his own.

As they approached, the doors to the great chamber were thrown open by immaculately uniformed guards clad in the finest mail with filigree-inlaid helmets, boots gleaming with polish, and brightly burnished spears. The Count of Tripoli's name was announced in a loud voice by an officer.

The murmur of many voices in the great chamber gradually died away as nobles, palace officials, soldiers and merchants alike stopped talking to observe the Count and his two companions walk slowly down the wide avenue strewn with beautifully woven carpets from Persia and Afghanistan. There was silence as the three men approached the throne upon which was seated the Sultan.

The Sultan's sons and brothers were arrayed on either side of Salah Ed Din. Talon recognized at least two of the sons, Al-Afdal and Al-Aziz, while just to the Sultan's right was one of his more capable brothers, Taj al-Muluk Buri, and at his side stood Al-Adil, whom Talon considered to be the most ambitious of the brothers. Other men Talon recognized as the generals who had helped the Sultan win his battles for Mesopotamia and Syria. The most capable and trusted of the generals stood closest to the throne, General Muzaffar ad

Din-Gökburi, a Turk, and probably the man most to be feared should the army invade.

The small group of visitors knelt respectfully when they arrived at the foot of the dais and stayed there with heads bowed. Salah Ed Din rose from his throne and walked down the steps to take Count Raymond by the hands and raise him to his feet.

Talon remembered the man he had met in Egypt well over a decade before. The Sultan wore simple white robes and a loose turban rather than the huge, imposing turbans many of his followers favored. Taller than most of his followers, he had the bearing of a man who was used to command and who had seen his share of life. There were graying streaks in his beard; two deep lines running either side of his mustache crossed some scars. His brown, deep-set eyes regarded the newcomers without hostility but missed no detail. The lines around the corners of his eyes deepened as he smiled at the Count.

"*Salaam Alaikum!* My Lord Raymond, it is always good to see you," he said in a clear, firm voice. He spoke Arabic, in which language Raymond responded.

"*Wa-Alaikum Salaam*, my Lord, Your Excellency," Raymond addressed the Sultan with the utmost respect. "I come in peace."

Salah Ed Din gave the Count the kiss of peace and smiled warmly. "I, too, give you peace, Raymond; but... there is much to say and not all of it is pleasant."

Raymond dipped his head, then said, "My Lord, I bring with me two men whom I trust implicitly and whom I wish to present to you."

Salah Ed Din turned to stare at Talon and Reza. There was a smile lurking in his dark eyes as he intoned, "It is an honor to meet with you. Anyone who is with Count Raymond is an honored guest." He regarded both men from under his dark brows, and neither had any doubt that he knew them. However, he gave no overt sign recognition.

Raymond's expression showed his surprise; he had thought the Sultan would acknowledge his companions. But then he collected himself. "Lord Talon de Gilles and Lord Reza, both of whom are familiar with your language and customs, have come with me to see you in the sincerest hope to God that we can maintain peace between our people."

Salah Ed Din nodded politely in turn to Talon and Reza, then took the Count by the arm and said, "We shall move to another chamber, my Lord, where you may have refreshments and we can talk more in private."

They were ushered into a much smaller room by the Sultan, accompanied by his brothers and sons and General Gökburi, who maintained a stiff silence even as the others whispered to one another.

When they were all seated on a huge carpet, tea was brought and laid out with sweetmeats. Salah Ed Din dismissed the servants and gestured to the Count to speak. Raymond hesitated, coughed, then spoke slowly and deliberately.

"Your Excellency, my Lords, General. As God is my witness I come with peace in my heart, even as I know of your anger, indeed rage at the most recent crime perpetrated by Châtillon. I carry that shame in my heart because he has spoiled the good name of our people and dishonored all of us. I come to ask for peace because war will serve no one. Even though I and the lords of Edessa and Antioch do not always agree with Jerusalem, we must seek a peaceful path on behalf of the Holy City for the benefit of all."

Talon shot a glance at Reza. What was the Count saying here? Reza gave an imperceptible shrug and focused on what else the Count might say. However, Al-Adil interrupted. "Your Christian lords, in particular Châtillon, have broken the agreements again and again. Are you here to speak for that... bandit, robber and rapist?" The last word, which he spat out with venom in his voice, created a stir amongst the others. Salah Ed Din raised his hand for silence.

"My brother is enraged and disgusted by the actions of that man... as am I and all my people." he said, with a frown at his brother. "I shall not labor the details of the crime, of which I believe you are aware, Count." Even so, he was angry. It showed in his eyes, which flicked to Talon and Reza as though to gauge their reactions, too.

Raymond coughed again into his sleeve and nodded. "Your Excellency, I am appalled, and I refuse to dignify the errant lord with excuses. I came despite the awful crime to ask that you reconsider your intentions, my Lord. I see with my own eyes the host that you have gathered; but the Kingdom of Jerusalem is not helpless, and despite the formidable numbers I see on display here, to go to war would be disastrous for all. Do not forget the Orders who will form the core of the army, my Lord."

Talon could see that the Count had struck a nerve, because the expression on the Sultan's face hardened and his eyes flicked again to Talon. He knew that Talon had been at the battle of Montgisard, where the army he had brought with him from Egypt had suffered a resounding defeat.

Salah Ed Din shifted his weight and looked thoughtfully at Talon and Reza, then addressed them. "The Christian Kingdom is not well endowed with men like you, who know our ways and respect our civilization. Most of the people who rule are fanatics and thieves who use God to make excuses for their excesses. Why now, after this the heinous crime in a long list of crimes, should I listen to one whom, while I respect, I know to have little or no influence over men like Châtillon? How can we believe you when you tell us that he can be controlled and this kind of thing will never happen again?"

"Because I intend to go to Jerusalem and persuade the King to arrest Châtillon and put him in prison. There will be a trial and then punishment, my Lord."

"What assurances can you give for that? All we have seen from this Christian king is ignorance and arrogance; by his very inaction he condones the unforgivable crime perpetrated against my sister."

"Before God I swear that I shall do everything in my power to ensure that he is punished, Your Excellency," Raymond countered forcefully, but neither he nor Talon not the alert Reza missed the deep skepticism on the Sultan's face and evident in the visages of his advisors. Al-Adil, even shrugged dismissively.

Raymond looked from one to the other and saw only sardonic disbelief. Finally, he shook his head, coughed again, then said, "What can I do to convince you that I am sincere?" He sounded almost as though he was pleading.

"It is not that I don't believe in your sincerity, nor that of your two companions," the Sultan stated, eyeing Talon and Reza. "But it is indisputable that you are here in the north in Tripoli, while that animal is far south of Jerusalem, and he is still in control of the castle Kerak. There is no one, least of all that weak king Guy de Lusignan, who can stop him from breaking yet another truce unless he is removed from that castle. Do you intend to do this, my Lord?" his tone implied that he doubted it very much.

Raymond looked uncomfortable. "I do not have the direct authority, Your Excellency, but I still have influence in Jerusalem and I intend to go there and carry out my promise!"

They talked for several hours, making little progress as far as Talon could see, and the deadlock was creating a tension that had not been present at the start. Finally, Gökburi, who had said nothing at all up to this point, interjected; "Your Excellency, if I may?"

Salah Ed Din waved his hand for him to continue.

"Perhaps," said the General, addressing the three emissaries, "if there were a show of faith, then we could take some steps back from a dangerous consequence?"

"What do you mean, General?" Salah Ed Din demanded.

"I am sure it has not escaped the notice of our guests that we have a large number of cavalry camped about this city," he said. It was almost as though he knew that they had come to spy as well as to negotiate. Talon looked across the carpet at him with new respect.

"Please get to the point, General!" Salah Ed Din said. His impatience was beginning to show.

"If the Lord of Tripoli would allow some of our horsemen to take advantage of the waters of the great lake and the surrounding grassland about it, then perhaps that could be construed as a gesture of goodwill which is acceptable to yourself, Your Excellency."

Neither Talon nor Reza liked what they had just heard, and it must have showed on their expressions. The Count responded by saying, "Your Excellency, I would like to confer with my companions before I respond to this suggestion. Will you grant me some time?"

Salah Ed Din looked somewhat relieved to be able to terminate the meeting. Then he offered something else, but it was so veiled that not even Talon grasped it at first. "As I recall, when you were the Regent of the Kingdom there was a long spell of peace, Lord Raymond." He smiled but said nothing else, leaving it to his visitors to make of it what they would.

"We can discuss this suggestion, and others which you might bring to us, tomorrow," he continued, rising to depart. "Would you like me to send my physician to attend to you, my Lord?" he asked as they were about to leave.

Raymond declined gracefully and led the way back to his apartments.

Once they were back in their own accommodation and had posted Junayd and Yosef to ensure there were no spies listening, they adjourned to the main living area to talk. The Count took a seat and began to cough. He wiped the tears from his eyes and dabbed at his lips surreptitiously, but he could not hide the light stain of blood on the fine cloth. After he had taken a sip of cold tea, he sat back and said, "Well, what do you think of our chances of winning him over?"

"You should take advantage of the Sultan's offer of a physician, my Lord," Reza told him. "Otherwise, I think the discussion went very poorly." His tone was curt.

"I agree with Reza, Lord," Talon said carefully. "One thing is clear to me. The Sultan is under a lot of pressure to go to war. What was done to his sister is unconscionable and there must be a reckoning."

"You hit a nerve with mention of the Knights, Lord," Reza remarked.

The Count nodded. "I wanted to make it clear that they would be in the forefront of any battle. Talon here can attest to the Sultan's fear of them."

"You mentioned punishment for Lord Raynald of Châtillon, Lord," Talon said in a lower voice.

Raymond looked up at him, then glanced at Reza, who had gone very still. Both men were staring at the Count with looks that chilled him. Raymond's eyes widened with realization, then he shook his head vehemently. "Oh God, no! God forgive me for even thinking it, but I cannot allow that. His chastisement must be seen to in the eye of the public!" he said with emphasis. "If we do something like that we are no better than—" he stopped. "My friends, if I understand you correctly, and I am aware of what you are capable of doing, I simply cannot allow it!" he continued. "I do feel very cornered, though." He pinched the bridge of his nose between a finger and thumb, then shook his head in a weary gesture, suppressing another cough.

"The County of Tripoli is independent of the crown in Jerusalem, is it not, Lord?"

"Yes, but not quite," Raymond responded. "Tripoli, Edessa and Antioch have sworn fealty to Jerusalem, although we can and have made independent truces with the Sultans before. Nur Ed Din, the Sultan's predecessor, honored them, as did we, for the most part."

"Then you can make your peace with the Sultan again and it would be up to Jerusalem to do the same, would it not?" Talon pressed.

"I dare say I could, Talon, but who would you suggest is suitable for negotiations in *that* court?" The Count curled his lip with contempt. "There is no one like Guy de Veres any more. His own people abandoned him to a terrible death at Jacob's Ford!" He shook his head with acute frustration. "Besides, without Jerusalem we would all fall, one after the other. It would be just a matter of time. No... we need to hold the Kingdom together. But how, when they themselves seem intent upon breaking it into pieces? How glad I am that I could bring you both to this meeting. You have been able to follow everything that has been said... and left unsaid." He sighed.

"I wish I could somehow, just *somehow* be more in control. That bitch Sibylla and her wretched mother, along with Rideford, put Guy on the throne. No one is less qualified to rule!"

"From what you have told us they play silly palace intrigues as though the Sultan were not sitting on the border waiting for his opportunity to destroy them," Reza remarked with a scowl. "You should allow us to take care of Châtillon. The Sultan would know exactly what had happened and would probably accept a peace overture because of it."

Raymond gave him a smile and shook his head, albeit with reluctance. "No, Reza, but... one might wish it, for he deserves it more than anyone. I wish I had done more to protect the kingdom when I was Regent. I should have acted then to change it for the better, despite opposition from those foolish people."

Talon looked at Reza, who glanced back. "Would the Sultan countenance something of that nature? That you could be Regent again?" Talon asked the surprised Count.

"If you mean what I think you mean, Talon," the Count gave Talon a long look, "he might, but I would have to put it to him very carefully. At this point in time I don't know how it would be possible, with all our enemies in that pit of vipers arrayed against us."

Later in the day, a messenger arrived to escort the Count to a very private meeting between with the Sultan.

As it was getting late, Talon and Reza returned to their quarters to eat some food and ponder the day's discussions with their own men.

"That was a mistake on the part of the Count. He should have insisted that we come along to listen," Reza said through a mouthful of meat and *nan*.

"The Sultan is a chess player, and by the look of things he wants to move his knights deep into Raymond's side of the board. There they will wreak havoc, especially if General Gökburi is in charge," Talon told them. "Raymond has no bargaining power, and he knows it. At any time, the Sultan and his army could march through his lands and there is nothing he could do to prevent it. What the general was really saying was that if Raymond wanted to stay out of the coming war he could formally allow them to cross his land and he would be left unharmed."

"It would not be very long before Guy and his nobles learned of such a move and sent and army to try and throw them out," Reza stated. "And they will accuse this good Count of treachery."

"I fear so, Reza. Our visit here has not been entirely in vain, but there is little doubt in my mind that Raymond is going to have to make a separate arrangement with the Sultan if he is to survive. The Sultan has every intention of invading. His brothers and generals will see to that."

That evening, when the Count came back from his meeting, it was as though he had made a decision and his mind was more or less at peace.

"I have decided to allow the cavalry access to the lake," he told his unhappy companions, who held their peace and pondered the implications. Talon put his left hand up to his mouth and rubbed his beard in a gesture that Reza was all too familiar with. Reza shook his head in dismay.

"It is only a temporary thing," the Count hurried on, seeing their expressions. "But there is another factor which has not been discussed, and it is an important one. Time is not completely on the Sultan's side. The rains will come in September. The farmers and tribesmen in his army will become restless and will want to leave to deal with their own tribal concerns. If we can delay a confrontation long enough by making a concession like this, then we will have succeeded. In time, he will have to disband the bulk of his army., and he would not dare attack without those forces." Raymond tried to sound optimistic.

"It is still a dangerous concession, my Lord. And yet, I don't know what else you could have agreed to. They have most of the pieces on the board," Talon conceded.

"Good. Then we leave tomorrow at dawn, as I have to get home and see to alerting my people. I shall beg of you one more favor, Talon."

"What may I do for you, Lord?'

"When we return to Tyre we will leave soon after for Tiberius, where my wife is at present. When we have settled in, take a contingent of my men and go south to warn the Lord Ibelin, the Bishop of Tyre, and the forts to the south of Tiberius. I do not want any skirmishes or unnecessary alarms. The cavalry will come in about two weeks; they will water their horses at the lake, stay for a week, perhaps a little longer, then go home. By which time I shall have completed my own preparations to go to Jerusalem and make the case to prosecute Châtillon."

Chapter 10

A Pact with the Devil

I shall drink your wine,
take away your food,
deprive you of shelter
and dry up your well.
You have hurt me
just once, and must pay.
—*Herbert Nehrlich*

Zenos arrived in Beirut a few days after his departure from Famagusta. He had not sailed to Paphos, as he had told everyone. As his ship was rowed into the large harbor, under the glowering walls of the main Crusader castle held by the Ibelin family, he felt a familiar rush of excitement.

Two coastal castles protected the harbor: Ibelin's and another looming to the north; beyond these he could just make out the Bab ad Darkeh castle, which was much larger and held most of the garrison of Crusader and Templar warriors. Beyond the garrison, surrounded by the cluster of red-tiled roofs of the town, was the Church of Saint George, with its round, copper-clad dome and huge iron cross.

Off to the north across the wide shallow curve of the bay was Mount Sannine, still with a light cap of snow. A cool breeze coming off the mountain ruffled the waters of the harbor. The quayside was teeming with people of all races and origins: sunburned or pale, newly arrived Frankish would-be Crusaders, who stubbornly refused to wear local garb, sweating themselves sick in the heat; half-naked Nubian laborers, brought to the city by their Arab masters, who dominated the population, along with their Greek counterparts; and Jewish merchants.

Everyone wore their distinctive ethnic clothing like a badge of honor, from the plain robes of the peasants and laborers to the finely sewn, silver- and gold-embroidered robes of the merchantmen. The Arab merchants vied with one another as to whom wore the largest turbans; the Byzantine Christians wore silk and wool hats that were totally inappropriate for the hot weather. The Jews, ever self-effacing, wore their flat, saucer-like *kippots* pinned to their long curls. All the women went about veiled. The occasional Templars or Crusaders could be seen, usually in pairs, sauntering along the quayside. For the most part they were ignored by the population.

Half-naked fishermen were busy unloading their catches, with vigilant seagulls wheeling and screaming overhead, looking for scraps of fish. Sweating slaves labored to bring ashore heavy sacks to be stacked in great heaps on the quayside before being moved to warehouses by patient donkeys or lumbering camels. The city relied upon fishing and trade. Zenos knew that Beirut, because of its distance from Jerusalem, had been somewhat sidelined by Acre, but this had not inhibited merchants from every country on the eastern seaboard of the Inner Sea and deep inside Syria from using Beirut as a prime market. It was his experience that almost anything could be purchased here... for a price.

As he and his bodyguard stood at the rail, his man pointed at a ship anchored in the middle of the harbor. "Wonder what happened to them?" he remarked. "Looks like they had a fire."

Zenos stared at the ship as they were rowed past. The sound of carpenters' hammers and saws drew his eye to the activity going on at the after end of the vessel. It had certainly sustained some fire damage. The rails on the upper deck were shattered and splintered.

When he stepped ashore, all the familiar noises, sights and smells assailed his senses. Warding off the pleas of beggars and vendors, Zenos walked briskly away from the busy quayside, heading towards the slopes where the richer merchants resided. He refused to be carried by palanquin, preferring to hear and see the city as he walked. The men who called out the offer cursed him behind his back. A rich man who refused a palanquin? Whoever heard of such a thing?

He was accompanied by his bodyguard, one of the many mercenaries belonging to Isaac; he glowered at anyone who tried to come too close and shoved aside any beggars who made a bid for alms. Zenos noted a group of men seated at the entrance to a tea house on the side of the quay and realized that they were watching him with interest. One hawkish-faced man wearing a large turban stood out from the others, but Zenos was too preoccupied to pay much attention; he strode on with his bodyguard taking the lead.

They were soon climbing rows of steps that led up the hillside and walking along narrow, quieter streets where there was less jostle by laborers and they passed better-dressed merchants, stepping aside from time to time to allow a camel to lumber by with its impossibly huge load. These animals could have come from as far away as the Arab sea or Constantinople carrying anything from silk bales to pottery and tea, even porcelain from distant Cathay. Shortly he arrived at his father's agent's house. It overlooked the harbor, allowing anyone from its balcony to see the full span of the sheltering bay—and any ships or boats that came and went.

They greeted one another warmly. The man was Greek, originally from Thessalonica, but he spoke several languages, hence his position of trust with his father's business. If Himerius didn't know the name of a person within the city, then he was of little consequence. After the customary embraces and long drawn out greetings, which included enquiries into each other's heath and that of their parents, they went to the garden for more privacy.

Tea was brought by a slave girl, whom Zenos sized up appreciatively. She was clad in a simple cotton shift which did little to hide her figure. Only when she had left did they get down to business, as they sipped the scalding tea in the shade of a prized mulberry tree. Zenos realized how much he had missed the calm of the high streets and the excitement of the port. Compared to Beirut, Famagusta was a small, dull fishing port, the palace notwithstanding.

Himerius looked over the rim of his tea cup at Zenos, taking in the expensive new clothes, the well trimmed beard, his manicured nails, and the hands adorned with rings of gold and silver.

"You appear to not have to work in the manner you once did, my friend," Himerius remarked with a smile.

"Indeed, I do not. You do know, do you not, that I am working directly for the Emperor of Cyprus? My tasks now are... more administrative these days, but I still hunt with him and keep my health," Zenos could not help bragging to his old acquaintance.

"I have heard the rumors. So it is true; in which case I must congratulate you. That is great news, and I am sure your father is very pleased." His tone was just the least bit dry. It was common knowledge that Zenos and his father did not get along very well, and now Zenos was to all intents and purposes working for the wrong side. The behavior of Isaac Komnenos, the so-called Emperor of Cyprus, was disparaged by the merchant class far and wide, who valued stability above all else.

Ignoring the tone Zenos said, "I do my best to protect him from the, shall we say, excesses of the Byzantine Emperor." His tone was a trifle sharp.

"I take your point, Lord," the agent said with an ingratiating smile. "So what brings you to our humble home? A caravan with a load of porcelain and silk arrived the other day from Persia; it came by ship from China. I managed to purchase some, although God help me, it was expensive! I hold it in our warehouse. I have already sent a message to your father in Larnaca about it."

Zenos shook his head. "No, my friend. I have come to seek... people." He lowered his voice. "Of the mercenary kind, if you take my meaning."

Himerius's eyes opened wide with surprise. "Is the Emperor looking for men?"

"After a fashion he is," Zenos stated. "But this is to be kept secret. No one, and I repeat, *no one* is to know, other than you and I, about the reason."

"Naturally, Lord." Himerius reverted to being very polite. "This town is swarming with mercenaries of all stripes. Even pirates have taken up lodging with us recently."

Zenos looked surprised. "What does that mean?" he asked.

"It means that when Abdul-Zinad, a distant relative of Salah Ed Din himself, takes up residence, we have pirates for guests." He leaned forward. "If I might digress for a moment, what do you know of a sea battle that was fought on the north side of Cyprus quite recently?"

Zenos frowned. "I did hear something of that. If there were any witnesses, however, they have not passed the news along to me." He resolved to correct this oversight when he got back to the island. "What do you know?" he asked, curious.

"Well, and this is mainly rumor you understand, but it is noised abroad that the man known as Lord Talon defeated Makhid and Abdul-Zinad in a sea fight, and even sank one of their ships. A third ship has not been heard of since the fight.

Perhaps it was captured. Abdul is here in Beirut, and his ship was mauled."

Zenos sat up. Now he was very interested. "You are telling me that Abdul is the owner of the ship that looks like it was on fire, here, in the harbor?"

"Oh yes, and word has it that he is hopping mad and would like to take revenge for the death of his two brothers and his nephew, who disappeared in the fight. You won't hear this from him, but he was lucky to get away himself. That Talon fellow has a diabolical weapon which he used on their ships. They do say he is a magician... perhaps it is true?"

There was that name again. "This Talon sounds like a formidable enemy," Zenos remarked casually.

"Oh, yes indeed. But I also hear that he is here in the 'Holy Land', as those Latins call it. Word is that he came at the bidding of the Count of Tripoli and even now is negotiating with the Sultan Salah Ed Din." Himerius paused to observe the reaction of his guest. "But perhaps we should get back to the main point of our discussion?" He took a sip of tea. "Common mercenaries are two a dinar here, so that won't be a problem. How many do you need?"

Zenos sat back on his seat, feeling a sense of justification. This news confirmed one thing: the leader of the people in the castle on the hill was absent from home. If he was going to gain access to the castle of Kantara, this was an important factor.

"I need people who are clever at gaining entrance to difficult strongholds and who can work with my people, but I also want to talk to this pirate, Abdul-Zinad," he told Himerius, who looked thoughtful.

"There are... other people, not mercenaries but are very dangerous, and skilled in the arts of war as well as gaining entrance to difficult places," he said slowly. "If you are contemplating gaining entrance to a fort similar to the one we are talking about, mere mercenaries will not be enough. You should be warned, however, that these people are very dangerous and will demand high payment. They should be treated with the utmost respect."

"Whom are you alluding to?" Zenos demanded.

"Why the *Batinis* of course, those ghosts from the mountains behind this city. You know of them, everyone does. The Assassins!"

Zenos felt a little cold prickle creep down his back. He nodded slowly, a frown on his face. "Yes," he said. "We all know of them, but they are invisible! How could I even speak to them of what I have in mind?"

Himerius looked sly. "Even those people come to Beirut. To spy, to buy, and sometimes to offer their services," he replied.

"You mean...?" Zenos didn't finish.

Himerius nodded his head vigorously. "Oh yes, they are for hire too, but they charge a lot of dinars for what they do. They have never failed. And... no one has ever failed to pay them, either." Himerius gave a dry chuckle, a wide-eyed expression on his pock-marked face.

"Can you arrange a meeting with these men?"

Himerius pursed his full lips thoughtfully, "That will take some time. Their leader is lodged deep in the mountains, and he has to give permission. You had better talk to the pirate first. This project sounds like a difficult one. I hope it is worth it for you and your Emperor. You appear to be playing a dangerous game, my friend." He finished his tea and called for some arak. He noticed the look Zenos gave the serving girl when she came out again.

"You must be tired and in need of refreshment, Lord." He gestured towards the girl. "Perhaps a little relaxation will help?"

For the next three days Himerius put the word out that mercenaries were wanted for a short job, the destination to be given out to those chosen for the work. The would-be recruits were told to come to a deserted warehouse on the outskirts of the city, where selection began. Zenos was to meet some of the most villainous and mean-looking hard cases he had ever encountered.

"These men make the crowd working for the Emperor look like babes," he remarked to Himerius after a long day of recruiting. They had chosen half of the twenty or so they were interested in hiring, out of the nearly fifty men who'd paraded in front of them and told lies about their backgrounds and experience. Himerius used one of his own men to help with the choices. They all had to be riders, and they all had to have had experience in storming a fortress. There were not so many of these to be found.

After several grueling days they had their twenty men, who were told to report for duty within the week at the quayside.

The agent had also arranged a meeting with Abdul-Zinad, who, after playing coy with the request, had finally expressed interest. It was to be at the same tea house Zenos had passed when he first arrived.

He presented himself there late one humid evening to find the place almost deserted. Abdul had used his influence to empty the place. He was introduced by Himerius, who then discreetly went and sat by the entrance with the bodyguards, leaving the two men alone.

"I hear you are looking for men to take with you to Cyprus," Abdul said, as he sucked on a water pipe. The smell of hashish was strong in the air. Zenos wrinkled his nose but said nothing. The meeting was too important for him to breach good manners.

"I am looking for a little more than just a few armed men," he responded. "I hear that you had a small altercation with the man called Talon, who lives in the castle Kantara."

Abdul-Zinad frowned. "Where did you hear that?" he demanded.

"I didn't have to go far to find out. Word is on the streets everywhere. I knew almost the moment I arrived, and your ship tells its own story," Zenos retorted. He didn't add that the rumors were also rife on the island of Cyprus about the sea battle which had not gone unnoticed by people on the coast.

He noticed a brief flash of anger on the dark, hawkish features, brought quickly under control by the pirate. "I will have my revenge... one day."

"That opportunity might be closer than you think. It is partially why I am here," Zenos replied. "Rumor has it that your cousin is held hostage. Would you not like an opportunity to release him?"

"Yes, yes of course I want to release him," Abdul said, but Zenos didn't detect much enthusiasm in his words and wondered at that. He decided to carry on, although this was something to bear in mind. Perhaps there was bad blood between them.

"What is your interest in this, this castle on a hill?" Abdul demanded after a small silence.

"I have business of a similar sort. The Emperor wants the castle back, and I intend to take it back for him," he lied.

"So, you need my help and I need yours," was the dry response.

"Yes. Your task would be to create a diversion, and while the occupants of the castle are otherwise distracted I shall take the fort by surprise."

"Is that all? It sounds *so* simple when you put it like that."

Zenos ignored the dripping sarcasm. "You will share in the spoils of what we find in the castle, and whatever else you pirates do, you can do to the village. You have raided not a few of our towns already," Zenos told him.

"Indeed we have," Abdul replied with a smirk. But silently he thought to himself that such a castle was well worth taking and holding onto, if he could manage it, and be damned to the Emperor of Cyprus.

Two weeks later, Zenos found himself standing alone on the edge of a large Muslim graveyard. It was late and dark, although the stars were so bright that he could make out the gleaming piles of limestone and the contours of the land which sloped down to the beach on his left. The muted sound of surf did little to calm him. He was facing north and trying to keep his nerve. This meeting had been arranged by Himerius, but that worthy had told Zenos that he must go alone, with no escort, or the person who was going to talk to him would not show up.

An owl hooted in the small copse on the edge of the field and several dogs barked in the distance. Some dogs, he'd noted, barked all night long. He shivered; there was a cold breeze coming across the bay. He had already been standing exposed and nervous for half an hour. Out of the dark a voice spoke.

"What have you come to Beirut for, Zenos, son of Spiros, who is a merchant in Larnaca?"

He jumped with fright and whirled about. Standing not six feet away was a tall man dressed in long robes of some light cotton which moved in the breeze. He wore a loose dark turban, but his face was completely covered, showing only his eyes, which gleamed in the starlight and regarded him with an intensity he found unsettling.

"I, I, er, I wanted to talk to someone of your people. My, my Emperor has work which can only be d... done by people of your kind," he stammered. "Er, there is payment, much payment," he concluded.

"So you know who we are?" the stranger asked, his voice strong and sibilant.

"Yes, er, yes I do, and I am here to buy your help." Zenos was trying hard to bring himself back under control. He gulped. The sudden appearance of the man had unnerved him. He had not heard a whisper of noise.

"What kind of help do you want?"

"There is this castle, on Cyprus," Zenos began.

"Ah, yes, Cyprus, where that erratic King Isaac lives. Do you work for him? Has he asked you to come here?"

"Well, not exactly. You see, it's about gold." Zenos hadn't meant to gush it out like this, but he was frightened and wanted to hold the stranger before he vanished again.

"We, that is, the Emperor, well, not him really, the Ambassador from Constantinople and I think... no, we are sure, that a huge amount of gold was stolen from the treasury of Constantinople and has found its way to this castle."

"Which castle is this?"

"Um, Kantara. It is on the mountain behind Famagusta. A man called Talon stole it from the Emperor and we want it back."

He did not hear the sharp intake of breath by the man standing opposite him, but the tone of the stranger's voice changed markedly. "Talon, you say? A Frank?" he hissed.

Taken aback, Zenos said, "Yes." He peered at the stranger, alarmed by the change of tone.

"So that is where he now has his lair!" the man said, almost to himself. "You will tell me about this castle and... the gold you say is held within?"

Zenos was very willing to oblige.

After he had finished, the man was silent for a long while. Then he said, "You will hear from my people within a week. You will pay one third of what is discovered in the castle."

Zenos, who had formulated a pretty good idea of what might be up in the castle, gasped. "A, a third?" he stuttered. "I cannot be sure of what is up there at this time. We are sure, yes, but I have not personally seen it!"

"I will take a third of what you find," the stranger said comfortably. "My people will take the castle and open the gates, that is my pledge. It is what you want, isn't it?"

"Yes, yes, it is," Zenos whispered, wondering what else he might have just agreed to of which he was unaware.

"You will speak to no one about our agreement. Not that fat agent of yours here in Beirut, and not that foolish 'emperor' of yours, either. No one! Do you understand?"

Zenos nodded energetically. He had been worried about how this private arrangement would sit with these people. Best to keep it private, oh yes!

"Then we have an agreement, and payment will be delivered when the castle is in my hands," the stranger said.

"I have an agreement with Abdul-Zinad as well." Zenos wanted to make sure that the stranger knew about that part of the plan.

"What do you mean?" The voice held menace.

"There was a sea fight, and Abdul and his cousins lost ships and lives. Abdul wants revenge. We planned on his creating a diversion down at the village."

There was a long, ominous silence, but finally the faceless man nodded his head. "A diversion would be in order. Abdul is only just capable of something as simple as that, so yes, a diversion. But the castle is for *my* people to take, and to open for *your* men afterwards!" he snapped. Zenos nearly jerked back, the words were so sharp.

"Yes, yes, of course. It is all about timing." He tried to sound reassuring. 'The diversion and then we take the castle."

"Our agreement stands. Do not break it. Do not betray me." The words were delivered as softly as the light breeze that disturbed their clothing, but Zenos had no doubt that his life would be forfeit should he fail to keep his word.

"Turn away and do not look behind you. To do so will mean death," the stranger ordered him. Zenos hurriedly complied and turned to face the sea. He never heard the man leave, but he dared not turn for fear of being caught doing so. Eventually he began to walk away from the meeting place without looking back. His route took him through the burial field, which did little to comfort him. He arrived back at the house of the agent tired and frightened, but also with the feeling that he might now be able to accomplish the impossible.

Watching him go from the darkness and concealment of the small copse of olive trees, Rashid Ed Din's usually harsh features were thoughtful. Unwittingly, this idiot Greek had provided him with several good options. If this man was right and there was indeed much gold in the castle of Kantara, then it was a prize well worth the endeavor. For some time now the rumor of a vast amount of treasure missing from the vaults of the palace of Blachernae in Constantinople had floated about the eastern seaboard. Word of it had even reached the ears of the School Teacher. He might at the same time be able to settle an old score. It was time to take down Talon and his family once and for all. Rashid had a long memory, and the killing of his people by Talon when he had lived in Egypt still rankled. But for that man, Salah Ed Din would be dead today and a threat to no one.

There was another matter that caused him to think hard. The castle of Kantara was reputed to be not dissimilar to the castle of Alamut in faraway Persia: perched high on an al-most inaccessible mountain ridge. Perhaps yet another opportunity had presented itself.... One thing was for sure, this Zenos man would be cut out of the final play. The castle would not fall to some treacherous lackey of the so-called Emperor of Cyprus. And the pirates could fight it out at the harbor, but they would never be allowed to get to the castle either.

He would ponder these interesting ideas on his way home to his own refuge deep in the mountains of Lebanon, across the dangerous country now belonging for the most part to that hated man Salah Ed Din. It would never do to be discovered here in Beirut by any of his spies. The hatred that existed between them was white-hot. He flicked his hand and a group of men detached themselves from the dark shadows nearby and surrounded their leader. He issued terse instructions before he turned towards the east and began the long journey home.

Eight of his men went in the opposite direction towards the city, where they would wait for a few days before presenting themselves at the house of the Greek.

Chapter 11

The Springs of Cresson

For their history trails away to the dark and bloody day
When the Christians made their stand in the troubled
*   Holy Land*
And the followers of the Christ ruthlessly were sacrificed.
There amid the inky gloom shown the Templar's spotless
*   plume.*

—Edgar A. Guest

Talon, Reza and their escort of riders crested a rise and immediately stopped their horses. Off to their left and further south, a full league away and not far from the great lake Tiberius, otherwise known as the Sea of Galilee, was what could only be described as an army.

"They are the same horsemen who came by the other day," Talon commented to Reza, who sat his horse quietly, contemplating the distant Arab cavalry.

"Just what are they doing here?" Reza asked. He knew the reason why, but it still bothered him. He sounded to Talon as though he would rather be elsewhere.

"We both know Salah Ed Din is testing the treaty with Lord Raymond, Brother. These people have Raymond's permission to ride through his lands, but this is still very provocative and can lead to no good. They also arrived swiftly; much sooner, I think, than Lord Raymond anticipated, so that makes us late to tell the bishops."

"Lord Raymond is playing a very dangerous game, playing one side against the other like this." Reza's tone was sour.

"It could be seen as such," Talon agreed. "But it is because he wants to survive in stormy seas. He doesn't see a problem with living alongside the Arabs, but the people in Jerusalem do. And he genuinely wished to avoid war."

"Which is why *we* must avoid that army and warn those Christian friends of yours, eh?"

"Something like that," Talon agreed. "Come on, we have no time to waste."

The small group of horsemen had little trouble bypassing the large force of cavalry, which were resting near to a spring which their guide, one of Raymond's men, informed them was named Cresson.

Not long thereafter, they noticed a cloud of dust rising in the distance where the road went over a saddle between two low hills, and before very long they could see that it was a body of Christian soldiers. The black and white square denoting the Templars and the black banner with a white cross of the Hospitaliers were distinct, even in the distance. Talon estimated that there might be as many as a hundred and fifty of the knights, accompanied by some dignitaries to the front, while behind the horsemen were many men on foot.

The two parties came together near the crest of the saddle where there were some stunted trees but little else. Talon recognized Lord Gérard de Rideford as the leader of the Templars, and groaned inwardly. There too was Joscius, the Archbishop of Tyre, riding a smaller palfrey and looking diminutive compared to the stocky de Rideford seated on his huge destrier. The portly bishop was sweating profusely in the heat. His jowls were bathed in perspiration and his mouth was set in a petulant grimace. He was not enjoying the heat and the dust. His small, black eyes never seemed to rest on anything for very long before flicking away toward something else.

Talon raised his hand, signaling his men to halt, then they waited for the small force of heavily armed knights to approach. Rideford himself halted his men about twenty paces away and called out.

"I see the banner of Tripoli but I do not know you. Who are you and what do you want?"

Talon then realized that he was not only unrecognized by the Master of Templars, but he and his men, including Raymond's two men who accompanied them, looked very much like a group of Saracens rather than a Christian delegation come to warn them. Their clothing and chain hauberks could easily be mistaken for that of the Saracens. Indeed, both Talon and Reza had taken their fine mail shirts from dead adversaries. Their loose turbans, their small round shields and their bows denoted them as Turkish light cavalry rather than anyone belonging to the Count, let alone the Christian community.

"I am Sir Talon," he called over. "I have come from Lord Raymond de Tripoli to warn you of the army of horsemen camped below this ridge." He pointed eastwards. "They number far more than you."

"Sir Talon, did you say?"

"Yes, Master Rideford, I am Talon."

"You come from Lord Raymond?" Rideford seemed to be hard of hearing.

"Yes, Lord, I do, and you are in great danger," Talon insisted.

Rideford made a gesture of irritation. "Lord Raymond is a traitor, so why should I listen to him? And you are a deserter from our cause, so again, why should I listen to you? I know about those infidels down there. I have mustered my knights from all around this region and I intend to attack them and destroy them."

Talon gasped. "You cannot be serious, my Lord! They are come in peace! Besides, they outnumber you by ten to one!"

Rideford sneered from his position in front of his sweating men. All were clad from head to foot in heavy chain. Barely a breath of air stirred the dry, sun-browned grass under their sweating horses' hooves.

"My Lord!" Talon put a pleading note into his tone. "These men are led by General AL-Muzaffar Gökburi. He is known as the Blue Wolf and is a Seljuk! He is one of Salah Ed Din's best generals. Salah Ed Din's son, Al-Afdal, is in charge of the bulk of the army. This is not just a band of skirmishers."

Rideford stared at him, his bearded mouth turned down in a look of disapproval and disdain as he glowered at Talon. Talon had a creeping feeling that he was talking to a fanatic. De Rideford's eyes, staring beyond Talon, had the blank look of one. He noticed that the Master of the Hospital, Roger Des Moulins, was seated next to the bishop; both looked very unhappy at the news.

"My Lord Des Moulins, can you not reason with the Master? There are far too many of them!" he called out.

"Perhaps we should reconsider, Lord Rideford. If Sir Talon is to be believed, we are too small a force to take on such an army," Des Moulins offered. He took off his helmet and wiped his damp face. There was much grey in his beard. The man was too old for this kind of thing, Talon decided. Perhaps he could prevail over this madman?

"Pshaw!" exclaimed Rideford. "We are the Knights of the Temple! God is on our side, and who can withstand our charge? Remember Montgisard! You yourself were there, *Sir* Talon. You rode with us then before you were corrupted by the infidels and their Godless ways."

Talon remembered the battle only too well. Despite the fact that Salah Ed Din had been defeated, it was the stuff of later nightmares for Talon. This was insane. "I urge you to reconsider, Lord!" he called over. They are expecting you, and to underestimate Gökburi is sheer folly."

"I, too, urge that we do not engage until our numbers match theirs, Gérard," the red-faced bishop said to Rideford, his nervousness evident. Talon became aware of the crowd gathered behind the knights and realized that they were poorly armed peasants, not men-at-arms at all. They were impatient and began to wave their fists. They were tired of waiting in the sun.

"What are they doing here?" he demanded pointing to the restless crowd.

"They are come to find rich pickings when we are done with those infidels," Rideford smirked.

That was when Talon knew he was dealing with a mad-man. "You, Lord, are insane. For the last time, I urge you not to throw away the lives of these good men in some insane and reckless venture."

One of Rideford's attendants shouted, "You will show respect for the Master!"

"You are all cowards!" Rideford shouted at Talon, then turned to Roger. "Are you, too, a coward, Master of the Hospitals? Are you so craven that you dare not do God's work? He is with us and we are invincible!" he shouted again. "Leave, *Sir* Talon. You are not wanted here," there was spittle on his beard as he spat out his final words.

For a long moment Talon stared at him. Finally, he called out, "I came to warn you!" He looked up at the knights behind Rideford. "You go to your deaths because of this man." He pointed directly at Rideford then he turned his horse away, shaking his head in despair and disgust.

It happened just as they turned to leave. Someone from among the gathered knights and followers shouted, "Leave, you infidel-lovers! God curse you!" and hurled a spear at them.

Neither Talon, Reza nor their two attendants were prepared; they had their backs to the Templars and the Hospitaliers. They both whirled about in their saddles to confront the shout, but the spear struck Reza high on his right side, tore through his chain mail and penetrated his chest. Had he not reacted by twisting as he did, he would have taken the spear in his side and it would have been fatal. His shield had been hanging off a strap from the back of his saddle.

He lurched backwards and would have fallen had not Yosef seized his left arm with a vice-like grip and steadied him; then, in one swift motion, Yosef dragged the spear out from Reza's side. Reza gasped with the pain and slumped in the saddle, blood rapidly staining his tunic and dripping down his side. He reached up and pressed his hand against the wound in a desperate attempt at stopping the bleeding. His hand became dark with blood, which continued to well from the wound. Reza groaned in agony.

Without even thinking about the consequences, Talon snatched his bow out of its scabbard and knocked an arrow. Still twisted half-way around in his saddle, he loosed the arrow at the man who had thrown the spear. The arrow went true, straight into the attendant's throat. The man gurgled with shock and agony, then sagged in his saddle and toppled off the horse, which skittered sideways as his spur gauged its side. There was a stunned silence from everyone as they contemplated the dead man at their feet.

"Murderer!" exclaimed one man.

"No. *He* tried murder; this was *justice!*" Talon snarled. "A life for a life!" Talon's anger was white-hot. He knocked another arrow and aimed it straight at Rideford.

"If anyone moves in our direction or attempts to try another spear, you will die!" he called to the cluster of men. Even though they numbered about two hundred, there was a significant pause. Men reined in their mounts and looked to their leaders for direction. All knew without doubt that Talon meant exactly what he said. Rideford appeared to be unsure, but then collected himself and sneered. "Go back to that dog, Tripoli! You are cowards. God is on our side and we will prevail!"

Talon glanced at Reza, who looked up at him with an agonized grimace. His normally dark features were grey with pain. "It tore my front to hell, but I think it glanced off my ribs. Didn't go in..." he gasped in Farsi.

"Can you ride?" Talon asked. He was nearly choking with rage and concern.

Reza nodded and reached for his reins. Yosef helped him with them, and then to settle back into the saddle.

"Take him away. We are going back to Tiberius," Talon ground out to his men. "I shall follow. Hurry!"

Yosef and the others rode close to Reza, supporting him when he slumped in his saddle. Dar'an tore a strip from his own tunic and tied it around Reza's upper chest, then knotted it behind him. The cloth quickly became bright red. Talon watched them moving down the track that led north to Tiberius.

"You are a fool, Rideford!" Talon called over to the hostile gathering of Templars and Hospitaliers. "There are five thousand of Salah Ed Din's men down there, spoiling for a fight." He waved his arm to the east just beyond the rise of the hill. "You have only a couple of hundred men. What do you hope to achieve by sacrificing them? None will live to tell the tale!" He glanced at the unhappy faces of the other leaders. Roger de Moulins, the master of the Hospitaliers would not meet his eyes.

In the silence that followed Talon snorted with disgust.

"Run away, you traitor, you coward! We will do God's work without you. He will protect us!" Rideford bellowed.

Talon glared at him. "Somehow I doubt he will. Is it not written, 'Tempt not the Lord thy God?'" he turned away contemptuously and settled his horse into a canter.

As he turned, he heard something that would stay with him for a very long time afterwards. The Marshall of the Templars, Jacques de Mailly, entreated them against the idea of attacking the Arab host.

Rideford rounded on him and declaimed, "Do you love your blond head so much to want to not lose it?"

Jacques de Mailly finally lost his temper and spoke contemptuously to the Grand Master Rideford. "I shall die fighting as a brave man, but you! You will run away as a traitor!"

With those words ringing in his ears, Talon reined in on the side of the hill where he could see the Arab army gathered around the water of the springs of Cresson. Some were mounted, while others were taking their ease. He could not see the Knights from this angle, but then he heard the trumpets blare from their location, and the alarm was raised by the Arab horsemen. There was much pointing and gesticulation within their ranks, but within a few moments they were all mounted, and almost as though they had rehearsed it they formed up to face the Christian knights, who were charging straight down at them.

Talon could hear the muted battle roar of the knights as they hurtled down the slope. They made a fine sight, with their banners streaming behind them and their lances in a steady, disciplined line. "*Beauséant! Deus lo Volte!*" they shouted, as they crashed into the packed ranks of the Arabs. But then something strange happened, which surprised and shocked Talon. The Arab ranks give way, and the knights were swallowed up by the Arab cavalry. The only thing that indicated they were still alive was the swirl of activity in the midst of the mass of Arab riders. General Gökburi had lived up to his reputation and had swallowed up the Knights into a deadly trap.

Sickened, Talon turned his mount away and galloped after the riders ahead of him. They had to hasten now, as the Arab army would soon be on their way home, and Tiberius was along their route. Anyone caught on the road would be killed in the prevailing tide of bloodlust; or worse, taken prisoner. He could not let that happen to his men. He had a puddle of bile in his stomach from what he had witnessed, but also a deep concern for his brother. He prayed that Reza would live.

He soon caught up with his men. Talon rode up alongside Reza, who was being held in the saddle by Yosef and Dar'an riding on either side of him. "How are you, Brother?" Talon asked. Reza looked up, his face grey with pain and loss of blood, and grimaced. "Hurts a little, and I am dizzy," he muttered.

"We must get him into the citadel before he loses more blood," Talon told his men. "The Arabs are bound to come soon. They have just slaughtered the Templars."

"Have those people ever listened to good advice?" Junayd asked.

"Few if any of them seem to learn, much less possess any common sense, Junayd. The Arabs, on the other hand, have learned how to deal with the Templar charge. I just witnessed it. If any of the knights survive they will be very lucky indeed," Talon grunted.

"It is urgent we stop the bleeding," Junayd interrupted them. Reza had slumped in the saddle, his head hanging close to the pommel. Blood was caked on his legs and clothing. The city was within easy ride, but Talon knew that to hurry too much would jar Reza's wound and make matters worse. He turned and stared back along the track. A small brown cloud of dust was rising on the slopes to the south west. That indicated horsemen, and they were coming towards them. The Arab army was going home.

"Hang onto the saddle with all your strength, Brother. We have to hurry," he said to Reza, who merely nodded. The others also looked back and saw the reason for Talon's concern. They were in danger of being captured. "Come on, Lord!" Junayd called to Reza, and kicked his horse into a canter. The other men did the same, pulling Reza's unwilling mount with them. Yosef slapped it on the rump with his whip.

The distance to the city shrank, but not fast enough for Talon. "Go ahead of me, and hurry. Get inside the gates!" he called, and dropped back to the rear. "You too, Yosef," he said, when his faithful follower made to stay with him. Yosef reluctantly rejoined the others ahead. Taking out his bow, Talon knocked an arrow on its string while continuing to canter behind his men. Only a few hundred paces to go now for Reza, he told himself, and watched with relief as the gates began to open to receive the riders. The duke's men had ridden forward and shouted the alarm to those on the walls.

But it would not be long before the advance guard of the Arab army caught up with them. The scouts had seen them and increased their speed. Talon twisted in the saddle while allowing his horse to continue cantering towards the open gates, judging the distance between him and the furiously galloping riders behind. The distance rapidly closed to two hundred paces, then a hundred and fifty. There were about fifty horsemen. In one fluid motion he raised his bow and loosed an arrow. It sped into the sky and briefly vanished; then a thin, dark streak made its descent and struck a rider somewhere in the middle of the group, who threw up his arms and fell. The arrow was so unexpected that the rider tumbled off his horse and was trampled before the other horsemen realized what had just happened. They slowed in confusion. Already another arrow had arced into the sky, and another man fell from his horse with a cry, clutching his side.

Talon faced forward and saw his horse had reached the very gates to the city. The sentries were shouting down at him from the battlements to get inside and to hurry up about it. He needed little persuasion and kicked his mount through the opening, then heard the crash as the huge wooden gates slammed shut behind him, cutting off the yells of rage from his pursuers. Just before he dismounted, he noticed Lord Raymond on the battlements above the gates.

The Count waved down at him. "You appear to have cut it a little fine, Talon. Impressive archery!" he called.

Talon wasted no time. "Do you have a physician here, Lord?" he demanded.

The Count nodded and pointed to the area of houses near to the citadel. "There is one there who is very good. What has happened, Talon?"

"My brother is sorely wounded, and we must get him to a physician. Not one of those useless leeches, is he?"

Count Raymond noticed the activity around Reza and said shortly, "No!" He glanced briefly at the departing Arab horsemen, then ran down the steps to the courtyard.

"Bring him along at once, and treat him with care or you answer to me!" he called out to his men-at-arms. Attendants ran to do his bidding, and Reza was carefully eased from his sweating and nervous animal onto a portable pallet, then carried hurriedly after the duke, who was striding rapidly off towards the aforementioned house.

The physician was a wizened old man with a long beard, his hair pulled back into a pony tail. He wore a loose, plain cotton robe that looked like the Egyptian *thobe* worn by the *fellaheen*. The first thing Talon noted was that the man's clothing and hands were clean. This was a good indicator, he decided. A Leech would have had blood-stained clothing and filthy fingernails and hands.

The Count greeted the physician politely and gestured towards the recumbent Reza, who was gritting his teeth with the pain and on the edge of passing out, even though the attendants had been very careful with him.

"This man is in my care, Artemus. I want you to keep him alive," the Count commanded.

"I never guarantee people their lives," was the laconic answer. "But we shall see what we can do, Lord."

"God willing, you will manage," the duke responded, apparently unoffended. "We will leave him in your good hands." He glanced at Talon. "I shall be on the walls when you are ready. Join me as soon as you can."

The old man waved the attendants to place Reza on a long wooden table, then gestured for them to leave. They hurried out. Artemus leaned over Reza, took his pulse, and then reached for some scissors. He carefully snipped the crude bandage and let it fall away to expose the bloody chain hauberk. "We must get him out of this and the rest of his clothing underneath," he rasped to Talon in French.

They lifted Reza up to a sitting position and as gently as they could undid the straps and eased his hauberk over his head. Reza gritted his teeth and at one point groaned out loud, but they managed to take off the cumbersome chain mail, then eased him back down into a lying position. He gave a deep sigh of relief.

The doctor wasted no time snipping off his under shirt. Having removed the bloody garment, he examined the exposed ugly rip in his chest. It was still seeping blood, so he dabbed at the entrance of the wound with a clean cotton cloth and then examined Reza's chest more closely.

"Good, it's not pulsing," he murmured to himself. He peered myopically at his patient's rib cage and pressed with his long fingers in a couple of places, making Reza wince and grind his teeth.

"Tell me he isn't one of those awful Christian Leeches you keep telling me about?" Reza asked Talon in Farsi.

"I think he is Christian, but he appears to be more like one of those Byzantine doctors, and the Count seems to trust him. I'm just a little worried about his eyesight," Talon told him with a tight grin.

Reza rolled his eyes, then jerked and yelled as the doctor's probing fingers struck a nerve.

At that moment the doctor looked up. "What are you speaking? It isn't Arabic."

"No, it is Farsi, but we can speak Arabic if you insist," Talon told him.

"I don't really care," was the terse reply. "Now, I have to clean this wound or it will become infected."

Talon began to respect the matter-of-fact way the man went about his business.

"Go ahead, Master Physician," Reza replied. "Get it over with."

"Good. Then let's get started," Artemus said.

Leaving Dar'an with Reza, Talon and Yosef joined the Count on the battlements overlooking the main road that went past the city. The Count had already been alerted that the army of cavalrymen was on its way north to Damascus.

"There must be nearly five thousand horsemen!" the Count commented, as he watched the triple ranks of the Arab army trotting along the road, raising a cloud of dust as it moved. Among them, linked by ropes and chains, were many of the peasants who had not been able to flee after the Templars had been destroyed.

"I cannot see for the dust. What are they brandishing on their sp—" he didn't finish his sentence, as the horror of what they were witnessing became apparent.

"Those are the heads of the Templars and Hospitaliers, my Lord," Talon murmured. "I wonder how many lived to tell the tale. If any."

"I hope that one of those heads belongs to Rideford," the Count snarled. "What an utter waste!"

They watched in stunned silence as the Arab army rode past. It was very clear that there could not have been very many survivors from the engagement; there were too many bloody heads being carried on spears by the triumphant horsemen. The long, unkempt beards hanging down from the pallid faces and the blank, dead eyes made for a ghastly spectacle. The Arabs roared their contempt as they rode by city.

"We will be back for you, Christians," they chanted.

They finally disappeared with their gristly trophies, dragging their wailing prisoners behind them into the northern foothills, leaving a pall of yellow dust hanging over the road. During the long silence that followed, the men on the battlements avoided one another's eyes. Finally, the Count turned to Talon, his face pale and his lips tight.

"Did you witness this... this massacre, Talon?"

Talon looked him in the eye. "I watched its commencement, Lord. I could not stay to watch its conclusion."

"Had you warned them of these people and their numbers? Who was there? Was Ibelin present? Why didn't he stop them?"

"Yes Lord I did. Lord Ibelin was not there, but Roger de Moulins, the Master of The Hospitaliers, was, as was Jacques de Mailly, and both tried to reason with Rideford, but he would not listen. Even the Archbishop of Tyre tried, to no avail. No one could prevail upon Rideford to leave well alone! He is quite mad, my Lord."

Talon went on to tell the Count what had been said, and how Reza had been wounded. The Count listened to him in tense, fuming silence until he had finished.

Talon's anger surface at the last. "Rideford was a complete imbecile! I hope he went down with his men. They did not deserve to be led by such a man!"

Raymond was just as angry. "The arrogant, stupid fools! They do not realize what they have done!" He gave a ragged sigh and began to cough. It lasted some time, and when he stopped and wiped his mouth, his features were haggard.

"The truce we negotiated is at an end, Talon, and we are now at war! They attacked men who were under my protection. The Sultan may even be lead to believe I arranged a trap for his army, in defiance of all the laws of hospitality! Curse those zealots who come to this land and know nothing of its ways. God help us all now!

The Count pounded the underside of his fist onto the stone battlements. He stared out at the lingering dust cloud, just beginning to take on a shade of red from the setting sun. He groaned then, and put both hands to his face, resting his elbows on the stone. He rubbed his eyes with his finger tips as though to obliterate the image of what they had just witnessed.

"We are surely lost... unless... unless the King can be persuaded to lead an army and fight Salah Ed Din in a place of our own choosing," he muttered.

"The King and his remaining army are in Jerusalem," Talon reminded him.

"Yes, and he is quite unaware of what has just taken place. I shall send a messenger to him today."

"And what will you do, Lord?"

"I have no choices left!" the Count cried, waving his hands in a gesture of acute exasperation and resignation. "I must join the King, and we must all fight for our lives and our lands," he finished, then looked at Talon. "I assume you will be coming with me?" it was a question.

"My friend, my brother, is grievously hurt. I would take him back to my home and to a physician who is one of the very best. If anyone can bring him back to full health, it is she."

"A woman?" The Count sounded incredulous.

"Yes, Lord, a woman." Talon shook his head and smiled at the surprised count. "The Byzantines of Constantinople train women to be physicians who are every bit as good, and in some ways better than men."

The Count was a man of the east who knew and respected the Arab physicians, but he still shook his head in amazement.

"Can you not stay with me and send him home with your attendants?" The Count put his hand on Talon's arm and gripped it. "Talon, I need... I need someone I can trust. Someone whose judgment and level head I can rely upon when I go to Jerusalem, and then later when we come upon the Arab army. Jerusalem is a nest of vicious and very stupid vipers, and I have few friends there other than Ibelin. Will I have to beg you?" His eyes pleaded with Talon, and Talon became aware of how hard the Count's decision to join the King's army had been.

He was fully aware of the distrust that existed between the Count and the allies of Sibylla. The Count had been at peace with Salah Ed Din to the extent that most Christians thought he was a traitor in league with the Sultan. Few of them bothered to work out the subtleties necessary for coexistence in this country, not appreciated how many attacks and retaliations had been prevented by Raymond's treaties.

Talon sighed and shook his head. The Count looked deeply disappointed, but Talon said, "Very well, Lord, but I must be sure that my brother is well on his way to safety with my people before I follow you to Jerusalem. I will not leave Reza's side unless I am confident that he is safely on my ship and in the care of my men."

The Count nodded. "I understand the sacrifice you are making, Talon. But know this: I am leaving Tiberius to join with the King, and should Salah Ed Din come this way he will surely lay siege to this city. My family is here. All that I possess and all my people will be in peril."

"Then we must waste no further time, Lord. I shall prepare Reza for the journey and instruct my men."

"I shall provide a large escort for Lord Reza to Tyre," Raymond assured him.

Talon knew the journey to Tyre would be very hard. Reza thought he could ride, but the Armenian physician was adamant. "If you are going to move him, Lord, which by the way I do *not* recommend," he told Talon, his faded old eyes flashing with annoyance, "then do not let him ride. He must be carried on a litter." Talon looked over at Reza, who was resting on a bed with his chest tightly bound, his eyes half closed.

Artemus said, "I have stitched him up. There was a deep wound from some kind of spear, which runs across his chest through his right chest muscles. It glanced off his ribs, which are not broken as far as I can tell. There is, however, always the risk of infection. I doubt if the metal was clean. Above all, keep him away from those Latin Leeches. They will kill him." The old man's lips curled with disdain. "Be it upon your head, Lord, if he goes with you."

Talon spoke rapid Farsi with Reza. "The situation here is going to be untenable before very long, my Brother. The Arabs killed all the Templars, and Count Raymond thinks Salah Ed Din will be back very soon, so I want to send you to Tyre and put you on the ship. I am sending you home."

"You're not coming with me, Talon?" Reza croaked. He sounded incredulous.

"No. I am keeping Yosef with me, while Junayd will go home with you and everyone else. Yosef has agreed to stay and keep me out of trouble." Talon grinned at his friend, trying hard to hide his concern. Reza looked pale and weak from loss of blood and the recent ordeal, and although the distance was manageable Talon was concerned about the journey. His brother still managed to protest. "I can recover while here."

Talon shook his head vehemently. "Don't argue with me, Reza. You are out of this mess, and I want you to do as I ask. I will not be able to work with the Count if I am worrying about you, too."

Reza stilled the protests forming on his lips and lay back. "When do we leave?" he murmured.

"Tonight." Talon turned to Junayd. "I entrust him to you, Junayd. Keep him safe."

Junayd nodded. "I shall, Lord. Will these people provide a litter?"

"A litter and a strong escort," Talon assured him. "The Count is to be trusted, and so are his men. The distance to Tyre is about forty leagues, which will be very tiring, but Guy's ship is there, our ship. You are to leave Tyre the moment you get to the harbor, and make haste to Cyprus. Rostam will get you there."

"I am sure he will, Lord," Junayd smiled. "That boy is a navigator." He paused. "But what of you and Yosef, Lord? How will you get back to us?"

"Have Henry come to Tyre when you get home, and he can wait there for us there. I think that city is safe for the moment. Warn him to be careful, however. Things are changing very rapidly. A war is about to begin."

Junayd looked alarmed. "Is it as bad as that?"

"Yes, God help us, I think it is, Junayd, which is why I want Reza out of the way as soon as possible. The moon is high and your escort will be large enough to deter any bandits, so you should be safe enough."

Reza spoke up. "*Khoda Hafez,* my Brother. Come home as soon as you can. This is no place for you either," he gasped, as speaking made his chest hurt. "I don' t think it is your fight." They clasped hands hard, and Talon had to turn away; there were tears in his eyes. "*Khoda Hafez,* my Brother," he whispered.

"And keep him from talking too much! He never stops and it is bad for his chest," the physician said testily, speaking Greek as he washed his hands.

"What did that grumpy old man say?" Reza grunted in Farsi.

"He said you talk too much," Talon told him.

Reza snorted, then winced. "Might be right. But he wasn't very gentle with that needle, the old bastard."

Talon grinned with affection at his old friend. "Be safe, both of you. God protect."

He and Yosef watched as Reza was carefully placed on a litter. The escort formed up and the gates were opened. The small cavalcade with the horse-drawn litter moved off out into the dusk. Reza, looking unhappy at being for the first time in his life completely helpless, lifted his hand tentatively, and then they were gone into the night.

"It is a clear road and my men know it well," the Count assured Talon. "I thank you for staying. We leave on the morrow. I must alert the nobles, especially Ibelin." He turned away. "In the meantime, I have work to do."

Sir Matthew began to shout orders to his Frankish men, who formed up in the square in front of the citadel. The Count addressed them in French.

"All the Saracen men who have been staying at this garrison are to be removed. Not one is to be allowed to stay. Do not harm them, but ensure they are all gone by the morning. Every one of them!" he finished sharply.

Sir Matthew and his men immediately sought out the confused Arab and Turkish men-at-arms who had been sent to help garrison the city and, roughly at times, marched them out of the gates. The bewildered men left, shouting imprecations and curses at the watchers on the walls.

Talon understood why the Count had done this, but Raymond was at pains to explain himself early next morning as they watched the dawn spread across the clear sky to the east.

"I can no longer sit on the fence. Our arrangement with Salah Ed Din is at an end, regardless of who started that battle yesterday," he told Talon. The bright light slid over the formerly dark hills of the Golan Heights, which reared up on the other side of the leaden-colored waters of the lake. The still, dark slopes of the hills bore a strangely ominous feel today. From the walls Talon looked west to where he could just discern the twin peaks of Hattin. Past those hills the road led to Acre. The land around was dry as a bone this time of year, which seemed incongruous when there was a vast lake right in the middle of the valley.

"They accuse me often enough of being in league with Salah Ed Din," the Count ruminated, as they stared over the still waters. The usual fishing boats were missing this dawn. Even the fishermen were staying home, fearful of what the future might hold.

"They conveniently forget the three basic rules we *pullani* have had to live by: diplomacy, trust and gold. All of which are in short supply now. Those zealots in Jerusalem think all this is just about God. I wonder sometimes if God has had enough of our squabbling over his holy places and will leave us all to go the Devil."

Talon wondered if he wasn't right.

Chapter 12

Reza

Horror of wounds and anger at the foe,
And loss of things desired; all these must pass.
We are the happy legion, for we know
Time's but a golden wind that shakes the grass.
                                        —Siegfried Sassoon

Reza succumbed to the pain, passing out for long stretches of time during the journey to Tyre. The men who formed his escort were as careful as they could be, but the lurching and jolting took its toll. By the time they had crossed the low mountains to the north of Tiberius, Reza was feeling terrible. His chest felt as though it was on fire, and although Junayd did his best, changing the dressings as per the instructions of the irascible doctor every dawn, it became clear to him that there was a problem; infection was setting in. He noticed how blackened and tight the stitches had become, and the edges of the wound appeared inflamed. They arrived within sight of the city at dawn of the third day, by which time the entire party was exhausted, including their mounts.

Good news could travel speedily, but bad news flew faster than the wind, and people had already heard of the crushing defeat the Templars had suffered at the Springs of Cresson. People who normally made their living in the country were making for the safety of the walled city of Tyre. It took several hours for the small cavalcade to push and shove their way along the narrow causeway which separated the mainland from the island city. It was not designed to handle so many carts and refugees at one time. The men used their spear points to make a path through the frightened throng of peasants and merchants. At one time they came across a heavy cart that had a broken wheel blocking most of the road. The oxen stood stoically amid the chaos, placidly chewing cud while all around them men shouted and women screamed at the luckless carter, who stood helplessly looking at the broken wheel.

The commander brusquely told his men to shove the cart off to the side of the causeway. They took him at his word, cutting the oxen loose. The wagon toppled over and, before anyone could stop it, tumbled down onto the stones below the causeway, then rolled into the water with a big splash, its belongings sinking with the overladen vehicle or floating away, to the wails of despair from the family to whom they had belonged. The crowd cursed the men-at-arms, waving fists and calling on God to punish them, but no one wanted to physically dispute passage with such grim and well-armed men, so they gave reluctant way.

Junayd was grateful that the commander of the party was known to the nervous sentries on the walls, because they were admitted almost immediately. To his immense relief, Guy's ship was still tied up to the quayside. Guy hurried on deck at a shout from one of his crew, quickly followed by Rostam and Junayd. They were aghast at the sight of Reza, lying on a litter and looking much the worse for his uncomfortable journey. Without ceremony they brought him on board, while the commander of the escort, clearly relieved to hand over his charges, hurried off as soon as it was decent to do so, taking his men with him.

"What happened, Uncle?" Rostam demanded as they shifted Reza below decks.

"Questions can wait, Rostam. We must get him comfortable and dress this ugly looking wound," Guy warned.

Reza had only a hazy memory of the final stages of the journey as they'd jolted along the road, and the worried face of Junayd hovering over him.

"Where are we?" he croaked as they lifted him onto the bunk. He became aware of familiar faces looming over him, Guy's and Rostam. "Hello, where have you all been?" he asked.

"I think a fever is beginning," Junayd said. "We must leave as soon as possible to bring him to Kantara."

Guy nodded, his features grim. "How long will we be at sea?" he asked Rostam, who looked up at the deck above their heads and made a mental calculation.

"We will have the wind behind us for a day or so, which could bring us to the peninsular. After that it will be in God's hands, because the proximity to land can play havoc with the direction of the winds," he finally replied.

"Then it will be all hands to the oars and a prayer to God," Guy stated. "We have sufficient provisions and water. We leave at once. I'll make sure our prisoner is chained up until we are out of sight of land."

He stepped out of the cabin to deal with their departure. Rostam could hear him shouting orders, and in a very short space of time he felt the ship shifting under his feet and knew they were about to exit the harbor. The oars slid out and soon the regular beat of the drum heralded the familiar sound of the creak and grind of many oars pulling hard in time.

He leaned over the dozing Reza. "You are safe with us now, Uncle. I shall come back later when we are at sea. We have to get you to Auntie Theodora. She will put you back on your feet." He kissed his uncle on his hot forehead and left.

"What has happened to Father?" he demanded of Junayd, who was on the steering deck talking with Dar'an and Guy.

"He chose to remain, Rostam," Junayd replied, sounding dispirited. He usually called his young lord by his first name. He had known him for a long time and they were close friends.

"Why would he want to do that?" Rostam shook his head. "Mama said that it is not his quarrel, that they don't like him and would harm him at the least excuse."

"I cannot disagree with you, Rostam. Look what they did to Reza. But your father avenged him. Oh, yes he did, by God!" Junayd nodded his head, remembering the speed of Talon's reaction. He went on to tell them what had followed.

"I did not see the battle, but Lord Talon was a witness. He told us the Arabs used a new tactic. They opened their ranks, swallowed the charging knights, then destroyed them."

"I still do not understand why he stayed. It sounds like there will be war, and he should not be involved," Rostam stated, his young features frowning with exasperation.

"I am almost sure it is because of Count Raymond of Tripoli," Guy interjected. "He has some kind of hold over your father." He sighed. "Talon has always had this 'honor' compulsion. I think the Count has taken advantage of it, damn him!"

They were just passing between the two towers that protected the harbor, and the thump of the oars was a reassuring sound to Rostam. They were going home, well away from this cloying atmosphere of uncertainty and fear. He gazed aloft to see which direction the wind was blowing. It was a steady breeze that would pick up as they went further out to sea. The banner at the top of the center mast streamed in a north-westerly direction. Almost as though reading his thoughts, Guy commented on the wind.

"We might have a good wind all the way home, young man. God willing." Then he glared at the steersmen, who had allowed the ship to come too close to the starboard promontory. "What the hell you are doing? Keep us in the center of the entrance or you'll answer to me!" he bellowed.

Rostam sent a glance back at the harbor as they left. He could still smell the stink of offal and effluence from human living. The seagulls still wheeled and clustered about the idle fishing boats; the large, brightly emblazoned banners still streamed from the tops of the jumble of towers that made up the citadel. But for how long? Was it his imagination, or did he see storm clouds on the eastern horizon?

He could now see the causeway. It was black with people all moving in only one direction, fugitives seeking refuge in the city. He was glad to be leaving, but the anxiety for the safety of his father left a heavy feeling in his stomach.

He started when Dar'an put a hand on his shoulder. "You must not worry too much about Lord Talon, Rostam. He is wise and resourceful, and besides, he is with Yosef!" Dar'an tried to put on a lighter tone for Rostam's sake. "I am sure we will see them both before very long. Our job now is to get your uncle to safety and a full recovery. You are our navigator, Rostam; Captain Guy and Master Reza needs all of your skills now."

Rostam look up from his contemplation of the distant harbor and the city of Tyre and nodded. Dar'an, Junayd and Yosef had been his instructors, but they were also among his closest friends. He knew he must focus and make sure that they were at sea for the least amount of time for the sake of Uncle Reza. "You are right, Dar'an. I shall concentrate on that."

The ship was cutting through a narrow gap between the four small islands that ran in a line to the north of the city. The passageway was not for every ship, least of all the great, lumbering Templar ships that plied the sea routes from Aigues Mortes far to the west of the Middle Sea, but Guy knew the way, and his vessel with its shallow draft could slip just above the rocks without difficulty. This route would shorten their journey by several hours. They arrowed through the opening, the sides of the vessel only a short stone's throw from the city on one side and the nearest island on the other. Boys and men who were fishing waved as they passed and called out greetings.

Almost before they had cleared the hazard, Guy roared for his crew to raise the sails. Willing crewmen scampered to their work, while the rowers, all facing aft, still driven by the drum, continued to march three paces forward, drop the blades into the churned water, then haul back for three paces. The sun blazed down on them, and despite the fresh breeze from shore they were sweating as they worked. Others brought water in skins for the sweating men to drink, and poured some over their shoulders to cool them off.

Within moments the sails were set, cracking and snapping as they were hauled taut. The galley heeled slightly as the wind caught the sails and they began to move at a good pace, leaving behind the city and its string of small islands. Rostam glanced at the sky, noted the position of the sun and estimated their course. "Captain Guy, we should steer four more points to the north from west."

Guy nodded. "You heard him. Get to it, men! Rowers, in oars!" he bellowed.

The rowers thankfully stopped what they were doing and hauled their dripping oars in and onto the deck. Once they were stacked, the panting men were allowed to rest. Leaving Guy to harass the crew for the slightest sign of delay, Rostam made his way below to look in on Reza and was relieved to see his uncle asleep. As though sensing that someone was there, Reza opened his eyes and looked up at Rostam.

"Rostam! Are we at sea?" he croaked, trying to sit up. He winced and fell back, looking flushed and hot.

Rostam stepped fully into the cabin and leaned over Reza. "You are on board the ship and Guy is taking us home,

Uncle. You have to rest. Dar'an, Junayd and I will come and help care for you later, but for now you must sleep. Are you comfortable?"

Reza nodded, his breathing shallow. "Hurts to breathe deeply, but yes I am. This is a lot better than on the road. That journey was not what I would call enjoyable, although Junayd did his very best."

"He told me all about that. We are only a couple of days' sailing from home, Uncle. It is very important that we clean you up later, and that you do not stress yourself. Junayd told me the wound is deep."

"Very well then, I shall rest. Do you remember the way?" He attempted a grin, and despite himself Rostam had to laugh. "Be careful, Uncle, or I might drop you off in Famagusta! I am sure the Emperor would be very happy to put you up... in one of his dungeons!"

"I shall be good. You know that Talon remained behind?" he asked.

"Yes." Rostam looked unhappy.

"I did not want to leave him, but that is one stubborn man at times," Reza muttered, wincing again as he adjusted his position on the bunk.

They sailed all that day under a burning sun, their prow cutting a foaming path through the azure waters, leaving a wake that was as straight as a spear behind them. The wind was faithful and kept their sails full, for which Rostam was very thankful. Their lookouts perched high above the deck kept a sharp eye open for any other vessels, but although there were some sails to be seen on the horizon none came near them as they sped towards their home.

As evening approached the wind dropped off, but the light breeze was enough to keep them moving at a decent pace. Guy and Rostam agreed that if they sailed all night they would in all probability make landfall by early morning. Then it would be a matter of sailing along the long arm of the island of Cyprus until they made port. Guy was optimistic. "I think we have a good chance of landing by early afternoon tomorrow, if the winds are kind," he told an anxious Rostam.

"You need to sleep, boy," he continued. "I can steer by the stars along the lines you have indicated. If we bump into land I'll wake you. Go now and rest. I need you to be sharp and clear-eyed for the morning."

Rostam reluctantly headed for the cabins. Before he went to his bunk, he and Dar'an tended to Reza. Dar'an pointed wordlessly at the stitches, almost hidden by the puffy, inflamed flesh around them. Rostam nodded. In silence they swabbed the area of the wound with hot salt water while Reza gritted his teeth. They then wrapped a clean bandage around his chest and allowed him to lie back with a deep sigh of relief. He went to sleep almost immediately.

"The wound is infected. I hope our physician lady can deal with it," Dar'an muttered. He had great faith in Theodora, who had learned her trade in Constantinople, but he didn't like what he was seeing.

They were about eight leagues out from the coast the next day when they saw a rocket flare in the sky, which pleased Rostam enormously. It meant they had been seen by lookouts at the castle. He gave a great sigh of relief.

Before very long, they could see the harbor and a ship racing towards them. Henry was clearly on the alert and had mustered his crew to meet the possible threat.

"Send up the recognition flag," Guy ordered, and within moments Talon's standard with the ship and lion emblazoned on it was fluttering high on the mast. A similar flag was hauled up onto the ship approaching them, and before long the crews were cheering as the two ships drew alongside one another.

Henry was braced against the rail, looking over at them. "What news?" He shouted.

"Urgent to get into port and we will explain there. Reza wounded!" Guy roared back.

Henry looked alarmed, but waved them past and set about turning his ship to follow them into port, where a small crowd of onlookers had gathered.

Guy took the ship in at a fast pace, using his rowers, who were willing enough. They slid into place alongside the quay and were rapidly tied up. The gangplank was lowered and men carried Reza off the ship almost before it had stopped moving. Dar'an and Rostam accompanied Reza, while Junayd escorted the pirate leader, who was again in chains. Two crewmen came with him to make sure he didn't try to escape. Junayd warned him, "Don't do anything stupid. We haven't got time to chase you. I'll just shoot you with an arrow."

The chained man nodded silently and watched as willing hands placed Reza on a light pallet to be carried by four men for the uphill journey. They left the port behind and began the long, steep climb to the castle on the ridge. A messenger on horseback rode ahead to notify Theodora that Reza would need her urgent attention.

Rostam looked down at his uncle as he lay on the swaying pallet. Reza was only semi-conscious; his fever was getting worse. When Rostam placed a hand on his forehead, it was clammy with sweat and very hot. "Hold on, Uncle!" he murmured. "We are nearly there." He urged the panting and straining men to hurry.

They were met at the gates by a small contingent of the family. Theodora was foremost. Rav'an had her arm around Jannat, who was tense with worry and red-eyed. The messenger had not been able to tell them anything beyond the fact that Reza was grievously wounded.

Theodora immediately took charge. She briefly checked Reza's bandage, which was pink with blood, then placed her hand on his forehead.

"The fever is setting in," she muttered, then she looked up at Rav'an and Jannat. "We must hurry! Bring him into my rooms. I must examine him immediately."

"Will he be all right?" Jannat was wringing her hands with worry. Rav'an put her arm around her shoulders again. "Theo will do all she can, Jannat. We must allow her to do her work. There is no one better."

Max was there, wanting to know more of the story, but he made sure that Reza was safely with Theo before she chased everyone out of the chamber, allowing only Jannat and Rav'an to stay.

Downstairs, Max and Rostam plied Junayd with questions. He was willing enough to tell them, recounting in detail the confrontation with Rideford and his men before the battle.

Max shook his head in disgust. "No one ever listens to Talon. He knows better than anyone, other than perhaps the Count of Tripoli, how to deal with our enemies, but still they don't heed him. And now he has gone to Jerusalem with the Count?"

"I do not know, Max. I left them at Tiberius, in the small city by the lake. I do not know what is in store for them!" Junayd sounded very distressed. "Those people over there are quite mad."

"Hmm, I don't disagree," Max muttered, almost to himself.

They talked for hours that afternoon, and then, after eating, well into the evening. The story was told several times as other people of the household gathered to hear it, and each time Max became more and more convinced that there was a disaster looming. He glanced over at Rostam, who was eating bread and olives with some cheese and smoked sardines. Damian, Theodora's young son, had wandered into the room and had been listening wide-eyed to the story. He sat next to

Rostam, who attempted a smile at him. "Will Uncle Reza be all right, Rostam?" the boy chirped.

"He will be all right, Damian. Your mother is going to take care of Uncle Reza."

It was late in the evening when the women joined the men, who by then were on tenterhooks with worry. Theo looked exhausted. "Tell us," Max said gently.

"His fever is high, but I think I can control it. I have given him drops of frankincense and mullein. Both are good at controlling fevers and inflammation." Theodora looked down at her hands, which were pink from washing, as though reassuring herself that they were hers. Max sat next to her, while Rostam embraced Rav'an and Jannat in turn.

"I had to reopen the wound," Theodora said. Her tone flat. "As I suspected, the physician in the Kingdom, while good, had still missed a piece of cloth that was forced into the wound by whatever struck Reza. We had to open it right up to expose the scrap and remove it."

"I would never have known about that, but she knew exactly what to do!" Rav'an said to the assembly, her tone awed. "She has sewn him back up and he is resting. It is in God's hands now."

"I shall have to stay with him until the fever breaks, and to ensure the drain I have placed in the wound is working properly," Theo stated.

"I shall be with you every minute, my Theo." Jannat began to sob very quietly. Rav'an quickly moved to take her in her arms. "He lives, my darling. We must be thankful for that." Her own fears for Talon were temporarily forgotten as she comforted her adopted sister.

Theo departed with Jannat in tow, leaving Rav'an to see that Damian went to bed, and then to look in on the children. The remainder stayed to continue discussing the situation. The fact that Talon was with the Count of Tripoli somewhere in the Kingdom was hardly reassuring.

Eventually, everyone went to bed, but before he did so himself Max went on the prowl to see that Palladius and his men on guard were wide awake. He took Junayd with him. He also intended to check up on their two prisoners. Palladius, the Sergeant of the Guard, was full of curiosity about what had happened to Reza.

Then they went down into the dungeons to have a look at the prisoners. The boy and his father were separated by an empty cell, so that if they wanted to communicate with one another they had to call out, thus allowing the sentry to hear what they said. Max had asked for a sentry who spoke Arabic to be posted. The boy sat cross-legged on the floor, looking sullen; he barely looked up when Max and Palladius arrived. The father, however, came to the bars of his cell and asked, "Is the Lord Reza going to live?"

Max barely understood him, but he guessed what he was saying and replied, "You should hope he lives, because if not you die." The grim look on his face must have spoken volumes, because the pirate retreated and went to sit on his pallet. There were no further words between them. After making sure they had water and some food, Max and Palladius left.

The next day, another ship was observed making its way towards the harbor. The flare went up and the intruder was intercepted by both scout ships as it approached.

As Henry and Guy stood off from the newcomer, it became apparent that this was the same ship that had escaped from them during the engagement some weeks prior. The railing on its starboard side was still in a state of disrepair. Henry wrinkled his nose at the smell emanating from the vessel. There were slaves aboard. It was a slovenly ship, but he knew better than to underestimate the men who sailed it.

The rough-looking crew clearly became apprehensive when the two ships pointed their bows at their vessel, but a lean, finely dressed man wearing a huge turban waved, indicating he wanted to talk.

"What do you want?" Henry shouted across the water.

The man on the pirate ship put a hand to his ear and shouted something back.

"My Arab is poor," Henry told his steersman. "Who speaks the Arabic on our ship?"

One of the crew stepped forward. "I do, captain."

"What is he saying?" Henry asked his man.

"He said he has come to parley for our prisoner, Captain."

"Parley? About what? Tell him to be quick, or we'll sink him right now!" Henry told his translator, forgetting for the moment that they now held a prisoner at the castle. He glanced towards the bows, where several of his crew were standing by, one with a fuse coil ready to fire the Scorpion spear with its deadly explosive load.

The man on the other deck shouted across the water. "You have my cousin and his son prisoners. I want them back. I have come to parley for them. You still have them, don't you?"

Henry looked blank for a moment, but Guy, who had been listening also with a man who understood Arabic, shouted back. "Yes, we have them. You lead the way with your vessel. No stupid moves, or we sink you. Anchor in the middle of the harbor. No one is to leave ship without our permission. We will take you up to the castle."

"The castle?"

"Yes, that place up there!" Guy pointed to the distant castle perched high on the mountain.

"Ah, yes," Abdul-Zinad said quietly to his nearby lieutenant. "I would very much like to see the inside of that place. Very much indeed."

Chapter 13

Frankish Treaties

Perhaps the revealer of depths, the Lord,
will show me where wisdom lurks—
for it alone is my reward,
my portion and the worth of my work.
                                        —Shelomo ibn Gabirol

The bell of Tiberius cathedral dolefully beat single notes throughout the morning, the stroke of a hammer marking the death of each of the fallen. The priests had gathered inside and a Latin mass was being said for the dead, punctuated i by the muffled sound of the bell tolling above the heads of the congregation. Count Raymond of Tripoli and his wife, Eschiva of Bures, were present to hear the solemn service. Just as the priest finished one long intonation and was about to begin another, there was an interruption at the door of the church and all heads turned.

After genuflecting at the doorway, Sir Matthew strode along the nave, his spurs rattling and his leather hauberk creaking and clinking as he approached the Count, who had also turned to find out what was going on.

"What is it?" he demanded sharply.

"My Lord, there is a party of horsemen sighted on the road. They appear to be coming from the south. We think they are Christians."

The Count shrugged. "Very well. I shall come." He looked over at the priest, who was waiting to continue with barely suppressed impatience.

"Finish the service," the Count ordered, then turned to his wife. "You should stay here and be seen to represent me," he said, then he was striding out of the cathedral into the blinding light of the noonday sun. He shrugged off his ceremonial cloak and looked around for Talon, noticed him standing with his phantom attendant Yosef on the walls overlooking the entrance to the city, and made in their direction.

"I missed you at the service, Talon," the Count said pointedly as he came alongside. Talon was leaning on the parapet, gazing at the oncoming horsemen.

"I thought I should keep an eye on the road, Lord," Talon replied. "If I am not mistaken, that is Count Balian of Ibelin, to whom you introduced me in Jerusalem."

"Yes it is," said the Count, and if I am not mistaken the two persons dressed in their usual finery are the Bishop of Tyre and Nazareth respectively." He shook his head.

"They make no concessions to the heat, do they?" he remarked. "Preferring to retain their dignity above all else, including the sensible comfort of light robing. Which is probably why their thinking is always so addled," he added caustically."Well, I can imagine why they are here. We should make them welcome, I suppose. Sir Matthew!"

"Yes, Lord."

"Open the gates, man! We have company, and it is from the Church. Honor guard and all the trappings. You know what to do."

Matthew hurried off to carry out the Count's bidding. A trumpet blared, and men-at-arms formed a rough line of spearmen near the entrance of the city gates. The large wooden portals were pushed open by four strong men. Not long after, the party of dignitaries and armed knights clattered through the archway and rode into the main courtyard.

The Count, meanwhile, had stationed himself at the top of the stairs leading to the entrance of the citadel, with several of his knights in attendance. He had requested that Talon join him, so Talon and Yosef stood just to the right of the waiting Count.

The visitors dismounted, Ibelin with practiced ease, but the two bishops needed assistance to clamber off their mounts. Pages held their horses and the two older men hobbled slowly after Ibelin, who strode up the steps with his arms wide. The two Counts embraced. "These are sorry times, cousin," Ibelin murmured to Raymond. "We must talk as soon as possible."

"We will, Balian, we will. But you are very welcome, even under these tragic circumstances. You will need some refreshments, I think. It is thirsty work riding this time of year."

The two bishops had by this time arrived at the top of the steps and were waiting to be greeted. Instead of kneeling and offering to kiss their rings, the Count greeted them tersely. "I trust you are well after your ride, Bishops?"

Nazareth frowned, but Tyre, who was used to this treatment, nodded and said, "Indeed, Lord Raymond, the road was wearisome, but infinitely worse is what occurred in Cresson." He was almost wringing his hands with distress. They had ridden past the battlefield on their way to Tiberius and had beheld the gristly sight of the unburied and headless knights lying where they had fallen. His restless eyes darted to the right and to the left; he recognized Talon and stared. Talon gave the bishop a sardonic half bow; he scowled and looked away.

The visitors were ushered into the citadel's great hall and seated at the head table to be plied with bread, cheese, olives, goat meat and wine, even some dates. The Count, who had already eaten, sipped a silver cup of water and watched the bishops stuff their mouths with food. Ibelin was more circumspect, eating sparsely and taking an occasional sip of the rough red wine provided by the Count's steward.

The Count's wife passed through the hall on her way to the upper chambers and was greeted respectfully by all. "I shall be in my chambers, my Lord," she addressed the Count pointedly. "You will bring me news there?"

He nodded without saying anything. Talon was struck by the coolness between the Count and his lady.

As soon as the bishops appeared sated, Raymond stood up and said, "We will convene in my chambers upstairs, my Lords. I wish to bring Sir Lord Talon with us, as he witnessed the disaster."

Ibelin nodded in recognition. "I do remember you, Sir Talon. I am pleased to see you again." He smiled. "There have been many rumors about you, not least from Acre. I would like to hear your side of things some time."

The reaction of the bishop of Nazareth was different. "Is this the heretic of whom we have heard who uses witchcraft?" he demanded. His tone was hostile and he fingered his rosary.

"Yes, it is," the Count snapped, irritation plain in his voice. "But I have known him for a long time, and while I know much of his skills, witchery is not one of them!" he winked at Talon. "Or... is it?" Talon tried hard to remain impassive.

Ibelin added his note to the discussion. "All I have ever heard of *Lord* Talon,"—he used Talon's new title—"is that he is an exemplary warrior and has always remained true to our cause... despite the efforts of the bishop of Acre and others to gainsay him. King Baldwin IV gave public notice of this, my Lords." His tone carried a warning.

"This means that he is under my protection at all times. I do hope I am clear on this point?" The Count asked the unhappy bishops. His manner was polite, but there was an underlying steel.

"Now you will hear from his lips what transpired yesterday, as Lord Talon here was my emissary not only to yourselves but to Lord Rideford and his Templars." The Count showed them into his chambers, which were cool compared to the hall, well lit and comfortable, with a distinct Eastern flavor to them: low brass tables, and cushions distributed on expensive carpets. There were several thick, leather-bound manuscripts resting on one of the tables, denoting that the Count was a scholar as well as a warrior.

A light breeze filtered through the slatted shutters and disturbed the window drapes. Talon noted they were made from Gaza cloth, an expensive material which almost transparent. The Count knew the bishops could not sit on the cushions, for neither would have been able to get up again without assistance, so he led the way to an alcove where there was a large desk and the rounded, carved wood and leather chairs that were popular with the Franks.

Both Nazareth and Tyre, sweating after the climb to this floor, lowered themselves heavily onto their seats, one with a heaved sigh, the other with an audible expulsion of flatulence. Ibelin and Talon chose to stand. The Count took his place in a chair on the other side of the desk where he could, if he turned, see down into the courtyard.

A silent page provided more wine and water, then vanished.

"*Lord* Talon," the Count emphasized Talon's rank for the benefit of the bishops, "has told me of the encounter with the Master of Templars. He tells me you were there, my Lord Bishop."

"I was not there for the aftermath of the battle," Talon said, looking directly at the Bishop of Tyre. "But you were there, were you not, my Lord?" he asked the bishop, who looked shifty.

"We... we made our escape, and later in the day we ran into Lord Ibelin, who was trying to catch up with the van," he muttered.

Talon wondered how hurried that escape had been, with the nimble Arab cavalry chasing stragglers all over the countryside after their sudden victory. He almost smiled as the image of the plump man's panicked retreat.

"Did anyone else survive?" The Count interrupted his thoughts.

"Lord Rideford and three other knights managed to escape. All were wounded, but by the grace of God they managed to escape," Nazareth answered.

Both Raymond and Talon were stunned into silence by his words. The Count was incredulous. "He lives?" He shook his head as though to banish the unwelcome thought from his mind.

"Well then, where is he?" the Count demanded. "You say he is wounded?"

"They all were, my Lord. Not seriously, but wounded nonetheless. God protected them by his good grace. Lord Rideford's followers are now with the saints in heaven," the bishop added piously.

"And not much use to us of the living, are they?" the Count barked, his voice harsh and dripping with sarcasm.

Both bishops looked offended, but wisely kept their mouths shut.

Ibelin, who up to this moment had said nothing, stirred. "It was a disaster of huge magnitude that has weakened us badly, Raymond. Rideford stripped several of the local garrisons of their knights to go into this reckless venture. Now we must try to pull ourselves together to face the looming threat." He paused to take a sip of wine; he savored it, appearing to think about what to say next.

Finally, he placed his cup carefully on the desk and looked directly at the Count. "I know that your relationship with the King has been... difficult, even hostile, and even more so with Châtillon."

"Châtillon should have been gelded at birth!" the Count snarled. "He is the cause of all this mess. But I am listening. I believe I know why you are here, my friend."

"Yes, indeed," Ibelin said slowly. "It is time for us all, all of us who are of the faith, yourself included, to put aside our animosities and join forces. We, myself and both my Lords of the Church here, have come from Guy de Lusignan, our King, to ask you to join us in holy battle against the Saracen. Will you join us, my Lord?"

The Count threw a glance at Talon that said, "I told you so." He nodded his head once. "Yes," he said, his tone reluctant. "I had already decided upon coming to Jerusalem and was making preparations when you arrived. I will throw my support and my army, such as it is, on the King's side."

What Raymond refrained from saying was that his own men in arms were restive. Arabs had plundered his land and taken slaves, despite the treaty with the Sultan. There were murmurings of mutiny if he did not throw in his lot with his King. He had bowed to the inevitable and taken the only path open to him. He had shared this with Talon the night before, just prior to expelling the Muslims.

There was a collective sigh from the three men. Talon watched as the bishops visibly relaxed and become more effusive. Then he realized just why the bishops had come to this meeting. It had been to add their weight with the threat of excommunication, should the Count have wavered. He frowned to himself. There were too many pressures on Raymond. The only other person in the room who considered the Count a friend was Ibelin, but he too had come for the sake of the King.

The banners made a pretty sight fluttering in the light, warm breeze that came off the waters of the great lake. The knights were assembled with their squires at hand; the bishop of Tyre stood on the steps, waiting to bless the soldiers gathered in the great square of the citadel of Tiberius. Eventually the Count and his lady appeared, and all went to their knees for the blessing. When it was over, Raymond, Count of Tripoli and the lands of Tiberius, bowed over his wife's extended hand and kissed it in a gesture of farewell, but hardly with affection. He turned, and without looking back he descended the steps to where his horse was held by a squire.

At a signal from the Count the gates were swung open and the cavalcade of counts, bishops, knights and attendants rode out of the city towards the main road leading south to Jerusalem. Talon and Yosef rode just behind the Count, who was engrossed in a conversation with Count Ibelin. The bishops and their attendants were close behind him. Talon could almost feel their outraged stares burning holes in his back. Despite what the Count had said, these men feared what they did not understand, hence Talon remained to them a man of dark powers. He was sure that their rosaries were becoming worn out from all the fingering they were being subjected to.

He ignored the bishops and focused on the road. This was the very one along which he and his companions had fled only days earlier. It was not long before they could see the macabre evidence of the battle of the Springs of Cresson. Despite the efforts of a burial party sent out by the Count the day before, there were many headless corpses yet to bury. The sky over the battlefield was dark with carrion birds, crows and vultures competing for the spoils of the slaughter. The stench of the rotting corpses wafted in the direction of the Count's column, and men were forced to place cloths over their noses to mitigate the nauseous stink.

Several of the younger, less calloused squires retched or lost their breakfasts. Older soldiers averted their eyes and rode by, while the bishops, looking sick, lifted their arms in pious benediction and made the signs of the cross in the air. Talon wondered how many men in this column of men realized what a hideous error of judgment had been committed by Lord Rideford. The Count of Tripoli shook his head as they passed and snarled, "God forgive him because I cannot."

Leaving the gruesome slopes of the battlefield behind, the small army continued south, picking up the pace so that they could cover as much ground as possible. No one knew if there might be another army of Arabs lurking on the other side of the river, and all yearned towards the safety of numbers that Jerusalem would provide.

They rode most of that day on the road parallel with the river Jordan, stopping sooner than the Count wished because the fat bishops were worn out from riding. The next day, the Count insisted that they hurry and complete the remaining distance. He was driven by the fear that Salah Ed Din would move earlier than he had anticipated.

Towards evening they swung west and took the hilly road towards the ancient town of Fort St Job, a fortification held by the Hospitaliers which was just a few leagues from Jerusalem. Before long the country became hilly, with more cultivation than Talon had seen for some time. Proximity to the city of Jerusalem was enough to protect farming, which was important to the inland city. Supplies came regularly from Jaffa and Acre, but the essentials of food had to be grown locally.

At Fort St Job, as banners fluttered and men clad in chain and leather sweated. Talon noted with some interest the two leading lords at Guy de Lusignan's side were Rideford and Châtillon. The Grand Master of the Templars, who had somehow survived the massacre at Cresson, wore his arm in a sling.

Just off to the side of the throne, Sibylla stood with her female attendants dressed in simple white. It enhanced her features, although Talon would not have said the queen was a beautiful woman. The column came to a halt and the Count of Tripoli, attended by Count Ibelin and the Bishops of Nazareth and Tyre, walked up the wide stone steps to kneel before the King, who smiled and took both the Count's hands in his.

Talon was too far from the group to hear the conversation that ensued, but before very long the King and Count Raymond exchanged the kiss of peace and embraced. This appeared to be the signal for cheers from the King's attendants, which were taken up by the Templars, although with less enthusiasm, then spread to the men-at-arms and eventually the citizenry, who had no idea why they were cheering but it made them all feel better. The King led the visitors away, followed by his close advisers. The Count motioned to Talon to accompany him.

"Lord Talon is with me, Your Highness," he told the King, who glanced incuriously back at Talon. "Have we met before?" Lusignan asked.

"My Liege, Lord Talon was responsible for bringing the Templars from Gaza to the battle of Montgisard."

The King didn't respond.

The gesture and comment from Raymond were not lost on Raynald de Châtillon, who started with surprise. He made a surreptitious sign of the cross and then nudged Rideford, who turned and glared.

"I didn't expect to see *you* here, Talon. I hear you are a *Lord* now?" he added with what might have been a sneer. Bit young to be one of those, eh?" he added sarcastically.

"I didn't spend as much time in Arab prisons as some others, my Lord Rideford," Talon retorted with a pointed glance at Châtillon, who sent him a venomous glare. The other two men turned with a swirl of their cloaks to follow the King's retinue into the depths of the gloomy castle.

After the "reconciliation" had been completed, the King and his entourage mounted up and together with the new arrivals they rode the short distance remaining to Jerusalem. As they approached that city it became evident that there was a huge encampment around its walls. The King had already gathered a large army.

Their arrival was greeted with the blare of trumpets. The walls and streets were jammed with curious citizens, eager for firsthand news of the disaster at Cresson. Rumors were rife and fear was pervasive as the uneasy citizens watched the colorful cavalcade make its way along Furrier's Street towards the Temple and the palace of the King.

The last time Talon had been in this city had been just before leaving for Acre, and it had been a sad place then. Baldwin the Leper King had been about to die. Now the air was charged with tension. Servants scurried about, but they were markedly nervous and kept well away from the armed knights that strutted along the corridors. Talon guessed that many of these knights were part of Châtillon's force.

Rideford was in command of the Templars, who were generally well behaved and housed in their barracks at the Temple. Talon could tell that others were from Edessa and Antioch by their surcoats, while many men served minor lords who held small garrisons up and down the country. The King was clearly getting ready to counter the massed army that Salah Ed Din had assembled.

In the wake of Count Raymond, Talon bumped into Sir Matthew and his large Saxon companion.

"Lord Talon!" Sir Matthew said, with a smile of welcome to Talon and Yosef. "I had hoped that you would come in with us to the court, Sir. The Count is about to join the King in conference and asked that you be present.

They were admitted to a crowded chamber filled mainly with lords and senior knights. The atmosphere was stuffy and full of tension, as loud, opinionated men drank wine and traded arguments. Both Grand Masters were there. Talon noted that Roger de Moulin's replacement had already been chosen, but he didn't recognize the man. Sir Matthew saw where Talon was staring.

"That is Armengol de Aspa, the new Grand Master of the Hospitaliers. Lord Rideford is still with us." He shrugged with a wry dismissive gesture. "The Lord God moves in unfathomable ways."

Talon walked through the crowd to join Raymond, who was in deep discussion with the King.

"Ah, there you are, Talon," he said, looking up. "Perhaps you can add your argument to mine." Raymond sounded frustrated. "I have been telling his Majesty of our visit to Salah Ed Din and offered some ideas of strategy."

He turned back to the seated king. "My Lord, while it is good that we are assembling here, we must move the army to place it between the lake of Tiberius and Acre, both of which are vulnerable. Lord Talon knows both the terrain and the Sultan, as well as I do and better than most men. He speaks the Arabic and has spent time in their world."

"So much time that it is hard to decide on which side he is any more," Rideford sneered from just behind Talon, who turned to face him.

Raymond stepped in. "I know that reckless and rash decisions will lose any advantage we might be able to gain against the Sultan, my Lord. You yourself have just demonstrated that, and we have lost many good men as a result of your folly. Who, then, is the traitor?" Raymond was having difficulty controlling his temper by this time. He glared at Rideford as though daring him to violence

Rideford's bearded face flushed with anger "You left the field, like a coward, Lord Talon," he ground out.

"You and your kind are ignorant fools who come out here under the pretext of serving God when in reality you seek your fortunes like common mercenaries," snarled Raymond.

Rideford stepped closer and reached for his dagger. At this moment Talon slipped in front of Tripoli and seized the wrist of the hand that held the dagger. This placed him and Raymond between the King and Rideford. Talon fingers held Rideford's wrist in a vice-like grip. He stared straight into the Master's eyes and hissed, "You are inches away from death, my Lord. Both I and my man here will see to it if you harm a hair on Lord Tripoli's head."

The silent confrontation continued for a moment more until Rideford's maddened eyes slowly cleared and his strength gave way to Talon's. "Sheath it! Do it now!" Talon whispered. Rideford shook his wrist free and sheathed his dagger. He stared across Talon's shoulder with eyes filled with such hate as Talon had rarely seen before, nevertheless he stepped back, a sneer contorting his features.

"Your heretic friends are here to protect you yet again, Tripoli!"

A knight who had been near enough to see the silent battle of wills bared his teeth and moved to step forward as though to confront Talon on behalf of Rideford, but Yosef intervened, using the handle of his dagger enclosed in his fist to strike the man in his solar plexus. The blow was unexpected and incredibly fast, and despite the man's chain armor it had the desired effect. Abruptly the knight began to choke, and his knees gave way while he had a fit of coughing. The distraction this provided took away any further interest in the confrontation between Rideford and Tripoli, but Raymond still had one last word.

"I should perhaps remind you, Rideford, that Lord Talon was my emissary when you foolishly sacrificed those precious lives," Raymond snapped. "He was not yours to command. He was sent to warn you of the peril, but you chose to ignore him. As a result, many good men lie dead, their bodies dismembered by hyenas and dogs and their heads decorating the Arab spears. It was *you* who led those unfortunate men to their fate, and then abandoned them. He was under strict orders to return to me, not to throw his life away on that madcap charge, which I heard you personally ordered."

Rideford glared but held his peace for once, while others helped the breathless and confused knight out of the crowded chambers. "It must be the air in here, it is somewhat stifling," someone nearby said with a small chuckle. Count Ibelin had witnessed the whole thing; his expression told of his approval without his saying a word.

"Your Majesty," Raymond turned back to the King, who was listening with interest, as was Sibylla, who sat to his left. Neither of them had witnessed the incident.

"Lord Talon did his duty, and furthermore, he has the knowledge to counter the army of Salah Ed Din. We should listen to him."

"Anyone who has spent time with the Saracen has most probably been seduced by their heathen ways!" snarled another voice. Châtillon approached, with a short bow to the King. He swayed, and from the smell of him it was apparent to Talon that he had been drinking heavily

"Why should we listen to these *pullani,* my Liege?" Châtillon sneered. "They have been here so long they have forgotten the whole purpose of our presence here, which is to carry the true cross to the infidel and send them to hell wherever we can."

"While you break every hard-won truce time and again, dishonoring all of us while doing so!" Raymond shouted, his temper, ever quick, was now on a razor's edge. "You bring no honor to any discussion whatsoever. You caused this war, and you should be in prison for it!"

Châtillon put his hand on the hilt of his sword. "I do not need to listen to you, traitor!" he shouted. Talon and Yosef stiffened, wondering if the drunk lord would break even more rules and draw his sword in the presence of the King himself. Châtillon, however, while he might have been drunk was not insensible. He stood back with a sneer and called for more wine instead.

"I would listen to what Lord Talon has to say." A clear voice cut through the acrimonious dispute, that of the Lady Sibylla, who touched Guy on the arm. "We should hear what he has to say, my Lord," she insisted. Slowly the chambers quietened as people nearby gestured to others to quieten.

The King lifted his hand as though to say no, but then nodded. "Very well. What do you say, *Lord* Talon? If that is indeed what you are?" He sounded skeptical.

Talon gave the queen a thin smile and half bow of acknowledgment, then addressed the King directly. "Lord Raymond is right, my Liege," he heard a snort of derision behind him from Rideford, but continued.

"We cannot wait for Salah Ed Din to come here to Jerusalem. Almost the entire Arab population would come at us with overwhelming numbers, and Jerusalem is not equipped to withstand a siege. He must be intercepted. We should march north and ensure that we are in a position of strength, with access to water, thereby forcing him to come to us. That is the only way we can defeat him decisively."

His words were greeted by many who were nearby with approving nods and words of agreement, but Rideford, ever the man to oppose anything that came from the Count of Tripoli or members of his group, shook his head and shouted, "We destroyed Saladin at Montgisard and we will do it again! My Templars are all we need to cut him to pieces."

"You demonstrated that amply well at Cresson!" Raymond retorted. "Montgisard was won by leaders far more capable than you will ever be! How many battles have *you* actually won, Rideford?" he demanded.

Talon lifted his hand and shook his head at Rideford, who appeared about to lose it yet again and attack Raymond. With an ugly look at Talon and Yosef, Rideford subsided.

"Where do you think we should go?" Guy asked Talon.

"He will try to cut Acre off as early as possible, because that is a significant port of entry to this land; so the army must intercept him before then by placing ourselves between Acre and Tiberius," Talon replied.

Raymond brightened for the first time and slapped his thigh. "Yes, of course! I know exactly where you mean, Lord Talon. The springs of Sephoria! There is ample water and grazing for us there. We would be right across his path, and he would have to come to us across the dry lands. No water anywhere between Sephoria and Tiberius. His army would be badly weakened by thirst."

Talon nodded. "Yes, my Lord. Your Majesty, the Sultan has somewhere between twenty-five and thirty-thousand men. They would be exhausted by the time they arrived to do battle, after a twenty-league march through waterless terrain. The battle would be on our terms."

He received a long look of approval from Lady Sibylla, and Guy himself seemed persuaded. "Very well. We now have almost twenty-thousand men of our own. We should make our move as soon as possible. Give the orders, Marshall," he told the senior man standing nearby, listening with great attention. "Lord Aimery," he called out to his brother, "Prepare the army. I want every able-bodied man to meet the army outside of Acre, and then we will move to Sephoria."

Talon and Raymond, accompanied by Balian, finally left the King's chambers. "I am exhausted," the Count said, and coughed. He looked weary and his cough had not improved. "You did well, Talon. We are the only voices of reason in that crowd of zealots." He coughed again. "I shall go to my chambers now. Good night." He left with Matthew and his Saxon in tow.

Balian and Talon watched them leave. "Lord Raymond is not a well man," Balian remarked, then he put a hand on Talon's shoulder. "You know this country like the back of your hand, Talon. I thank God that you were able to persuade the King, and not those hot-headed lords. But what did your man do to that unfortunate man earlier? I didn't see anything, but I am could swear he did something to make him keel over.

"I really wasn't paying much attention, my Lord," Talon responded briefly. "The man might have eaten something that disagreed with him, perhaps?" He glanced over at his impassive companion. Yosef, who understood perfectly, said nothing, as usual. Talon's own mind was preoccupied with the alarming lack of understanding for their collective predicament within the court.

"It isn't the same as before, my Lord," he said, forcing a change of subject. "There is willful ignorance here that bodes ill for all of us. Under the former king, God bless his soul, there was much listening before decisions were made; and men like Sir Guy of de Veres were in command, men who underwood the worth of strategy, and valued the lives of the men they commanded."

Count Balian gave a bark of rueful laughter. "Yes, indeed. I miss that, but we are in God's hands now. Let's see what transpires when we get to the Springs of Sephoria. Good night."

Chapter 14

The Springs of Sephoria

What more does war need?
A road, someone living, someone dead,
a river of sacred mud,
and the devouring heat of June.
                              —*Nadia Tueni*

In late June the primary army of the King of Jerusalem arrived on the outskirts of Acre. There gathered knights, volunteers and men-at-arms to augment those already in the army of the King. The Templars and the Hospitaliers had almost denuded their castles in order to bring as many men to the anticipated battle as possible.

As Talon and Yosef rode into the encampment, he noted large numbers of Genoese mercenaries, cross-bowmen for the most part, their elaborate badges and bright red tunics a clear indication to their origin. Volunteers from as far south as Gaza and as far north as Beirut were present, but not all of these men were well armed, nor were they disciplined. The knights of the Orders kept very much to themselves while they awaited the next move.

The meetings, which the King held each evening, became more and more acrimonious, which to Talon's mind was astonishing. There were even scuffles actually inside the King's large tent, as men who knew what to expect in a war argued with and shouted at the fanatical supporters of Rideford and

Châtillon, who responded with sneers and shouts of 'Cowards!" and *"Pullani!"* which was now used as an insult. His respect for the King, already low because of the manner in which he had taken the throne, dwindled even further.

"It is dangerous to have as king a man who has not the slightest idea as to how capable his enemy is, nor the consequences of ill-considered decisions," the Count lamented.

News arrived that Salah Ed Din had crossed the Jordan just south of the Sea of Galilee near to the village of Sennabra and was disbursing his army, some to the nearby hills, while others set off to besiege the city of Tiberius. Rumor arrived hot on the heels of this news that the city of Tiberius had fallen, and that Raymond's wife and her guardsmen had withdrawn to the citadel, preparing for a long siege.

The debate that followed the arrival of this news was loud and contentious. "We should march now and drive the infidels into the lake at once!" bellowed Rideford.

"My Lord," Raymond pleaded with the King, "Remember that beyond Sephoria the road to Tiberius is bone dry, a desert without access to any water for an army. Yes, engage the enemy, but on *our* terms, not his. He *must* come to us or fail in his overall mission. Do not allow yourself to be provoked! If we camp at the springs there is water aplenty and good grazing for us while we wait, whereas his army will be dry and without any food for their animals. They will be seriously weakened by the time they arrive before us!"

"Pah!" Rideford sneered "You, Raymond are a proven traitor and in league with Saladin. We have the strength to kill him and his rabble in front of the gates of Tiberius, but you want to skulk in the hills while he sacks our places of worship and our city!"

"I should perhaps remind you that it is not *your* city but mine under attack!" Raymond shouted.

"Where is your reason, Rideford?" he demanded acidly. "You have already destroyed two hundred men in an act of reckless insanity at Cresson!"

Talon and his companion Yosef stood aside, appalled, as the acrimonious shouting match continued. Then the King held up his hand for silence and said, "We will relieve Tiberius, but we will march in two stages. We go to the Springs of Sephoria, and then I shall decide what to do." Raymond and his adherents had to be content with that.

The King's army arrived at the springs of Sephoria late in the afternoon of July the second. The land was green and well-watered; as Talon and Raymond had surmised, it could easily support the nearly twenty-thousand knights, men-at-arms and hangers-on who now spread out over the low pastures around the springs. There was much good fodder for the animals.

Talon and Yosef stayed close to the Count, who looked around him with satisfaction and said, "We can easily defend this place. Look over there towards the east. It is bone dry, almost desert. They must come from there, marching over twenty leagues to reach us. We will be fresh and ready, while they will be parched and exhausted."

Talon agreed and made preparations to settle in for the night. That evening, however, things were to change. Another desperate messenger arrived from the Count's wife, begging for assistance. Tiberius was being attacked from all sides. She was not sure if she could hold out for more than a week. It set the council off once more on another round of acrimonious debates, but this time the Count's own sons stood up and begged the King to help their mother.

Their father raged at them, but they became stubborn and defensive. "Our mother is being besieged by the infidels, Father!" One of them exclaimed, "while we sit here in comfort! It is unconscionable! You have never been fond of her, but she is *our* mother!" He almost shouted this in front of the knights and the King himself.

Raymond seethed and took his sons aside, but they were angry with him and clearly worried more about their mother's fate than the good sense of waiting for the Sultan.

Guy began to waver. Others put in their words in favor of staying, but the words with the most impact were those of Raymond. The exasperated Count stood up in front of all the nobles present and called out for all to hear. It was an impassioned plea for common sense.

"The lady in question is *my wife*, that is true! The city under siege is *my* city, that also is true! However, everything I and others present have told you is also true!" he shouted.

"I am a Christian first and foremost, and although I love my wife and my city, I also know that to leave this place would be the *utmost* folly! It would be precisely what the Sultan wants. Don't you see? He is laying siege to Tiberius to draw us into a trap! I would rather lose my relatives and my lands than lose the Holy Kingdom of Jerusalem, as we would surely place it in peril if we leave the Springs. I beg of you all to listen to reason. We can defeat him here but not at Tiberius. He knows this and awaits us for this very reason."

He paused, then continued. "Hear me!" he begged. "I say again to you, all of you, that we would never arrive in any condition to fight, should we leave these springs. Do not forget that Salah Ed Din's army is between us and the lake, so we would have to fight to reach water, and that after twenty leagues of dry, dusty road. If the heat of the day—it is July, for God's sake—does not kill half our men, then thirst will drive the rest mad!" He turned to the King imploring him. "I beg you, my Lord. Stay here and we will win. Leave and we imperil the Kingdom itself! I have seen many an Arab army, but this is the largest by far. We *must* be prudent!"

"You would try to frighten us?" Raynald de Châtillon sneered. "We all know you prefer Saracen company to ours!"

"I am no traitor, my Liege!" Raymond stated to the King, and then turned his venom on Châtillon. "It is common knowledge, Châtillon, that you like to rape Arab women! Your crimes have brought us to this, you filthy scoundrel!" he retorted angrily. "But listen to me when I say that unless we use a sensible strategy we will all die."

Rideford could not hide his hatred of Raymond any more. "Traitor!" he shouted. "You have dealt with the enemy to enrich yourself at the expense of all others. You are a wolf in our midst, and I, for one, will not put up with it any longer!" Many of his followers took up this cry.

"I have said it often enough in the past, but I shall say it again," Raymond shouted over the noise of arguing men. "The Arabs have an infinite supply of men, horses and material, but we Crusaders must go to distant lands to beg for men and equipment from parsimonious kings who are slow to provide what we need, and when they do it is always slow in coming. We must be prudent and pick our battles. We must not be reckless at this time!"

Others joined with Raymond to persuade the King to stay, despite the vitriol spouted by Rideford and Châtillon. Finally Guy de Lusignan gave a reluctant nod. "We stay," he said. Raymond and Talon, along with many others, breathed a huge sigh of relief.

Later that night after a short discussion with Tripoli, Talon and Yosef went to bed in the open next to their horses. "What do you think, Lord?" Yosef asked sleepily.

"We are to stay... for the time being, but Tripoli has few friends here," Talon remarked. "Not even his sons will talk to Raymond now." He rolled into his cotton sheet. The night was warm; the July heat took some time to dissipate.

*****

During the night, under the blaze of stars when most men slept, with the exception of the pickets and guards, Grand Master Rideford slipped into the tent of the King and woke him.

"My Liege, you must hear what I have to say!" he insisted.

The King was tired after the long journey from Acre and the endless debate that had followed, but he sat up and sleepily waved Rideford to a chair.

"You *know* that Tripoli is a traitor, Lord! He made an alliance with Saladin, which he is still holding to. These *pullani* are all the same! They are as dishonest as the people they live with! He certainly cannot be trusted, and neither can anyone trust his words. That other fellow who is with him is also in league with the infidels. His reputation is terrible! Ask Châtillon about that!"

Guy stirred uncomfortably. "But what about the water issue and our strong position here?" he asked feebly.

Rideford pressed his case. "Tiberius is a Christian city and we must defend it! And Tripoli is lying about the water. There are springs at Hattin, on the slopes, where we will dominate. Are we going to sacrifice Tiberius for the sake of a traitor and a coward, my Liege?" he exclaimed. "Why, my knights will cut through the Saracen ranks like a knife through butter, I can guarantee it. They are thirsting for revenge after the betrayal at Cresson. We will not only reach the lake in a timely manner, we will take the city back without much of a fight." He looked hard at the tired King, slumped in the lamplight. "You do know that it was he who betrayed my knights at the springs of Cresson, don't you, Lord?" he lied. "I have supported you in every way, my Lord. You do owe it to me to listen," Rideford finished.

"What do you want me to do?" Guy finally asked.

*****

Talon was woken to the sound of trumpets in the very early hours of the morning and the bustle of a large army waking up in the darkness. He stumbled out of his light cotton covering to find that the entire army was preparing to leave the safety of the springs.

He found the Count striding about, beside himself with rage and frustration. He coughed, then snapped, "I said that this king was so stupid that the last person to whisper in his thick ear would be heard! Well, Talon, we are now all going to hell. You had better prepare yourself and get ready to leave. We are under orders to go to Tiberius."

"Why the change of heart?" Talon asked, his own heart sinking.

"That imbecile Guy couldn't even offer a good reason. Simply that we must prepare to leave for Hattin." Raymond sounded thoroughly unhappy. "Rideford, the swine, got to him last night and made him change his mind."

"It makes no sense to march during the day," Talon stated, as he peered up at the first streaks of light in the east. "It is going to be dangerously hot today!"

"That does not appear to have occurred to the King, nor to any of his closest idiots," the Count retorted, shaking his head in disgust. "I have instructed my men to bring as much water for themselves as possible. I would do the same if I were you."

Talon needed no persuasion. He instructed Yosef to fill their skins and to find or steal two others. Yosef hurried off to comply, while Talon saddled their horses and made preparations for the long march to Hattin. He had a deep sense of foreboding. He looked around him as the army began to move off. Already there had been numerous desertions by the volunteers and even among the mercenaries. Always nervous about bad leadership, many of these men had decided that the wind blew the wrong way and had departed in the darkness.

As the army lumbered into motion, Talon took it upon himself and Yosef and some of the lighter horse scouts to explore the road that led through the foothills to the west of the Sea of Galilee, and soon they were well ahead of the army. As light from the east began to flood across the hills, he realized what a dangerous move this had been. They could now make out distant bands of Turkish cavalry waiting for the army to take the winding road into the hills and he knew without a doubt that Salah Ed Din was already well aware that the Christian army was attempting to go for Tiberius.

"Salah Ed Din must be feeling very pleased with himself," Talon remarked to Yosef, as they trotted their horses along the stony and dust-laden track which passed for a main road between the city of Acre and Tiberius. He spotted yet another band of mounted archers lurking along the skyline ahead of them. "Those are Turks without question, and they will sting," he muttered.

"We should be very careful not to become too exposed ourselves, Lord," Yosef cautioned. They were by this time some way ahead of the van of the army, which was being led by the King, Guy de Lusignan, and Lord Raynald de Châtillon with his unruly men. The Templars, under the leadership of Grand Master Rideford, took up position at the rear of the army, while in the middle, ostensibly protected by the heavy cavalry at either end and the spearmen, marched the Genoese archers, the ragged majority of the volunteers in charge of the wagons, and donkeys carrying the rations and baggage of the army. There were almost no trees other than low shrubs in small patches on the sides of the hills, hence no shade whatsoever from the blazing sun.

As they ascended into the foothills that formed a low barrier before the basin of the Sea of Galilee, Talon became uncomfortably aware of how exposed they were. It was not long before his fears were confirmed. Salah Ed Din had sent light, mounted bowmen to harass their progress. Talon wanted to see one thing for himself before he rejoined the army and relative safety.

"Come, Yosef, we will be able to check the position of the Sultan's army from the crest of that hill over there. We have to move fast. Follow me!" he called to the scouts.

They set their horses into a gallop and drove them hard up the shallow incline, their bows ready for trouble should it appear on the crest. They were lucky; the enemy horsemen were intent upon a much larger and easier target, and a few distant, isolated horsemen didn't present any danger to them. As they crested the hill Talon reined his blowing horse in and stared around, then gazed east towards the great lake, shading his eyes from the glare of the sun.

His heart sank. The army still had fifteen leagues to go before it came within reach of the precious waters. Slightly to the north were twin peaks of bare lava rock hills known as the Horns of Hattin. Just below and between the horns he knew there was a spring that lasted well into the summer, but he realized that the dark mass in the distance was an army, and it was encamped with the spring behind it, protecting it from the Christians. They would not reach it without a fight.

He wiped his brow with a cloth. "We will need to conserve every drop of water that we have, Yosef. The Sultan has positioned himself well."

Yosef wiped his own brow. Even this early, the heat of the day was well advanced. "Why do you stay with these people, Lord?" he asked. "They do not respect your advice, nor the Count's. They insist upon doing stupid things and getting themselves killed for it, and they will again this time."

Talon smiled at his longtime companion. "It is about honor, Yosef. Something you understand perfectly well. The Count needed my help, so I am here; I cannot leave now and live with myself. I am not a coward, and neither are you. We must go where the dice are thrown now, and God protect us in doing so."

"We had better get back to the army then, Lord," Yosef remarked, pointing. A small group of curious Turkish horsemen had appeared on the top of another hill adjacent to theirs and had seen them. Their shouts and yells could be clearly heard as they raced their horses down the slopes with the aim of cutting Talon and the scouts off from the Christian army. Talon, Yosef and the scouts had enough distance, however, and easily evaded them to rejoin the van of the Christian army

The danger was not past. The Turkish horsemen took advantage of the ability of their smaller, nimble-footed mounts to scramble up and down the slopes of the hills, while the lumbering Christian army was confined to the road, which in places was narrow enough for only four men to ride abreast. The Turks, shouting their battle cries, loosed arrow after arrow into the ranks of the Christians, who would have had to stop and shoot their crossbows to respond. The King, looking hot and confused, ordered the army to continue its march. Casualties began to mount as the arrows found the less well armored men and horses.

"What did you see?" Tripoli demanded of them. He already looked exhausted and was coughing again.

Talon spoke for the scouts. "The Sultan has taken up a position astride the springs of Hattin. We will have to fight to get to the water."

Raymond of Tripoli beat his hand on his thigh. "Do you hear, Your Highness?" he called out. "Salah Ed Din has placed himself on the wells of Hattin. We must now fight for water, as we cannot go around him."

The King threw him a resentful look, but then just stared ahead, saying nothing. His brother, Lord Aimery, looked apprehensive, and even the normally arrogant Châtillon, sweating copiously in the heat, seemed uneasy. He was continually wiping sweat off his sun-reddened face.

The army had been marching for two hours but had covered only about five leagues. Little was said by anyone now; they were too thirsty. The only sounds were the creak of leather, the clop of hooves or a click as the they struck a protruding stone, and the muted rattle of accoutrements. Abruptly there would be a flurry of yells as the Turks galloped up to within fifty or so paces and discharged arrows, the whisper of death and the thump of the missiles striking a shield or a man, or worse, a horse. The beast would whinny and either fall, taking the rider down, or stand trembling from the shock of its wound while the rider took what he could carry and abandoned it to the mercies of the Arabs and Turks, who were becoming ever more bold.

The heat was taking its toll. The surrounding air all about was dense with the dust raised by the plodding hooves of horses and feet of marching men. The men who wore heavy chain mail hauberks, the knights of the Orders or those who served as knights for a lord, suffered the most. There was no relief within these leather and iron corsets, the links of which became hotter and hotter as the sun beat down on the luckless men. By mid afternoon men were suffering from acute dehydration. Some fainted and slid off their horses, or just lay down by the side of the road, and no amount of shouting could persuade them to get up and rejoin the ranks.

Then the Turkish riders began to circle around the army to come in from behind to attack the closed ranks of the Templars. They would ride as close as twenty paces and loose off arrows directly into the stolid ranks of the knights. Sergeants and commanders shouted to their men, "Do not leave the ranks. Stay closed up! March on!" The order had come back for no one to retaliate. Men and horses fell from the arrows, to be abandoned and plundered where they fell. Briefly, some of the exasperated knights broke ranks and chased the cavalry off, but they knew they were running into traps, so they didn't pursue them far. To the jeers of the enemy they would return to their ranks, even more frustrated than before.

Genoese bowmen were used to drive the Turks off if they came too close, but their bolts, although very dangerous, were nowhere near as effective as the slim arrows of the hated Saracen. Talon yearned for a few Welsh archers, who would have inflicted horrendous damage upon these roving bands with the greater range of their strong bows, but there were none to be had with this army.

The Christians had few men who could ride and shoot bows, only Talon and Yosef and a few of the scouts, but the Count of Tripoli insisted that they stay with him.

"Their leader knew what he was doing when he sent these men to harass us," Sir Matthew said to Talon, as he wiped his dusty face and beard with a rag.

"There is worse to come, I fear," Talon answered, watching the numbers of enemy increase. They were nearing the crest of the low hills to arrive at a point where a sharp eye could just make out the Sea of Galilee and the city of Tiberius in the haze. By now the army was almost entirely out of water and desperately thirsty. Men who were not experienced at marching in the desert had drunk their water and had none left, having been assured that there would be a plentiful supply at the end of the day. But by late afternoon, as the army crawled within sight of the lake, the realization that they were in serious trouble became apparent even to the most ignorant of the men-at-arms.

Arrayed before them was most of the army of Salah Ed Din, and it was in possession of the only available water before the lake itself, and that was to be denied the Christian army.

Raymond no longer bothered to be polite to the King. "If you had only listened to me, we would not be in this predicament!" he snarled. "The Sultan has achieved what we could have had if only you listened to the right voices, but no! You listened to that imbecile Rideford who whispered in your ear. Now we are to die on the Sultan's terms! Our only hope is to break through the Sultan's army to get to the water, and I suggest we do this without delay!"

Just then an exhausted rider arrived from the back of the army and, bowing to the King, reported that Lord Rideford and his men could not continue but needed to stop and camp for the night. "They are exhausted and completely out of water, Your Highness," the man said, through parched lips.

Guy, who was suffering as much as any one, turned glazed eyes on Raymond and croaked, "What should we do, Lord Tripoli?"

"There is no turning back now! Half our army would perish on the way back to the springs, and if we camp for the night we will be no less thirsty tomorrow! We will only be a target for raiders in the dark. We must continue whatever the cost, my Lord!" Raymond stated, his voice cracked with anger and thirst.

Then Rideford himself rode up and began to harangue the King. "We cannot continue in this condition. We have to rest. I am told there are wells near to the Horns. We cannot fight in this condition! I shall not move my men another step," he shouted.

"The wells of Hattin are taken! You are madder than even I imagined!" Raymond raged. "Don't you see what will happen? Salah Ed Din has not only denied us water but will surround us if we stop now. We must attack as soon as we can!"

But Rideford had the King's ear yet again, and after more insults and shouting Guy gave the command to halt the army. Talon, himself close to despair and incredulous, watched as the Count turned away almost in tears at the utter stupidity of the order. "You, Rideford, will be the death of this army. You are a complete and utter fool!" he raged.

The King, still unable to understand the predicament they were in, again turned to Raymond. "What should we do now, Lord Tripoli?

Raymond shrugged and rudely turned his back on his King. As he walked away he called back, "We must take the high ground at the base of the horns and hope to God that we can live through this night. Make your tent up there," he waved his hand towards the two peaks overlooking the Sultan's encampment. They were a mere three leagues from the lake itself, but the vast army was between them and the water.

The King sent men up the boulder-strewn slopes to find out if the wells in the area of the horns were, as Rideford had insisted, full of water. The dismayed men, wild-eyed and half crazed with thirst, came staggering back, croaking from parched throats that there was none.

Talon cast a look at Rideford to observe his reaction, but that man just seemed to shrug and ignored the frightened men. By now many of the volunteers and mercenaries had had enough, and no amount of discipline could control what happened next. Groups broke away from the ranks of the main army and fled down towards the waters of the lake. The rest of the dust-caked, exhausted men watched with horror as the deserters were intercepted by light horsemen or spearmen from the Sultan's army and butchered. None of them reached the lake.

The utterly dispirited army of King Guy de Lusignan dismounted and prepared to settle down for the night. Even under these conditions Guy's servants were ordered to put up his royal tent; it was red and distinctive, clearly visible to the waiting army below. There was food, but it was of little use to those who were too parched to swallow. Talon and Yosef shared what water they had with Count Raymond, Matthew and Brandt, the burly Saxon of few words, but Talon was firm about not distributing it further. "We have little enough for you, Lord, so please do not ask me to spread it around. I most certainly will not be providing any to Rideford, nor the King."

Raymond gave him a tired smile. "You have been a staunch friend, Talon. I am so sorry for this. Dear God, but I wish it were better circumstances. I absolutely fail to understand the workings of that man's mind." He was referring to Rideford, who was keeping clear of the Count. At least he had the wits to do that, Talon observed.

There was nothing to be done before dawn, when the battle would surely begin. Talon and Yosef kept a small supply of water for the morning and settled down to get what sleep they could. Exhausted men took their beds wherever they stopped, sleeping outside in the hopes that the cool night air would alleviate their misery. Many hoped that a few charges by the Knights of the Orders would see them clear to the waters of the lake, and went to sleep with that comforting thought in mind.

Salah Ed Din, however, had other plans. Talon woke to the acrid smell of smoke. He sat up, throwing his light covering aside, and found Yosef wide awake and staring down the hillside. The hill was no longer a dark black band above the lighter grey sheen of the lake. Instead, all about the Christian army were the bright glow of fires, consuming bushes and bone-dry grass. A choking cloud of smoke wafted over the dismayed men of the Christian army.

Talon seized Yosef by the arm. "Wet some rags and we will put them over our faces. We must try and protect our horses, too," he said, his tone urgent. Yosef hurried to obey, and then they listened to the wailing and crying of the demoralized men all around them.

———————————

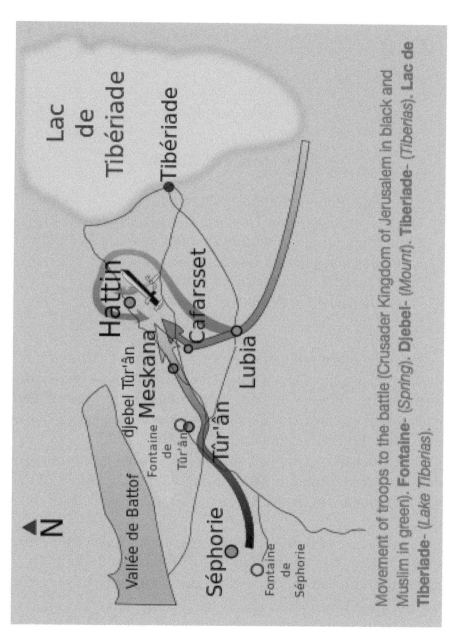

The Battle for The Horns of Hattin

Chapter 15

The Horns of Hattin

See, yonder come the foes of Christendom,
And we must fight for God and Holy Faith.
Now say your shrift, and make your peace with Heaven;
I will absolve you and will heal your souls;
And if you die as martyrs, your true home
Is ready midst the flowers of Paradise.

—*Song of Roland*

As dawn arrived, the scene was one of turmoil and mounting despair. The choking smoke drifted slowly over the army in dark clouds. Worse, Talon saw that the enemy had encircled them during the night. There was no way out of the trap Salah Ed Din had devised.

The Christian army had shrunk during the night, but any deserters were probably dead or enslaved at the hands of the watchful enemy in the hills. There was no refuge left for anyone.

The Bishop of Acre set up the gold inlaid relic of the True Cross before the assembled men and blessed them in a cracked and dried-out voice. He failed dismally to keep the despair out of his voice.

"God bless this army of God Himself, who will protect us all in our time of need!" he bleated. "Today is the Feast of Saint Martin Calidus!" he called out, as though this made any difference to the mostly illiterate gathering.

"I wonder how many here appreciate the great irony," Raymond said to Talon. "Our Lord preached his great sermon of peace for all men on this same day." He gestured back towards the King with his thumb, no longer caring to hide his contempt.

"I despise that man as much for the vacancy of his soul as for the impoverishment of his mind! All three of them brought us to this. Châtillon, Rideford and Lusignan!"

Talon could only nod his agreement. Few were really paying much attention to the bishops after a day and a night without water; their attention was focused on the stretch of gleaming water that was just out of reach. But the knights of the Orders still shrove one another. This was their act of repentance before dying for the Cross. The red tent of the King and the few surrounding tents made a pretty backdrop for the bishops, but even while presenting a brave sight, the King's red tent was stained dark with smut from the numerous fires that were still burning.

At that point Talon came very close to leaving the doomed assembly. In his opinion the King and his advisor Rideford could not have done a better job of destroying their own army with their ignorance, coupled with an astonishing and unwarranted degree of arrogance. He sighed in resignation, then turned to Yosef.

"I cannot leave, but you should, Yosef. This is not your battle. Save yourself while you can, my friend."

Yosef stared back at him with red-rimmed eyes and dirt-caked features. "I do not leave you, Talon. You saved my worthless life in China and made me into a warrior! I shall not desert you now." Talon almost wept, but he had no tears. He just wiped his face with a grimy hand and embraced Yosef.

"Then we die together. I can think of few others I would prefer to have with me. Other than perhaps Reza," he grinned. He held Yosef by the shoulders with both hands to look at his long-time friend with deep affection. "But he would have had something to say about that, I dare say." They both laughed, even with dry throats they laughed, and men nearby who had not understood what they were saying were puzzled by these two strange men among them who could laugh in the midst of this catastrophe.

Dawn was well advanced and the Orders had mounted up. Talon and Yosef, themselves mounted, joined the Count and his men; then they waited in serried lines for the King to join them. As they waited, morale broke altogether among the Genoese archers and the infantry. Abandoning all pretense at discipline, a large number of men-at-arms and volunteers panicked and broke ranks. Thirst-crazed, they charged on foot down the hill to attack the enemy and try to break through to the water they so craved. Once again the men on the hill watched in grim silence as the mob was butchered by the Arab army, or rounded up and bound to be sold into slavery. Their battle was over before it had even begun.

Talon was to ride next to Sir Matthew, who was to the right of the Count. Their horses, tired, agitated and thirsty, fidgeted and snorted as the smoke continued to burn eyes and nostrils.

Talon heard the shouted command, "Advance!" called from the center of the Templar ranks and repeated along the line. Talon glanced their way. The black and white banner of the Temple was raised high, as was that of the Hospitaliers. The Templar and Hospitalier lines closed up into tight formation. The Count's men followed suit; now Talon could feel Yosef's knee next to his right and that of Matthew on his left. He remembered the last time he had been in the middle of a Templar charge at the battle of Montgisard. He had been terrified then, too.

"Stay close. Stay close together at all times!" he shouted. Yosef nodded wordlessly. This was the first time for him, and he was clearly terrified, although he controlled it well.

"Stay close, Yosef. I have been here before, and if we stay close we will survive," Talon reassured him. "Don't be afraid of fear, my friends. Denying that fear is what courage is all about, but even so... my teeth are chattering, too!"

Matthew heard him and spluttered with laughter, then Yosef snorted. "You? I don't believe that is true, Lord."

"Oh, y-y-yes it is!" Talon replied. Sir Matthew choked, whereupon the three of them began to laugh.

"How can you be laughing at this time?" demanded the Count in an incredulous tone. "Is this such a laughing matter?"

"Because we are scared shitless, Lord," Matthew informed him. "God help me, but I am about to lose the few teeth I have left because they are chattering so much! I shall blame Lord Talon for this!"

Even the Saxon understood this time. He gave a bellow of laughter and swore. "Fuck the bastards down there. I shall laugh in their teeth even as I chop them out!"

So it was that as the Templars began their charge down the hill at the massed Arab and Turkish horsemen, Raymond's men were laughing like idiots.

"I always thought you were slightly mad, Talon," the Count shouted, his tone more admiration than rebuke. "God love you, but now I know it for sure!

"Follow the Knights!" he bellowed, and they too began their charge. Their own trumpets blared and their standard rose high. The aim of the Templars and Hospitaliers was to break through the Saracen army and then race for the lake. Raymond and his men were to take the flanks and clear the path after the knights had cut through. Châtillon and his men, positioned on the other flank, were to do likewise. The

Genoese bowmen were to run behind the horsemen and add their arrows to the melee, inflicting as much damage at close range as they could to the flanks.

Talon felt his horse jump into the charge and held the eager animal in a tight rein, making sure his mount kept pace with the others in the line. Yosef was yelling his head off as he spurred his mount.

"Stay in line, Yosef!" Talon shouted over the thunder of hooves and the screaming lancers. He lowered his own lance and took aim at his first victim, a wild looking man with a silver filigreed helmet who was brandishing a long spear. Talon braced for the impact. The famous battle cry of the Templars rang out. "*Beauséant!*" they bellowed as they crashed into the Arab Army. "*Deus Lo Volte!*"

Talon's lance drove right through his target's small shield, through the man's chain armor and out the other side. He winced as the shock of the strike nearly took his own shoulder off at the socket, and the lance was torn from his grasp. He barely noticed the expression of horror on the face of his victim when his helmet was torn off by the impact. His horse rammed past and another man loomed up in front of him. He barely had time to draw his sword to parry the thrust from his opponent. A quick feint up, and then under the shield to strike; his sword flexed ever so slightly, then went in deep. The man fell away, his mouth gaping, a round black hole as he screamed, to join others on the already bloody sand.

The packed ranks of the Arab army's finest took the shock of the Templar charge, wavered, but recovered and began to flow up on either side of the Knights. Raymond realized what was going on and screamed at his men to ride closer to the knights, to hammer at the enemy as they tried to outflank the Templars. They collided with a clash of horses, lances, and shields, smashing into each other with tremendous force; the animals biting and thrashing with their forefeet, while their riders thrust lances forward again and again, hoping to find a weak spot. In the melee lances shattered, or lodged in their victims too tightly to be withdrawn; then swords were drawn, or maces and axes were taken up, and the hacking began. Talon saw dark, bearded faces in round helmets crowding close. His sword cut through the shield of the third man he killed, his weapon an instrument of death for anyone who faced it.

Beside him, Yosef, still yelling himself hoarse, slashed and struck with deadly efficiency, and men fell. Sir Matthew, an experienced horseman and warrior, was taking his victims down one by one. The Saxon, using his ax with horrible efficiency, was clearing a path, all the while cursing and swearing in his own language. But something was wrong. They had stopped moving forward! The press of men, horses and bodies was so great that they had completely lost the impetus of the charge. Talon noted with sinking heart that the Templars had also been stopped. Salah Ed Din had enough men that day to absorb the famous and formidable charge of the Templars and arrest them in their tracks!

Then he saw with fury and disgust that Châtillon and his men had failed to support the Hospitaliers, with the result that the Arabs had managed to inflict more damage to the Knights on that flank. The men who had caused this dreadful situation now shirked their duty. Not only that, the Genoese appeared to have given up the ghost. Many archers had fled back up the hill and had scattered, some sitting or lying on the charred ground, their weapons discarded; some were even crying.

Focused on surviving and striking with deadly effect at anyone who came close, Talon listened for the trumpet that would recall them. He was not surprised to hear its brazen sound, ragged but clear, cutting through the screaming and howling of fighting men and the shrieks of those wounded and underfoot being trampled to death.

He banged Yosef on his shield with the pommel of his sword and jerked his head back. He glanced to his side to shout the same words to Sir Matthew, but found he had disappeared, cut down, no doubt, by one of the enemy. The wild Saxon was still laying about him with his bloody axe. The Count bellowed to his men to disengage. Sergeants and commanders of the Templars and Hospitaliers yelled for their men to pull back. The Saxon hauled around his horse to follow Talon and Yosef. Others who had not heard or who, in a fury of battle lust, refused to retreat, stayed behind and were slaughtered.

The survivors rode back up the hill to stop just below the red tent of the King, panting and shaken by their experience. Talon was impressed by the speed with which the Templars formed up to present a solid line, even though they had been forced to retreat. He remembered the discipline. Now he prayed that they would be successful, but he felt a deep sense of unease and foreboding. Salah Ed Din had endured the worst that the Templars could hit him with. The lessons of Montgisard had been harsh, but his people had learned how to absorb the charge. Their tactics at Cresson had been the foretaste for this battle. The Sultan had guessed or known that they would attack his strongest point, at the center, and had probably hoped to lure them in and then kill them all, but Raymond had anticipated that countermove and had thwarted the effort.

All the same, the much feared and deadly Templar charge had clearly failed. With a sinking heart Talon watched Raymond's men as they reformed into a ragged line on either side of the Count. Some of them, including Matthew, were missing, lying wounded or dead in front of the regathering Saracen army. With a glance at the lines of Templars he grimaced to himself with a sense of acute unease. The Christian forces would have to do better than this if they wanted to succeed against now appeared to be very determined foe.

The trumpet sounded and they charged again, thundering down through the dust and ash and smoke to crash into the packed ranks of the enemy. But once again the force of the charge was absorbed in the fighting that ensued. The packed ranks of the Arab army gave a little, but the Sultan managed to bring up sufficient support to hold his line and push back.

Men fell, screaming, and many of the wounded died under the feet of the panicked horses. Riders mad with blood-lust slashed and stabbed at one another with ferocious intensity, and yet again the charge failed. Men pulled back, then straggled back up the hill, either on foot or on horses as weary as themselves to re-form, leaving even more of their comrades behind to be finished off by the triumphant enemy.

Talon and Yosef's mounts were exhausted, their sides heaving and streaked with dried sweat, their heads lowered as they stood with legs apart, awaiting the command to charge again. Men and horses, all were covered in dirt and blood, from other's wounds and their own. Their confidence had been badly shaken and some men wore expressions of despair, while others bore a look of blank resignation, yet all were brave and none wilted as they stared down the hill towards their implacable foes.

The Count himself appeared resigned to his fate, to fall here on the fourth of July at the Horns of Hattin. Talon glanced over towards the center of the Templar line and wondered what the Grand Master Rideford was thinking. The man had been utterly wrong in every decision he had made, Talon reflected with despair.

Talon and Yosef had not escaped unscathed. They were bruised and battered. Talon had garnered a cut on his sword arm; Yosef had a slash on his calf. Yet their wounds were light compared to some.

"Are you able to ride?" Talon asked, looking down at the bloody leg.

"It is nothing, Lord," Yosef said briefly. "It looks worse than it is."

Talon hurriedly dismounted and tied a clean rag tight around Yosef's calf. "That should help, but you need to clean it and dress it when you can," he grunted as he remounted.

They rejoined the group that was sorting itself out prior to another attempt.

*****

Below them the Sultan observed the weakening army opposite and felt deeply relieved. And yet, despite the heat, the thirst and the fires, they were still readying a third attempt. Much hung in the balance. He could hardly believe that his men had weathered two charges from the much vaunted Holy Orders of the Frans. If they had brought all their forces to bear on that first charge, if the archers had brought their arrows into play instead of fleeing and the other flank guard had joined the charge instead of holding back, he could not be sure that his own men would have been able to hold their ground. He had observed the fierce efforts of the Count of Tripoli, a man whom he respected. He knew that respect was reciprocated, but there was not much he could do for the Count with the Templars and Hospitaliers driving so hard at the heart of his own army. He glanced beyond the assembled horsemen, who were clearly making preparations for yet another charge, to the red tent of the Frans King. That was the prize which he could almost taste, it was now so close. He gave an order to his men to bring forward the camels.

None of the Christians had any water, so it was utterly demoralizing for them to see camels arriving at the base of the hill, carrying water which the Arabs then poured into the ground around their former comrades, all the while taunting the grim and silent men on the slopes above them. They grunted with rage, frustration and humiliation, but they had no energy left for more expression. Some licked parched lips with wooden tongues, but most just stared. Many were barely able to lift their swords, while others began to contemplate the hopelessness of their cause and the stark reality of their looming deaths.

For Talon it was almost the final note in this desperate but futile battle for the Holy Land. Fools had squandered all the opportunities, and brave men were now dying for the want of them. The trumpet called, a ragged sound blown by a herald who could not even spit. The bloody and exhausted men formed up one last time.

It was foolhardy but typical of the Templars to aim for the strongest part of the Saracen army, right where the Sultan was seated on his palfrey, watching events unfold before him.

The Count pulled his trembling horse alongside Talon's and pointed to the right flank of the Saracen army, where the auxiliaries and footmen were formed up. "I've had enough of working with Lusignan and Rideford. That is where we will go. We feint for the center, more or less in the same direction the Templars will take, then we veer for the weaker point. Let them break their lances in futile charges. All that will happen is that they will die of exhaustion before he lets them through."

Talon nodded his head, then turned to Yosef. They exchanged looks from bloodshot eyes above parched and cracked lips.

"God help us, Yosef, and may God protect you," Talon told his young friend.

Yosef looked back at his friend and mentor of many years. "God Protect, Talon. *Khoda Hafez*," he croaked, then leaned down and patted his trembling mount's neck, murmuring gentle words.

They tightened their reins and looked to their weapons one last time. Yosef and Talon gripped the shafts of their replacement lances, provided by the frightened stores-men and squires, then moved the short distance to form up knee to knee with the other knights of the Count's army. The rancid smell of horse sweat and of unwashed men all around, coupled with the pervasive stink of fear and blood was almost overpowering, but they were ready.

The trumpets blared; a feeble sound, the trumpeters had no moisture in their mouths, dried out by dust and ash. They tried hard, but their efforts were almost lost in the din of shouting men from the other side and the incessant, nerve-rasping noise of wounded and dying men and horses lying in heaps below the Christian position which only added to the obstacles they had to overcome in order to destroy the Arab army.

Talon felt the line move and flicked his eyes at the Count, who was in the center of his line, next to his banner bearer. Talon heard a roar on his left and glanced over at the depleted ranks of the Templars and Hospitaliers. The double line of knights and sergeants began to move down the hillside at a walk which became a trot, followed soon after by the cry of "Charge!" and then the shout of *'Beauséant!'* As the warrior-monks dug their spurs into the bloody sides of their exhausted mounts, the destriers wearily lurched into a lumbering gallop.

Talon and the men supporting the Count followed, but they kept their eyes on their leader, who was watching for his moment. As they came within fifty paces of the braced enemy, the Count swung his arm to the right.

His entire force turned their mounts at a sharp angle. Instead of smashing against the solid, armored horsemen expecting them, they crashed into the ranks of the foot soldiers and horse auxiliaries, who were quite unprepared for this change in tactics. Raymond and his men swiftly cut through the first ranks, but gradually the resistance stiffened. Suddenly, without any warning, the ranks of the footmen opened and the Count and his men were through and free from the surrounding Arab army. The Count was as surprised as any of his men, but after a short glance back at the hill from where they had just come, he turned to face ahead and spurred his mount forward. Raymond and his men rode on, leaving the field of battle behind.

As he surged forward, an arrow penetrated Talon's thigh a hand's breadth above the knee. He felt the point grate on the bone as it penetrated. He looked down and saw the fletch on one side of his leg and the barb protruding from the other. Before he could react, other than with an involuntary cry of agony, his horse began to fall. An arrow had struck his mount almost at the same time. Talon knew then that he was a dead man. He and the horse fell together to join the bloody bodies on the ground, and as he tumbled over its head he could see the rest of the Count's party leaving him behind. With a feeling of utter despair he allowed himself to fall with the horse. His sword went one way and he another as his mount screamed and nosed into the sand. He tried to roll, but because of his wound, it was more of a sprawl. Talon had just risen to his hands and knees when he felt a terrible blow on the back of his head. The world went black and he sprawled face down into the bloody soil, while the battle raged all around him and the Count of Tripoli drove on to safety with his men.

Yosef was not aware that Talon had fallen until he had ridden a good forty paces ahead. When he did notice that his lord was not with them, he could not go back to find him. The Saracens had closed ranks, and he faced an impenetrable hedge of spears, and worse, flying arrows. Anguished, he whirled his horse and rode after the departing Count. He swore he would be back, but there was black despair in his chest. The Count did not look back, even when Yosef called out to him. The only man who did was Brandt, who reined in and joined Yosef to face a bristling ranks of infantry who were beginning to take an unhealthy interest in them.

"You saw him fall?" the Saxon asked.

Yosef shook his head. He was weeping with anger and frustration at being unable to help Talon, but their own situation was becoming untenable, with hurled javelins landing nearby. He whirled his animal and galloped off, with the Saxon just behind. When they were clear of the struggling armies he reined in again and took a mental fix on where the Count had broken through the Sultan's infantry. He would be back that night.

It was clear to him that the Christians were on their last legs. The third, desperate charge by the Templars and Hospitaliers had failed, and the weary knights were trailing back up the hill towards the red tent of the King of Jerusalem. He noticed that the footmen, the Genoese and the auxiliaries were just milling about without any purpose. The end was very near.

Brant joined him and began to speak rapidly in his own tongue, which Yosef could not understand. Cursing, the Saxon pointed to the crest of the hill, still occupied by King Guy Lusignan and his officers. Then he turned his horse and slowly rode after the fleeing Count.

Yosef came back later at night. He left his horse in a small grove of low trees by the waters of the Sea of Galilee, hoping that no one would discover the animal. If they did, he was in for a very long walk. Taking a chance, he brazenly walked through the encampment of celebrating soldiers and camp followers, then made for the battlefield itself. There he wandered about the area where he thought Talon might have fallen. No one challenged him, for he was easily mistaken by the pillagers and scavengers for one of the Arab foot soldiers. He was, after all, dressed very much like them.

There were many that night who prowled the field, plundering the corpses for their armor, weapons, ornaments, gold and coin, or whatever else they could take off the dead.

Yosef saw a man hold up an odd looking sword and examine its workmanship by the light of the thin moon. Yosef recognized the curved blade immediately; it had belonged to Talon. At the sight of it his heart lifted. He hastened up to the man, who staring at the weapon curiously. Yosef's hand closed over the scavenger's mouth and he slipped his knife into the back of the luckless fellow, who struggled violently for a few long moments before sagging in his arms. Yosef laid him down on the ground and retrieved the fallen sword. In the dim light of the nearby torches, he knew without a doubt that the sword belonged to Talon.

He slipped the weapon into his sash, careful of its incredibly sharp edge, and continued to search for any sign of his leader. It was fruitless, gruesome work which brought him close to retching, as he turned over one disemboweled corpse or headless body after another. He could not find any sign of Talon anywhere. He searched until dawn lit the sky on the horizon, when he concentrated even harder on finding his fallen Lord.

Most of the scavengers were gone by then, some chased off by friends of fallen comrades, to whom they wished to give proper burial. Salah Ed Din's army had not won without heavy losses. To his growing despair Yosef found nothing. He did, however, find Talon's horse. It lay on its side, stripped of its saddle and accoutrements, with an arrow protruding from its chest. Yosef recognized the white mark on its forehead and the white sock on its near foreleg. Someone had obviously put it out of its misery; its jugular had been slashed open, but there was no sign of its rider.

Yosef cast a bleak look about him. The field was littered with the dead, horses and men lying in heaps where the fighting had been at its most savage, but also scattered thinly about over a wide area. The carrion birds were already coming in from everywhere. The stink of death had brought them in great flocks: black crows and vultures converging on a feast beyond reckoning.

The human scavengers who had swarmed the field during the night had succeeded in stripping the dead of their clothing and anything remotely valuable, leaving only naked corpses and broken shafts of spears, useless scraps of leather and iron, and the odd broken sword hilt. The stench of blood and faeces was so powerful so that it forced Yosef to cover his face with a part of his loose turban. The ground was blackened by the fires that the Sultan had ordered his army to light the night before the battle.

A thinning pall of smoke still hung over the battlefield from fires that continued to smolder. In his wanderings Yosef drifted towards the area where Salah Ed Din had accepted the surrender of the King of Jerusalem. The headless bodies of many former Christian men were sprawled in scattered heaps. Piles of heads were massed nearby.

He paled with horror as he stared at the pallid faces and dead eyes. His first fear was that Talon might be among the dead here, but then he noticed something significant. All the heads were bearded, unkempt, with long, straggling hair. He was certain Talon was not among these corpses. Just then another man, one of many still poking around the field, ambled over. Jerking his thumb at the headless heaps, he said, "God has had his revenge. The Sultan took the heads of all the Templar infidels. These and these alone he beheaded. I think it is because he fears them so much. Nonetheless, he broke one of the laws."

Yosef was almost too shaken to say anything. He just nodded, but then he asked, "How did he break a law?"

"The law says that when a man surrenders he is to be protected, but the Sultan broke that law." Then he walked off.
Yosef was glad of the man's lack of interest in his presence.
As far as anyone was concerned, he was just another soldier
who had been in the battle.

A few dozen paces away, a couple of foot soldiers were
arguing over a piece of gold chain they had found. "This is
meagre fare compared to the ransom some of those infidel
lords will be able to pay," one of them complained. "We only
get the scraps, we who did all the fighting, while our masters
get all the gold from the ransoms!"

"There were few enough of them taken for ransom, even
after the Sultan, May God preserve him forever and forgive
him for sinning, executed all those Templar whoresons."

A tiny flicker of hope arose in Yosef's breast. He wandered over to where the two men were standing. At their feet
were several half-naked corpses, Franks without a doubt, but
as far as he could tell, Talon was not one of them.

"God's blessings on you, friends. I could not help over-
hearing you," he said with an ingratiating smile. "Did you say
that some of the Frankish lords were captured and are now
prisoners of Lord Sultan, may God protect him always?" he
touched his heart in a pious gesture as he spoke.

"Very few, but some. God be praised, the King of the infidels was captured, as were some of his lords, God damn
them. Not many others, though," one of the men responded
without looking up.

———

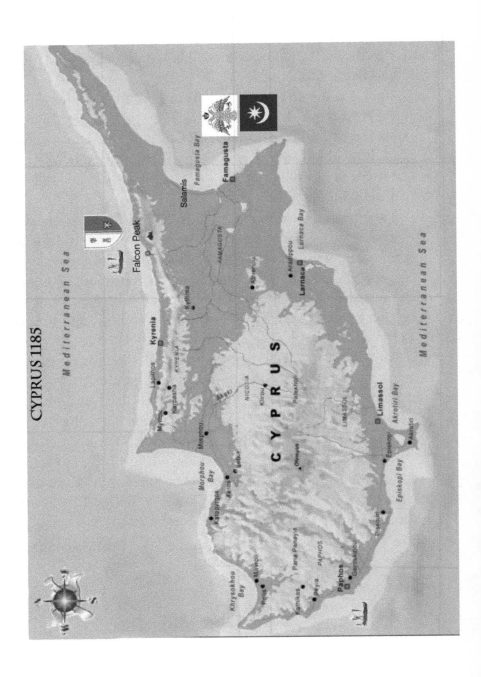

Chapter 16

Intruders

Treacherous time has put me in prison
where I've chirped away like a bird in a snare.
How pure and fine my inspiration
is, and was, and will be there.

—*Yosef Giqatilla*

As dawn brightened over Tiberius to illuminate the carnage of the Battle of Hattin, the skies above were dark with
carrion eaters. They had come to feast.

The sun also rose over the palace in Famagusta, the capital of Cyprus. Diocles the Chief Minister awoke after a restless night, during which he had worried over reports con-
cerning not only the Emperor but the Ambassador. It wasn't
exactly news to Diocles that Isaac had regained his virility;
there had been a lessening in the intensity of the all too familiar rants echoing along corridors, and the general behavior of the erratic man had calmed down; the eunuchs had informed him of the visit to Tamura's quarters. They also told
Diocles of something else that had occurred at more or less
the same time the previous evening.

Without doubt, they reported, the Ambassador had been
seen leaving the palace, disguised as an entertainer, escorted
by Siranos. They believed that the Ambassador had been in

Tamura's apartment at more or less the same time the Emperor had arrived!

Diocles was consumed with alarm and curiosity. When a suitable hour arrived, he paid a visit to Tamura, who greeted him calmly enough and offered him wine and sweet cakes as she normally did. However, she appeared to be brimming over with barely suppressed excitement.

The Chief Minister allowed himself to be led to the table where the sweetmeats were laid out and a silver beaker stood full of wine beside two cups. He sat down, keeping his face impassive. He poured wine and raised a cup to Tamura, who responded in kind, but then blurted out, "I have news!"

"I dare say you have, my Lady," Diocles replied. "Pray do tell me."

"The Ambassador is here for the gold," she said in a low, conspiratorial manner. Diocles frowned and said, "I think we more or less agreed that he probably was."

"But he is *only* here for the gold, nothing more! And I think he and Zenos are hatching a plan."

"How do you know this, my Lady?"

"Well, I, er, I invited him here, and he told me!" she exclaimed.

"Yes, I know, my Lady. Have you any idea how foolish that was? You not only endangered his life but your own!"

She shook her head impatiently, making her curls jump about her flawless features.

"I needed to make sure. He is here for the gold that was stolen by Pantoleon. He actually said it!" She chortled with glee.

Diocles frowned again. 'The problem with this, my Lady, is *how* you obtained the information."

Tamura looked annoyed. "I didn't do what you are thinking, Diocles!" she protested indignantly.

He shook his head and smiled. "No, I am sure not, my Lady, but don't you see that the Emperor or the Gatherer of Information will *assume* you did, should you say anything at all?" He shook his head again.

Tamura looked hurt, then pensive. "What if we warned them?"

"Warn who?"

"You know perfectly well who I am talking about, Diocles." Her pretty eyebrows came together in a frown.

"Yes, yes I do," he conceded. "We should warn the Lord Talon. Leave it with me. I'll deal with it... somehow," he ended, sounding vague.

He had a lot to ponder. When Zenos had left for Beirut, Diocles had had one of his eunuchs search the man's private quarters. Later that day the man had brought a bar of gold to him and described where he had found it. The stamp and the other markings matched the gold bars in the treasury. Diocles had gone on his own to the locked chamber and verified both the amounts against his records and the similarity of the bars. The tally had been one bar short. After that, there had been no doubt in his mind that Zenos had helped himself to the bar.

This alone was enough to have the man executed, but Diocles wanted to find out more. If there was something going on between the Ambassador and Zenos, he would need solid proof if he was going to denounce the two of them to the Emperor and remove them both. Going after Zenos precipitously might warn the Ambassador to be more circumspect. Thoughtfully, he returned to his room and summoned the eunuch, giving him instructions to replace the gold bar where he had found it, and followed to watch as he did so. He had resolved to bide his time.

Events were to take an unexpected turn. Diocles and the Commander of the Guard finally managed to persuade Isaac that the depredations of the pirates called for some defensive or retaliatory action on his part. Weeks before, Diocles had suggested a visit to the harbor of Limassol to inspect some towers that the merchants had begun to construct, pointing out that the Emperor should be there to endorse them and also to help finance them. The commander of the mercenaries, when consulted in Isaac's dilatory way, had agreed. Three days later, Isaac abruptly departed with his usual entourage—but without Diocles. Nor did he take Tamura, and she was uncertain what that meant. Was he growing tired of her?

"I shall see what can be done about those pirates the merchants are always complaining about," the Emperor had told Diocles. "They will have to pay me for my endeavors, of course!" No doubt he wanted to avoid hearing Diocles plead with him to pay for the construction with money from the treasury. "Make sure that those roof repairs are carried out, and keep a close eye on that so-called ambassador. I have no reason to trust him, but as long as he is kept under a close watch there isn't much he can do. When I get back, I shall decide what to do about him."

Diocles was quite sure that the Emperor had no intention of paying for any deterrence that would ward off the pirates, even though their depredations were becoming a real problem. His intent, Diocles was sure, was to gouge the merchants for what he could squeeze out of them, and take their young daughters to bed. Now that he had regained some of his vitality, he seemed intent upon spreading it about again as much as he could. Diocles had watched the Emperor and his colorful mercenaries depart with mixed feelings.

Zenos returned from his travels a day after the departure of the Emperor. There was a distinct change to his manner that did not go unnoticed by Diocles, whose antennae were always well tuned. Zenos, for some reason, appeared much more confident, and addressed the Chief Minister with less respect than before. He was also accompanied by some new faces, which the minister found very disturbing. These were rough-looking, and, while they were not unlike the Emperor's men in appearance, these seemed to be loyal to Zenos.

Like all the people with any influence in the palace, Diocles had his own cadre of spies, eunuchs for the most part, who drifted about the palace on one errand or another, watching and then reporting. The Chief Minister ordered that Zenos be watched even more closely, and learned that he paid another visit to the villa housing the Ambassador. He also visited a place where some very sinister men, youths really, were now living, and these men had arrived more or less at the same time Zenos had returned. They kept to themselves and didn't go out into the town, which was somewhat odd, as there was much to entertain young men.

Diocles began to wonder whether it had been a good idea for Isaac to depart after all, but he had already left for Limassol and Larnaca, taking with him the bulk of his personal bodyguard. This left the palace guards outnumbered by the newcomers, which was profoundly disturbing to Diocles. He wondered if a coup was about to take place. Zenos might feel inclined to some excess or other.

Then there was the unsettling news that finally reached Diocles, informing him that Zenos had not traveled to Paphos at all. Where, then, had he been? Diocles vowed to confront the Gatherer of Information. It was not that man's provenance to bring complete strangers into the palace without asking the Chief Minister. Diocles, however, did want to tread carefully, because the unpredictable Emperor might have sanctioned Zenos's behavior. All the same, he felt that he did have enough cause for alarm to send out a warning to the people on the mountain, and he set about preparing a letter which could be delivered via pigeon.

What Diocles didn't know was that some of Zenos' new acquaintances were roaming the palace, unremarked by the palace staff and unnoticed by his spies. These were young men who looked fresh-faced and innocent; residents assumed they were new additions to Isaac's collection of hostages. And so they investigated every corner they could access without drawing attention to themselves, and one of them noticed something.

The old, balding man who seemed to be in charge of everything occasionally went alone up the winding steps of a tower. Out of sheer curiosity, the assassins decided to investigate. They found a collection of healthy looking pigeons. That would have been normal enough; people kept pigeons, primarily for food; but as they examined the contents of the room, it became evident that these birds were kept for another purpose.

The next day, one young assassin brought Zenos up to the tower. There, amid the sounds of rustles and throaty cooing, he showed Zenos the birds, but also the bands that fitted around their legs, and a small copper tube on a shelf. There was even a scrap of paper with some writing on it. Although he could not make out the message, Zenos was deeply alarmed. The Chief Minister was a spy! But for whom? And did that fool Isaac know? Zenos saw an opportunity here. It might be his chance to get rid of the old man—and take his place.

"We lay a trap for him. Let me know immediately the next time he comes up here. I want to catch him at whatever it is he is up to," he ordered the youth.

Two days later, one of the newcomers came sidling up to Zenos and whispered into his ear. Zenos jerked upright, terminated his meeting then and there, and followed the youth out of the main palace. Together they hurried across empty gardens, heading for the small tower. They slipped up the steps and found Diocles holding a pigeon in his hands, just about to release it. Zenos could not fail to see the small copper cylinder attached to one of its legs.

"Stop what you are doing this minute!" he called out as he mounted the final step and charged into the small chamber. Diocles was caught by surprise, but not completely. He made one step towards the window and released the bird, which fluttered away.

The youth beside Zenos moved with lightning speed. He had equipped himself with a bow when he had assumed surveillance of the tower, and this he now unslung from his shoulder. The assassin darted outside onto the parapet, an arrow appeared as though from nowhere, and the bow string twanged. It was a virtually impossible shot by any standard, but the arrow struck its target and the stricken bird fluttered to the ground just outside the walls palace. Diocles was aghast, but Zenos was triumphant.

"We have you now, you traitor!" he snarled, as he strode forward and struck the old man in his face. Diocles raised his arms to protect himself, but Zenos struck him to the ground. "Guards!" he roared, "To me now!"

Sentries and some of the newcomers who had heard him crowded into the small chamber. The Emperor's mercenaries looked shocked and unsure, but the newcomers were ready enough to follow orders. "Take this man to the dungeons and keep him under lock and guard. Now!" Zenos bellowed. "Someone go and fetch that pigeon."

As the bewildered sentries lifted the dazed and bleeding Chief Minister to his feet, Zenos hissed at him, "You are a dead man now, old man."

Once they had all departed, leaving Zenos and his assassin alone, he turned to the youth and said, "With the Emperor gone, now is the best time for us to act. However, there are other spies in this palace. One of them is the eunuch of the Princess Tamura. I want him watched and followed wherever he goes outside. Nothing must get in our way, and the very last thing I want is for the Emperor, or anyone else, to know what we are about." The youth nodded and went off to talk to his companions.

One of the sentries returned and handed Zenos the dead pigeon. Removing the arrow, he studied the fletching. These strange youths who belonged to Rashid Ed Din were Djinn; their skill in the arts of death was all they existed for. Then he examined the pigeon's leg. Sure enough, there was a small copper cylinder attached. This he removed, then pulled off the tight fitting cap. Inside he found a tiny roll of paper with very small writing on both sides.

Scanning it, Zenos became frustrated. It was no language he recognized. Realizing it was some kind of code, he cursed, but then shrugged. It would be easy enough to extract information from the old man, he told himself. Meanwhile, the day after tomorrow was the day for their plan to go into effect, and he had preparations to attend to. The old man could stew in prison until Zenos was ready to 'talk' to him.

It would only complicate his plans to inform the Emperor at this stage, he decided. The last thing he wanted was a precipitous return, so keeping the minister out of the way and under wraps until he had obtained the gold was probably the best course. Who knew? Perhaps the Emperor himself might.... He let that thought drift away. First things first.

Unbeknownst to the Gatherer of Information, Siranos heard of the arrest of Diocles very soon after the event. He watched from the shadows as the old man was hurried down the stairs towards the dungeons. Then Siranos, who was himself becoming good at moving about the palace unobserved, sped to his lady's chambers, and after a light knock was bid to enter. Martina, Tamura's servant girl, let him in. Her eyes widened with alarm at the expression on his face.

"Oh, my Lady, all is lost!" he moaned to Tamura, sinking to his knees in front of her.

"Oh, for Goodness sake! What is it this time, Siri?" she demanded impatiently. She wasn't in the mood for his dramatics today. "Martina, be a dear and bring him a cup of water," she commanded.

"The Gatherer of Information has arrested the Chief Minister!" Siranos wailed. He looked sick.

Tamura put her hand to her mouth in astonishment and alarm. "Tell me, tell me everything!" she commanded, trying desperately to keep calm. Siranos told her what he had seen.

She turned away, horrified, murmuring, "Oh, the poor man! But there is nothing to connect us... is there?" She tried to recall if Zenos had ever seen her talking with the Chief Minister. "What was he doing in the dovecot?" she demanded, curious.

"I... I believe he was sending a pigeon somewhere, my Lady," he sobbed.

Tamura went pale and sat down hard on one of he cushions. "He was trying to send a message to the people on the hill!" she whispered, as the realization struck her. "Oh God, what will we do now?"

"One of those terrible new people hanging around Zenos killed the bird," Siranos choked. "He shot the pigeon in mid flight! A servant I know was sent to retrieve the bird, and he showed it to me."

Martina nearly spilled the water, her hand shook so badly as she handed the goblet to Siranos. She, too, gave a low moan of terror; her eyes were like saucers as they stared at Tamura, looking for reassurance. Instinctively Tamura reached out for the girl and embraced her, although she was in dire need of comfort herself. Holding the sobbing and fearful girl to her breast, she thought hard.

Now Diocles would be accused of treason, and executed. Zenos would see to that. The Emperor would feel betrayed, and thus be vengeful. She shuddered, feeling very alone. Diocles had provided some kind of sanity in an otherwise chaotic world where unpredictability was the norm and no one really knew how to anticipate the moods of the Emperor.

Her mind raced. There was no doubt that Zenos was involved in something underhanded. The constant visits to the Ambassador, the strange and sinister youths who had arrived from God knew where and only did his bidding, and now this. It all added up to something very menacing, but against whom? Was it the man on the mountain, as she and Diocles had begun to suspect? But what if a coup was planned against Isaac himself? She finally concluded that, either way, it was about the gold. How could it not be? From what she had gleaned from Diocles, the treasure was vast. These people would stop at nothing to get to it, of that she was now sure. But what to tell the Emperor?

Siranos had by now regained some of his composure. His next words echoed her own thoughts. "My lady, have either you or the Chief Minister shared your concerns with His Majesty?"

She shook her head. "No, other than telling him we didn't trust the Ambassador at the onset, we were not sure enough of anything else."

"And now the Chief Minister is in prison, accused of treason." Siranos paused, a frightened look on his young face. "If he is tortured, he might reveal that you are in his confidences, my Lady. You will be implicated!"

"Think how that would look to His Majesty, my Lady," Martina interjected. "He would see it as a double betrayal, and decide against the Chief Minister in favor of the Gatherer of Information. You mustn't warn the Emperor, or he will suspect you take Diocles' side. And if that man accuses you, you must deny everything."

Tamura stared at them aghast, knowing full well that Martina was right. She could be quite level-headed on occasion.

"They are definitely up to something evil," she said. "I wish I knew how to stop them and make sure the Emperor is not misled. I'm almost sure it is about that stolen gold."

Siranos nodded his head vigorously. "I agree with you on that my Lady. You must write a warning to the Greek in the town. He will know where to send it."

Tamura agreed. "I shall write the letter tonight, and you must take it to him tomorrow, Siranos."

Tamura spent that evening composing a letter, outlining all she knew and whom she suspected, then spent a restless night. The next day, early in the morning, Siranos slipped out of the palace with his usual care and headed for the wine house, where he hoped to meet with Dimitri. He was unaware of a slim figure waiting in the street, who began to shadow him. The Assassin quietly followed at a discreet distance; Siranos appeared to be more cautious than the average man simply out for a stroll or running an errand. The frequent backward Siranos cast behind forced the youth to lag more than he usually would. As a result, the youth almost missed the doorway into which Siranos disappeared.

Siranos had felt uneasy almost as soon as he left the palace, but no matter how many times he checked for followers he could not see anyone. Nevertheless, his fears persisted, so that by the time he was able to slip onto a bench next to the messenger he was sweating, and it was not from the heat of the day. This time the messenger was not Dimitri himself, but one of his servants. Without pausing to exchange greetings, Siranos thrust the letter into the man's hand. "Something terrible has happened in the palace. You must give this note immediately to your leader," Siranos stammered, with a long glance at the curtained doorway. "I am sure I was followed, but I did not see anyone."

Khuzaymah gave him a sharp look as he tucked the letter away in the depths of his loose robes. His glance flicked to the doorway, but there was no one there. Whoever was following Siranos, if indeed there was someone, was obviously not going to fall into the trap of walking into a place like this without looking it over carefully first. He gestured to Maymun, who came over and sat on a bench nearby.

"He thinks there is someone following him," Khuzaymah told Maymun in a terse undertone. "We'll follow him back to the palace, but not just yet. Let's lay a trap. If there is anyone, they will follow him to the market." He turned back to Siranos, who had just gulped some of the sour brew that the proprietor called wine. "Do you have money on you?" he asked.

"Y... yes, I do." Siranos reached for his coin, thinking that he was going to have to pay for the drinks.

"Good. Go spend it in the market, as though you were sent on an errand," Khuzaymah told him. "We will be following, so don't worry about your back. Now get up and walk out slowly. Don't look back, not even once! Just go and buy something, then go back to the palace. D'you think you can do this?"

Siranos's head bobbed up and down. He stood up, knocking over the rest of the wine with a spasm of his right arm, and forced himself to saunter out the door of the inn.

"Do you think he can do something as simple as this?" Maymun asked, sounding doubtful.

"He's shitting himself, but self preservation is part of being a spy. I think he will manage," was the laconic response. The two men eased themselves out of the bar. They were just in time to see Siranos disappear around a corner, but their sharp eyes saw something else of interest.

There was indeed a follower. Both men tensed, then fell back into their roles of hunters. Reza had trained them well, so they were extremely careful. Their caution was justified, for the man trailing Siranos behaved in a manner familiar to them both. Maymun shot Khuzaymah a concerned look. This one knew what he was about; it was almost as if he, too, had trained under Reza.

Siranos made directly for the market and loitered casually near the herbs and soap stalls. The market was not very crowded, as it was still early morning. People were eating breakfast, making preparations for the day ahead. Siranos examined the scented bars of soap, feeling and sniffing them, while glancing about surreptitiously. He eventually paid a few coins for a small package, which the owner of the stall presented to him. He turned away and strolled towards the palace. His eyes were still nervously searching, not only for his follower, whom he was sure was still there, but also for the two men belonging to the Greek.

He saw no one at all even remotely resembling anyone who might be tracking him, nor the other two. At one point he did run into a young man with a covering over his head, who appeared to be in a hurry. They disengaged with a grunt of apology, and Siranos continued on his way. The encounter would normally have been unremarkable. People were forever bumping into one another in the narrow streets; it could have been an accident, or at worst a pickpocket trying his luck. In his present state of paranoia, however, Siranos was shaken and looked back over his shoulder. The man had vanished, and again neither of the Greek's men were to be seen.

*****

"Did you deliver the message?" Tamura demanded, as soon as Martina let him inside the chamber. He looked pale and frightened.

"Yes, my Lady. The Greek was not there, but two of his men were. But I know I was followed," he all but whimpered.

Tamura went cold all over. "So he suspects!" she whispered. "But they have the message?" she repeated.

Siranos nodded and sipped a cup of water Martina gave him. "They have the message, and they told me to go to the market and make a small purchase as my reason for leaving the palace," he told her. "I never saw them after that, but someone bumped into me when I was on my way back here. I think it was the man who followed me! His head and face were covered but... there was something familiar about him."

"What do you mean?" she asked.

"The way he moved so quietly reminds me of those youths who accompany Zenos, my Lady. Maybe even the one who shot the pigeon. His hands were everywhere on me! He was looking for something. If he had done that before I delivered the message.... Oh God, I am so scared," he whispered, his face was as pale as a ghost.

Martina gave a low wail and Tamura closed her eyes. "Then we must pray to God that the people at the castle act upon my letter, or we are all lost," she said.

*****

Khuzaymah and Maymun had not failed to notice the incident. They were well versed in this tactic, and its familiarity disturbed them. The youth who had bumped into Siranos had checked thoroughly for any kind of letter or message.

"It's a good thing we have the letter, or it would have gone badly for that boy. We have to follow this one and find out where he is going," Khuzaymah muttered. Maymun nodded agreement.

"The boy should count himself lucky the other only wanted to search him. I thought for a moment he was going to get knifed," Maymun commented. "I nearly broke cover to grab him."

To their astonishment, the figure they shadowed also went to the palace and was allowed entrance by the guards. He disappeared inside the grounds while the two men looked at one another.

"Tell Dimitri what is going on, Maymun. Take the letter with you," Khuzaymah told him. "I shall stay here and see if that man comes out from the palace again."

Dimitri's initial response was to shake his head and sigh. "More palace intrigues! Can't these people get along for just a little while?" After he read the letter, however, his whole demeanor changed. "Maymun!" he called. Maymun hurried into to the room to find his chief looking very out of sorts. "You two were right to follow that man. There is big trouble brewing at the palace. Khuzaymah is watching there?"

"Yes, but there are many entrances. He can only watch the one."

"Get back over there, and take two of our men with you. You are just to watch and find out whatever you can. Most certainly do not be noticed." Dimitri went on to tell him of the contents of the letter and his concerns. "I must send a pigeon out tomorrow morning. It's too late now, and we need to know more, if possible, before I send a message."

That evening Maymun and two other men joined Khuzaymah in the shadows of the narrow streets near the palace. Khuzaymah told them what he had seen thus far.

"Four more men of similar dress went into the palace not long after the first one, but nothing since."

"Dimitri says that we should find out where they live in town," Maymun said. So they waited while the sun set in a blaze of red and orange colors and the air cooled, bringing more people out onto the streets. Candles were lit, and it became less easy to see who passed through the entrances to the palace. Yet their patience was finally rewarded. Not long after dark, eight hooded figures emerged from the trader's entrance and made off towards the eastern gates of the city.

The four companions followed at a discreet distance and observed them leave through the gates, after having presented the guards with some document or other allowing them to depart. The curfew being in place, the document had to have come from some authority within the palace itself. Khuzaymah and his companions made their way back to their lodgings to report to Dimitri.

"They appear as skilled in stealth as we are. And they were carrying bows, quivers and swords," Maymun responded, when Dimitri asked him for his opinion. "But whatever mischief they are here for, it seems the palace is safe from them—at least for tonight.

Dimitri and his men spent several hours trying to piece together the events of the day. Finally Dimitri decided that, although he did not have all the facts, since the Chief Minister had been thrown into the dungeons for trying to send a pigeon to the castle, it was incumbent upon him to send a message to the castle in the morning. Pigeons didn't travel at night, otherwise he would have sent one there and then. There was even a full moon, but he knew better than to chance a bird's life with the predators of the night.

As the first light of dawn paled the sky to the east, Dimitri sent the creature on its way and watched as it gained height and then turned north. Its destination was the castle of Kantara.

Chapter 17

The Shield Walls

Sword, how fair and bright thou art.
Come thou forth and view the light,
Long as I can wield thee here
Charles my Emperor shall not say
That I die alone, unwept.
—from *The Legend of Roland*

A few leagues to the west of the Kantara harbor there is a long, deep inlet that could easily harbor a ship, either to protect it from the Mediterranean storms that can spring up in a moment, or to hide it from prying eyes. It is the nearest of several inlets along that particular stretch of Cyprus coast.

It was for the latter reason that two small ships stealthily nosed their way into the inlet during the night. The full moon allowed the captains and their men to see their way clearly, and they had little difficulty guiding the ships past the dangerous rocks on either side of the narrow channel. The bright moonlight gleamed off the water, and the only sound was of low ripples that pushed up and drew back from the small sandy beach with a gentle rustling sound, almost as though the sea itself were breathing quietly in its sleep. Once they were through the neck, the inlet opened out just enough to allow the ships to be turned with oars; then anchors were lowered, without splashes, into the water.

On either side and overlooking the beach were low cliffs, atop of which grew small, stunted pines forming the beginnings of a forest which extended up into the mountains several leagues to the south. The trees here were interspersed with grassy spaces where goat herders could take their flocks. Aware that some might be in the vicinity even now, the crews were silent, apart from the occasional hoarse whisper. Quietly they rowed to the beach where they assembled, waiting for the order to set off.

Their objective was the village harbor of Kantara, and they wanted to get there just before dawn. Some men hefted spears, sabers, and shields, while others checked their bows and arrows. Upon a low-voiced order, all of them followed the scouts up a narrow dirt path leading to the top of the cliff. Below them, the ships gently rose and fell with the swell from the sea. The men were alert and tense, but apart from the hoot of an owl in the distant forest and the rustle of small animals in the undergrowth, all was quiet. They crested the cliff and set off in single file towards the distant village.

*****

Just one half league from the inlet, Kostas woke up and listened to the night. The boy was well tuned to the sounds around him during the day, but particularly at night when the larger predators, such as foxes, would roam the hills and sometimes try to pick off a sheep, lamb or goat caught unawares. He usually slept close to his animals, which were quite used to their human guardian and remained bunched up in his vicinity at night.

Kostas rubbed his eyes and stared at the animals. They were absolutely silent, but every one of them was clearly listening, their long ears pricked to catch the faintest sound. By the bright orb of the full moon he could see that they were all wide awake and nervous, staring in the direction of the long inlet to his north. Thinking there might be some large predator nearby, he fumbled for his spear and moved into a crouch and stared hard in the same direction as his animals.

Then he saw them. Below the hillside, a long line of dark figures was moving stealthily in the direction of his village. He could see that they were heavily armed, their spears glinting in the moonlight.

He glanced up at the sky and estimated that it was some hours before dawn. There was no time to lose. His heart pounding, he slipped away from his animals—they would have to fend for themselves while he was gone. He trotted along a path only he and the other boy shepherds knew. Once well out of sight of the animals, he began to run as fast as he could through the long grass, nettles, and brambles that tore at his bare legs.

Kostas arrived at the village outskirts to find that there was no one to challenge him. He shouted as he ran among the huts and finally found two of the guards who should have been further out keeping watch. Both had been asleep.

"What is it?" they demanded gruffly of the breathless boy, who pointed behind him. "P-pirates! They are coming!" he gasped.

"You sure?" One of the guards demanded skeptically, but he pushed his mate. "Go and warn the captains, now!" he ordered, and then seized the boy by the arm. "You're not playing the fool now are you, Kostas?" he growled.

"No! Do you think I would leave my sheep unguarded for a joke? They are coming. There are many of them! Ouch, you're hurting me!" The boy wriggled free and ran off. "Sound the alarm! It's real!" he yelled.

The guard shook his head. Pirates! "Dear God, is there never peace from these people!" he muttered, then began to run and shout, "Alarm! Pirates! Go to the harbor!"

People came to their doors, bewildered and rubbing sleep from their eyes. "What is it? Who? Where?" they demanded.

"To the west, at least that is what Kostas is saying. Go to the harbor! Hurry!" the guard shouted.

By this time the second guard had alerted the men who guarded the houses where the captains slept. Henry, Guy, and their men tumbled groggily out of bed and scrambled into their clothes.

"Are there ships? Did the castle send up a flare? Where are they coming from?" Henry bellowed, as he ran outside with his jacket only half on.

"The boy said they were coming overland, Captain. They are going to be here very soon."

"Get everyone we can onto the ships. Move!" Guy shouted. His men rushed off to obey. Already there were people hurrying onto the quayside with small bundles of belongings. Sleepy and frightened children were wailing, while their mothers tried to hush them. Some families even had their domestic animals in tow.

An excited donkey began to bray; sheep bleated in panic while dogs barked, adding to the general sense of chaos, alarm and peril.

"No animals! Leave them, leave them behind or we leave you!" Guy shouted at a stubborn villager. "Get all the women and children onto the boats. You men, get over here with my guards and form a group." The village men had brought spears and some shields, for Talon and Reza had decided some time ago that the village should be able to defend itself and had provided arms and training. Even so, Henry was fully aware that they would be no match for a large band of determined pirates.

"Guy!" he called over to his friend. "How many men-at-arms do we have? Other than crew."

Guy looked around the busy quayside. "Ten at best, and the villagers, which brings us to about thirty able men. Some of the fishermen are gone out fishing already."

Henry cursed under his breath. "We keep the men here on the street with us, but send a rider to alert Max!"

Guy nodded and detailed off a young man, who rushed off to the stables to saddle a horse. Within minutes the lad was galloping up the track to the castle on the mountain. "I wish we had rockets that could warn them up there, as they can us," Henry muttered, but then he had an idea.

"Nico, you know how to use the scorpion, don't you?" he called to one of his crewmen, who was helping some women and children onto his ship.

"Yes, Captain."

"Get two men and load it, then point it as high as you can. Send off a rocket! Now!" Henry yelled. The man darted away, pulling two other crewmen with him. That was going to take a while. Meanwhile the women, young children and older people were being hustled onto the three ships tied alongside the quay. All they had to do was to stand off from the shore, but they needed to hurry. The nervous husbands and youths were being shepherded into squads on the quayside.

Guy grabbed a passing man-at-arms. "Find another man, and go tell the guards in the two towers to make their Scorpions ready for a possible attack from the sea, and to lock themselves in. Then get back here; we need every man," he ordered.

The wide-eyed man rushed off to tell another, and the two of them scampered towards the squat, almost completed towers that dominated the entrance of the harbor.

Henry shook his head. He was sure he knew who it was who was bringing the pirates. Abul-Zinad had returned. He couldn't help thinking that if Talon or Reza had been in command of such a raid, they would have made a better go of it. They would have sent in burning fishing boats to ignite the moored ships, and stealthy scouts to neutralize the towers before making any kind of land attack. He was very, very glad Abul-Zinad had not done so.

If the pirates cannot hear this noise they are as deaf as stones! Henry thought, as he looked over the milling, wailing, shouting crowd on the quayside. Just then there was a gasp from one of the villagers, who called out, "Fire! God help us, the pirates are here!" The man pointed to the east of the village, where a glow of light that did not come from the moon was beginning to grow.

Henry whirled. "Form the men up here with me!" he bellowed. "Shield wall, now!" Men ran to assemble in a ragged line, facing one of the two eastern exits that led onto the quay. Their shields were interlocked and the front row had spears pointing up, while the second row placed their shields overlapping those of the front row and held their spears at the ready. Men who lacked spears clustered on the wings, fingering their swords, axes, and clubs. Henry was pleased that no one stabbed anyone else by accident this time. During the drills, small accidents had occurred frequently. They finally managed to sort themselves, then Henry and one of his lieutenants guided them so that they were stood wall to wall between two buildings.

Guy followed suit with his group of men, so that both entrances to the harbor were now blocked by armed men. This tactic had been worked out with Talon some time ago. His experience in Byzantium during a huge battle against the Turks had convinced him that a shield wall could be effective, even with relatively inexperienced troops.

Henry looked behind him. Almost all the women and children were now aboard, and the ships' crews were waiting for his orders. "Push off into the middle of the harbor!" Henry called to his coxswain. "All the boats. Arm the Scorpions." He turned his gaze to the east and noticed that the red, flaring glow had become more intense. Anyone who had been left behind must now seek the shelter of the castle or the forest. He could do no more for the village.

There was a sizzling sound, then a loud twang, and an object rushed up into the sky overhead. His men had fired the ship's Scorpion. Villagers gasped and cringed, and some even wailed with fright, but Henry looked up and clenched his fist.

"Pray the infernal thing goes off in the air!" he muttered, as the rocket arced into the sky. Just as Henry thought it might fall to the ground, there was a bright flash that lit up the sky over the village, followed by an explosion. The sound reverberated over the village, causing more cries of dismay. The donkey jerked desperately at its rope and brayed with fright, the goats bleated and bolted down the empty streets, and the villagers on the ships wailed. The men around Henry murmured and crossed themselves.

Henry and Guy exchanged grins of savage glee. Life had become just a little boring up to this night. "If that doesn't scare the life out of the brigands, I don't know what will!" Guy shouted to Henry.

*****

High up on the mountain, the castle of Kantara perched on a long ridge overlooking both the southern plains and the harbor. The two guards on the north side were sleepy and bored, but they were also keeping an eye open for their Sergeant Palladius, who might appear at any time and berate them for not being alert.

One of the two men lifted his tunic and began to urinate over the parapet. "You better watch out the Sergeant doesn't catch you at it!" the other said. The moon threw everything into sharp relief, and he stared out at the sea to the North and the dark patch of the harbor. He realized that if he squinted he could even see the tiny shapes of the ships in the water. Then he started with surprise. "Oi, what's that?" A small flash and a distant boom had come from just above the village.

Then they noticed an orange glow emanating from the area of the harbor. "Oh, Lord! There's trouble down there!" The second man forgot what he was doing and stepped back. "Damn and stab me with a spoon!" he exclaimed in disgust as he wet himself. But then the urgency of what they were seeing took hold.

"We've got to sound the alarm!"

The first guard began to run off and called out, "I'll go. Stay here and keep an eye on the village."

He ran down the steps, shouting and yelling at the top of his voice. "Alarm! Alarm! Attack!"

Palladius stumbled out of the guardhouse to confront him just as he arrived at the entrance.

"What is it? Where is it?" he demanded, hastily buttoning up his jacket.

"There is a fire down at the village, Sergeant, but something else too. There was a flash and a bang. Never seen anything like it down there before."

Palladius suspected that he knew. He threw a glance at the sky, which was just beginning to lighten in the east; the moon was fading to a pale white. He made a decision.

"Go to the keep and wake everyone up: servants, the ladies, and especially Sir Max. And the Lord Rostam. Hurry!"

He turned back to the barrack room to arm himself. Just as he did so, two of Reza's ghosts appeared beside him. He gave an involuntary start. They scared the shit out of him, these people, but they were on his side, and that was all that mattered. He recognized Junayd and Dar'an; there was a third lurking about in the background.

"What is going on, Sarg'ant?" Dar'an asked him in poor Greek.

"There is an alarm, Dar'an. The men on the parapet saw what might have been a rocket, Sir." Palladius was always respectful to these men.

Dar'an nodded, and the three men sped off. Palladius watched them leap the steps to the northern parapet, taking them two at a time. He shook his shoulders and shivered, Phantoms! Then he turned back to his own responsibilities.

"Get up and form a line!" he shouted unnecessarily to the already bustling men-at-arms inside the barracks. Within a few moments they were assembled, and he detailed them off to their positions along the walls to join the night guards already there. By which time, Max came striding out of the main hall, strapping on his sword.

"What is going on, Sergeant? Why the alarm?"

"The men on the walls saw what they think was a rocket above the village, Sir Max. I suspect an attack. There might even be a fire."

Max glanced up at the manned walls. "You did the right thing. Good man. Come, we must check this for ourselves."

The two men hurried up the steps and joined Reza's phantoms, who were staring intently towards the village and harbor to the north. They were joined by Rostam, who had heard the commotion and was eager to know what was happening. He greeted the others quietly.

"See, there is a fire," Dar'an murmured and pointed. "The guards said they saw a flash of light and heard an explosion over the village. It might be that Henry wanted to attract our attention and used a Scorpion to do so."

Max nodded agreement. "Very glad that he did. Well now, we are awake, and I hope we can be of some use."

Palladius, who was still glowing from the rare praise from Max, pointed to the road that curved up the hillside. "There is a horseman, Sir Max. He seems to be in a hurry."

"Go and let him in, Sergeant, and bring him to me," Max ordered.

It took some long minutes for the horseman to arrive at the gates, which were immediately opened by Palladius and his men. Palladius escorted the excited youth to Max while his men shut the gates and saw to the exhausted animal, which was lathered with sweat.

The youth went down on one knee before Max. "Pirates have come, Sir!" he blurted without waiting to be asked.

"Tell me all you know," Max ordered.

The youth told him what Henry had been doing with the villagers, and how they were getting everyone onto the ships.

"Max turned to Dar'an. "So it is confirmed. We must send some kind of signal to tell Henry and Guy that we know and will be providing reinforcements."

Dar'an grinned. "I shall take care of that for you, Max." He gestured for Junayd should stay with Max, but took Na-suh and Dar'an with him.

Grimly, the men on the battlements watched the distant, spreading glow of fire.

Some time later, there came a whoosh from above their heads and a rocket tore into the sky above. It left a trail of sparks behind it, and then burst high in the night, a bright flash that would most certainly be seen by everyone in the harbor and the village. Then there was a quiet patter of approaching feet, as Rostam and the others returned.

"We must not forget the other villagers who are on the slopes by the vineyards," Rostam reminded everyone.

"No. That is why we must muster who we can and get ourselves on the road to protect them," Max responded. "You'll come with me, Rostam?"

"Try to stop me, Max," the boy said with a laugh. "I think we must hurry, though."

"Then we must arm ourselves and prepare to leave very soon," Max replied. "We need to inform your mother and your aunt first."

Henry and Guy saw the signal and understood its message, but their attention was fixed on their own predicament. They faced at least a hundred well armed men who were boiling into the streets ahead of them, with the clear intent of breaking through and ravaging the buildings along the quayside, then taking the ships.

Their yells of victory at their easy access to the village itself had emboldened them, even as the lack of human prey infuriated them. They had fired several houses, which now burned furiously in the grey light of dawn. Guy worried that the entire village would catch fire, or that the pirates would burn everything out of sheer spite, but there was nothing he could do. They had to defend what they could.

"Brace yourselves!" Guy shouted to the men. Most of them were unfamiliar with the scrimmage of battle, but they were backed by some of the veteran crew and the men-at-arms. His shield wall, such as it was, appeared very weak to Guy. He shrugged; it would have to do.

Shouting, "Allah akbar!" The pirates charged along the narrow street, brandishing spears and swords and screaming battle cries, and hurled themselves at his flimsy shield wall. To Guy's astonishment it held.

"Hold! Hold fast!" he roared, then shoved his big frame into the middle of the shield wall and rammed a spear straight into the belly of one of the foremost pirates.

"Hold the line!" he bellowed, and his men took up the chant. "Hold the wall! Hold! Hold! Hold!" They shouted with increasing confidence and stabbed at any face or chest that came too close.

The men in the front found themselves face to face with the surge of angry pirates, who rushed forward only to be stopped by the line of interlocked shields bristling with spears that jabbed out at them, drawing blood and wounding many.

Guy's men cursed and spat, some even voiding themselves with fear, but they held the line. Where possible, those who were wounded were dragged back out of the scrimmage, while corsairs who fell were savagely stabbed to death where they lay. Some of the more fanatical pirates tried to leap up onto the shields and cut their way through, but the second line of spears met them and skewered them or cut at their legs, whereupon they tumbled to the ground and were finished off.

"God almighty!" Guy swore, utterly surprised at how effective the tactic was proving. "It works! Go for them, men! Hold the line!"

The frustrated pirates cursed and howled and hacked with their swords, some of which bent or even broke on the shields, but they were making no headway. They could not flank the line because of the walls of the mud brick buildings, and so their corpses piled up in front of the two thin walls of shields. But it was not all in favor of the men from Kantara. During the pushing and shoving where men were so close they could almost bite one another, a pirate would stab across the gap, and someone would fall back with an agonized cry, with an eye missing or a newly gashed face.

Psellos, the Greek priest with the misshapen face who had been one of the victims of Lord Châtillon's visit to the island, had joined the group. He called out to Henry over the din of the fighting, "They are my flock, Henry. I must fight with them."

At one point, Psellos popped his head up to see down the street and came face to face with a pirate. The startled man took one look at the grotesque face glaring at him and almost fainted with horror. Psellos took advantage of the man's hesitation and rapped him over the head with a club.

"Be at peace, my son," he intoned. The pirate fell unconscious at his feet, and Psellos ducked back down behind his shield. His villagers, crushed alongside him shoulder to shoulder, howled their approval and gained heart. But then arrows began to whisper in, and men began to fall.

Henry and Guy had their own archers standing at the back of the shield wall. "Archers!" Guy yelled. "Kill those men!" He pointed to the pirate bowmen at the side of the unruly mob. Their own arrows flew, and not a few found their mark.

Henry felt someone tugging at is sleeve. "What is it?" he demanded impatiently.

"Look behind you, Captain!"

Henry whirled. He noticed his ship was very close to the quayside and directly in line with the street. "Why is that ship so close?" He demanded. "Is he..?" he asked the dripping wet crew member who had juts swum to shore.

"Yes, Captain. Nico asks that you and your men get out of the way and then he will loose the Scorpion."

Henry rubbed his face with a calloused hand and sized up the pirates, who appeared to be hesitating, baffled by the unexpectedly sturdy defense.

"Very well," Henry said reluctantly. "Signal him when I have moved the men out of the way." The crewman nodded and waved to the ship. He received an answering wave. "He is ready, Captain!" he called.

And then they began to withdraw. The pirates retreated, but only to regroup before attacking again. Henry bellowed for quiet among his chattering men. They had only a few moments to do this.

"On my command, all of you split away from the center and *hug* the walls. On my command! Are you ready?"

He received bewildered nods from the men, who braced to run. "Now!" Henry yelled, and ran for the wall along with half of his men. The other half raced for the opposite wall and glued themselves to it. He heard a distant twang of a very large bow and something whistled overhead to smash into the roof tiles of a house a hundred paces away at the end of the street. There was a stunned silence, then there was a huge bang and the roof of the house exploded outwards, sending tiles and splinters of wood high into the air, which then rained down upon friend and foe alike.

"Bugger!" Henry exclaimed. They didn't have many opportunities left. He braced himself to reassemble the line, but a shout from the ship delayed his order. The pirates, disconcerted, were gawping at the gaping hole in the house roof when one among them gave a shout and pointed at the gap in the road to the quayside, and Henry's men hugging the walls.

The second arrow from the Scorpion was too low. It sped past the cringing Henry and his men and ricocheted off a stone in the middle of the street, creating a shower of sparks as the arrow veered off its intended course and hurtled into the sky to explode with a noisy bang in the air over the harbor. Everyone instinctively ducked as a shower of sparks descended upon pirates and crewmen alike.

There was a pregnant pause while both sides gawped up at the sky or slapped frantically at the burning sparks now landing upon everyone. This allowed just enough time for the men on the ship.

"Will you aim the fucking thing properly! You halfwit bastards!" yelled Henry. "IF I survive this I'm going to skin the lot of you alive!"

"Stand clear, Captain!"

"Oh Good God, protect us!" Henry groaned as he hugged the wall again and shut his eyes. He was sure he was about to be spitted by the next one.

"Look out!" came the yell, and, "Stay where you are!" Henry bawled, just as the Scorpion twanged again. The hissing spear sped past Henry's cringing men, trailing a wisp of smoke. This time it was at waist height. The pack of pirates had just begun to charge, and it took the leader full on and hurled him back, to skewer yet another man right behind him. The two men were driven into the crowd behind them, tumbling other men to the ground. While the skewered pirates twitched in their death throes, the men around them faltered.

As the shocked pirates stared at the two bodies, there was another explosion as the fuse lit the small canister of gun powder attached to the arrow. The pirates were tossed about in all directions, many to lie where they fell. Wounded and dying men began to scream.

Henry gave an exuberant shout. Then, realizing this was a golden opportunity, he bellowed. "Follow me, men!" and charged down the street, brandishing his sword in the air and howling like a banshee. The sight of the wild old man with murder in his eyes, his mouth wide open displaying terrible teeth as he screaming obscenities, was too much for the survivors. The ones that could stumbled away as fast as their legs could carry them. After the briefest hesitation, Henry's men charged after him.

"He's as mad as a jelly fish, you know?" one of them observed.

"Mad or not, I'll follow that old bastard anywhere after this. Follow quickly, before he gets himself killed!" another crew member called out, and they charged after their captain, hollering and screaming, and then the slaughter began. No one was spared.

Guy heard the screams and realized what was going on. "Hold men. Just hold! Henry is going to be with us soon," he bellowed.

But the pirates facing him also realized their danger. Those who could faded away, and within moments the street was deserted except for the dead and a few wounded.

"Come, men, we still have work to do!" Guy called, and he led the way at a run to where he met a very bloody and wild-eyed Henry. "What happened over there, Henry?" Guy demanded after they had embraced.

"They didn't like Master Reza's little toys, Guy!" a jubilant Henry shouted with glee, brandishing his bloody sword.

"We must go after them before the vindictive swine burn down any more houses. But one of us must find their ship or ships and destroy them. You or me?"

"I'll go," Guy grinned. "I think I know exactly where they are, and I can deal with them."

"Go, my friend." Henry clapped him on the shoulder and pushed him towards his ship. "Be safe, Guy. We will send men over the land side to thin them out before they get to their ships."

"God protect, Henry!" Guy called after his friend, who had already turned away. "And God help the pirates if that old buzzard gets hold of them." He laughed.

Chapter 18

A Strong Defense

Let your blades drink blood like wine;
Feast ye in the banquet of slaughter,
By the light of the blazing halls!
Strong be your swords while your blood is warm,
And spare neither for pity nor fear,
For vengeance hath but an hour;
                                    —Sir Walter Scott

"Who will you leave behind to guard the castle?" Rav'an demanded, after she had been informed of events and Max's intentions.

"Junayd and Dar'an will remain with you, my Lady. I shall take half the men with me. Palladius will mutiny if I don't allow him to come, but Gregory can work with Dar'an and will do as he is told. He is a tough man and a good soldier; he will make sure the castle is secured."

"And Rostam?" Rav'an looked over at her son, standing beside Max.

"Your son wants to come with me, my Lady," Max murmured.

"He is not fully a man!" she exclaimed.

Rostam was going to protest vehemently, but Max forestalled him with one hand on the boy's shoulder.

"Enough to have fought the pirates at sea and to have saved Reza's life," Max reminded her. "This is a dangerous world, my Lady. Better he is prepared for the worst, and we can pray for the best."

She gave a reluctant nod. "He will at least be in good hands," she commented. Max nodded at the compliment.

"Then you must go. Time is pressing," she told him. "Rostam, my son," she turned to Rostam. "Do as Max says, and do not question him."

Rostam looked sheepish. "When have I not, Mother?" He then grinned and kissed her on the cheek. "You and Aunty Jannat and Theo will hold the castle while we are gone! Don't forget to arm the Scorpions before you shoot them!" He danced away from the gentle slap his mother would have delivered. "Mind your manners, young man," she told him. "Go! And God protect."

At that moment Junayd rushed into the main solarium and called out, "My Lady! Max! There are villagers running up the hill towards the castle."

Rav'an followed the men as they climbed the steps leading up to the top of the keep. Staring northward towards the road to the harbor, they could see women, children, and old men straggling up the steep hillside. Despite the steep incline, they looked as though they were hurrying at the best speed they could manage.

"I can see some armed men about a quarter of a league behind them," Max said, peering down. "Junayd, your eyes are good. Tell me what you see," he demanded.

Junayd stared hard for a brief moment and then replied, "The men following the villagers are not ours, Sir Max. I am sure of it."

"Then we must go! Rostam, get the horses ready. Junayd, you and Dar'an must stay and guard the castle with your companions. I don't want anyone to slip past us and get inside while we are away. I shall take the Franks and some of the Greeks."

Junayd and Dar'an nodded reluctantly. "We will stay," Dar'an said.

Rav'an sent a thankful look at her two retainers. "Thank you," she said.

Max and Rostam rushed off, while Rav'an and Jannat headed for the sick chamber to tell Reza and Theodora what was going on.

Dar'an and Junayd went down to see Max and his men off. Leading ten horsemen and twenty footmen, Max hastened out of the gates and to the junction of the road, which turned south and north. There they encountered the first of the terrified villagers, who were gasping for air after the long climb, and crying with both fear and exhaustion from their flight.

"What has happened?" Max demanded. He was answered by a babble of Greek, which Palladius helped to sort out. "They were woken up by a messenger sent from the port, but all he told them was that pirates were attacking and to seek shelter in the woods or go to the castle," Palladius informed him.

More villagers were still struggling up the hill. Some were carrying crying infants, while others were helping older people negotiate the slope. Others carried possessions in bulky loads. A few reluctant donkeys were being cursed and dragged up the hill. Among the villagers were several men whom Max recognized. He called them over, and with Palladius acting as translator he managed to find out more details.

Apparently, the pirates had split into two large groups. As soon as John, the leader of the village, had understood that they were under attack, he had ordered all the women, children and aged to flee for the castle while he tried to create a diversion with his able-bodied men. They now had better weapons than in former days, Lord Talon had seen to that, and they had tried to lead the pirates away and ambush them.

Unfortunately, it had not quite worked that way. The pirates, after looting the village, had brushed the village men and boys aside, killing several and wounding many others. John had been killed, after which the rest had fled into the woods. Then the pirates had set off in pursuit of the women and children, who were now gathered in a wailing crowd before Max and his men.

Max wasted no time. "Go to the castle and be quick about it!" he ordered the frightened people. "Hurry!" He waved them towards the walls behind them.

Already he and his men could see the band of pirates well on their way up the mountain road. It seemed, however, that the pirates were not yet aware of Max and his men.

"Ambush is our only hope," Max said to Rostam. "Dismount everyone except the bowmen! I want you and your lads with bows to be mounted behind us while we form a shield wall."

"Why don't we just charge them?" Rostam demanded impatiently.

"Had they been further down at the base of the hill it might have worked, but not now, because they will see us coming and simply step aside while we gallop past them, and then they will beat us back up the hill. Can't have that," Max answered. "The battle ground is ours to chose, and I choose to be on the up-slope. You and your bowmen will do the most damage. Our job is to prevent them getting past us to you and the castle. Do you understand?" This last was delivered sharply, as Rostam still seemed reluctant.

"I understand, Uncle Max," he said, and then called to his men, "Stay mounted and prepare to shoot. Join me behind Sir Max."

While the archers were preparing, Max and Palladius moved their men into position across the narrowest part of the road, not far from the crest. These men were well practiced in the formation of a shield wall; theirs spanned the road at the entrance to the woods which covered the upper slope. The castle was at their backs but a good hundred paces away; this left them more exposed. However, Max had spoken with Dar'an and Junayd earlier and they were preparing a surprise.

The first of the pirates marching up the curve in the road saw the silent line of men with their shields just in time to receive an arrow in the chest. Rostam had sent it, and Max nodded with approval as he noted the accuracy and the distance. "Nice shot," he murmured to Palladius, who nodded his own approval.

*****

Rav'an and Jannat silently entered the chamber that had been prepared for Reza, and beckoned to Theodora. She held a finger to her lips. "He sleeps," she whispered.

"How is he?" Jannat whispered, her concern very evident.

"I think he might just be getting beyond the fever," Theo told her, as they moved into the corridor.

"Thank God for that, but I thank you more, my sister," Jannat said. She embraced Theodora.

"What is going on out there?" Theo demanded. Her red hair was bound back in a copper-colored ponytail, there were dark rings under her eyes, and her pale, oval face showed tired lines. "I have not heard alarms like this for a long time! Is it one of those practices the men are forever having?"

"No, Sister. Not this time," Rav'an told her. Theo's eyes widened with alarm. They told her in short, whispered sentences what they knew, and had nearly completed their report when they heard a pained grunt from Reza. The three of them tip-toed into the chamber to find Reza awake. He looked pale and gaunt, but there was certainly more color in his face than before.

"My Love, we didn't want to wake you," Jannat told him as she leaned over to kiss his forehead.

"I have been awake longer than you think, and I have heard a lot of disturbances going on outside," he responded, touching Jannat's arm.

"We don't want to alarm you, Reza my darling, but...." Jannat looked at Rav'an and Theodora. "May we tell him?" she asked.

Theodora was reluctant but shrugged. Rav'an sighed and said, "You must promise not to get too excited if we do tell you, Reza."

"Excited about what? What is going on?" he demanded, plucking at the covers.

"The pirates came back early this morning and started to burn the harbor," she bluntly informed him, and watched the look of astonishment on his face. He tried to sit up, but groaned again.

"Reza, you must not move! Is that clear?" Theodora told him. Reza rolled his eyes, then reluctantly bowed to the inevitable. He simply did not have the strength to rise, let alone to fight. I cannot, even if I.... Help me to sit up," he ordered. The women complied, but it was a slow and painful process. Finally, when he was propped up more comfortably he said, "Henry and Guy can probably manage down in the village, as long as they were not caught napping. They can always take to the boats. But what about the second village?"

They explained that Max and Rostam had gone off to confront the pirates. Then Rav'an cocked her head. "If I am not mistaken, some of the villagers have already arrived," she stated. The noise made by the refugees was beginning to make itself clearly heard, even through the thick walls. "I shall have to go down and see to them." She made to depart, but Reza said, "Wait one minute, Rav'an. I need you to send me Dar'an. How many men did Max take out with him?"

"I think about twenty men-at-arms and several of your young archers, including Rostam," Jannat told him.

He did some thinking then. He was sure Max would be able to delay the pirates; he hoped he could do even better than that. But out in the open there was the risk of being flanked. They had precious few men left to guard the large enclosure of the castle itself. It might have been better to leave the villagers to their fate and concentrate on defending the castle and all therein, but not even he would have been able to countenance that. To his mind Max had done the right thing. He urgently needed to talk to Dar'an.

"Send Dar'an. It is very important, Rav'an," he told her, and she hurried off. Jannat stayed with Reza, while Theodora went off to see to her other patients. Some were still in her care from the sea battle.

"I am glad that you seem to be recovering, my Reza," Jannat murmured. Tears shone in her huge eyes as she held his hand. He squeezed back. He glanced over at his sword propped up against the wall nearby and fretted. "I should be taking care of this myself !" he grumbled.

It was Junayd who appeared, however, and seeing the look on Reza's face he hastened to explain. "Lord Reza, Dar'an apologizes for not coming and sent me instead. He said you would understand. He is down in the basements preparing his barrels and those other infernal things, and as I cannot do that work he sent me." He knelt before the bed.

Reza gave a wan smile. "Dar'an has anticipated me," he said. "Good. Who is manning the walls, and who is in charge of them? We are so few!"

"It is Gregoree," Junayd said, mispronouncing the name. "He has posted men all around the walls."

"Tell him to get all the boys and old men from the village onto the walls where they can help defend should the need arise," Reza ordered. "We might as well keep them busy now that they are here."

He went on to discuss other aspects of the defense, should pirates get past Max, which he fervently hoped they would not. While they were talking, Theodora came back and took Reza's pulse, then brusquely ordered Junayd out of the room.

"You must rest, Reza, or the fever will return and I cannot answer for anything after that. Jannat, you can stay."

Reza gave a frustrated grunt but waved Junayd off. "Keep me informed," he called after the youth. Junayd smiled disarmingly at Theodora, who pretended to glower at him before he slipped out of the door.

*****

Max and his men were busy. The pirates had come running up the slope in a ragged group, yelling as they came, and despite several of them going down to arrows they had charged the shield wall. Most of the local men were unused to battle, but most of the Franks were familiar with the solid formation and they helped hold the line alongside of Max and Palladius.

The pirates were courageous and confident that they could break past this thin wall of men, and then the castle would be theirs. All that stood between them and their plunder was the stubborn hedgehog of sharp, stabbing spears coming from behind a solid wall of large shields. They would try to seize the shaft of a spear only to be stabbed by another. If one or more managed to breach the wall or reach over the first line of defense, the men just behind would hammer them with their swords, or pierce them with even more spears, or hack at them with long-handled axes. Worst of all was the deadly accuracy of the bowmen.

Nevertheless, there were many more of the pirates than the small group of men in front of them, and if some fell to the spears or arrows that just meant more loot for the survivors. They pressed on, howling and cursing.

The delay was exceedingly annoying for their leader Abul-Zinad. He shouted encouragement from behind a small bodyguard who protected him from the arrows with their shields. He glanced behind him down the road and could see there were fires in the port. That meant Waqqas had kept his side of the bargain and was in control of the entire village and the port itself. Soon the wealth of the castle would be his, if only he could get past this damned barrier. They fought unlike any villagers he had previously encountered in his coastal raids, and an uncomfortable feeling began to take hold. That dog Zenos had not mentioned that the resistance would be so well disciplined and hard to overpower.

Just then the men of the shield wall began to retreat towards the castle, giving ground slowly but holding their defensive formation. "Perhaps they have had enough?" he wondered hopefully. He wanted that orderly retreat to become a rout and began to exhort his panting men, who had paused to rest. "Get up there and kill them! Look, they retreat! They give way! *Allah akbar!*" he shouted, and pushed his guards out of the way. It was time to lead.

Max and his men were tired. They had been pushing and shoving, stabbing and clubbing the pirates for over an hour. There was a small pile of torn and bleeding bodies in front of them and scattered about at a further distance to attest to the skill of Rostam's bowmen and their stubborn resistance. But they needed a break, which didn't seem to be forthcoming. Thirsty and bloody men wished they were anywhere else but this place. Then Max bellowed another order.

"Back another fifty paces. Hurry! Form up at the base of the castle!" He shouted at the men. The Franks wasted no time in obeying this welcome order.

"Rostam, keep those arrows flying. We need to delay them," Max tried to shout, but it came out as more of a croak. He was not even sure the boy heard him. Sweat was pouring off his face, and he was drenched with perspiration underneath his armor.

"I'm much too old to be doing this any more," he muttered to himself. "I wonder why they are so determined?" he said aloud to Palladius. "Pirates usually go for easy targets, but these savages seem dead set on getting past us."

Palladius nodded agreement. He, too, was dry-mouthed and perspiring hard. "I agree it is unusual. They should have left by now. There isn't much profit to be had here."

Max glanced up at the castle walls as they moved towards their new position. One figure waved to him. It was Dar'an, and he lifted a dark looking device high and pointed to it.

"Ah," murmured Max with satisfaction. "Now it will get interesting. Form up, men." he called, as the pirates began racing towards them again. "Here they come. Rostam, where are our arrows?"

Rostam and his companions loosed their missiles into the screaming ranks of the advancing pirates at short range. Many of the enemy stumbled back and fell dead or wounded, no longer interested in the fight, but a dense mob of them with spears aimed ahead in a kind of arrow formation came charging straight towards the center of Max's new wall.

Max knew a moment of real concern as he watched the screaming, turbaned crowd of fierce fighters charging towards them. These men seemed to be determined to break through and this time they might succeed, after which he could not contemplate the consequences. Rostam called over that his arrows were running short, and the men were hot and tired. Grimly Max lowered his own spear and braced for impact.

The front of the horde was a scant twenty yards away when a short, dark tube with a tendril of smoke trailing from it tumbled through the air and landed in their midst. The object actually struck a man on the shoulder and laid him out before it exploded with a flash and a loud bang. The men of the shield wall ducked instinctively and fragments of the bomb rattled off their shields and helmets. One man cried out in pain and surprise as a splinter struck his exposed ankle.

"Keep down!" Max shouted, as he cowered from the blast. A moment or two later, he peered over his shield. A small cloud of evil looking yellow smoke obscured his view. He was just in time to see something else fall from above. Dar'an had tossed a Greek Fire hand bomb, and it landed directly in the midst of the wailing, keening pack of wounded and dying men. Max gasped. It had come terrifyingly close to him and his men. Now dismembered men, some still alive and on fire, were strewn all over the road. The stench of burning flesh added itself to the already rancid stink of blood, voided bowels and fear.

A few survivors, dazed and bleeding, were staggering about. Those who had been at the back realized that the fight for the castle was over and began to make their escape.

At that moment Max made a fateful decision.

He was influenced by the sight of the still burning villages, having no knowledge of the success that Henry and Guy had enjoyed; he thought that they were in peril and that the pirates were still at large, plundering, looting and committing other unspeakable crimes. He needed to bring his men to the fight down in the valley, and the castle appeared to be secure.

"Mount up!" he shouted. "We must finish this and go to the aid of Henry and Guy. They need our help!"

Rostam and his archers, unburdened by heavy shields and armor, mounted swiftly and charged past him, racing down the slope, chasing after the pirates who fled for their lives. Some fell to the vengeful riders, while others took to the woods and trees, hoping to find refuge and eventually make their way back to their ships.

Chapter 19

Assassins and Punishment

The battle grows more hard and harder yet,
Franks and pagans, with marvelous onset,
Each other strike and each himself defends.
So many shafts bloodstained and shattered,
So many flags and ensigns tattered;

—The Song of Roland

Even as the fighting was taking place on the east side of the castle, the gates located at the south side of the castle had been opened to admit the frightened villagers, who trooped into the bailey in ragged groups.

"Hurry through, we have to shut the gates!" the excited and nervous guards shouted. The men were sorted as they arrived and told to report to the battlements. But, unnoticed by the guards, another group had joined the villagers. Those few villagers who noticed the strangers and who tried to raise an alarm were slain, swiftly and silently, before they could cry out, their slumping bodies passing unnoticed in the press, as many of the villagers had collapsed in exhaustion. Now a small group of hooded men were within the bailey of the castle, mingling with the crowd that was milling about, waiting to gain entrance to the main part of the castle.

It was Junayd who noticed that something was wrong. He had been watching the crowd of refugees gathering below with half an eye. The activity on the other side of the castle to the east was taking up most of his attention, but then he noticed a small cluster of villagers making their way towards the opened gate that allowed entry to the main courtyard. Something about them bothered him. They were like.... Suddenly, he had it. Their purposeful movement through the crowd of wailing and calling villagers reminded him of the way Reza has trained the companions to move through a crowd. His instincts began to clamor.

"Shut that gate!" he shouted down to the men below. The gate men stared up at him, bewildered. "Shut it! Now!" he screamed, and then groaned as he saw one of the sentries falling aside as an assassin buried his knife in his stomach. Junayd had his bow with him. With the speed that Reza's hardest training had instilled, he loosed an arrow which struck the lead assassin in the chest, causing him to fall back; but it was not enough to stop another from leaping forward, and then two more. Before anyone else could react, the three dark-clad men had escaped into the main courtyard of the castle. Two of the other sentries had the presence of mind to slam the gate shut in the faces of the men who tried to follow. The outer gates were shut and the towers manned, so there was no escape for them, but now there were some well armed and determined assassins inside the main courtyard of the castle, and they were hard to pick out among the milling villagers.

Frantically, Junayd called out again and again to Dar'an who was focussed on the fight at the base of the outer walls. Then an alert sentry called Dar'an's attention to the frantic Junayd, so he raced back along the battlements towards his friend. "What is it?" he called.

"Assassins! They are inside the castle!" Junayd shouted, pointing down into the bailey. "Some are still there before the gate!"

"Gregory!" Dar'an yelled. "Guard the people in the bailey! There are assassins among them!"

"Where are they?" he demanded, as he un-slung his bow.

They are there somewhere in the crowd." Junayd told him, then he pointed. Three figures were slipping through the chattering villagers clustered in the main yard, heading towards the main hall.

"We must protect the women in the keep. That is where they will go! I'm sure they have come to kill our Lords," Dar'an called out as he began to run.

Gregory mustered his men and they lined the battlements overlooking the bailey, trying to spot the intruders, who now tried very hard to make themselves invisible. It was not an easy task, for they stood out by being able bodied men, and armed. The men on the parapet pointed them out to one another, marking them.

"Gregory, use the other companions to stop them opening the gates and escaping. Now!" Dar'an yelled.

"Where have they come from?" Junayd demanded, as he and Dar'an raced towards the keep.

"I don't know, but they look very dangerous. We have to get to the women and Reza before they do," Dar'an gasped. His stomach was churning with fear as they ran, dodging stray children and women who dotted the courtyard.

"Get out of the way!" Junayd yelled at one mother and her child, who insisted on blocking the way, demanding attention. Other men-at-arms, seeing the two making for the keep with such urgency, began to follow them. Dar'an beckoned them to keep pace and to keep people away from the main hallway entrance.

They were too late. The three assassins ran swiftly up the steps to the keep, where they paused briefly to see where their pursuers might be. Dar'an and Junayd were ready, and their bows twanged together. One man fell with a choking cry to roll down the steps. Unfortunately, the other had just moved behind him, so Junayd's arrow flew wide to chip the stone of the tower.

He cursed as the two other assassins disappeared into the main hall. Dar'an didn't even pause. "Leave him to the men-at-arms," he called, and gestured to the dying man. Three men-at-arms gathered around the fallen man. One kicked his sword out of the way and the others pointed their spears at the wounded man.

Dar'an and Junayd raced towards the archway that led to the stairs, which in turn led up to the living quarters of Talon and the families. They came across two servants lying in pools of blood, while others huddled in a terrified group off to the side. One mutely pointed to the steps. There, waiting for them, was one of the assassins. Seeing the bows drawn, he moved until he was just out of sight in the gloom of the tower steps. Anyone trying to use a bow in these close quarters would be severely handicapped, and Dar'an knew it.

He handed his bow to Junayd. "I'll go first. See to it that you follow close."

Junayd tossed the two bows onto one of the tables nearby and drew his own sword. "I am here," he whispered.

"Where have you come from?" Dar'an called out in Arabic. Their opponent was darker skinned than a Latin.

"The Master sent us."

Dar'an was incredulous, 'The Master? The Master from Persia?"

The man snorted. "Of course not! My master. The School Teacher, El Rashid Ed Din. Are you so ignorant?" He sounded disgusted.

Dar'an and Junayd were barely listening. The third man was getting ahead while this idiot gave them a history lesson. Dar'an had an idea. He reached for a jug that was on the table near their bows, among which were other small bowls of salt. "I shall toss this at him, and then the two of us go for him. It's vinegar," he whispered, when Junayd gave him an incredulous look.

"Very well. We have no time, but he has."

Dar'an put his sword, his Japanese sword, into his left hand and dived for the entrance. When he was one pace away from the steps he hurled the jug at the wall above his head to the left. The jug smashed, splattering vinegar and shards in all directions. It distracted the assassin just enough to allow Dar'an to dash up the few steps that separated them. Dar'an ducked and went onto his knees as a vicious swipe of a sword went past. The assassin cursed as his sword struck sparks off the stone wall, but Dar'an's sword swept in low and severed his attacker's foot at the ankle.

With a shriek of agony the man tumbled forward, to be spitted on Junayd's sword. Junayd brutally hauled his sword from the dying youth, who rolled further down the stones groaning in agony, then he sprinted up the remaining steps after his companion to the floor above. It was eerily silent.

Dar'an cast about him wildly, trying to divine where the assassin might have gone. Huddled in a blood-soaked bundle on the floor of the corridor leading to the infirmary was one of the children's nurses. His heart sank. Then both men heard a sound coming from the chamber that Reza occupied. Junayd slipped a long knife out of his belt, flicked it over so that he carried it by its blade, and crept forward, following Dar'an, who peered cautiously through the entrance of the half-open doorway.

Reza was lying on the bed propped up on pillows, but on the other side of the bed was Rav'an, holding his sword in the position of on guard. Crouched just behind her, Jannat was holding a chamber pot in her hands and watching the third assassin through narrowed eyes. He stood near to the end of Reza's bed. No one seemed to be hurt so far, but that was not going to last.

"You will not come one step closer," Jannat hissed, raising the pot.

The assassin laughed. "You know why we are here?" he demanded, with a smirk of derision at Jannat.

"To kill me..." Reza croaked.

"No, but it's good for us that you are here. It is a bonus. We are here to disable your people and open the gates."

"To the pirates?" Rav'an demanded.

"And others." The youth began to make his move. He was watching Rav'an, who was holding the weapon. Reza was clearly incapacitated, and the silly girl with the pot was of no consequence. However, he was to be surprised. When he thrust his sword contemptuously in Rav'an's direction he was taken aback by her reaction. With only a very small flick of her wrists she parried and then lunged, just as she had been taught by both Reza and Talon.

The assassin danced out of the way of the deadly blade with a surprised look on his face, which was when Jannat gave a scream and hurled the chamber pot as hard as she could at his head. He had no time to react. The pot left an arcing trail of mess that splattered everywhere when it shattered right on his forehead. The assassin's eyes crossed, but it didn't knock him over. He staggered back, grunting with anger and pain and shaking his head, which sprayed more mess about. Then he made the mistake of putting his hand up to the cut on his forehead. It masked his view of Rav'an for a crucial moment.

At that same instant, Dar'an dived into the room with a great shout, and right behind him came Junayd, who, with a shout of his own, flung his knife with all his might at the assassin. Their shouts disconcerted the assassin just long enough. The knife flew true and buried itself in his shoulder, which made the youth howl with surprise and pain, but it didn't stop him lunging for Reza.

Dar'an just managed to parry the blade, but it was Rav'an who whirled and slashed hard at the man's exposed neck. That blade, which had been made by one of the finest Japanese swordsmiths in the world, slashed through the cloth wrapped around the assassin's throat and cut deeply. The man dropped to the floor, where he floundered about for a couple of long moments before he went still.

There was complete silence while everyone in the room took in what had just occurred. Then, with a cry of relief, Jannat scrambled to her feet and ran to Rav'an, who was pale, shaking, and looked sick.

Dar'an delicately removed the sword from her trembling fingers and wiped it clean with great care before slipping it into its scabbard. He replaced the sword reverently against the wall next to Reza's bed. He knew Reza could not bear to be parted from it.

Reza was his usual self. He wrinkled his nose. "God, what a mess!" he exclaimed, sounding indignant, and looked accusingly at his faithful followers.

"What took you two so long?" he croaked. Dar'an and Junayd merely shook their heads and grinned at him. "We were somewhat delayed, Master," Dar'an murmured. At that moment Theodora appeared in the doorway, having heard the commotion.

"What...?" She gasped at the sight of the dead man lying in a pool of blood at the foot of the bed.

"We had a visitor," Reza explained, "and I am covered with shit and piss!" He wore a look of disgust on his face. "Where did he come from?" He directed this question at his men.

"The other one said they came from Rashid Ed Din," Junayd informed him

Reza looked alarmed. "The School Teacher? What others?"

"Three of them managed to get into the courtyard. They are dead now, but we have others to deal with, Lord." Dar'an said.

"Go and deal with them. You did well. I shall comfort the ladies. And someone *please* clean up this terrible mess!"

Junayd retrieved his knife and the two of them loped off. "Remind me to never to cross the Lady Jannat... ever!" he panted as they ran. Dar'an snorted with amusement.

"Nor the Lady Rav'an!" he replied as they skipped down the steps, avoiding the crumpled corpse at the bottom. "We must make sure the one we capture doesn't kill himself before we talk to him," Junayd said, when they had snatched up their bows in passing.

He waved to the servants and attendants. "You are safe now, but you must go upstairs and attend Lady Rav'an and the Lady Jannat. Go!" he ordered them. After a frozen moment, they scampered to obey.

The two companions employed several of their fellow comrades and men-at-arms to keep a watch on the assassins in the bailey; they were most concerned about more assassins getting into the castle by stealth.

The remaining assassins knew they had lost every advantage of surprise and disguise. Dar'an and Junayd shouted down to them that they could surrender, but both knew the unwelcome visitors would not allow themselves to be captured.

The assassins then began to kill some of the villagers, but well aimed arrows from Junayd and the other companions killed one of them and wounded another. The remaining two retreated to the far end of the courtyard, leaving their comrades lying on the ground. Immediately Dar'an ordered the gate to the main courtyard opened, and the remaining villagers poured through. There were now only two men and the wounded man left.

"Kill them, Junayd," Dar'an said, knowing that Reza would have ordered it. "We keep the wounded man."

And so it was done.

The gristly task had just been completed and the wounded man picked up by the men-at-arms when a new danger manifested. One of the men on the lookout to the south towards Famagusta gave a warning shout.

"Bind his wound and take him to the dungeons," Dar'an ordered, but just as the men-at-arms were turning to leave with the prisoner, something Talon had once said occurred to him. "Search him! Now!" he barked at them. The men-at-arms dropped their charge none too gently on the ground and searched him all over. They turned up a knife. "How did you know?" Junayd asked, surprised.

"Lord Talon knows of these things. He mentioned it once," Dar'an said. "Come, there is another alarm!" They hurried up to the parapet to stare out in the direction the sharp-eyed sentry indicated. There, in the distance, on the road that led to Famagusta, well below the castle, was a cloud of dust, and it was sizable.

"Seems we have unwelcome company from every quarter," Dar'an commented. His sense of unease grew. What was going on?

"Sound the alarms. Inform my Lady Rav'an of what is happening, Junayd. Gregory!" he called, as Junayd rushed off, "get every able-bodied man onto the ramparts. We have visitors and I do not think they are welcome."

Gregory bellowed orders to his men, who sorted out the villagers, pushing the bewildered men and boys towards the steps that led up to the ramparts. "Buckets of shit from the stables and the midden!" Gregory shouted. "Hurry! Bring them up here, and make sure there are plenty of rocks and other missiles.

Junayd, in the meantime, had raced back up to the private quarters of the ladies. He knuckled his forehead respectfully to Rav'an and said hastily, "Khanom, Dar'an asks that you come to the ramparts to the south. I will escort you."

"What is it, Junayd?" Two thin lines formed between her brows. She was petting one of the two hounds lying nearby.

"We appear to have visitors from Famagusta, Khanom. Dar'an is making preparations for them."

You mean unwelcome visitors, Junayd?" Jannat said with a concerned look. She had just re-entered the room.

"Yes, Khanom. I fear so." He nodded briefly. "Will you please inform Lord Reza and ask him for any advice he might have, my Lady?"

Jannat nodded. "I don't know how we are to keep him in his bed with all this excitement going on around us," she said to the world at large.

"He must stay there, Sister," Rav'an said to her. "Just tell him we are going to take a look and we will let him know what is going on. Come along, Junayd."

They arrived on the parapet to find it crowded with men-at-arms instructing the village boys and young men in their duties. Piles of rocks were growing, and there was a noxious stink from the buckets placed strategically along the south ramparts, which caused Rav'an to wrinkle her nose. As soon as she was seen, everyone stopped what they were doing and knelt respectfully. She realized that she was expected to say something and cleared her throat. Her thoughts were out-pacing her words, like deer dodging and jinking as they fled from hunters. With a fierce effort of will she forced herself to be calm, and then spoke.

"Some of you have already lost loved ones to the pirates. It would seem that they were trying to work in concert with men from the Emperor, who are now on their way to attack us. They have not succeeded so far, and we have the oppor-tunity to surprise these new unwelcome visitors. Do as you are instructed and fight hard. God protect all of you!" she turned away as the cheering started, to be hastily suppressed by Gregory and his men.

"We must surprise them!" they called out. "Silence!"

"My Lady, please come to the tower over by the main entrance," suggested Junayd. "That way we can observe without being in the way."

"Where is Dar'an?" she asked, looking around. Several of the trainees that formed Reza's group of young men were also missing.

"Here I am, my Lady," Dar'an called out. His arms were full of the deadly tubes he was so fond of throwing at people, while his men gingerly carried boxes filled with round objects that looked like spherical jugs with something sticking out of them. He noticed her look.

"Greek Fire, my Lady. A very pleasant surprise for anyone who decides to attack." He threw a glance at the distinct shape of the Scorpion squatting nearby. We have two of these, and then there is the trebuchet." He nodded his head towards the bailey, where the huge frame stood unattended.

She smiled. "You think of everything. But we are not sure yet, are we, that they are the enemy?"

"I'd bet Junayd's bow on it, my Lady."

Junayd scowled at this jape. "It was something the assassin said that warned us. They were hoping to gain control of the gates and to open them for allies they expected. Not just the pirates." Junayd pointed down the slope. "They are hopelessly late for their appointment, so it is our turn to surprise them." His eyes gleamed with excitement at the coming confrontation.

Rav'an regarded him and Dar'an with affection. "Talon would be proud of you two," she stated. "I am confident we can overcome this new danger with your help."

Both men's stern, dark features went darker still as they flushed with embarrassment and pleasure. "Will you be staying, Khanom?" Dar'an asked.

"I shall indeed. You and the hounds will protect me." She smiled and fondled the ears of one of the large dogs, which had followed them onto the ramparts.

"Very well, my Lady, but please do not stand too close to the parapet if they come this far. Their crossbowmen can be very accurate at short range," Junayd warned her.

"I shall do as you ask. Now, can we see what they are about?"

"They are in a hurry. They must know they are late and are still hoping for success, I suspect," Dar'an muttered, as he stacked his deadly little treasures against the wall.

"Gregory! Get every one out of sight," he called to the Greek soldier. "No one is to move until I drop my tube." The soldier waved back from his position on the eastern wall. They then waited in tense silence as they observed the approaching horsemen, who were flogging their mounts up the hill towards the junction of the roads. When they reached the turn, they halted briefly and milled about.

"Their messenger is not there to greet them," Dar'an muttered. Despite their evident concern, someone must have issued an order, for the riders began to gallop along the narrow track that led along the southern walls of the castle, making for the main gates. Everyone crouched behind the ramparts could hear the thunder of approaching hooves and the voices riders calling to one another as they galloped confidently towards their goal. From their perch on the tower, Dar'an and Rav'an could overlook the road and its approaches. They glanced at one another. She raised an eyebrow as though to say, When?

"We let them come close, my Lady, and that time is... now!" He struck a flint and the stream of sparks struck the fuse of his bomb. The hounds whimpered with fear and crouched as far away as possible. Dar'an held the weapon, spluttering and hissing, then stood up and tossed it casually over the ramparts. "Keep down, my Lady," he cautioned, holding his fingers to his ears.

Rav'an grimaced and copied him, her eyes wide. The boom followed quickly, shaking the air around them. No sooner had Dar'an's infernal device gone off, wrecking death and destruction below, than the ramparts erupted with men and boys of every age hurling rocks and pushing boulders over the ramparts to crash into the terrified horses and men. Some riders were unhorsed as their mounts bucked and reared. Others were hammered by the falling missiles, some of which struck the outcroppings of the walls and rebounded to slam into the riders from their flank, maiming and wounding.

Junayd hurled a smoking Greek Fire bomb into the chaos below, creating even further havoc. Some of the villagers, emboldened by their success, began shouting imprecations and taunts and tossed effluence onto the nearest riders, thereby adding insult to injury. It quickly became evident to the survivors that there was no hope of surprise, and the shouts of anticipated victory turned to shouts of dismay and calls to retreat.

Those that could whirled their horses and spurred them savagely over the corpse-littered roadway, seeking escape. It was a fearsome gauntlet, and only half of the original number made it back to the junction, for the bowmen on the ramparts had clear shots at their unguarded backs. The survivors urged their mounts down the pathway heading towards Famagusta.

"Dar'an!" Rav'an called over the noise and screams. Her ears were numb from the noise.

"Yes, my Lady?" he was right there with an exuberant Junayd, who was almost as ready to dance as the jubilant villagers. "Use the trebuchet. Use it, Dar'an!" Rav'an shouted.

He blinked, and then an almost feral grin crossed his dark features. "Yes, Khanom. At once! Come on, Junayd.

Bring some men." He snatched up one of the bombs and they rushed down the steps to the bailey. Rav'an waited impatiently on the ramparts, watching the panicked enemy galloping headlong down the road. She glanced down at the frantic preparations about the trebuchet.

"Come on. Come on!" she exclaimed, impatiently pounding the stone with the underside of her clenched fist as she watched the distance shrink between the foremost riders and the flat space that marked where Talon and Reza had sent many practice missiles. As the distance closed, Junayd raced up to join her. "All ready, my Lady. Shall I call it?"

Rav'an glared at the fleeing riders. "No, Junayd, I want to call it."

Those plunderers would not be allowed to simply flee. She wanted to teach them a lesson they would never forget.

Gauging the distance against the time it took the fearsome weapon to loft a boulder into the air, she raised her arm. Then she brought it down sharply. Dar'an lit the fuse of the bomb seated in the cradle, then hauled off the lever that retained the long arm.

The arm hesitated for a fraction of a second, and then the huge bar whirled in a long arc up, carrying its deadly package with it. A thin streak of smoke trailed behind, which reassured Dar'an that his fuse was still lit. The Counter weight, barrels full of sand, thumped into the ground, the arm pivoted and slammed into its padded stop. The bomb, hissing like some creature from hell, was hurled high into the air over the heads of the people on the ramparts, who cringed as it sped overhead, and then they all stared intently in the direction it was expected to fall.

Dar'an had ducked out of the way after releasing the lever. He was never sure if the whole contraption would shatter into pieces when it operated. But it held together, and when the missile cleared the walls he raced up the stairs to join the others. Rav'an noted with dismay that most of the riders had passed the flat space. To her chagrin she had mis-judged the timing. But then the watchers on the ramparts saw something astonishing. A dark streak fell directly in among the riders, who were all just past the flat space. They saw a flash go off right in the midst of the distant group, and felt a small concussion in the air just before they heard the distant explosion. Luck or skill, they had achieved their ob-jective.

Rav'an and her two attendants gasped. She was still get-ting over her surprise when Dar'an said, "My Lady seems to have an unexpected skill with this device." He laughed, shook his head in amazement, and slapped his thighs with delight. Then both he and Junayd forgot themselves and did a small skipping dance, linking arms and crowing with glee. The cheering began from all around on the walls. This time the noise was wild and joyful. Men waved their hats and weapons in the air. Rav'an herself was silent, mostly with surprise, but she smiled with her lips pursed, and her eyes were wide with triumph.

Collecting herself, she looked down at the tiny dark fig-ures strewn about on the hillside. "Someone must go down there and deal with them," she told the happy companions, who could not stop grinning.

"And you can stop behaving like a pair of monkeys right now," she admonished them, a smile tugging at her mouth. They both sobered up quickly and ducked their heads re-spectfully.

"Yes, my Lady. We will deal with them at once," Dar'an said, trying but failing to keep the grin off his face.

"I wonder if it is over now?" Rav'an asked herself. She left the ramparts to find Jannat and Theodora and tell them what had befallen. Her two faithful attendants proudly es-corted her all the way.

Ah, Talon, she thought, as they made their way down the steps and then across the crowded courtyard full of cheering villagers and their own men-at-arms, *Where are you? It is you who should be here doing this, not I. How I miss you!*

It took an immense effort of will to walk calmly up the steps that led to the main doors of the hallway. Everyone in the courtyard had by now learned what had occurred and regarded her as endowed with the same magic as her husband. Some crossed themselves surreptitiously while others called out greetings, but most cheered her all the way to the doorway.

She turned, smiled and waved at them, then said, "Dar'an and Junayd, I leave you in charge. Please let me know as soon as Max and my son return. Thank you both." Rav'an turned away and entered the gloom of the hall, accompanied by the hounds. While they padded ahead of her she leaned against the cool stone of the entrance wall and found that she was shaking and close to tears, but there was a sense of exhilaration too.

"What would they have done to us had they gained entry?" she asked herself, after which she felt stronger. She wondered what kept Talon away for so long. Praying that he was still alive—surely she would sense it were he not—she dashed away the tears, then climbed the stone stairs, glancing down as she passed at the wet places where the servants had cleaned away the blood of the dead assassin. It reinforced her resolve. Gathering her skirts in both hands, she went up the stairs to her family.

When she arrived at the Solarium, Jannat silently presented her with a message from Dimitri's pigeon, warning of something dire about to happen, he knew not what.

Chapter 20

A Pyrrhic Victory

Fill the bright goblet, spread the festive board!
Summon the gay, the noble, and the fair!
Through the loud hall, in joyous concert pour'd,
Let mirth and music sound the dirge of Care!
But ask thou not if Happiness be there
                                        —*Sir Walter Scott*

Down in the valley and in the area of the port, the hunt was on for the pirate survivors. No one was inclined to give any quarter. Some of the wounded were found lying in dense bushes, where they had crawled to hide. Others were chased by dogs and men until they either gave up and surrendered or were killed by the eager bowmen on horseback, led by Rostam, who now began to appreciate the long hours of training Uncle Reza had insisted upon. The accuracy of their shooting was their testimony, as desperately fleeing men from the sea were brought down, one after the other. Then the villagers would take over and, howling like a pack of dogs, set to with knives, swords and axes; they were not in a forgiving mood.

"The pirates have fallen, but others have fled. May I go after them, Henry, Max?" Rostam asked the two men.

Henry pointed east in the direction of the same inlet that Talon had used to reconnoiter the castle. "Guy is very sure they came from there, Rostam. You will find them all heading in that direction, I am sure of it. Be careful!" he called, as the eager young man began to turn his horse.

"Do not get isolated!" Max called to Rostam as the boy galloped off. "They are like rats; they will turn on you! They have nothing to lose now!" He doubted that the boy heard him.

Max had met Henry on the outskirts of the port where Henry and his men were trying to put out the fires and prevent the total destruction of the village. Some of Henry's men mounted and rode off to join Rostam and his horsemen.

"Impetuous young fools." Henry shook his head, but there was pride, too, as he watched them leave. "So, Max, you came all this way down here to help me out?" He laughed and clapped Max on the shoulder. "That was nice of you, but we managed well enough."

Max was a little chagrined. "It would seem so, Henry. But all I could see were the fires. We had no idea you had done so well. Thank God for that. Where is Guy right now?" he looked around.

"He divined that the pirate ships were probably still in the inlet and went to block it off so that they cannot escape."

"How many ships were there?" Max was curious.

"Two, we think. There were too many men for just one ship, and you met with more from what I hear."

"Can Guy deal with them on his own?"

Henry laughed. "Guy has two Scorpions, Max, and his men know how to use them. As long as he can stay away from their Greek Fire he can kill them from a distance, and that is what he will do. I am sure of it. A bigger problem is to salvage anything afterwards, and there will be stragglers in these forest for some time. We will need to flush them out or they will do harm."

Max nodded soberly. "Then this has been a successful repulse. Tracking down pirates could be an interesting task for

Reza's hounds." He was not referring to Rav'an's hounds but to the young trainees who were being schooled in the arts of stealth and murder by Reza, who was one of the best.

"Very well," he continued, "then I need to get myself and my Franks back up to the castle. I left it closed up with the villagers safe inside, but guardians were a little thin on the ground. If you don't need me, I shall depart. Can your men and the villagers get the fires under control?"

Henry nodded. He was covered in other people's blood and filthy from the smoke, his face and beard smeared with dark smudges from the effect of the fires. His chain hauberk was ripped and he looked tired, but he seemed to Max to be very happy with the way events had turned out.

"Go, Max. Report to our Lady that all is under control, and I shall send messengers to inform her of anything untoward should it happen. Wish them well."

Max saluted, clambered upon his mount, which was being held by a village boy, thanked the boy, then looked over at Palladius. "We march back to the castle, Sergeant. Are the men ready?"

Palladius bellowed a command, and the men formed up on the road. Max then led the way up the long, steep, grassy slopes towards the distant castle. It appeared to him that they had done very well with their limited resources. As they marched past corpses of the pirates they had engaged earlier, they began to see activity on the crest of the hill. Wary and alarmed, Max and Palladius stared upwards, but then the people on the castle walls noticed them and waved. Reassured, they finished the weary climb to encounter an extraordinary sight.

Corpses littered the road that led right up to the castle gates. Dead horses and men were strewn about, their form of dress unmistakably Greek, which could only mean to Max that they were mercenaries from Famagusta. A few of the dead men were more ornamentally clad, with gold adorning their chain armor and shields or persons. Surprised and shocked, Max hurried past them and the work gangs, ignoring the called out greetings, and rushed into the bailey where he found yet another pile of bodies.

"What happened!" he roared up at Gregory, who was supervising the clean up.

Gregory pointed with his thumb at the main hall. "While you were away, Sir Max, we were attacked. All of us have been very busy, but our Lady and her phantoms did the most damage. I swear she is akin to Lord Talon and Master Reza. She, too, is a magician!"

Max dismounted with some care. He was feeling his age sometimes, and now was one of those times. "Dear God, but I hope they are all right," he whispered to himself, Theodora being foremost in his mind.

He emerged at the top of the steps and clumped his way breathlessly towards the Solarium. He heard soft voices, and his relief was profound when he saw all three women seated on cushions, looking as though nothing had happened.

"Ah, Max, there you are. We were beginning to wonder where you might have been," Rav'an greeted him with a sweet smile of welcome. "Would you like some tea?"

"I... er... I... er... went to see if Henry needed help," he rumbled, looking from one of the beautiful women to another as though searching for a clue. They all looked quite calm and composed, but he knew something was up.

"As you can see, Max, we have been enjoying the warm late morning, and I do think you should have asked me if it were wise to gallop off down the hill in your present condition," Theodora told him with hint of a frown. Jannat gave him a sweet smile. "Max, you have been missed. Will you not tell us all about the port and if all is well?"

Max looked around the room warily. "Is Reza all right, Theo?" he demanded slowly. Then he shook his head. "Very well, Ladies, stop this! What has been going on while I was away?"

The women began to laugh. Then Rav'an said, "Sit down, Max. You look tired, and we will of course tell of what happened. Just after you left to help Henry, we were attacked from an unexpected quarter. Fortunately, we were alerted just in time. We were almost taken by surprise."

"Dimitri actually sent a warning, but the message arrived right in the middle of the conflict, so it really didn't make any difference," Jannat said. "We have dealt with the enemy who came here to do us harm, but there appear to be problems in the palace."

Max dropped tiredly down onto a cushion next to a smiling Theodora and accepted a little bowl of tea. "Tell me everything, my Lady. I beg of you."

"First, please, tell me where is my son?" Rav'an demanded with a slight edge to her tone.

"Don't fret, my Lady. He is in good company. He and his little gang of 'Assassins are sweeping up the remainder of the pirates. Henry thinks that their ships are in the same inlet that we used ourselves."

*****

Rostam and his men moved warily through the woodlands, keeping a sharp lookout for anyone who might be preparing an ambush. He was grateful to Max for trusting him with this task and took it seriously. Behind the horsemen, a group of armed villagers were spread out in a manner they employed when beating for game. They had already flushed out three of the pirates, all of them wounded, who had been summarily put to death as they begged for their lives. Rostam had at first almost weakened, but his closest companion, Andreas, a tall boy who was mature for his age, told him, "Rostam, you must think as would Master Reza. These people came to plunder, rape, and murder your people. Reza would show no mercy. They have none. As prisoners they would be a burden on us now and a danger later. You must tell them, the villagers await your order."

Rostam looked down at the dirty, disheveled and bleeding man kneeling in front of him. The man called out piteously for mercy.

Realizing that Andreas was right, Rostam reluctantly indicated to his companions to carry out the gristly work. For the first time he understood the harshness of battle and its consequences.

At the approaches to the inlet the riders dismounted. Telling the villagers to stay back and watch for straggling pirates, Rostam and his men slipped along the pathway, alert for any trap or attempt to block their way. There was no sound other than the perpetual hiss of the cicadas and a light wind that soughed in the upper branches of the pines; there was no sign of activity.

Nonetheless, they moved silently and very cautiously to emerge onto the cliff overlooking the inlet. It was deserted, as was the beach below, but there were clear signs of much recent activity. There was discarded equipment all over the beach, including mail shirts and helmets. The panicked crews must have been in a great hurry, Rostam thought, staring out towards the sea where he just caught a glimpse of the top of ships' masts moving slowly down the neck of the inlet.

"They are getting away!" exclaimed Andreas. Then they heard a boom further out to sea and saw a yellowish cloud rising in to the sky. It was quickly disbursed by the freshening wind.

"That way!" Rostam pointed excitedly towards the goat path which led to the promontory near the entrance to the inlet. "We can see from there!" Dismounting hurriedly, the boys and some village lads raced along the path, jumping over and dodging bare roots and rocks and ducking under low branches.

They emerged from the scrub and woods onto a bare patch of grass and rocks that gave them a grandstand view of the entrance to the inlet and a wide open view of the sea.

There, ahead of them, about half a league distant, Guy's ship was just turning around, the oars creating a froth in the sea as the crew went at their labors. Rostam could make out Guy very clearly as the captain gesticulated and bellowed orders. Men in the bows were bent over one of the two Scorpions. Others were running up the rigging to assist with the sails. The slim boat appeared almost to spin on its heels in a flurry of spume and spray.

One pirate ship, the one nearest to Guy's ship, was on fire at its after end. The crew were desperately trying to put out the flames, which had taken hold on the hull and were now threatening to engulf the rigging and the sails.

"The sea is rising, Rostam," one of his companions observed as they stood, braced against the wind on the furthermost point of the promontory. He was right; the wind had come up and a heavy swell was developing at sea. Guy's ship rose and fell to such an extent that Rostam wondered how they might be able to strike the second ship, now making its way out of the inlet. He could see it was a struggle for the depleted crew of the enemy ship to negotiate the exit against a head wind, but they managed, and before long the second pirate ship was nosing into the swells. Spray flew all the way back over its deck as the ship caught the wind from the north quarter and heeled.

There was no doubt that, in skillful hands, this kind of vessel could sail very close to the wind, and Rostam formed a grudging respect for the captain as his men maneuvered the nimble ship past the dark teeth of the rocks on either side and made for open water. The vessel was within reach of a long bow-shot, but the spectators were caught up in the drama unfolding below and had no thought to try to hinder the passage with puny arrows. Rostam gave a start when he recognized the captain of the ship, who, looking up, waved to him in a gesture of bravado that made the young man grin. Abul-Zinad was making his escape, and despite all the setbacks he was still defiant.

Their ordeal was not over, however, for Guy had his ship facing the right way, and even with the growing swell he had the oars out and sails set, and his ship was ploughing a furrow through the waves like some monstrous water bug intent upon its prey. He shortened the distance between him and Abul's vessel at a rapid pace. It was a fine spectacle to watch as the pirate ship exited the inlet and attempted to head north and away from the menacing approach. Both ships were now under full sail, rising and falling in the waves with spray flying high over their sides and bows.

Guy's ship was now only a few hundred paces away from the pirate vessel, and from his vantage point on the promontory Rostam could see the activity in its bows as the crew attempted to prepare the Scorpions. He shook his head. Guy would have to get very close in these seas if he wanted to be sure of a hit. The bows of his ship were rising and falling in the green spume-laden swells, which were growing in height. Guy appeared to be determined, however. The distant, regular beat of the drum came to the watchers on the cliff as the chase unfolded almost right under their eyes.

Abul-Zinad had successfully turned his vessel towards the north. His ship heeled as his sails caught the strengthening wind, but the turn delayed him just enough for Guy to come within sixty paces. Guy must have decided to try his luck, because the spectators saw one of the Scorpions jump and a long dark arrow sped towards the pirate ship.

"They shoot!" one of Rostam's companions shouted excitedly, pointing.

But the rolling waters made aim chancy. The shaft flew over the pirate ship almost at head height and disappeared into the sea with a splash fifty paces beyond. There was a collective groan from those on the hill, and all eyes turned to the pirate vessel.

It appeared that Abul-Zinad had a trick or two in his own arsenal. The watchers on the promontory could just hear the shouted orders, then the vessel turned into the wind and they all heard a thump from the ship's waist. A small, dark, round object flew into the air towards Guy's ship, which was ploughing furiously towards it. The object left a thin trail of smoke behind.

"Oh, God protect them!" Rostam gasped. "He has Greek Fire—and a catapult!"

Everyone on the cliff top held their breath as the missile arced across the intervening space and struck Guy's ship almost at the water line just aft of his bows. It exploded in a silent splatter of blue fire that reached up as high as the hand rail, then sped along the hull at water level as the noxious liquid flared. There was a collective groan as they witnessed the deadly fire, every sailor's nightmare, take hold of the hull.

Moments before the Greek Fire struck Guy's ship, his second Scorpion jumped in the bows and another long, black Scorpion strike hurtled across the gap, and this one struck home, even though the fleeing ship had begun to turn away as soon as it had sent its own missile. There was a flash, then the muted blast of an explosion. The ship trembled, and the watchers could all see the rails shredding and men falling, but it continued to turn; and when it was facing north it sped away. The crowd on the cliff could just see a gap in the side on the main deck, but the ship was seaworthy enough to take to its heels.

Apparently Abul-Zinad had no stomach for a closer encounter, for even while Guy was forced to deal with the potentially deadly blow his ship had received, Abdul used his advantage not to attack again but to make his escape. Rostam turned his attention back to Guy, and saw with relief that the fire appeared to be contained. Guy's crew knew that the only way to stop Greek Fire from spreading was to smother it with sand, which they were now doing with great energy. Their frantic efforts paid off, leaving a huge smoldering black patch, over which men poured water and sand in copious quantities. A pall of stinking black smoke blew back over the spectators on the cliff, but as soon as it passed they could see that Guy and his crew were out of immediate danger, so they cheered.

Rostam glanced northwards to see the pirate ship already two good leagues away, hurrying from this unfriendly coast.

"I hope we meet again. Then we shall see," he murmured, as he watched the retreating vessel. Once he ascertained that Guy would be able to take his ship safely to port, he led the way back towards the horses.

"Keep looking for stragglers, and capture anyone who makes it to shore from that first ship," he ordered the villagers. "We want some prisoners for their information." Rostam wanted to know where the pirate lair was located.

Later that day when the sun was about to set in a blaze of red to the west, the family and the two captains convened in the dim Solarium. Candles were lit, and food and drink for the thirsty captains and warriors were laid out on low tables. Guy and Henry were eating their way through a mound of meat and vegetables, sopping up the gravy in their bowls with bread as though they hadn't eaten for days.

Reza had been carried in on a pallet by attendants; Junayd and Dar'an placed themselves on either side as though on guard. Jannat seated herself nearby and fussed over her husband. Reza was enjoying the attention, but Theodora was keeping a sharp eye on him for fatigue, having threatened to remove him at the first sign of exhaustion.

Having done her best to see that Reza was going to live through the experience, she sat beside Max, who took her hand in his and rubbed it. "You look tired, my Theo," he murmured and handed her some warm spiced red wine, which she sipped gratefully.

"I am thankful you have all come back safely," she said, and gave him a wan smile.

"Well, Mother, you have told us all what happened here, and we have given you our accounts of what happened below in the village. What now?" Rostam chirped up.

Rav'an looked out over her family. Apart from the children, who had been taken away by their nurses, and the conspicuous absence of Talon, they were all together. She was grateful they had survived the several engagements, but there had been a heavy cost, particularly to the villagers.

"We have lost many of our people to the pirates, and you, Guy, were very nearly lost. I give thanks to God for your deliverance, and ours, but it was a close thing."

"Indeed it was, my Lady." Guy lifted his cup. "But everyone played their part, and we overcame the scoundrels. What we have to find out is why they attacked. We know Isaac's men were involved, even though we have an informal truce with the Emperor."

"You ask why the pirates came?" Reza interjected. "Why, to try and save that cousin of his in our dungeons, of course."

"There is more to this than a rescue, Reza," Rav'an stated with a thoughtful frown. "Besides, I don't think Abul-Zinad tried very hard to regain his cousin. Do you, Max? Why did he not send a messenger with an offer of ransom? That is how these situations are customarily resolved."

"I am beginning to have my suspicions, my Lady," Max responded.

"There is something odd that I am seeing here, or rather not seeing," Jannat spoke up.

"What do you mean, Sister?" Rav'an asked.

"The message from Dimitri says that Diocles is in prison, which might be why we have not heard from him. It is unusual for him not to send a pigeon once a week. Dimitri tried to warn us that something was going to happen. He reports that there have been strange ships in the harbor, and much activity at the palace. The Emperor is away, the most senior person at the palace is now the man called Zenos, and he appears to have brought in people from outside the island."

"Ah. So we can be sure that the palace indeed had a hand in this attack, and it may be the Emperor knows nothing of it," Reza said. "Dar'an and Junayd know that Rashid Ed Din is involved, so it seems we were attacked from not just one but three quarters. Tell them, Dar'an," he said, and leaned back with a sigh of pain.

"My Lady, Sirs," Dar'an said in his quiet way, "we talked to the assassin who survived." Rav'an knew it had been more than a talk. The screams had percolated all the way up from the dungeon.

"He was sent with a small group to gain entry, sow panic, and open the gates to the men from the palace, who would then claim it in the name of the Emperor. The pirates were to be a diversion, to be paid with a share of the plunder once they had taken the villages. But while that might have been the initial agreement, Junayd and I found out that the assassins were in fact going to kill all of us and hold the castle for Rashid Ed Din. They had orders to *not* allow the riders, nor the pirates, access to the keep."

There were exclamations of surprise at this. "And their plan very nearly worked," Max muttered. He was still angry at himself for having misjudged the situation.

"Do not blame yourself, Sir Max," Dar'an said, seeing his discomfort. "We were all caught by surprise." He smiled at Rav'an. "But Lady Rav'an and Lady Jannat saved the day."

"And made a smelly mess!" Reza murmured.

"Quiet, my Reza, let him continue," Jannat chided him.

"The assassins know who within the palace ordered the attack. It was that man Zenos, but there is another man, called Aeneas, from Constantinople, who came to investigate the whereabouts of Pantoleon," Dar'an continued.

"That man again?" Jannat breathed. She was referring to Pantoleon who had come to the island using the alias Exazenos.

"Yes. It was Pantoleon who brought the gold to the island, my Lady, and this Aeneas came to find it." Dar'an gave her a reassuring smile. "However, I think we stopped this one in his tracks, my Lady."

"Seems like Zenos hatched an elaborate plan to get the gold back for him," Max commented, "only to be betrayed by his allies."

"If Zenos is breaking the unspoken treaty between Talon and the Emperor, we have a problem," Reza said. "You say Diocles has been arrested, in which case I do not give much for his chances. That Isaac is a vengeful person. Someone must to go to Famagusta and talk to Dimitri."

"But that has usually been you or Talon. Who can we send?" Jannat asked the question that was on all their minds. There was a brief silence as everyone contemplated this remark. Reza was clearly unable to go, and no one knew where Talon might be.

"I will go!" Rostam volunteered.

Rav'an gave him a sharp look and almost said "No!" right there and then, but Max sat up and said, "My Lady Rav'an. Rostam has proved himself an able soldier, and Reza has good reports on his abilities within that shadow world of his. Those are the skills that are needed. And Rostam need not go alone; he could take Dar'an or Junayd with him."

She still looked hesitant. "But he is only—"

"A boy, Rav'an?" Reza wheezed. "He is a man. I promise you that. *We* were only boys when we escaped from Alamut, and you a young girl, but we did well. *You* did well. He is growing up, Rav'an, and this will be a good experience for him. The travel is no longer as dangerous as it used to be," he insisted. Rostam gave him a grateful look.

"Very well," Rav'an conceded reluctantly. "But Junayd or Dar'an or both must go with him. And which of you captains will take him?"

Henry looked uncomfortable, and to buy himself time to think about his answer he tore at a piece of bread with his bad teeth. Finally he spoke. "My Lady, Guy's ship needs repairs, as the Greek Fire badly damaged the side. The wood is so charred at the water level we cannot leave it afloat for much longer. The ship will have to be beached and patched."

"That leaves your ship then, Henry."

"We need a good ship to protect the harbor at all times, my Lady. One with Scorpions mounted."

Rav'an frowned. This didn't appear to be going very well. She took a sip of wine to help bring her frustration under control.

Rostam raised his hand tentatively. "There is another ship in the harbor, Mother. Remember the one we took off the pirates?" Rav'an looked as though she would rather not remember that, but finally she nodded.

"I can navigate that ship, and captain it too, Mother."

"Oh, no," she protested, but Guy hurriedly interjected.

"My Lady, he does know how to navigate, and I am confident that he will see the ship safely in both directions. I shall lend him my best crewmen to ensure he is well assisted."

The scruffy, uncouth pair of captains were conspiring to get her son into a hazardous mission. She frowned, giving them both a disapproving look; she was by now thoroughly vexed with them. Henry looked uncomfortable and avoided her glare, while Guy wiped gravy off his beard with his sleeve, looking sheepish.

There was more discussion, but finally she conceded, and then the party broke up. Reza was taken back to his infirmary, where Theodora fussed over him for a while. Having reassured herself that he was comfortable, she left Rav'an and Jannat with him and went in search of Max.

Rav'an and Jannat sat on the either side of his bed in companionable silence.

"You are not to worry about Rostam, my Sister," Reza said finally.

"I am his mother, Reza; it is my duty to worry about him. Is he truly ready for all this?"

"I didn't tell you before, but he saved my life on the ship in our first engagement with the pirates. I would have died had he not been there at the right moment. The men like and respect him, too," Reza responded.

"Talon has become fond of saying, 'Hope for the best but be prepared for the worst,'" Reza continued. "Your boy is as prepared as we are able to make him, and should now be given the chance to prove himself independently. I would stake Jannat's pigeons on it being a safe mission." He smiled with deep affection and patted her hand.

"It is hard for you, I am sure. But it is necessary if he is to become the warrior he aspires to be. And we have to know what is going on in that den of iniquity. Don't forget that Dimitri and his men will be there to make sure nothing happens to him, as well as Junayd."

She nodded and smiled through her tearing eyes, then took his hand. "I am so uncertain, Reza. I miss Talon dreadfully, so that any thought of Rostam being in danger is too awful to think about."

Jannat leaned across Reza and kissed her on the cheek. "He is his father's son, but a huge part of his courage comes from his mother, Rav'an. Have faith, and we will all pray for his and Talon's safe return."

A servant appeared at the door and beckoned to Jannat. "You asked me to tell you the moment a pigeon arrived, my Lady. Here is the message." He handed the small roll of paper to Jannat, who opened it and stared at the message. By now she could read the code as though it were in clear language. Her face went white and her fingers holding the message shook as she looked up at the assembled family.

"What is it, Jannat?" Rav'an was the first to ask, her tone full of concern.

"This message is from Boethius in Paphos." She stopped as though trying to collect herself.

"Jannat, what is it?" Rav'an insisted, reaching for the paper in Jannat's trembling hand.

"There has been a great battle," Jannat whispered. "The Latin Christians have been utterly defeated. The Kingdom of Jerusalem is lying in ruins."

———————————

Chapter 21

Aftermath

My Thoughts no longer seek an end to tribulation;
My vision's gates are sealed, there is no revelation.
My eyes no longer picture the time of my salvation.
Foes amass before the border of my home like thorns
That pierce my side when I fall in pain.
                              —*Shelomo.ibn Gabirol*

Talon awoke with a splitting headache and a deep, aching pain in his right thigh, and a lesser pain on his upper left arm. He had trouble focusing his eyes. He lay still for a moment, feeling nauseated, trying to orientate himself, listening to the murmur of voices around him. He could hear the groans of wounded men, and the calm, low tones of someone talking to one agitated man who appeared to be crying.

He moved to sit up and look around, but his head threatened to burst and his leg screamed at him. He must have groaned aloud because a dark, bearded face under a loosely wrapped turban leaned over him, then the orderly called out to another person at the other end of the tent.

"The infidel lives and breathes, Doctor!"

Moments later, a thin-featured man with a well kept beard, wearing a more formal turban, peered down at him, while cool fingers lifted his wrist and took his pulse. From that one gesture Talon realized that he might be in some kind of temporary Arab hospital, or *Bimaristan* as they were known.

"Am I in hospital?" he croaked.

The doctor looked surprised. "He speaks Arabic! Now that is unexpected. Good, then you can tell me how you feel," he demanded, not unkindly.

"I feel like a horse fell on my head, and I could do with a drink of water," Talon rasped. He managed a weak smile.

The doctor nodded and gave him a bleak smile in return. "Yes, it might well feel like that; but a drink would be all right. Amman, go and fetch some clean water for our Infidel."

Turning back to his patient he said, "You have been unconscious for a day and a night. It was a good thing that you were wearing some protection on your head, otherwise I don't think we would have been talking today." His tone was dry. "Someone tried very hard to bash your skull in. Someone else saved your life and had you brought here. No one knew who you were until the Sultan's brother recognized you and told me to do what I could to patch you up."

Talon fingered the bandage around his throbbing head, then touched his thigh.

"What...what happened to my leg?" he asked, as he accepted the grudgingly given cup of water from Amman. "Did I break it?" His mind flashed back to the chaos on the slopes of Hattin, trying to remember what had occurred during those last nightmarish moments.

"You don't remember?" the doctor asked.

Talon nearly shook his head but thought better of it and croaked, "No," instead. He drank the water slowly.

"You took an arrow through the middle of your thigh. Don't worry, we took it out, and you are going to be able to walk again. The bang on your head must have addled your memory, but that, too, should come back to you... eventually.

Now I must notify the prince that you are awake, as he wants to see you."

The doctor got up, and as he left Talon thanked him. He stopped and said, "You might not have much cause to be grateful, but at least there is hope where there is life. So much is lost for these ridiculous causes men keep inventing to kill one another." He shook his head, a disapproving expression on his lean features.

"I thank you, nonetheless. Go with God," Talon said, and shut his eyes. He felt very tired. A wave of despair threatened to overwhelm him as he slipped back into the darkness.

He woke to someone shaking him by the shoulder. The none too gentle orderly helped him to sit up, pushed some cushions behind his shoulders, then gave him water to drink and a bowl of lentils and scraps of lamb meat to eat.

"You are named Talon? You are a Lord?" he asked, as he handed a round disc of *nan* to Talon and then made him comfortable to prevent the bowl from falling. Talon felt faint after he sat up, but when his eyes ceased to cross and the tent stopped moving, he could take stock of his surroundings.

They were in a round tent with a center pole that allowed a man to stand upright near the middle. It had become stuffy from the breathing of too many men and the hot sun beating down on the fabric with unrelenting force, but it was preferable to being outside, he reasoned. All the same, the flies had found them. One of the other men lying on a pallet nearby was being fanned by an orderly to keep the buzzing creatures off a heavily bandaged, bloody wound in his abdomen. Talon flicked a couple away that had begun to show an interest in his bowl of food.

"You speak our language very well for an Infidel," Amman remarked. "I suppose you must be a lord, or else they would have killed you on the field, wounded as you were. Not much use as a slave!" he finished with a scornful sneer.

"Yes, I am named Talon, and yes I... I am a Lord." Talon responded. He spooned up more lentils and lamb from the soup. As he ate, he realized that he was famished and proceeded to finish off the soup, wiping the rim with some of the soft *nan*. "Where are we?"

"We are on the outskirts of Tiberius. Your battles are over, Infidel," Amman told him, then left to tend to one of the other wounded, who was calling out. Talon realized that he was with men from the Sultan's army. He wondered what might have become of any other of the Christian lords, if any had been captured. He sank back against the cushions, suddenly exhausted.

Later that day, Talon was again woken. There was a stirring at the entrance of the tent, and Amman was pulling his bedding into a neater shape. He whispered urgently to Talon.

"It is the Prince! Be very polite, or your head will roll, Infidel!" He struggled to move Talon into a sitting position as the Prince Al-Adil was ushered into the tent. He was in full armor and attended by two well armed footmen, who stood guard impassively at the entrance to the tent while he strode in and made for one of the beds.

Ignoring Talon, he stooped over each of the men in turn. Two of them were awake and keen to show their loyalty. One even tried to rise from his pallet to kneel before the prince, who pushed him gently back and spoke some encouragement, then moved on, motioning to an orderly to take care of the gasping man he had just left. The physician appeared and murmured something to the prince as he approached Talon's bed.

"*As-Salaam-Alaikum*, Lord Talon."

"*Wa-Alaikum-Salaam*, my Lord Prince." Talon responded.

"I had not thought to see you under such circumstances, Lord Talon."

"I am alive, thanks be to God and fate, which counts for something, Lord." Talon gave the prince a wan smile. "I am relieved that your doctor is very capable."

"Better than those Frans Leeches I have heard about?" the prince gave a derisive chuckle.

Talon smiled agreement and said, "It is impolite of me to lie here in front of you, Lord. I apologize for my incapacity, but I am honored to be in your presence." He knew the prince would come to the point eventually, and he suspected what it might be about.

"I trust the health of my Lord the Sultan is good?" Talon inquired.

"It is good, and becomes better by the day," the prince responded, looking smug.

He waved the hovering orderlies away and stepped a little closer. "God goes about his work and we are only able to ponder its meaning. You were lucky. Others not so."

"I can only imagine how fortunate I have been, Lord." Talon's tone was dry.

"In that you are right, Talon," the prince replied. "Your horse fell, and you were already wounded. One of our more eager warriors did not know your rank, so he tried to kill you. You owe your life to one of his officers, who recognized your dress and the coat of arms emblazoned on your shield and stopped him."

"I hope one day to be able to thank that officer from my heart," Talon said. "Who else lives, if I might ask Your Highness?"

"Your King, the Lord de Rideford, and others of that house, but... that evil man Châtillon does not. He has gone to hell." The prince sounded very satisfied with that.

Talon sighed. He wondered why it was that de Rideford, the cause of this utter catastrophe, was still allowed to live. The man had survived not one but two disasters of his own making, where all who followed him had perished. A sardonic thought occurred to him. Perhaps God didn't want de Rideford in heaven?

"I shall not mourn Châtillon. He caused much trouble between our peoples," he told the prince, who nodded.

"Then you will be pleased to hear that when the King surrendered he was escorted to our Sultan's tent, where he was treated with great courtesy... as it should be between kings." He shrugged. "Châtillon was with him at the time. They were all suffering from a terrible thirst, so Salah Ed Din gave a cup of chilled water to King Guy, who took some, but then handed it to Châtillon, who gulped the rest, just like the pig he was." The prince paused and looked straight at Talon. "Our Sultan, may God guide his ways, was incensed and rebuked the King, saying, "Let it be written that it was you who gave that man the water, not I.""

Talon bowed his head. "The Sultan, having given water to his prisoner, would not then harm him, but Châtillon merited no such protection," he murmured.

"I see you know our ways, Lord Talon," the prince said, with a wry twist of his mouth, then he continued.

"The Sultan then angrily listed the crimes of Châtillon for everyone to hear. They are too numerous and terrible to recount, but I am sure you are aware of many," the prince said.

"Yes indeed, my Lord. I know many of them, only too well," Talon agreed.

"When the Sultan finished, Châtillon still could not resist provoking him further and insulted him, so my brother struck off his head with his sword before all who were there."

"Châtillon will not be missed by anyone, Lord. I am glad that he is gone, and I am sure it is to hell," Talon said. He wished that de Rideford had gone with him.

"So he was also hated amongst the Frans?"

Talon grimaced. "He was despised, Lord. No one will mourn him."

The prince took a deep breath. "Well, now it is over, and we are about to take the citadel of Tiberius. Your Count Raymond is fled to the north, but his wife remains. The main part of the city was taken several days ago, but she still holds onto the citadel. Will she sue for peace, do you think? The Sultan, whom God has blessed with this great victory, is about to enter the city. I think he would be magnanimous."

Talon thought about that. "I am sure she will, Lord. It would be pointless to hold out. Will you sack the city?"

"Not unless they resist. Why should you care?"

"There is a physician there who is very skilled. He would be a useful addition to your own group of physicians, and he speaks Arabic."

"That could be useful," the prince agreed. "There is an acute shortage of skilled physicians at present. I shall pass the word. What is his name?"

"Artemus, and he is an old curmudgeon but he knows what he is doing, unlike the Latin Leeches. He was educated in Constantinople at the *Bimaristan* there. I would willingly pay for his release, if you wish."

The prince chuckled. "I shall take that into consideration, Lord Talon. I have never known a physician who is not condescending and aloof. Fear not, I shall have him found and protected. The rest, however, I fear will be enslaved; you know how things are."

Talon shrugged mentally. This was the way of things, and he could do no more.

He was clear in his mind as to what lay in store for the rest of the crusader world. First Tiberius, then Acre no doubt, after which the Sultan would proceed to mop up all the other cities, his ultimate goal being Jerusalem.

The prince changed the subject. "My brother has been notified that you are alive and in our care. He says that he
hopes you have a full recovery, but, alas that you are still a
prisoner... unless, that is... You understand that this is a delicate matter?" He finished with a gentle wave of his right
hand.

"I shall do my best to raise whatever is asked of me, Lord.
Please let me know the conditions, and I shall send a letter to
start proceedings."

The prince looked relieved. "Ah, yes, just so. The amount
would be for some ten thousand dinars. Not too much for
someone like yourself I hope? You are, after all, a *Lord* now,
is that not right?" There was just a trace of sarcasm in his
tone, which was not lost on Talon, but he ignored it.

Talon pretended to look concerned by the amount, but it
was nothing when compared to his fortune. He nodded, appearing to be reluctant. "I... agree to the amount, Lord. I
need, however, the means to write a letter to my people in
Cyprus, and then have the amount delivered to anywhere
you wish."

"That is so good of you, Lord Talon." The prince waved
both hands in a gesture that resembled that of an armored
praying mantis. Even his eyes had taken on the glossy look of
one. Talon began to wonder if the prince was handling matters on his own rather than on behalf of his brother the Sultan.

"The other condition would be that, once the payment is
made, you must leave and not fight again in this land."

"Perhaps there is another way we could manage this, my
Lord," Talon said, without acknowledging the terms; his
tone, however, was tentative and respectful.

"Hmm, what would that be?" the prince asked, cocking
his head, never taking his dark eyes off Talon's.

"Do you know where your cousin is at present, Lord?"
Talon asked softly.

"My cousin? Which one? I have so many!" the prince said with a depreciating gesture and a puzzled smile.

"Yes, of course. Forgive me, Lord, I meant Makhid, your cousin from Dalmatia, the corsair leader. The pirate," Talon added. He noticed a flicker of annoyance in the black eyes.

"He is not a pirate, Lord Talon," the prince responded sharply. "He is a sailor, and a very good one. He does the Sultan's work upon the seas. Why are you interested in him?"

Talon took his time answering. He could be on dangerous ground here, but he knew he had the advantage as long as the prince and Makhid were relatively close. More importantly, how much in favor with the Sultan was the pirate?

"Makhid and his ships ran into mine at sea, Lord. There was a battle... with heavy losses on his side. He became my prisoner. He is well, and by the way, so is his son. I am informing you of this because we might be able to negotiate an exchange... perhaps?"

Al-Adil slowly brought his right hand up to his bearded lips and frowned, as though pondering Talon's words. There was no doubt in Talon's mind that he was shaken by the news.

"He is in good health? Do you have proof of this?" the prince asked after a long pause.

"You have my word on it, Lord. I can assure you that he is in good health and will remain so until we can release him back to you."

"Where is he at this time?" Talon noted a sly look appear in the dark eyes. He knew what was passing through the prince's mind. The Christian lands lay prostrated before Salah Ed Din's army. They might be able to extract his cousin without the need to exchange him for Talon.

"He is on a ship, Lord. Because of that I cannot say exactly where he is at present," Talon responded, feigning regret. "I would have sent a message to you or the Sultan before this, but as we both know, events prevented communications. But now would be a good time to discuss arrangements, don't you think?"

The prince gave an abrupt chuckle. "Here we both are haggling like a pair of fishermen over a catch!" He grinned at Talon, but there was a gleam of respect in his eyes. "We will talk more on this, Lord Talon. I think that, although we have been enemies, we might yet become friends. Meanwhile, you must focus on getting well. God protect you. *Salaam*." He turned away.

"Peace to you, my Lord."

Talon relaxed back against the cushions with an effort and thought about his circumstances. His chances of making it to Tyre seemed very slim. If he couldn't get to the safety of the fort and his waiting ship, he might be a prisoner for a long time: months, even years. He had some experience of ransoms, having extorted one from the captain of a captured ship when he was just beginning to make his fortune. The negotiations could take many months to arrange, founded as they were upon a policy of mutual distrust.

He touched his leg and winced. He was a long way from recovery, and if he was unable to even walk, what were his chances of going anywhere? Not for the first time, he wondered what was going on at Kantara. He had left in April. It was now early July, and he and Reza had thought to be away a mere two weeks! Rav'an must be beside herself with worry. He hoped fervently that Yosef had made his escape. His thoughts turned inwards as he thought about his family and wondered how they might be, in particular Reza. He prayed that he had escaped this madness and was recovering.

How much he missed the community, his friends, and above all, his Rav'an! Thinking back on events, he felt a surge of anger at the arrogance and stupid behavior of the lords of the Crusader Kingdom. Even the Count Raymond had left his wife to fend for herself while he fled. Was everyone in the

Kingdom so venal? Sooner or later the Count would know of Talon's fate, and of Rideford's and others who had been captured. the jubilant Arabs would make sure the news was carried far and wide. He drifted off to sleep, thinking about what their lives had come to: him a prisoner and Rav'an without knowledge of his whereabouts.

*****

When he was informed of the fate of his cousin, Salah Ed Din gave a bark of amusement. "This *Lord* Talon, whom we have as a prisoner, wounded and at a physical disadvantage, is still one step ahead of us! I did tell you that he was once a slave in Egypt? Yes, that's right, and he played Chogan there too; a good player. He had the gall to steal a ship full of slaves, and disappeared off to Acre. Very cunning is our *Lord* Talon. Not to be underestimated at all. So he has our cousin a prisoner, eh?"

"So he claims. What do you want me to do about him, my Brother?" Al-Adil replied.

"I am sure of one thing," Salah Ed Din said. "I don't want another visit of the kind I was subjected to from his 'brother', Reza, as a reckoning. Lord Talon wants to do an exchange? We should agree I think, for our own sakes." He chuckled again. "He and his *'brother'*," the Sultan again emphasized the word, "are two of the most cunning people I have ever had the misfortune to encounter. We should deal gently with this man, because if he is harmed, then the revenge Reza will take, upon you certainly, and perhaps upon myself, will be awful. They are, or at least Reza is, even more dangerous than those *Batinis* that Rashid Ed Din keeps in the mountains north of Tripoli. How I would like to finish Rashid Ed Din off at the same time I conquer this land! My contentment would then be complete!"

Chapter 22

Escape

The Banshee's wild voice sings the death-dirge before me,
The pall of the dead for a mantle hangs o'er me;
But my heart shall not flag, and my nerves shall not shiver,
Though devoted I go—to return again never!
                                                    —Sir Walter Scott.

The citadel of Tiberius fell on the third day after the battle of Hattin. Talon had been dozing fitfully when he heard the roar as the Arab army swarmed into the city to celebrate and fully invest the town. The sounds of their triumph filled the air. From the excited chatter all around him, Talon gathered that the Lady Eschiva of Bures was under guard. Once relative quiet had been restored after the assault, Talon heard that terms for the disposition of the prisoners were being discussed.

Later that day, the physician came by on his rounds and stood over Talon. "Salam, Lord Talon," he said. "How are you feeling today?"

"Much better, thank you, Doctor." Talon struggled to sit up. "Is Tiberius taken?" he asked.

"Yes, and my work continues." The physician sighed into his beard. He administered the foul medicine that Talon had to drink twice a day, noticing Talon's grimace of disgust as he swallowed it. "That horrible tasting medicine has kept infection at bay, so you would do well to continue with it and not protest over much, Lord.

"I do have some good news for you," he continued. Talon looked up.

"Your request was heard, and I now have an assistant." For the first time the doctor smiled, albeit a wintry one. "The physician from Constantinople, Artemus, is under the protection of the prince and is safe with me. He continues his work in the city."

Talon smiled his thanks. "I am sure that, professionally, you will enjoy each other's company," he said in a voice loaded with irony.

His tone was not lost on the doctor, who shrugged. "Men insist upon making war, so there is always a need for skilled physicians, no matter from where, to patch them up. You will be moved, at least temporarily, to the city. I have asked that our seriously wounded be moved to where we can better aid them, and the Sultan agreed. The doctor Artemus informs me that his clinic would be a better place than this tent."

Talon could only agree. Despite the competent administrations of the doctor and his assistants, it was very hot in the tent, with little air flow to relieve the heat, and the flies were becoming not just a nuisance but a hazard. The man with the torn abdomen had died during the night, only to be replaced by another badly wounded man, who lay in a torpor for most of the time. When he was conscious he writhed with the pain in his chest and cried for his mother.

They moved Talon late that afternoon, lifting him onto a pallet, which was then carried by four sullen Arab infantrymen. They knew he was an infidel but dared not offend the doctor, who was adamant about how they should behave towards him. They lurched and weaved their way through crowds of men-at-arms and army followers who were moving back and forth between the encampment and the city.

The austere atmosphere that had characterized the place when the town was Christian had already been replaced by the noises and smells of street vendors and food stalls as the more enterprising camp followers cooked food for hungry soldiers. A light haze of smoke hung over the streets from the small fires, and the air was heavy with the aromas of roasting meat and vegetables.

As Talon's small escort entered the gates, now manned by Arab sentries, Talon glanced around. There was little evidence of looting or burning. Once again the Sultan had imposed his stern will upon his army and forbidden his men to sack the city, but there were other signs of the assault. He could see holes in the upper ramparts where the Sultan's catapults had succeeded in landing missiles. There were even blackened and burnt areas where Greek Fire, now in common use, had exploded. And of course there was evidence of hand to hand fighting in the form of discarded weapons and armor, still to be collected and redistributed.

They passed piles of corpses, which were being loaded onto carts to be taken out of the city for burial. There was no time to wash the dead, but the Arab corpses were wrapped in cotton cloth from head to foot. Those of the Franks were dumped unceremoniously into waiting carts. There would doubtless be a single pit for the Franks, while the Arabs would be interred with more ceremony.

His glance roved over the people milling about as they approached the large city square, and he gave a start. There were several lines of prisoners, squatting in chains, along one of the walls. He was sure he recognized one of the prisoners crouched among the others.

He called out to his carriers. "Stop!"

"What does he want?" one of the bearers grumbled as they lurched to a halt.

"Bring that man to me," Talon told them in their own tongue, pointing to the line of slaves. They put him down gently enough, with surprised looks on their faces. "You speak our language, Infidel?" one of the men demanded.

"Yes, but I need to speak to that prisoner, over there," Talon indicated the Saxon. "Bring him here," Talon commanded. He hoped that they would obey him, although there was no reason to, other than the authoritative manner he had adopted for their benefit. He was, after all, a prisoner himself. Still, they hesitated, so he forced himself to sit up and said in a low tone, "I shall reward all four of you very well, but he must come with us. He is my servant."

"Very well, but you had better not be lying, and you had better make sure we are paid," one of the men told him. Two of them reluctantly walked over to the overseer in charge of the prisoners. They spoke together for a couple of voluble minutes, and then all three walked back. The overseer appeared to be in an unfriendly mood; his swagger said a lot before he even opened his mouth.

"Who are you to demand the release of that prisoner over there?" The skinny man looked down on Talon with an arrogant stare. He spat at the ground, the gob of saliva just missing Talon.

"What is going on here?" another voice, this time with much more authority, growled from behind Talon's head. There was no mistaking the voice. It was a harsh, gravelly voice Talon would know anywhere.

"What are you doing, loitering in the square with an important prisoner?" Yosef demanded. His tone was imperious.

"We...we were asked to stop so that this infidel Lord could speak to his servant... over there, Sir," one of Talon's bearers said, pointing to the Saxon. His tone was now much more polite. Talon craned his neck to look up at his friend. It was Yosef, without a doubt.

"You are to take this man to the physician's house, over there," Yosef pointed in the direction of the house of Artemus. "Down that street, the second house to your right. If I see you stop for anything I shall be reporting you to the highest authority!" Yosef almost bellowed. "Now go! I shall be right behind you," he snarled. "As for you," he stared rudely at the overseer, who cringed. "His lordship has decreed that Lord Talon, this Infidel, is to have a servant. That one will do. Go and get him," Yosef ordered.

"Now!" he added sharply. "You will all be paid. I shall see to that," he said in a more conciliatory tone to the frightened men. "Now do as you are told."

The overseer ran over to Brandt, who had been dozing against the wall, and hauled him to his feet. Muttering imprecations and threats, he unlocked the dazed man from his neighbors, then dragged him, still bound by his ropes, to where Talon and his bearers were waiting.

"I shall pay you tonight. Or rather, the Prince shall pay," Yosef told the overseer.

"Allah be praised," he said as an afterthought. The man bowed and put his hand on his breast. "God's will, thank you, Sir," he answered, and returned to his charges.

"You!" Yosef seized the Saxon by the shoulder and shoved him roughly forward. "You go with us. Do not try to escape or I kill you." The confused Saxon understood not a word and was about to react to the rough treatment when Talon said sharply in French, "Do as he says, Brandt."

The Saxon gave him a shocked look of recognition, his light blue eyes wide with surprise, but he snapped his mouth shut and shuffled along after the bearers and Yosef, who had taken the lead. "By the Mullah's beard, hurry up, you lazy peasants!" he called back to the almost trotting men, who were sweating in the warm evening air under their burden.

"Just do as he tells you and we will talk later," Talon told the thoroughly confused Saxon, as they approached the house of Artemus. They entered the small courtyard inside the building.

Artemus was inside, treating some of the wounded from the Arab army. He didn't even glance at the new arrivals. "Put him over there," he commanded, and turned back to his bloody work. The bearers did as they were told, and then Yosef shepherded them out of the building. He sent them on their way with the reassurance that they would be paid, just as the Infidel lord had promised. They exchanged salaams, and the men walked off.

Yosef walked back into the house and closed the outer doors, after which he strode into the sick room with all the assurance of an officer in the army of the Sultan. Men made way for this expensively armored warrior, who appeared to be in charge; he made his way over to where Talon lay with Brandt kneeling in front of him, his arms still bound behind him.

Drawing out his short sword, Yosef cut the man's bonds and indicated that he should sit down. Brandt was willing enough to do so, while Talon tried hard to conceal his delight at seeing Yosef.

"I was very worried about you, Yosef," he whispered. "How in God's name did you find me, and where did you find that grand looking suit of mail?"

"By sheer accident, Lord, and the mail belonged to someone who was too drunk to know," Yosef replied, as he knelt on one knee beside Talon. "I was on my way out of the city to search one last time when I saw you being brought through the gates!" He grinned at Talon, who reached out and gripped his hand hard. "God be praised, but I am so very glad to see you." There were tears in both men's eyes.

"I found your horse on the field. And this." Yosef tapped the hilt of Talon's sword tucked into his sash. "I could not find the scabbard. I assume they took that off you."

Talon gasped with surprise and gripped Yosef's hand even harder, his delight showing in his eyes.

"We will talk later, Lord. I have to steal some money and pay the men who brought you here, or there will be questions," Yosef said as he stood up. Talon nodded agreement. "That should not be hard for someone like you, my lad," he smiled. Yosef grinned, then. "You are not to move from this place until I come back. Do you understand?" He spoke loudly, gesturing aggressively.

Talon looked meek and Brandt, taking his lead from Talon, bowed his head submissively. Yosef strode away, behaving like a lord himself.

"So now... there is some hope...." Talon murmured. "Are you wounded?" he asked the large Saxon.

"No, Lord. I was simply made to surrender along with everyone else in the citadel," was the low response.

"Ah, so it was surrendered. That is no surprise, but what has become of the Countess Eschiva of Bures?"

"I think she was granted safe passage to join the Count Raymond, Lord," Brandt said. "We peasants, of course, were made prisoners." He sounded bitter but resigned.

"I was not very hopeful before, but now that Yosef has appeared I feel much better," Talon said.

"When he thought you were lost he swore he would go and find you, but we were driven off the field."

"You stayed with him?" Talon was surprised. Self preservation was what he had expected, but apparently this man had felt otherwise.

"What happened to the Count?" Talon asked.

Brandt spat onto the rushes nearby, "He simply rode off with barely a backward glance. I am sorry, my Lord. I do not think he did the most honorable thing!" Brandt's tone was tinged with bitterness. Rather than follow the Count, I remained here to help defend the citadel."

Talon glanced up at glowering Saxon, re-evaluating him.

"Don't judge him too harshly, Brandt," he said in a low tone. "He is a sick man, and capture would have killed him most assuredly. He has already spent ten years in one of their dungeons. I am pleased that he did not fall on that field of shame and stupidity," Talon assured the Saxon. "And I am glad that his lady managed to negotiate a way out of this mess. However, I pity the poor people like you were who are left to the mercies of the Arab conquerors."

"While I am grateful to you for taking me away from that fate, can you tell me what is to become of us, Lord?" Brandt asked. His voice, while unafraid, was nonetheless a little apprehensive.

"Why, for a start you are now in my service, unless you would have it otherwise." Talon smiled up at the Saxon.

"That, Lord, is just as I could want it, especially under these circumstances," Brandt replied with a rueful grin. "I shall serve you to the best of my ability. Before God I declare this."

"Then that is settled. So now we shall do our best, with Yosef's aid, to escape."

"Escape? But you are badly wounded, Lord!" Brandt could not hide his astonishment at Talon's words.

"I can still ride, and with Yosef and you to help me... we shall see," Talon responded. "We have to get to Tyre before the Sultan, or our only means of getting to Cyprus will be cut off. Careful now, here comes the physician. Just sit there and say nothing."

Artemus shuffled up and stared down at Talon. "Ah, Lord Talon. I had heard you were here, but as you can see I have been somewhat busy. How are you?" he rasped in Arabic.

"Not at my very best, as you can see, Doctor. But better for having seen you," Talon responded.

"I am informed that I am under the protection of the Prince, and that is thanks to you, Lord." The doctor gave a brief nod of his head, the closest thing to a "Thank-you," Talon reflected, he was likely to get from the physician. He knelt, and took Talon's pulse, then placed a dry hand on his forehead, peering into his eyes.

"How long ago was the wound?" he asked, as he examined the ugly entry and exit of the injury.

Three days ago," Talon said, and winced as the doctor prodded the area around the wound.

"Well, I am glad to see that there appears to be no infection, and you are not feverish. Your eyes appear to be clear, which is a credit to the physician who treated you. I shall just ensure that the wound is kept clean and well covered," he stated. "Who is this?" He indicated the huge, filthy Saxon, who was squatting nearby, watching.

"He is my servant," Talon replied. "I have just purchased him back."

"I see. And that other man, he, too, is your servant if my memory serves me right?"

Talon tensed. "Yes," he replied in Greek.

"Ah. Just so," Artemus murmured in the same language. "How full of surprises you are, Lord Talon. If you plan to leave, don't worry. I shall be discreet. But I don't want any nastiness in this house. I gave my pledge not to escape, and my physician's oath is important to me."

Talon vented a silent sigh of relief. "My word upon it, Doctor. You will have no problems, of that kind, while I am in this house."

"Good. Then I shall leave you." He gave Brandt a disapproving look. "This man of yours can make himself useful by looking after you, firstly by washing his hands, and then by folding those burial cloths over there," he said pointedly, as he indicated a pile of whitish sheets in the corner near to Talon's pallet. "Despite my best efforts we still have to use them from time to time." The doctor rose and turned away.

*****

Yosef blended in easily amongst the wandering, jostling soldiery crowding around the food stalls and merchants carts. A couple of houses had been commandeered and converted into whore houses, and these were doing a roaring trade. The camp followers had moved into the city. He began to relieve some of the soldiers of their money by the simple expedient of cutting their purses with a tiny, very sharp knife that his mentor Reza has taught him to keep on his person. Despite the Mohammedan ban on alcohol, not a few of the soldiers were drunk, and these proved to be easy targets.

Before very long Yosef had collected a nice handful of coins. He then left the area and went in search of the overseer, who was himself drunk and seated in a mess of his own making not very far from the prisoners. One of the starving and thirsty prisoners begged him for water in French, which Yosef could just understand. He took up the skin near the overseer, who protested.

"You will not have any profit if you do not take better care of the slaves!" Yosef retorted contemptuously, and he tossed the full skin of water to the slave. "Make sure you pass it around," he said in French to the surprised and grateful man.

Yosef then tossed a couple of silver coins to the delighted overseer, and vanished into the milling crowd. He arrived back at the hospital several hours later, bearing a meal of *nan* and pieces of chicken for Talon and Brandt. Both men began to eat with gusto, while he settled himself cross-legged in front of Talon.

"We must escape, and it must be tonight," he stated simply. They were ignored by the other patients, most of whom were sleeping fitfully in their own alcoves, so the three of them had a small degree of privacy. Nevertheless they were still careful to keep their voices down. Talon and Yosef spoke to one another in Farsi.

"We need horses," Talon said.

"I have three of them in a grove near to the lake in a gully. Our problem is to get you out of the city." Yosef knew that under normal circumstances he and Talon could evade any of the sentries and simply vanish, but with Talon wounded and barely able to walk, not to mention their new-found and very obviously Frankish-looking Saxon in tow, it was quite another matter.

"I think the doctor was trying to tell me something earlier," Talon said, pointing to the now neatly folded pile of sheets that Brandt had stacked close by.

Yosef glanced at the pile. "Those are for the dead... ah....yes, of course," he murmured. "You both just have to die, Lord." His eyes gleamed with amusement.

"Not both of us, just me." Talon returned the grin. "But we will need transport to get us out through the gates."

"I have noticed that the carts are still moving in and out of the gates, even though it is quite late," Yosef replied. The removal of the dead continued, even as the celebrations got under way. "I shall find a cart and bring it to the door. Can you be ready?"

Talon looked at the silent Saxon, who had not understood a word. "Yes, I shall explain to him. We will be ready." Yosef got to his feet. "God protect, Lord. May He bless our enterprise. "

"Go with God, my friend."

Yosef disappeared, and Talon began to explain to Brandt what had to be done.

Roughly an hour later, Talon heard the sound of plodding oxen hauling a creaking cart come to a stop at the sharp command of their driver. He knew the voice. "Now!" he whispered to Brandt. Talon gulped a deep breath and became utterly limp.

With one swift motion Brandt knelt, scooped up Talon's limp body, and stood. Talon could not see anything; he was wound from head to foot in white cotton cloths, and he had to bite his lip to not cry out with pain. The Saxon carried his dead weight towards the door, weaving among the pallets of sick and wounded men.

Most of the torches in their sconces had gone out, but a single torch still flickered near the doorway, casting huge, moving shadows against the walls. The monstrous shadow cast by the Saxon and his burden was a sinister thing to behold for those still awake, wounded and already traumatized by the recent battle, some of whom cringed and whimpered with fear. Others who were conversing in low voices stopped as the strange sight walked past. The huge man who carried his limp burden, seemingly without effort, caused many to remember that it could be their corpses carried off tomorrow or the next day. One or two muttered, "God is Great. God be kind to that poor man's soul," as Brandt walked slowly by. Talon had to stay completely limp and hold his breath. It was a lot harder than he had thought, but he gritted his teeth and prayed they would soon be out of the building.

Standing outside in the dark alleyway next to the oxen was Yosef. Now he wore an ankle-length, dirty and stained cotton *thobe* with a hood that he had pulled over his head, half concealing his face. Instead of a sword he held a long stick with which to goad the oxen. "Hurry up, you Frans Infidel pig," he called out. "I don't have all night! We have other calls to make, not just this one, you know."

Now Brandt saw that there were other white-sheeted bodes in the cart already, which made him hesitate, but Yosef indicated to him to place Talon on the right side. This he did with care, and then Yosef rolled one of the stiff corpses so that it partially covered Talon. The pressure against his injured thigh elicited a low groan from Talon, but Yosef tapped him gently on the shoulder by way of reassurance and warning, then rolled some more shrouded forms closer to make a tighter bundle.

"Can you breathe?" he whispered.

"Yes, just."

Good, then we go." Yosef tapped the hindquarters of the oxen, and the beasts began to move forward.

Then came a call which made the two walking men turn. "Hold there! What are you doing?"

"What does it look like we are doing?" Yosef demanded irritably. "We are carting off the dead heroes from the hospital back there."

A man holding a spear stepped out of the shadows. "I'm the night guard and it is my business to ask questions," he stated pompously. He was poorly armed, wearing only a leather jerkin with round plates sewn on at widely spaced intervals. He came into the light of the single torch that was mounted above the lintel of the hospital and peered at the contents of the cart. "Ah, yes, you may proceed," he said, starting to back away, but then he gave a start.

At that very moment Talon had taken a deep breath, unaware that he had a spectator. "My God! Did you see that?" the man exclaimed. "One of those bodies moved, I swear it!"

He got no further. Brandt seized him by the head and rammed it against the side of the cart with a loud crack.

"What do I do with this?" he asked Yosef, holding onto the limp body by the back of its neck.

"Wait!" Yosef said, and disappeared for a minute back into the hospital, to reappear soon after with a length of cotton sheeting. "Wrap this around him and toss him into the back. Hurry!"

Brandt did as he was told, and the unconscious body of the guard joined the dead with a thump that rocked the cart. Talon gasped. "What happened?" he mumbled, his voice muffled.

Yosef leaned over the side. "Brandt just took care of it, Lord. I would not want to arm wrestle that Saxon for money, I can tell you!"

"You would probably cheat!" Talon chuckled." You never did like to lose."

Yosef snickered. "Probably. Hah!" He jabbed the oxen again to get them moving.

He gestured to Brandt and threw a filthy robe at him. "Put that on, and hurry!" he said. "You must put the hood up and stoop like you are old." He demonstrated an exaggerated stoop. Brandt didn't fully understand the poorly pronounced French, but the actions were clear, and soon two hooded cart-men were wending their way to the gates of the citadel.

By the time they arrived at the gates, the night was well advanced and the sentries were tired. Another cart was just returning, empty, with a tired and testy driver.

"I have been at this all night and I am worn out and hungry. Don't make life so difficult for me. Look! The damned cart is empty. By the hair on the Mullah's forehead, are you blind?" he shouted at the sentry, who was peering officiously into the vehicle.

Yosef took this moment to move his laden cart forward. He was not surprised when they simply waved him through; he was well aware that no one wanted to keep corpses lying around; burial services for the dead were a religious obligation. "God's blessings," he called out. He had noticed that the sentries were more interested in incoming traffic than the carriers of the dead, who were all heading towards the burial mounds closer to the lake.

"God is Great. They died for our Sultan. May God grant their souls quick entry to heaven. Bury them well," one of the nearer sentries said piously, and he tapped the side of the cart motioning them through. Even as he did so, the guard whom Brandt had knocked unconscious woke up, stirred, then began to sit up; but the quick-witted Brandt walking alongside the cart saw the movement before the guard turned his head in response to the muffled sound. His fist flew out and his knuckles connected with the luckless man's temple. He subsided in a limp heap, but the sentry peered at Brandt.

"Who is that with you?" he demanded, pointing to the Saxon who was again trying to make himself invisible by huddling next to one of the oxen. "He looks like a Frans!"

"Him?" Yosef said contemptuously. "He is, but he's *my* slave now. His master is among the dead on this cart. This ox digs the graves." Yosef prodded Brandt with the stick. "See how big he is? Ha ha ha!"

"Humph," the guard muttered. "Looks strong enough. Make him dig 'em nice and deep. Now get out of here, go on. Go in peace." The man walked back towards the brazier where his comrades were gathered.

"Peace be with you," Yosef intoned towards his departing back.

It took them another very uncomfortable hour to reach the place where Yosef had left the horses. They were approaching a copse of stunted trees growing alongside a small stream when Yosef became aware that not all was well. He noticed the flicker of something in among the trees where the horses should have been.

"We have a problem ahead," he muttered to Brandt, forgetting the Saxon might have difficulty with his bad French. Brand only partially understood, but lifted his head and peered into the darkness. "I see nothing," he murmured. Yosef scowled.

"There are some unwelcome visitors. Stay with Lord Talon and get him out of the cart while I go investigate," Yosef told him. "You understand me?" he asked, pointing to the bodies on the cart and pantomiming.

While Brandt began to roll the bodies off Talon in order to get him out of the cart, Yosef drew a long sword out from under the bodies nearest the front, then vanished into the darkness. Brandt felt the hairs on his forearms rise. The man was a phantom.

"Lord Talon?" he whispered.

"Are we there yet?" Talon wheezed from the side of the cart. "For God's sake, get me out of here, Brandt. I am suffocating and the smell is killing me!" His voice was muffled.

Brandt extracted his new master and cut him free of his wrappings. Talon sat on the back of the cart and rubbed his arms. "Phew! That was uncomfortable. Where is Yosef?"

Yosef, meanwhile, had crept up in a roundabout manner to the point where he could see who or what was near the horses. Crouched in the shadows, he made out the forms of two armed men, facing towards the city as though they might be waiting. Their horses were tethered alongside his.

They were far enough apart for Yosef to see each one clearly, but he waited to make sure there were no others. The men stayed where they were and whispered to one another. He strained his ears to hear what they were saying.

"When whoever tied the horses here come back, we can take them prisoner, and we'll be well rewarded, so stay where you are and don't move until I tell you," one of them said, making it easy for Yosef to pick who to come upon first. That man died with Yosef's hand around his mouth and sword buried in his heart from behind; he fell with just enough noise to alert the other.

"Ahmed?" the man queried, and turned just as Yosef appeared like some demon of the darkness and slashed at his neck with his bloody sword. Yosef spun around to make sure there was no one else, and then wiped the blade on the dead man's shirt. It was time to leave.

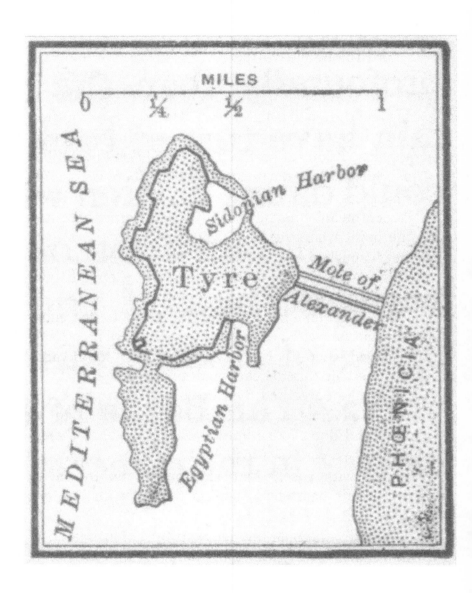

Fortress of Tyre

Chapter 23

The Siege of Tyre

I have been given my charge to keep—
Well have I kept the same!
Playing with strife for the most of my life,
But this is a different game.

—Rudyard Kipling

Prince Al-Adil's features betrayed his ill-concealed rage, even as he reported to the sultan the evening after Talon's disappearance. The sun had already set, leaving a crimson sky and high clouds streaked blood-red.

"He is gone, my Lord. Vanished into thin air like a ghost! No one saw him leave, and no one knows where he could have gone. We thought he must still be in the city, he was badly wounded after all; but somehow he managed to smuggle himself out last night." The prince looked nonplussed."I am almost ready to believe what people say about that man. That he is indeed a magician." He shook his head.

"How would that be possible?" the sultan asked sharply; he was clearly annoyed.

"Er, we think it might have been as a dead body, Lord," Al-Adil muttered unhappily.

"Are you quite serious?" the sultan asked. Now his voice sounded incredulous, but it was also tinged with amusement. "The cunning scoundrel! Ever resourceful," he murmured.

The prince did not hear him. "Once we had searched the city and the citadel, which took most of the day, we began to look further afield. Eventually a cart full of dead men was discovered near the lake."

Al-Adil had personally gone out to verify the report and had put a scented cloth over his nose; the stink of the sun-cooked corpses had been noisome. Even the oxen were disturbed and bellowing, which is what had drawn the searchers to the copse of trees in the first place. They were trying to pull away from the rocking cart full of the dead, which kept following them about.

"Such disrespect!" the sultan sighed. "Go on," he added. Al-Adil failed to notice the twitch at the corner of his mouth.

"We found two dead men in the copse, killed by some assassin, but also a poor man who had been tied up and left behind, Lord. My men tell me that the oxen must have walked about and trampled him, and one of them had even defecated upon the poor man. He was lying under their rears when help arrived and was almost mad with thirst and humiliation."

The sultan fished out a kerchief from within his robes with which he dabbed at his eyes, keeping his hand in front of his mouth at the same time.

"Is everything all right, my Lord?" the prince asked, his tone solicitous.

"Yes, er no, I have something in my eye." The sultan cleared his throat. "Please continue with your report." He coughed.

The Prince, who had vowed terrible retribution upon the fugitive if he caught him, went on. "We don't know how he could have jumped into a cart and escaped without help, Lord. The last time I saw him he couldn't even walk!" He growled through his teeth, "I personally interrogated the Greek doctor of the hospital. He claimed Talon was at the citadel, and Doctor Mehdi did verify that he was."

"Sooo, who could possibly have helped?" the sultan demanded, wiping his eyes again with the kerchief. He frowned. "Didn't he give his word, along with the others nobles, not to escape?"

The prince looked uncomfortable. "We were ... negotiating, Lord. We had not quite arrived at the point of parole."

The Sultan had to restrain himself from rolling his eyes.

"There must have been at least one other. He could not have escaped on his own, or slain those men, wounded as he was!" Al-Adil exclaimed.

Sultan Salah Ed Din felt a thin cold trickle along his forearms. "Yes, I think I can guess who it might have been," he said slowly. He had Reza in mind. He was glad of one thing. They obviously harbored no great ill will towards him, or he would be dead by now.

"Have you sent out search parties along the roads?"

"I have, Lord. Talon appears to have vanished into thin air. What seems to be the problem, Lord? Is something wrong? You seem, discomfited," the prince said almost accusingly. He thought he had heard the sultan make a sound suspiciously like a snort of laughter.

"No, no... it is nothing, Brother. I just have something in my throat; there is a lot of dust in the air today," the sultan said, wiping his eyes one last time and putting the kerchief away. That cunning Frank, *Lord* Talon, had slipped away yet again! He attempted to give his angry brother reassurance. His face resumed its normally stern expression as he said, "And no, I am not in the least bit amused by any of this, Brother. This rogue should be captured. Make sure you bring him in, *alive*," he told the prince. "If you can catch him," he finished under his breath.

Should they be captured, which he considered unlikely, he knew just what he would do with them. They could be set upon Rashid Ed Din, his mortal enemy who lurked in the mountains of Lebanon. These two might just succeed where others had failed, and remove a menace that had bothered Salah Ed Din for years.

He sighed. "Now we have more important things to discuss. Send out the word to the army that we are to leave for Acre in two days, and when we have taken it we will go north and take Tyre. After which we will fulfill our destiny."

"What do you plan for the infidel Rideford, my Lord? He is after all a Templar, and you have executed all the others."

"Ah, yes, but this man will be useful. He is still the Grand Master of the Templars. As such, by keeping him alive I will be able to forestall any election of another Grand Master. They have to obey him, even if I put him naked on a donkey before their gates and he requests them to surrender. That foolish man is my greatest ally in the Christian camp." The Sultan sounded quite pleased with that idea.

*****

Rashid Ed Din was at that moment pacing his chambers in a towering rage. Cringing before him was one of his young killers, who had just come back from Cyprus.

"You are telling me that both the corsairs and the men from the palace of that incompetent idiot *failed* in their mission, and that there is no news of any of our own men?" the man who was known as the School Teacher hissed at the groveling messenger.

"I, I, er, yes, Lord," the man almost wailed. "Lord, I could not find out anything of what happened during the battle, but I know the pirates were repulsed and even lost a ship, while those from the palace were decimated and the survivors came back with their tails between their legs. There is absolutely nothing heard from our men. The only conclusion is that they must have died or been taken prisoner, Lord."

Rashid Ed Din knew very well that none of his men would willingly allow themselves to be taken prisoner, but he was incensed by the failure of the mission, which would have provided him with a castle that was both strategically located and virtually impregnable. His cold, calculating mind contemplated revenge against that upstart "Information Gatherer" who had instigated the plan in the first place.

Some weeks before this debacle, one of his agents had been approached in Beirut, after he and his companions had completed a task, delivering to the Templar citadel a chest full of gold: the annual tithe agreed upon by that Order and the Master, as Rashid was also known. Rashid paid the Templars for the protection they afforded his castles from Salah Ed Din, the hated, Kurdish-born leader of the Sunni Arab world. This arrangement had only provided mixed results, and in the light of the very recent Christian demise at Hattin, which the whole world now knew about, Rashid felt it even more urgent to find a place where he could be more secure. With the Templars no longer able to protect Rashid, the Sultan would come after his castles in the mountains after he had dealt with his Christian foes.

News had come to him about the castle of Kantara, which the heretic Talon and his slippery companion Reza had finessed from under the nose of Isaac Komnenos. Rashid was grudgingly respectful of that accomplishment. Now, apparently, he and the Emperor had similar goals: the removal of Talon and his kin as soon and thoroughly as possible.

Having met with the Greek, Zenos, he had thought the opportunity ripe, especially with the capture of Makhid, the leader of the corsairs. Rashid had little interest in Makhid himself, but Makhid's cousin, Abul-Zinad, hated Makhid and wanted to replace him as leader of the corsairs from Dalmatia. Getting wind of this from his very active spies, Rashid's men had approached Abul-Zinad in turn, and the scheme had been set in motion. The prospect of gold had sweetened the pot for Abul-Zinad, although Rashid had been determined to keep it all, with the capture of the castle. Had they succeeded, Rashid might have rewarded the Information Gatherer; but, having failed, the Greek was going to hear from Rashid in no uncertain manner.

Rashid paused in his pacing and eyed with disgust the man on the floor in front of him. He was so frightened that his head was banging repeatedly on the carpet upon which he knelt.

"Stop that, and listen if you value your life," The Master barked. "This is what I want you to do. I want that upstart in the palace to be punished."

"How Lord?"

"In the usual manner. Now get out!"

*****

Talon and his two companions came within sight of Tyre three days after leaving Tiberius. They were exhausted and very hungry. It had been too dangerous to stop for any length of time, and equally ill advised to make a fire at night. Not unsurprisingly, the countryside was crawling with bands of Arab horsemen who roved at will, a good many of them probably on the look out for the fugitives.

With Yosef guiding them, they stayed off the roads as much as possible, and made their way across country. Herders, who had previously been numerous, had been quick to move their flocks deeper into the low mountains and kept themselves scarce, for marauders took what they wanted and left little behind. Whenever Talon's small band came across a shepherd by accident, Yosef paid for what they needed from their meager supply of coin stolen in Tiberius.

Without protest, Talon endured as best he could the jolting and swaying of the horse. Whenever they could stop near a stream, which were few and far between at this time of year, they cleaned the ugly entry and exit wounds and re-bound them with care. He and Yosef would scrutinize the area, trying to discern any sign of corruption, but found nothing to add to their other concerns. Talon felt clear headed, but utterly exhausted at the end of each day of the circuitous riding necessary to avoid any unwelcome encounters.

At one time they came across the corpses of peasants who had not been fortunate enough to escape. Marauding Arabs had found them, and what they had left behind was ghastly.

"Is it always like this, Lord?" Brandt asked, staring at the mutilated remains. A warrior used to battle, this butchery enraged and disturbed him.

"Often," Talon answered. "The men who did this were not true warriors."

The Saxon looked ill and wanted to bury the bodies, but Yosef said no. They could not leave any clues as to their passing.

"You are very close to the Lord Talon," Brandt remarked at one time to Yosef.

I have known him since we were young," Yosef responded. "But you, why do you serve him?" he demanded.

"I know of no lord who would have attended to their comrade the way he did for your wound during the battle. Then he picked me out from the slaves. There was no need to do so. He cares for his people," the Saxon stated simply. "I can serve someone like that. To the death, if need be."

Yosef nodded. He had wanted to know how true this huge man would be, should their situation become worse. So they continued on and passed more huts and farms, some charred by fire, others still smoking.

*****

Tyre was a welcome sight when they stood their horses on a low hill several leagues from the causeway. Talon noted that the surrounding countryside was denuded of peasants, caravans, and any normal activity by people. The fields, once well tilled in the fertile soil, were becoming patches of dust; the cottages and huts were abandoned. All these ominous signs indicated that news of the disaster at the Horns of Hattin had driven everyone to seek the shelter of the city, with its high walls and at least the illusion of security.

As they approached the still busy causeway, they could see the wreckage left behind by the refugees. They passed abandoned carts with a wheel missing or with broken shafts, some hanging off the edge of the road and others half submerged in the sea on either side. Possessions had been dropped in haste and abandoned, which attested to the panic that now reigned. Picking their way across the causeway, they arrived at the gates, which were firmly shut. Brandt had to call up to the men standing on the walls above. Despite the clear presence of a Frank, they still issued a challenge.

"Who goes there? Name yourselves!" one called down. Talon noted that a couple of Genoese bowmen were standing nearby. His contempt for these mercenaries was intense. They had proved t useless during the Battle of Hattin, fleeing at the first opportunity. Yet here were some of them challenging his arrival at the gates!

"Lord Talon requires entrance!" Brandt bellowed up at the surly men, who reluctantly pushed the gates open enough to allow them entry. Then the doors were closed with a crash and barred by the nervous soldiers.

Yosef led the way through streets packed with refugees camping where they had stopped, towards the harbor, desperately hoping that their ship would still be tied to the quayside. They were to be disappointed; there was no ship to greet them, merely an ominous quiet broken by the occasional shrill squawk of a gull. Only a few fishing boats were bobbing up and down in the greasy waters of the harbor. No ships of war or merchant vessels were to be seen.

"They are gone, Lord," Yosef said, his dismay written all over his face.

"God's will," Talon said unhappily as he surveyed the empty waters. His glance roved out to the twin towers protecting the entrance, hoping against hope that he would see one of his ships entering the harbor, so they could be out of this noisome place. Instead he could just see the white caps of the waves as the wind picked up. He glanced up at the banners, which flapped defiantly from the tallest towers, stating that this city still remained in the hands of the Christians, but that was poor comfort to those who only wanted to leave this troubled land.

"We must find accommodation," he said. Brandt nodded agreement. "I shall do what I can to find a clean, safe place until a ship comes, Lord. A ship will come, will it not?" he asked, his bright blue eyes fixed upon Talon hopefully. Talon smiled at him despite his misgivings.

"Yes, Brandt. Our ship must have taken Reza home. I just hope that they will remember to come back and pick us up before too long." He also hoped that it would be before Salah Ed Din and his army camped outside the city and laid siege to it.

Brandt dismounted clumsily—he was not a good horseman—gave the reins to Yosef, then hitched up his trews and ambled off to see what could be done about a place to stay.

It did not take long for him to return, bringing with him a man Talon recognized. It was the steward employed by Count Raymond, who hurried up and bowed courteously to Talon. "God's greeting, Lord! We, we did not know you still lived!" he stammered. "Stragglers who survived the battle have been arriving all week, but very few of the lords. I give thanks to God for your safe arrival." There was surprise written all over his lined face. "I am honored to greet you, even during these terrible times!" he exclaimed. "So tragic!" He wrung his hands. "All the news of the south has been just terrible. I don't know what is to become of us!"

"God's greetings to you, Steward. As you can see, I am here and alive, although in somewhat distressed condition," Talon said as he started to dismount, Brandt hastened to assist him, then held him steady while he talked to the steward.

"Is the Count here?" Talon asked. He had to lean on Brandt; his leg still refused to support his own weight.

The steward shook his head. "It saddens me to say that he is not, Lord Talon. He arrived some days after the battle with others, but then he went on to Tripoli. We have news that he is very ill. They say it is the pleurisy." The steward shrugged. "It is in God's hands now. Soon after he arrived there he took to his bed, and we have heard nothing of him since."

He seemed to collect himself and said solicitously, "Lord, you look weary, and injured. I can offer the same accommodations as before and the services of a physician for your wound." He glanced at Talon's dirty, blood-stained bandage.

Talon nodded. "I gladly accept your hospitality, Steward. God bless you. As to a physician, we shall see." He paused. "If the Count is not here, who is in charge of the city?"

The steward took his time answering. Finally he said, "It is Lord Reginald of Sidon, Lord. He is the leader of the city at present." He sounded unhappy.

Talon thought about that as he and his companions were ushered into the familiar chambers he and Reza had occupied before. He had told Rav'an that they would be away for only a couple of weeks, and now it was July. He had been away for almost four months!

News arrived that evening via pigeon that Acre had surrendered. While not unexpected, it was still a terrible blow to the morale of the city. Those with friends or relatives in Acre bemoaned their fate. Talon himself wondered what might have happened to Martin, the young monk who had been such a help in the past. The bells tolled single mournful notes and people crowded into the churches, seeking comfort in prayer and worship. Most knelt where they could, some beat their chests, while others wailed and tossed handfuls of ash over their heads, a behavior Talon had never fully understood.

He had his own injury to deal with, and he desperately needed rest; but word was out that he had survived the battle of Hattin. Before he had even managed to bathe, some men who were commanders were asking to see him. He wondered why they didn't go to Lord Reginald. Eventually Brandt was forced to keep them at bay by closing the main doorway in their faces.

Talon could envisage the entire countryside being crisscrossed by bands of Arab cavalry, with groups of desperate Christians seeking refuge wherever they could. In the middle of this chaos was the massive army of Salah Ed Din, composed of some thirty thousand men, perhaps more, now that he had won so decisively. He thanked God that he and his two companions had made it to the safety of Tyre. The question now was, would one of his ships come to take him away, or were they doomed to a long siege and possible recapture?

There was disturbance at the chamber entrance followed by a banging on the door. Talon, thinking it was yet another unwelcome visitor and being very tired, exclaimed, "Is there to be no peace tonight?" At the doorway, Yosef rolled his eyes silently and stood aside to allow the new visitor entrance.

It was Lord Reginald of Sidon himself.

Reginald was not a handsome man in any sense of the word. He possessed a huge nose, and the warts on his chin and lower cheeks had hairs sprouting from them that were longer than those of his beard, but his reputation for being a wise and very educated man was well known. Talon was resting with his knee propped up on some cushions when the Count was announced. He tried to get up, but the Count hurried forward and restrained him with an outstretched hand.

"Lord Talon! Forgive the intrusion. I am so very glad to see you are alive, albeit injured. You must not get up for me;

we can talk here. Lord Raymond has always had good things to say about you," he said, speaking in Arabic.

Talon was impressed by his fluency. Here was one more man on the side of the crusaders who could speak Arabic and understand the enemy! Talon wondered how little respect that had garnered Lord Reginald in the palace of Jerusalem. It was also said that the Count was very familiar with Arab and Persian literature.

"How did you manage to escape and come to Tyre?" the Count asked, with barely concealed curiosity. He seated himself with an expectant look on his face.

"It is a long story that I will tell later, Lord. But I could not have accomplished it without my companions," Talon replied, also speaking in Arabic. He gestured to Yosef and Brandt, who were hovering nearby.

"Who else was captured?" the Count demanded.

Talon recited the names of those he knew about, which included the King, Guy de Lusignan, Gérard de Rideford, and others of similar rank. There were some of lesser rank who would languish in Arab prisons for years to come, having little or no recourse to ransom. "Did Balian d'Ibelin survive, Lord?" Talon asked with some concern.

"Yes he did, God be praised. He has gone to Jerusalem," the Count affirmed. "God curse Rideford!" he muttered. "I did hear that Châtillon met a richly deserved fate. Because of those two, we are in our present predicament. God preserve the souls of those Templars and Hospitaliers who died after the surrender. That was a foul deed done by the Sultan!" He shook his head.

"Done by a man who feared them, Lord." Talon remarked. "They were the Christian fighters he dreaded the most, with good reason." He shook his head.

"He will go for Jerusalem now, won't he?" the Count said. He sounded glum.

"Yes, that is his ultimate goal. Therein rests his legacy to his people. I am sure of it," Talon replied.

"We have bad news from everywhere at present," Reginald stated. "You know that Acre surrendered, but so did Sidon, and Beirut will in due course. Our castles are tumbling like skittles one after the other, not least because they were stripped of men to feed Rideford's implacable greed for glory!" He sat back, gnawing at his heavy lower lip while he gloomily contemplated Talon.

"I doubt we will be able to hold onto Tyre," he finished abruptly.

"What do you mean, Lord?" Talon asked, surprised.

"Salah Ed Din holds all the cards, Lord Talon. He is invincible," Reginald replied, his tone more brusque than he might have intended. "We would be well advised to negotiate. If not, he will sack this city with horrendous loss of life. Look at the lightning fast way he has taken castle and city alike in the last week. To those who surrendered he was magnanimous. Those who did not, he slaughtered."

Talon stared at the man who was supposed to defend the citizens of Tyre and wondered, not for the first time, what drove Reginald, other than self preservation. Talon had witnessed the departure of Reginald and his men at the rear of the Christian army just before he had joined Raymond of Tripoli for his final charge and their own break out. It had occurred to Talon then that Reginald had not been fully committed to the battle and, having seen the disaster approaching because of Rideford and his Templars obdurate insistence on attacking the strongest part of the Arab armies, had simply chosen to break out and leave them to their fate.

"I do not feel that Tyre is as vulnerable as, for instance, Acre, nor Sidon, Lord. This city is protected by the sea on all four sides; it can be supplied from the sea and has plenty of wells. The harbor is out of reach of any land army, or their siege engines. It has strong walls on the side facing the land with a causeway in between." He must have sounded sharp because the Count frowned.

"Yes, but it's merely a matter of time. We need to negotiate with Salah Ed Din. He is a merciful man, a man of great honor," the Count replied. "You of all people understand that, Lord Talon." He looked as though he wanted to argue the point more, but did not. "I shall leave you to your rest and a full recovery, God willing." The Count got up to leave. "Do you have a physician to attend to your wound?"

"If you have a physician who does not call himself a Leech, then I would see him," Talon replied. "Lord, I think we should consider very carefully before we give the city to the Sultan. It is a vital foothold, one of the very last we have in this land. We should not give it to him as a gift," he urged. He sensed, however, that the Count was barely listening.

"That did not appear to go very well," Yosef said, after the Count had departed. he spoke in French for the benefit of Brandt.

"No, my friends, it did not. I was at a loss to comprehend the reckless behavior of our people at Hattin which led to the disaster; here we have exactly the opposite sentiment!" He shook his head. "This city can be defended almost indefinitely. Well, we need to rest. We shall see what morning brings."

Talon slept like the dead and woke feeling rested for the first time in weeks, but the morning did not bring much comfort. Scouts who had been out looking for signs of the Arab army came galloping across the causeway, to be admitted and escorted to the chambers of Lord Reginald, where they spent half an hour in conference.

The news was already out. The Arab army was nigh. Work that had been going on the landward fortifications took on a feverish pitch and continued throughout the following night. Talon got little rest that night, kept awake by the incessant banging of hammers and shouts of the masons and carpenters hard at work, so as the first streaks of dawn appeared in the east, he struggled out of his bed and asked Brandt and Yosef to help him to the battlements.

Yosef had managed to find a pair of crude crutches, for which Talon was grateful. Even so, the last few steps leading up to the ramparts were an effort. He propped himself against the parapet, feeling weak, and stared out towards the east. Yosef and Brandt stayed with him while he contemplated the distant coastline, still dark, but gradually they could discern activity.

A small cluster of Arab horsemen had gathered half way along the causeway, apparently watching the city walls. There was something ominous about that still, dark group of riders. More and more men arrived on the ramparts to stare at the newcomers. A babble of low voices could be heard all about as the defenders discussed what they were seeing.

A pair of strong looking, stocky men clad in what could only be described as rags sauntered up to stare out at the causeway, quite close to where Talon was standing. They smelt like badgers and they carried long staves that were their own height, which Talon recognized with a start of surprise as long bows. He had not known there were any long-bow men here in Tyre. Both men had long, dark hair bound at the back with string, and light grey eyes which stared out at the Arabs with calm interest. The leather caps they wore had done little to protect their faces, which were burned brown from the sun.

They spoke to one another in a language that Talon could not understand, but which he had heard before. Then it dawned upon him: these were Welsh archers! He assumed they were probably mercenaries, come like so many others for booty, rather than for any deep religious convictions. Their conversation ended and they lapsed into silence.

Speaking in French, he addressed them. "Are you from Wales?"

He received a surprised look from both men. "Yes... ah, Sir," said one hesitantly, who eyed him, recognizing a person of rank although he did not know who Talon was.

"Is anyone in charge of you? What are your names?"

"No... no, Sir," the other responded. "He is Dewi, and I am Caradog. We just arrived from Sicily with a contingent of men-at-arms. Had to fend for ourselves since then. No one seems to know what to do with a couple of archers, like."

Talon snorted. "Then you now work for me!" he informed them. "This man," he indicated the large form of Brandt, "is also with me. You will report directly to him and myself."

"But, but he is a *Saxon*, Lord," Dewi protested, staring hard at Brandt, who was now dressed in a heavy hauberk, with a huge ax in his belt along with a very large sword, and bore a large shield. He glowered back at them, looking dangerous. Talon suppressed a smile.

"Yes, and you are Welsh. I am a *pullani*, a man born here, and he," Talon indicated Yosef, who stood watching the two archers with cold, dark eyes, "is Persian, so get used to the strangeness and focus on the tasks I will ask of you. If you do not, then you will not live to go home, I can guarantee that. Other commanders, as you say, do not know what to do with longbow archers, so you would be wasted and either killed or allowed to be taken prisoner, and who would ransom you?. *We*, however, have work to do, and there is no time for differences!" he snapped, glowering at them.

"Yes, Sir," they both responded, sounding sour.

"I had some very good friends who were archers from Wales, a long time ago," Talon informed them. "They were the best of companions and helped me defeat a pirate ship."

Caradog perked up at this. "There is a tale put about in our land sung by the minstrels, about some of our people who did such a thing. It is in one of their songs." He turned to his companion. "Do you recall the name of the bard who sung that story, Dewi?" he asked.

Dewi scratched his beard. "Well, it might be that it was Llewellyn, or was it Dafydd ab Bran? Dafydd is defin'itely the better singer." His own sing-song voice reminded Talon of the Welsh archers who had aided him and Max in their defense of Talon's father and family, many years ago in Albi.

His companion begged to differ, but Dewi snorted and said, "You never had an ear for music, Caradog. With a name like yours, who would be surprised? Dafydd now, he could make a grown man weep with his harp playing!" Dewi sighed deeply. "No, I remember, it was Llewellyn. He's the one!"

Caradog opened his mouth to retort, but Talon interrupted. "My friend's name was Gareth, and he had four archers with him when he left Languedoc," he told the two men.

Dewi nodded. "It is in our songs, Sir! So the legend is true! Gareth and his companions came back with much gold, and he is now a chieftain, living to the west of our own tribe." Both men had become distinctly more friendly.

"Do you see those horsemen in the middle of the causeway?" Talon asked, pointing to the Arabs on the stone road. "How far do you estimate them to be?" He had his own idea as to how far, but wanted to test the two bowmen.

"Nearly two hundred paces, I'd say," Dewi answered, and Caradog nodded agreement. "Aye, well, give or take a few strides."

"A few strides!" his companion said, sounding scornful. "You never were any good at distances over a hundred paces."

"Lay you a bet?" demanded Caradog, his tone matching that of Dewi.

"You don't have anything to bet with," Dewi said. "We are broke, and the Sir here is wait'ing!"

Talon sighed. He remembered Gareth and his companions arguing endlessly about distances, and almost everything else. He thumped the parapet in feigned annoyance.

"When you two have stopped arguing over a couple of paces I want you to *listen!*" he snapped. His tone was sharp. They turned their attention back to him, looking sheepish.

"Now, I want you to put two arrows into their midst," he told them, pointing at the horsemen who were still observing the city, well out of arrow range—or so they believed. "Watch this, Yosef," he murmured in Farsi.

Both archers nodded obediently, bent their staves and strung them, then selected an arrow and checked the fletching with care, smoothing the goose feathers with spit-wetted fingers. After this, they carefully nocked the arrows just under a small knot tied to their bowstrings, and at a grunt from Dewi lifted their bows high and drew on the strings so that their huge longbows bent into the shape of arcs. They paused for a long moment, with their string fingers touching their cheeks just in front of the ear. Other men on the ramparts nudged each other and turned to watch. More than one could be heard muttering about fools and the wasting of arrows.

Then the twang of their bows, released almost simultaneously, reverberated in the air. The two arrows sped off into the sky, watched by all those nearby. Long moments later, Talon could just see the dark objects streaking down. The group of horsemen broke apart in consternation, and all departed back along the causeway at a gallop, except for one man and one horse, struck down by the well-aimed arrows. Talon was pleased to see that, even if they could not agree on the distances, both men could hit their targets.

"Good work!" he said, but his voice was almost drowned out by the yells of glee from the other watchers on the walls. Men were cheering and waving their hats, delighted by what they had just witnessed.

"*Dieu, Dieu Bachan*, what a bloodthirsty lot, bye *Godde!*" Caradog commented to Dewi with a grin. "I got the man, you got the horse."

"*Dieu Bachan,* but I did not! It was me as got the man!" Dewi retorted.

Men came up to congratulate them and cast wondering looks at the strange bows, the like of which they had never seen. Both archers were somewhat bemused by the effect of their handiwork on their audience, but Talon glowered at them. "Your work in the days to come is to kill or distract anyone who tries to set up a siege device at the end of that causeway. Yosef and I will deal with anyone who gets past that hurdle. Do you have a good supply of arrows and strings?"

"Could do with more, Sir."

"Brandt, go with these two and get them well supplied. There are blacksmiths and fletchers in this town, I dare say. Make sure they are put to work. Then ask the steward to provide food and drink for our group." Talon knew that the intimidating presence of Brandt would ensure that the Welshmen would get what they needed.

"Yes, Lord," Brandt replied sturdily.

"As they left, Talon overheard one of the archers say to the Saxon in bad French, "My word! So he's a Lord, then?"

"Yes, he is. 'Lord Talon' to you two Welsh louts, and you'd better remember that."

"Is he always so angry then, *bach?*"

"He is *fucking* angry just now," the burly Saxon said in his inimical manner. "We just came back from Hattin and we are all angry, *especially* the Lord Talon, so watch your step."

"And who is that sin'ister looking fellow who is with him....?"

Their voices died away as they trotted down the stairs to the courtyard.

———————————

Chapter 24

Lord Conrad Montferrat

This is where we wind up
We don't mean to but we do
Not where we started
but standing in the chill air....

It's not about return so much
as feeling the wind
and wondering what that was
that blew me here.

—Stephen T. Vessels

Talon almost laughed. Yes, he was angry, *very* angry, but it was at the sheer pointlessness of the battle they had survived; he was certainly not angry with these two Welshmen. They were a boon he had not expected, nor even hoped for. A good start to the day, as far as he was concerned.

"Yosef, you can stop gaping and close your mouth. They are now *our* men."

Yosef snapped his jaw shut, shook his head and grinned. "I have never seen the like before, Talon!" he said forgetting for a moment their difference in rank. "I have seen you and Master Reza do wonders with your bows, but never at such a range!"

"You and I are not in their league, Yosef," Talon said. "You just try and pull one of those bows! It takes a lot of strength that they build up from a young age." Somehow the arrival of the archers had cheered him up.

"You are smiling,Lord. It has been some time since you did the last time," Yosef observed. "There is not much to smile about as far as I can see. We are all trapped here in this prison!" He gestured around at the grim setting of the town and its citadel.

"But today we gained a small advantage, Yosef. The finding of those archers is more than I could have expected. You wait and see." Talon smiled again at his friend and clapped him on the shoulder.

Talon proceeded to tell Yosef about his adventures long ago with the Welsh archers, and how they had helped defend his family in Languedoc. "Ask Max what he thought of them. He, too, was amazed at their ability," he said. "That bow is a fearsome weapon in the right hands."

The commotion had drawn the attention of Lord Reginald, who came storming up the steps to the ramparts.

"Ah, Lord Talon! Didn't expect to find you here. What is all the noise about?"

"Just some archers of *mine* who were practicing, Lord Reginald," Talon replied casually, with emphasis on the possessive.

Reginald squinted to see the middle of the causeway where the two bodies lay. "At that distance? You had those people killed?" he said, and sounded oddly unhappy about it.

Talon shrugged. "Yes, my Lord. I just sent a message. The causeway is to be a path of death for those who are unwary."

"Wasn't that somewhat rash, Lord Talon?" the Count asked stiffly.

Talon stared at him in surprise. "I don't think so, Lord. We need to keep them at a distance and prevent them from being too confident when they approach the city. We have just shown them we can bite."

"What if they had been emissaries, Lord Talon?" the Count demanded with a scowl. He sounded not a little irritated.

"Then they would have shown the white flag of truce, which would have been respected, Lord Reginald," Talon replied patiently. "If we can make them wary of coming too close otherwise, it will be to our advantage.

"If the Sultan wants to parley, then I must be notified!" the Count snapped, and turned away to return to the citadel.

Talon stared after the Count, as he and his retainers left. One or two sent a glare of dislike his way, making him wonder what it was that he had said to offend the Count. He turned and stared across the causeway towards the approaching army, which was swarming down to the shore on either side of the road. "It seems the Sultan has arrived," he remarked to Yosef, who nodded, his face grim.

As he hobbled off, with Yosef helping him, they were jostled by men-at-arms and knights crowding the ramparts in preparation for the fight to come. A few men who had witnessed the bowshots were respectful and helped to clear a space for him. Words such as, "God protect you, Lord," and "We need a leader like you," could be heard.

That afternoon, Talon was resting on the bed with his leg on a cushion when Yosef came hurrying in.

"Lord! Are you awake?" he enquired.

"Yes, Yosef, what is it?"

"That Christian lord, the man who is in charge?" Yosef spoke in a low voice.

"What of him?"

"He led a delegation out of the city to talk with some people from the Sultan's army," Yosef said, sounding concerned. "I think he is planning to surrender, Lord!" he finished.

Talon sat up. "This could alter things in a very bad way. Help me up, I want to go back onto the battlements to see what is going on. Where are Brandt and the archers?"

"The last I saw of them, they were eating as though none of them had had a good meal for a hundred years," Yosef remarked in a somewhat prim tone.

"See if you can find them and bring them to the walls. I will start off now." Talon swung his legs off the bed and reached for his crutches. "Don't worry about me, Yosef. Go and get Brandt." With a concerned look, Yosef hurried off.

Talon was half way towards the steps leading up to the crowded walls when the gates were opened and Count Reginald of Sidon and his mounted escort of knights clattered into the courtyard. They carried a large white banner, but Talon's eye was caught by the other banners the riders carried with them. These flags were those of the Saracen army, banners that would have been displayed by the enemy in battle! It had obviously been a parley, but Talon wondered with a sinking heart what might have been agreed upon.

The Count noticed Talon propped up on his crutches, now joined by his tiny band. Brandt had arrived with the two archers in tow. Their quivers were full and they looked less hungry than before.

"Ah, Lord Talon. You should be resting that leg," the Count commented as he tossed the reins of his horse to a waiting groom and strode towards him. Despite their disagreements, the Count was civil to the only other Lord in the city at the present time.

"Good health to you, my Lord," Talon replied. "Have you been talking to the Sultan?"

"The Sultan was not there; he is still on his way here from Acre," the Count replied. "I talked with his brother, Al-Adil.

He asked after you by the way. We are going to meet with the Sultan when he arrives." He turned away and gestured towards the men carrying the Sultan's banners.

"Place them over the gates and on each tower either side of the gates," he ordered. His knights appeared unhappy with the request and hesitated, upon which the Count called out irritably. "Did you not hear me? Place them on the walls as I commanded!" He glanced at Talon and continued. "This is to ensure the truce while we wait to discuss surrender terms with the Sultan when he arrives," he said with satisfaction.

Talon stared at him, appalled. "Sir, you cannot do this!" he exclaimed. "We can hold out for a long time, long enough for the autumn to come, when the Sultan will be forced to disperse his army and allow them to go home to harvest their crops and tend to their tribal needs!"

The Count rounded on him, his ugly face suffused with blood. "Do not presume to tell me what to do, Lord Talon! *I* have been made the leader here, and I shall do what I deem best for the city. You should go and rest that wound of yours," he finished pointedly, and he strode off, Talon staring after him.

"That seemed to go well," Yosef said in an undertone.

"We have to find a way to leave this place. He will sell his soul to the Sultan, and that means slavery for the rest of us," Talon growled, thinking furiously. "Help me up onto the ramp. I want to think, and to see what the Sultan's brother is contemplating.

They arrived to find that the former crowd was dispersing, leaving a quiet space for them to stand and observe the activity across the causeway.

"They are already bringing up their siege equipment; look over there," Yosef pointed.

"A trebuchet, if I am not mistaken," Brandt added. A huge, cumbersome apparatus was being hauled towards the causeway. To Talon it didn't look as though Al-Adil was going to wait for the Sultan before he began to bombard the city.

"If they try to bring it along the road, see if you can disrupt them; I don't care what Lord Sidon says," Talon said to the two Welshmen. They nodded, propped their quivers against the wall, then strung their bows. Talon knew that what he was about to do could get him into deep trouble with the Count, but he was determined not to let the Arab army gain a solid foothold on the road. "Don't do anything until I tell you," he cautioned them.

They were thus positioned when they heard excited yells coming from the seaward side of the city. The calls caused people on the streets to look up, and men began to run towards the sound, which was rising in pitch to became a roar as more and more people joined in. Before long, the city bells began to ring in a much more joyful manner than previously. The air was filled with shouts of excitement and the clamor of bells. Even trumpets were being sounded.

"What is going on over there?" Talon asked. "Brandt, go and find out. It doesn't sound as though we are threatened with danger, but I'd like to know."

Brandt nodded his agreement and trotted off, leaving Talon and the archers staring towards the west of the city. Then Yosef noticed something. "It is a ship!" he called out, pointing in the direction of the harbor entrance.

Sure enough, first one ship, then another, and then another began to maneuver through the narrow opening of the harbor, using sweeps to make their way towards the quayside. From their mastheads the ships flew long, bright banners, which were without doubt of Christian origin, and if Talon was not mistaken in his reading of the crest on one of the banners, they belonged to Count Conrad de Montferrat. Indeed, men flocking to the quayside to welcome the new arrivals were shouting the Count's name.

Talon stayed where he was. He and his small group had a grandstand view of the harbor. The ships were packed with armed men, a sight Talon found very comforting, given how the garrison of Tyre was presently depleted. The first ship docked and tied in, with eager men helping, and then a gangplank was dropped to the quayside.

Talon saw a man in full chain mail stride down the gang-plank to the stone quay, where a hurried welcoming commit-tee had formed to greet him. Even Lord Sidon was there. Talon wondered sardonically how the newly arrived Conrad would react to the news that Sidon intended to give the city away. He turned his attention back to the invaders, who by this time had dragged the huge trebuchet to the causeway and were levering it into position to move it along the stone road.

Talon glanced back at the crowd and decided that they were preoccupied; no one was paying any attention to the east. "Are you ready?" he asked his archers softly.

"Ready, Lord," Caradog said sturdily.

"When they come into range, send some arrows to our friends over there," Talon murmured.

They waited for the lumbering machine to arrive at the mid section of the causeway, then the two archers drew their bows. Talon kept his gaze on the men below and heard the twang of the strings. After a brief interval, a man tumbled off the frame of the trebuchet. Talon thought he might have even heard the cry, although the distance was extreme. There was consternation, as those who had been working nearby clustered around the fallen man.

"T'was me who got that one!" Dewi said, sounding smug. Caradog was about to protest when Talon said sharply, "Again!"

"Oh, aye, but this is good!" Dewi muttered, and another two arrows were sent off. This time they landed in the middle of the distant group, which immediately dispersed, leaving two more of their number lying in the road.

"Nice work," Talon remarked with satisfaction, as he watched the enemy soldiers abandon the trebuchet. "Now all we have to do is to destroy it somehow," he concluded.

Yosef was grinning from ear to ear, shaking his head in admiration. "God help me, but if I had not seen it with my own eyes I would not have believed it!" he exclaimed.

Talon returned his attention to the harbor. The nobles had left the ships to their crews and disappeared into the palace, where no doubt they were discussing the situation. He had not been invited, he noted with a wry twist of his mouth. Brandt hurried back and confirmed that Count Conrad de Montferrat had indeed arrived and had brought with him a large contingent of men to augment the meager numbers of defenders.

Yosef silently pointed down at the causeway, and Brandt gave a wolfish grin when he saw the damage inflicted by the archers. "Good work, even if you are Welsh," he rumbled, giving them a sideways look of approval.

Their little action had not gone unnoticed. Several of the wall sentries had applauded and chortled with satisfaction, but someone must have informed the Count of Sidon, because soon he was striding across the stone courtyard and climbing the steps to the battlements two at a time. He was in a towering rage. Keeping pace with the angry count was a solid-looking man in full chain mail. Talon recognized the man who had walked off the ship to the cheers of spectators.

"Lord Talon!" Sidon roared as he approached. "I am informed that you have been engaging the Sultan's men against my express wishes! We have a truce with those people and you have broken it! I'll see you in jail for this!" he snarled.

Talon stood erect and faced him calmly, even though the pain in his leg was fierce. He put a hand on the parapet to steady himself.

"I do not see a white flag of truce, Lord Sidon. What I do see is a siege apparatus being moved into place by the Arab side. They clearly do not think there is a truce... Lord."

"I had the banners placed where I did to indicate we are not fighting them!" Sidon shouted.

Talon glanced at the fluttering banners; the wind had picked up. "Those are enemy banners, my Lord. I do not think they belong here—" He was interrupted by the man standing behind Sidon.

"Indeed, Lord Sidon. I agree with this man. Lord Talon, is it?" He smiled, showing bad teeth. It was a genuine smile of amusement, but anger also flickered there. "Why do you display the enemy banners when we are clearly at war?" he demanded of Sidon.

"I propose, as I told you in the palace, to negotiate for the city, Lord Conrad," Sidon spluttered.

In answer, Conrad reached forward to one of the Sultan's banners and lifted it up. Then, before the startled men, he hurled the banner into the water below. "You and you!" He pointed to two of the sentries on the walls. "I am taking charge of this city now! Remove the other banners forthwith!" The men hesitated. "Do as I tell you, by God!" Conrad roared. They hastily did as he instructed. All the while Sidon was rigid with confusion and pent up anger.

"I do protest, Lord Conrad!" he gobbled.

"I do believe, Lord Sidon," Conrad mimicked him, "by virtue of my senior birth that I am in charge here, and we will not be surrendering to *anyone*! Not any time soon!"

He turned towards Talon, who had been watching this exchange with interest. "We have not met before, Lord Talon. But already I am impressed by your determination.

Talon struggled to kneel. Brandt stepped forward to support him, but Conrad was having none of it. "Do not, I pray, kneel to me, Lord Talon. I see you are recovering from a wound. I will need your good advice in the near future, I think. Did your men accomplish that?" He pointed towards the causeway, which was now deserted, except for the three dead men and the abandoned trebuchet.

"Yes, my Lord. I felt that we needed to dissuade them from becoming too ambitious."

Conrad barked out a laugh. "Ha! Very good! Hear that?" He shouted to the men gathered on the battlements. "*That* is how we will treat with the enemy from now on!" He turned to Lord Sidon.

"Now, Reginald, we need to talk, in private and in the palace." He took the still enraged Sidon by the arm and marched him away. As they left, Talon heard Conrad remark, "Even with his wound that man is there, on the battlements, causing damage and confusion to the enemy. I hope there are more of him around. Ha! Ha!"

"Should I kill the ugly man, Lord?" Yosef asked Talon in Farsi. "You are a Lord, and he was very rude to you."

Talon chuckled and shook his head. "I am a very small lord, Yosef. I cannot field armies. We are not of his kind, in any case. I am a Merchant Lord, and different from those he is familiar with. Yet, much as I despise the Genoese and the Venetians merchantmen, we are more similar to them than to the Normans, who prefer their castles dank and cheerless. No, don't kill him. He will destroy himself sooner or later." Talon didn't add that he felt more powerful with his loyal, well trained people than any lord with a half-wit army.

Later that evening, a servant arrived to invite Talon to have supper with Conrad. He was helped to the palace great hall by Brandt, who grumbled about the Welsh as Talon hobbled along the darkened passageways.

"They feed like a host of locusts, Lord. And they never stop arguing! There have been times when I have wanted to use my ax to shut them up!"

Talon laughed, and paused to rest. "I recall the other ones were much the same. But don't forget, Brandt, their archery is unique in this part of the world. When we have endured this feast, I want to talk to you, Yosef, and the archers. How do you feel about a little expedition tonight?"

Brandt gave an eager grunt. "Arr, yes! That would be just fine with me, Lord. Why should the Sultan's men have all the fun?"

Talon arrived late, but there was a place for him at the head table with Conrad and Sidon. When he hobbled into the room there was a brief pause in the conversation around the hall as people recognized him. The whispering began, as men and knights and the very few ladies remaining in the city talked about him. Some furtively made the sign of the cross, because rumor had it that he had used magic to escape the clutches of the Infidels. No one else had escaped to tell the tale of captivity after the disaster of Hattin.

Conrad waved him over, evidently wanting to talk to him, for Talon's place was close to his own. A very disgruntled looking Count of Sidon sat further along the table, with some of his men and the bishop of Tyre. Brandt assisted Talon to be seated, then stood guard behind him. His glowering visage caught the eye of Conrad, who said *sotto voce* to Talon, jerking his thumb at Brandt, "Does he always look so fierce, Lord Talon, and are there others like him here in the city? You seem to attract some interesting followers."

Talon glanced back at Brandt and nodded to him. "He was formerly in the employ of the Count of Tripoli. I bought him from the slave line in Tiberius, and then he saved my life. The debt is mine, and I am more than happy to have him on my side. An axe is a truly weapon in his hands. He fought with us at Hattin."

Conrad gave Talon a sharp look. "Yes, I heard that. You have garnered quite a reputation, Lord Talon."

"I hope it is not all bad, my Lord?" Talon remarked as he sipped the wine from a silver goblet. He winced, not from the pain in his leg, which was almost constant, but because the wine tasted as though some enterprising soul had mixed mushrooms with acorns, stewed them for a week in animal pee, then bottled the result.

It was nowhere near as good as the wine from his own vineyards. Ah, but how he missed his home! He resolved to have a quiet word with the steward and put him right about serving horse piss to the new leader of the city. Talon knew there were good bottles hidden somewhere.

The Count was speaking again."Nooo, but there is much mystery attached to your name. Tripoli's steward, who now works for me, said that your followers are a strange crowd, and that you speak the Arabic fluently and know their ways better than almost everyone else, including Sidon over there. I would hear more of what you think about the 'Sultan', as he calls that man on the other side of the causeway."

"You mean His Excellency the Sultan Salah Ed Din, my Lord. He is a complicated man who has used our weaknesses to very good effect against us on more than one occasion."

"Hmm, Lord Sidon has alluded to that, and he thinks our best course is to negotiate. What do you think, Lord Talon?"

"We were badly led up to the battle at Hattin, Lord. But this city... Tyre is easily defendable, as long as we can keep him at a distance."

Conrad reared back in his chair, beaming with approval. "I agree with you!" He sent a sharp look down the table towards Lord Sidon. "*He* would give it all away, and this is the last of the secure port cities. I want to keep it! We *must* keep it!" Conrad banged the table with his fist. "So I have invited him to depart for his own lands, where he can do as he pleases."

Talon frowned. "He has agreed to leave, my Lord?"

Conrad tore some flesh off a thin looking rib he was eating; the grease on his fingers shone in the candlelight. "Yes. I don't want faint hearts here, and he appeared only too glad to get away from the responsibility of leading the city. I am now fully in charge, and he will be leaving in the morning on one of my ships. He can't leave any other way, can he? Ha ha!" Conrad tossed the bone to a hound lurking nearby, then wiped his chin with a linen cloth and took a swig of wine.

"The Count of Tripoli kept a rotten cellar, it seems," he remarked with a grimace, looking as though he were about to spit it out.

Talon could not have agreed more, and he was relieved to hear that Sidon was on his way out. That meant Conrad could defend the city in his own fashion, and he had experience, defending and organizing the populations of cities in Lombardy. Talon focused on his food, which was not nearly as good as that which he had become accustomed to on Cyprus, but a good deal better than what he had eaten recently. He wondered how long supplies would last if there were a siege. There was already a scarcity of goats and sheep, and not a cow to be found anywhere. They would be starting on the cats and dogs next, he surmised.

"I suspect there is better wine hidden away somewhere, my Lord," he remarked.

The Count nodded and attacked another rack of mutton ribs, tearing them apart with gusto. The steward had evidently decided to provide a feast tonight.

Speaking with his mouth full, Conrad told him, "My original destination was Acre, and indeed we arrived there, some two days ago. Almost from the time we saw the city in the distance there seemed to be something wrong. I think it was the lack of the Christian banners. As we approached the city, a vessel put out from the harbor and came within hailing distance." Conrad wiped his mustaches, then carried on.

"We learned then that the city had fallen, because some of our men understood what they called out to us. They had, in fact, invited us to enter the harbor. They were not clear as to who we were." He barked out a short laugh.

"I told our captains to leave, and smartly too. We came here with the prayer to God that Tyre had not fallen."

"I am sure *everyone* here is very glad that you did, my Lord," Talon replied, his tone dry.

"Hmm, yes," The Count cast a derisive glance at Lord Sidon. "What we saw at Acre tells me that this Saladin of yours moves very fast. And what do you think his intentions are next?"

"Oh, that is clear, my Lord. He will try the take this citadel, because this is a strategic city. If he controls it, he can deny all future supplies to the Holy Land. But his main objective is and always has been Jerusalem."

Conrad swiveled his head to stare directly at Talon. "You think so, eh?" His mouth compressed into a thin, grim line.

Talon nodded emphatically. "This was what the Count of Tripoli was so afraid of, and what neither the King nor his close advisers would understand. For Salah Ed Din it is the conclusion of his destiny, and he will not be denied."

The Count looked frustrated. "We cannot do anything about that, either. Who is left to defend Jerusalem if, as you say, the cream of our army lies dead on the slopes of Hattin?"

"Sidon told me that Count Balian Ibelin was going to Jerusalem, my Lord. Does he know anything more?"

"Pah, he is sulking and not very forthcoming at present. I say good riddance to that man, but I wish I could learn more about Jerusalem. Tell me what you know, anyway."

———

Chapter 25

Trebuchet

And so the warriors all go down;
they're slain although no blood is shed.
The dark fighters at times the victims,
the ones emerging triumphant are red.
                                    —*Avrahim ibn Ezra*

Pleading fatigue and taking his leave well before the end of the meal, Talon excused himself to the Count and hobbled off, with Brandt to aid him. As they approached their own chambers Talon said, "Brandt, find me a horse without iron shoes, saddle it and bring it to the gates within the hour. It's good and dark now."

"My Lord, you are not thinking of coming with us?" Brandt demanded, his voice full of surprise and concern.

"How else am I going to keep an eye on you and the lads? Watch from the battlements?" Talon retorted. "I can still use a bow and ride... after a fashion, to support what you are about to do. Go on now, I'll see you down by the gates soon."

Yosef was waiting at the chambers, fully armed. "Do you really think you should be coming with us, Lord?" he asked, as he moved to help Talon struggle into a hauberk.

"Yes, because someone needs to protect your backs as you and Brandt carry out the important part," Talon said, pulling on his gloves. "Did you get the other items?"

Yosef grinned and nodded.

"Then it is time we left. Come along, you two!" he told the waiting archers. They hurriedly finished off the food they had been devouring in the room adjacent to his bed chamber.

"They never stop eating!" Yosef exclaimed with a grimace. "Are you sure we can afford them, Lord?"

Talon snorted. "Tonight they earn their keep... or not, as the case may be. If not, I'll let Brandt deal with them."

Yosef picked up their two bows, then handed Dewi a sack full of something that rattled. "Be careful with it," he told the archer. Then he helped Talon limp down the steps to the outside courtyard and along one of the tunnels that joined the outside walls with those of the citadel. There they found Brandt waiting with a large horse.

"We took its shoes off, Lord. Seemed a better idea than to cal attention to ourselves by looking for one unshod."

Talon nodded. "Good. Help me up onto the beast, Brandt, and then we can leave."

He was almost flung over the horse by the great heave Brandt delivered. He managed to grab the cantle just before he went over the other side. Once he was settled, Yosef handed up one of the bows and a quiver of arrows, which Talon hooked over the high front of the saddle, ready to hand should he need an arrow.

Then Brandt strode ahead of them to talk to the sentries at the gate. Talon guided the horse after him; Yosef walked alongside, with the archers just behind. The gate swung open and they exited to a murmur of "God Bless and protect," from the guards, who had been among the men who'd cheered the morning's archery. They had been taken into Talon's confidence, so they knew what his men were about.

"Where are we going, Lord?" Caradog asked in a low tone. He sounded apprehensive.

"We are going to destroy that trebuchet before they start to use it, my friends. Your job and mine is to make sure that no one approaches while Yosef and Brandt set it on fire and chop it up a bit."

He received satisfied murmurs of acknowledgment from the two archers.

In the shadows of the city walls the night was very dark. There was no moon, for which Talon was grateful, but the sky was only sparsely covered with high clouds; they obscured the stars somewhat, but not altogether. There was just enough light to see the pale strip of the causeway, bounded by an undulating white line of surf on either side.

"It will be guarded," Yosef whispered.

"Yes. Do you think you can deal with that?"

"If the Saxon doesn't mind carrying the Greek Fire and can wait with you until I am ready, I can deal with anyone who is too close."

"Good. And you two," Talon muttered to the archers, "will be right behind to support Yosef. I can ride along the causeway and be in position to support at close range. I am the decoy." He smiled grimly. "Everyone ready?"

Talon led the way. The horse's hooves made a faint thubbing sound that was almost drowned out by the sound of the surf, nothing near to the noise they would have made on the stone had the horse still been shod. It fidgeted with unease as it sensed the tension of the men, but Talon used a light touch on its mouth and closed his legs, despite the pain, to calm it. Soon it continued quietly enough along the dark surface of the road.

The archers and Brandt crept as quietly as possible right behind the horse, while Yosef hugged the side of the causeway. Fully expecting to be challenged, Talon rode the horse towards the trebuchet, hoping to get as close as possible before any sentries noticed him. He was pleased when he arrived within twenty paces of the huge device unchallenged, and then he halted. Yosef had vanished. Talon could hear voices from the far side of the trebuchet; he called out in Arabic.

"I am here to talk to the Prince."

There was a muffled exclamation of surprise, but then there was a low cry followed by a thud, and then another half shout quickly stifled... and then silence. Yosef gave a hoarse call and Brandt loped forward, carrying the bulky sack. The horse pricked up its ears at one point, and Talon thought he heard a scuffle beyond the trebuchet, but nothing more. The air around them was thick with tension.

After a few minutes, they saw a stream of sparks as Yosef struck a flint, then a low flame. Moments later, they saw a dark, hulking figure high on the frame raise an axe, then came the sound of chopping. Yosef had shown Brandt where to cut the main bindings. Brandt chopped away in several places and the huge frame began to sag.

Suddenly, they heard shouts from the banks beyond the causeway. The alarm was being raised. The noise of the axe chopping might have alerted someone, and now the rising flames were clearly visible. Either way, torches were being lit and the sound of shouting increased in volume as the enemy became aware that something was going on with their equipment and rushed to investigate.

"Be ready!" Talon warned his archers.

Silence was no longer important, so Yosef called to Brandt, by now well illuminated by the flames. "Time to leave, Saxon! Hurry!"

Arrows began to thud into the frame of the device and hiss around the two men. Then Talon and his archers saw a dark form race towards Brandt, who was preoccupied with hacking at some bindings with a knife. The moving man raised a sword high in the air to strike at Brandt's exposed back.

"Now we can't have that, can we!" Caradog muttered, and he pulled back his bow string with an arrow in place.

"Better hurry with that one, *Bach*," Dewi's tone was sharp with urgency.

The arrow whispered above Brandt's bent back and thumped into the attacker's chest. He fell back out of sight with a choking cry.

Brandt realized with a shock what had happened. "Fuck me!" he shouted in surprise. He ducked hurriedly as other arrows went past him, then dived off the frame and followed Yosef at a run back along the causeway.

By now men with torches were rushing towards the stricken trebuchet, shouting and calling as they raced to intercept the intruders and attempt to put out the flames.

"Its time to use your bows!" Talon called to his archers, who were only too willing to oblige. In economic and fluid motions they loosed several arrows at the torch-bearers, whose calls changed abruptly to shouts of alarm and pain as the arrows found their marks. Talon could just make out the two figures racing towards him, one slight and agile, the other large and lumbering. He wondered what had happened to the small oil tubs that Yosef had brought along. Just as his two men came up to them, there was a whooshing sound and a huge flame burst out from the very heart of the apparatus, which had already become a bonfire. Its destruction was assured.

While very satisfying, the bright light betrayed the small group on the causeway. Yells of anger, followed by flying arrows, were directed at them.

"Time to leave!" Talon advised his men. He loosed an arrow of his own at a man who'd recklessly exposed himself by the side of the burning framework, then turned his horse. "Go! Run!" he called to Brandt and Yosef. "You Welsh, stay with me to cover their backs."

"Thanks for saving my hide, Welsh!" Brandt shouted, as he and Yosef took off running. Talon and the archers scanned the burning area for anyone who might be eager to fight.

"Hope he was worth the trouble," Caradog remarked, as he loosed another arrow towards the angry enemy. "Now who'll save our hides?"

"Looks like we have poked a hornets nest, *Bach*!" Dewi commented as he did likewise.

Sure enough, some horsemen charged right past the fire, oblivious of its heat and determined to avenge the ruin.

"Shoot them down!" Talon ordered, and readied his own next shot. The range was down to one hundred paces and closing rapidly. Three bow strings twanged and three arrows flew with deadly accuracy. Of the four horsemen, only one remained in the saddle, and after a shocked look at his fallen comrades he pulled his horse up, hesitating.

That cost him his life, for Dewi killed him before he could turn and flee back beyond the cover of the rising smoke and flames. Having thus discouraged any immediate pursuit, Talon and the archers trotted to the entrance of the city to join Brandt and Yosef. The gates were just opening.

The men were jubilant, and the guards at the gates slapped their backs and shouted congratulations as they strode through. The great wooden doors closed with a crash, and men gathered around, all laughing and shouting questions at the same time.

Talon just wanted to get off the horse and fall into bed, his leg was hurting so much. He leaned over the horse's neck, thinking that he was going to pass out from the pain. Yosef, ever alert to his lord, noticed and called for space, then with Brandt to help him eased Talon down off the animal.

"That should annoy Al-Adil no end," Talon managed to gasp, then he ground his teeth with the pain.

Abruptly the crowd cleared, and Conrad was standing in front of him, his hands on his hips, roaring with delight.

"You are one for surprises, Lord Talon! This is good work indeed! Some of us had said you were a traitor and might be leaving us, but they dishonored you with those thoughts. No prizes for knowing who that might have been, Ha ha!" He peered at Talon in the flickering light of the torches and his voice became concerned; he had noticed the blood on Talon's leg. "You look as though you are hurt. Are you injured?"

"No more than before, my Lord, but the wound is not yet healed and I am feeling it."

"I shall send my Leech to see you as soon as you have been taken to your chambers. God bless you for this!" the Count enthused. "Make way there, make way for these good men, do you hear?" he shouted at the excited gathering. "Go on, all of you, go home, there is nothing more to see!"

But there was much to see, and excited citizens and men-at-arms crowded the top of the walls to behold the great bon-fire in the middle of the causeway, pointing and exclaiming to one another.

Yosef and Brandt helped get Talon back up to his chambers and finally onto the bed and under a cover, while the archers chattering excitedly about the engagement.

"Just like one of those raids we used to do into the Saxon lands!" Dewi exclaimed without thinking to the room at large, for which he received a glare from Brandt. "One of these days, you black-hearted Welsh cattle thieves, I shall sort you out! Indeed I shall!" he threatened, grimacing fiercely at the two grinning archers.

Talon laughed then. "We should do this again some time. A good evening's work, I would say, on everyone's part. Now, you fellows, keep the insults down, find some food, and then get a good night's sleep. Yosef, if that Leech comes anywhere near me, you have my permission to cut his throat. Then he will see how he likes 'Bleeding'!"

Yosef snorted with amusement. "It will be my pleasure, Lord."

"I'm hungry," said Caradog. "Come along, Brandt, you must be hungry, too, after all that firewood chopping. Let's go and raid the kitchens." It was a peace offering. Brandt cast a look at Talon from under heavy brows. "This siege better not last very long, or we will be starving in a matter of days!" he rumbled.

Talon grinned. "Go on. There won't be anything left if they go on their own. Steal something for me and Yosef here; they didn't leave any food behind earlier."

No one was quite sure how the little dog managed to evade the cooks or the boys in the streets, who were eager to find any meat that lived on four legs by now, and find its way into the chambers. Dewi and Caradog blamed Brandt, who evidently had a soft spot for the little mutt. It was still just a puppy and looked half starved.

"You are just going to fatten it up before eating it all by yourself, I know it. You Saxons are all the same. Sel'fish you are," Caradog observed with a gleam in his narrowed eyes.

"You should remember to share it with us, *Bach*. Once its fa'tter, that is," Dewi said, sounding serious. "We looked after you, we did. Desper'ate it was, out there! Don't know how we all survived!"

"If either of you cattle thieves even thinks of eating this animal, I shall tear your fucking heads off with my bare hands!" Brandt threatened them. He shook his head so that his long blond hair fell about his bewhiskered face, and his blue eyes glared balefully at the two archers baiting him.

Brandt scooped up the little animal from the floor and held it protectively in his huge paw while he fed it a morsel of some indeterminate meat, which it gratefully snapped up. It was so small that it could almost sit up on one of his massive hands. It peered up at the two would-be predators with large brown eyes and wagged its stump of a tail. Brandt fed it some more morsels.

"Oooer! Now you are making me scared!" Caradog pretended to be terrified, cringing against Dewi, who put an arm around his shoulders.

"It's all right. I shall protect you, *Bach*. But I would certainly not call him by any name, Brandt," Dewi stated, gesturing at the tiny creature. He nodded towards Brandt. "He is really a nice Saxon, Caradog. Not too many of them about, are there, like? No name for the dog, though," he reiterated.

Brandt fell into the trap predictably enough. "Why the fuck not?" he demanded aggressively.

Caradog rolled his eyes. "Because you *never* eat an a'nimal you have named! It just isn't decent, and *Godde*," he looked upwards with a pious expression on his lean, sunburned features, "doesn't like it, *Bach*."

"Then I'll call it a name secretly then, and God doesn't have to know," Brandt sounded a little uncertain about this. He brightened. "You can give me a name! It is for sure that God has never been able to find out where you beggars came from!"

Dewi wore a pained expression. "Noo, and we wouldn't want to offend our ancestors by naming a mutt after one of them now, would we? But I'll tell you what we shall do instead, *Bach*. It's we will eat you first, and then enjoy it... for the afters, you know?" Dewi said, poker-faced, and he smacked his lips in anticipation. "I can just taste it!"

For the briefest moment, Brandt looked alarmed and surreptitiously shifted his axe around his belt to where he could get at it more speedily. But then Caradog shook his head.

"Nooo... I don't think he would taste good at all, he's a Saxon, after all!" he remarked, sounding mildly disgusted, while staring at the glowering Brandt as though sizing him up for a cooking pot.

"Its a *siege, Bach*! It doesn't matter how *bad* he tastes. Saxon or Norman, they're all as horr'ible as one another! You have to eat *whatever* you can when you are in the middle of a siege," Dewi said with knowledgeable emphasis.

"What would you two know about a siege? You live in mud huts where you come from!" Brandt retorted, sounding disgusted. "Not a castle between the lot of you!"

"Now then, there's no need to be *rude*!" Caradog said, appearing to be aggrieved .

Dewi shot back, "And besides, you *Sax'ons* didn't do too well with the *Nor'mans* now, *did* you! Hasting, I believe it was? Hum?" he added with emphasis.

"Pure chance was that arrow. God's will be done," Brandt snapped, looking ready to explode, but he sounded defensive. He was referring to the Norman arrow that killed King Harold at the Battle of Hastings. "You cheeky buggers! I don't know why the fuck I don't chop you into little pieces!" Brandt snarled, fingering his axe.

"Lord, they never stop bickering! But just when I think they will kill each other, they have competitions to see who can swear and curse the most horribly!" Yosef exclaimed to Talon, as they listened to the sing-song tones of the two mischief-making archers and the Saxon's growled responses.

"The other day, the Saxon boasted that he could poop in one of their boots and they wouldn't notice until it was too late! Who does that kind of thing?" he asked, sounding totally bewildered. "They nearly came to blows over that one!"

"Its just their way, I suppose," Talon told him with a grin. "Don't worry so much. I'd rather have them working for me than kicking about getting themselves killed or enslaved—or going hungry." Talon was still lying in the bed, recovering. He had warded off the leech and allowed only Yosef to tend to his wound, which, despite the pain, was not going septic.

Yosef drew back from the inquisitive puppy as it came over to sniff him. It gave a squeaky growl and he grimaced at it, showing his teeth. The dog hastily retreated into the other room towards Brandt, who swept it up into his huge paw and set it on his lap. "There, there, little fellow," he crooned. "Is he being mean to you?" He shot a baleful glare towards Yosef, who rolled his eyes and bared his teeth at him, too.

"This is all we need. Another smelly mouth to feed," Yosef complained. "I don't know which one of them stinks more, the dog or those three over there. God is punishing us, Lord. I am sure of it!" he stated with firm assurance.

"I think they are becoming friends. Brandt is just pretending," Talon said, without much conviction. He was amused that all three had to speak French to one another in order to communicate, and in doing so they mangled the language beyond belief, although the Welsh knew a lot of Saxon swear words, as well as many of their own.

"Are you sure, Lord? He looked like that during the battle."

"For all their teasing, the Welshmen definitely like him."

Yosef frowned. "How so, Lord? Doesn't sound like it to me."

"They want to eat him for dinner don't they?" Talon laughed.

Yosef gave Talon a look that implied that he too, was losing his mind.

"Are they all like that where they come from?" he asked, his curiosity taking hold.

"Probably. From what I hear, where those fellows come from it is always cold, wet, and miserable. I don't know how they can live without the sun. Maybe that's why they fight all the time, just to keep warm," Talon told him. "Mind you, it's not much better here, when you come to think of it."

Yosef put into words what Talon had been thinking. "This place is like a prison, Lord. There is no light anywhere inside." He cast a glance around their own gloomy chambers, "and every time I walk along one of the corridors I imagine a ghost will jump out at me."

Talon agreed. The stark stone structure was built for war and defense, nothing else; the Franks did not appear to be interested in the spacious, well aired rooms that he and Yosef were used to.

"I agree whole hardheartedly with you, my friend. I miss Kantara very much indeed," he responded. "I pray that we don't have to pass a winter within these walls."

Yosef nodded his agreement, then lowered his voice. "Those two archers... are they, are they... you know? They seem to be, er, together," Yosef finished, looking uncertain.

"I am almost sure of it, but they kill people efficiently enough, so I don't really care." Talon smiled at his confused young companion.

"Life is full of surprises isn't it, Yosef?" he sighed. "But I need to find something for you all to do before you kill one another." He looked hard at Yosef. "I, for one, am sick of the rotten wine that the steward is pushing out as being the finest in Tripoli's cellar. Is he hoarding the good wine of himself? Or is it all really that execrable? I would like very much if I could find out somehow without him knowing." He cocked an eyebrow at Yosef. "Any ideas? A person should always hone their skills," he added as an afterthought.

Yosef grinned. "I shall see what can be done, Lord."

After Yosef departed, Talon shifted his leg and stared at it resentfully. It was still very stiff and painful, but it was now beginning to itch, which made Yosef confident it was healing. He kneaded the area of his thigh around the wound. He was restless, and hated the confinement.

A week had passed since the night of the trebuchet, and the siege was well under way. The Arab army was firmly encamped along the coast inland; there were nearly twenty trebuchets perched on the far bank, hurling rocks and Greek Fire bombs at the city, but even for these formidable engines the distance was too great to do much real damage. The rocks would land in the sea, sending up tall spouts of water. Sometimes they would bounce on the water and then smash into the base of the walls with a shattering crash, shards of stone humming through the air past the defenders Or the Greek Fire would explode onto the rocks below the walls and a stream of flame would wash upwards, as though reaching for the defenders cowering on the parapet. This was alarming, especially for those who had never before seen fire that behaved as though it were a living thing.

The Arabs camped everywhere, even on the beaches, while the Christians, led by Lord Conrad, were cooped up in the high-walled city, fending off sporadic attacks and feints across the causeway. By now the Arabs were wary of that causeway of death, which was littered with dead horses and the corpses of men, all of them bloated and stinking. The remaining dogs and cats of the city were gone, and boys energetically searched for rats in every corner of the town. The price of bread had reached a point where the Count had ordered it to be issued at one small loaf per person.

Talon had learned that a siege consisted of brief moments of urgent activity followed by long periods of boredom, and with that came problems.

He turned his mind to how he and his men might get out of the city and go home. Kantara beckoned, but the problem lay with the lack of means. The only ships in port were the two left behind after the Count of Sidon had departed. Neither ship would be made available if Conrad had anything to say about it; and in his present condition Talon knew that, while he might be able to ride, he most certainly could not out-ride a gang of eager Arabs if he were observed trying to escape overland. The situation was bleak indeed.

His dismal thoughts were interrupted by a disturbance at the entrance to the main chamber. His three men jumped up and bowed respectfully to a person who entered without ceremony. It was Conrad.

"How is my Lord Talon?" he enquired briskly, striding into the bedchamber and bringing with him an air of confidence and authority. Without waiting for the invitation he dragged over a chair, sat down, and gazed at Talon with bright blue eyes. He gestured towards the archers and Brandt, who were standing respectfully in the other room. The puppy had vanished.

"I have rarely seen a more villainous group that this you have collected. They seem to be good at fighting, however."

Talon grinned. "They do well enough, Lord. But I am bored and tired of lying around being useless."

"I would not say you have been useless, Talon, if I might call you that, and dispense with formalities. Call me Conrad, at least when we are out of the hearing of others. Your little action the other night gave some backbone to the citizens, who were sorely in need of it."

"Very well... Conrad. How may I continue to be of service?" Talon smiled.

"Well, as you have probably assessed for yourself already, we have a rather rag-tag bunch of defenders, even with the men I brought over with me. I need every man of experience to ensure we do not have weak areas, nothing for the Arabs to exploit."

"Do you not have commanders who can be of help? Who do we have to work with?"

"In fact, there are only a couple of commanders, and Sir Philippe de Ypres, a lesser noble with few options at home. He is new to this part of the world, having only just arrived with me. He has told me that after what he has heard about you, he is content to let you take the lead. And yes, we do have experienced soldiers. Sir Sancho Martin is a very good warrior and just the kind of man we need; and there is another, Sir Hugh of Tiberius, whom you know already, but few other leaders, and they are lesser men. Among the many refugees we have people who could be trained, I suppose." He sounded doubtful.

"They have to learn some time," Talon remarked, his tone caustic. "It is their very lives they will be fighting for."

"Indeed. There are also many Genoese and Greek merchants here. Most had the good sense to send their wives and families away when the bad news arrived, but some, unable to pay the exorbitant fees charged by the ships' captains, remained."

Talon nodded. This explained why there were so few women in the city, other than those who had fled here as part of the influx of refugees form the surrounding lands.

"When I was in Lombardy," the Count continued, "I learned quite a lot about defending a city." Talon sat up, his boredom forgotten as he regarded the Count with interest. "The Lombardy nobles, and more recently, the new Merchant Lords, those who have made themselves rich trading with Byzantium and even with the Arab peoples, are a quarrelsome lot, jealous of their wealth, families and property. They get rich, as merchants appear to do effortlessly enough; by trading with anyone, and that includes our enemies; but when they come home laden with wealth, they are forced to protect it all. Each family, within each city and each little state, seeks to assert its influence, and to defend itself from challenges. If you think that nobles are contentious, try the merchants of Lombardy, Venice and Genoa!

"I learned that to be effective, we needed to establish *communes*," he nodded at Talon's questioning look. "Yes that is what they are called. Basically they are communities, cities, whatever, which swear allegiance for mutual defense, while keeping traditions going where they can, depending upon the circumstances of that particular *commune*. In our case here, I have managed to get the Greeks and those mercenaries the Genoese to agree to this principle. Perforce we are all in the same pickle, and unless we collectively look after one another's interests, we will fall together."

The Count sat back and said, "Then there are the knights and squires of those left behind by people like Lord Sidon." Conrad chuckled. "I only allowed him to take his immediate followers with him and packed him off in one ship. How he will manage I have no idea, and I could not care less at this time. He is sorely lacking in backbone, and I have no patience for his kind."

Talon smiled at that. "Very well, but what do you want me to do? I am not very nimble at present, although I would be willing to do whatever I can."

"We need to train these people to put up a coherent defense when and where it is needed. I hear that you know something of sieges, too. Yes, I am hearing all sorts of things about you, Talon. Some people think that you are a magician who practices black arts, but I shall settle for good soldier." He looked hard at Talon, who remained silent.

"There are several Knights Templar and Hospitaliers, about a dozen or so, who don't have a proper leader," he continued. "There are also spearmen and squires who need to be knocked into shape. These people predictably think they are better than the merchants, and it is probably politic to keep them separate for the time being. However, I cannot be negotiating with selfish merchants, soothing ruffled feathers of the knightly class, and administrating this city, as well as dealing with all the training, on my own. Can you help?"

"I would like nothing better," Talon grinned. "When do we start?"

Conrad laughed and slapped his thigh. "As soon as you feel like getting out of bed!" he said, and stood up. "You shall have absolute authority over the men I send to you. They will do as you damned well tell them, or answer to me."

"That should work," Talon said, his mind already planning hard.

"By the way, we need to do something about that awful wine the steward is giving us. My coin is on the good stuff being hidden away somewhere. I think I shall hang him for hoarding if service doesn't improve."

"Hmm. Working on that," Talon laughed. "I might have an answer for you soon, perhaps even by supper tonight."

Conrad grinned and lifted his hand. "Thank you. I shall tell the commanders to report to you tomorrow in the main courtyard. Meanwhile, God willing, your wound will continue to heal."

Talon waited until the Count had gone, then called to his men in the other room to come and join him. No sooner had the three arrived at his bedside when Yosef appeared, in his usual catlike manner. The Welsh and Brandt exchanged looks. None of them had heard him approach.

He addressed Talon. "I have found where the wine is being stored, Lord." He gave a conspiratorial grin and handed over a dusty bottle of wine that looked different from the usual bottles. "It is in an antechamber near to where the steward has his private chamber, Lord."

"Help me up, lads. We are going to see a steward about a bottle of wine," Talon told them.

Not long after, Talon was seated in a chair with his right leg resting up on the table in the room that passed for an office of the steward. That nervous individual was standing in front of the table facing Talon, with the fiercely scowling archers on either side and Brandt towering behind him. Yosef, his dark eyes intent on the steward, pared his nails with the point of a wicked looking knife. The steward sent him a fearful look and began to shake.

Talon eased his leg gingerly off the table down to the floor, then he leaned forward over the table to ask in a very reasonable tone, "All I am here to do is to ensure that my men are fed well, Steward. But also," he paused for effect, "they and I, *and* our illustrious leader, the good Count Conrad, want to enjoy their meager rations, rat, cat or dog, with a good wine. There does not seem to be much of that about. Can you tell me why?" The steward's frightened eyes followed his to the bottle that rested on the table. He still tried for bluff, however.

The Steward shrugged and displayed his hands wide, as though to say "I know nothing," but his voice quavered. "Lord. We are under siege. Wine, you say? I have provided wine to his worship the Count since he arrived. He has not complained. I serve the best we have!"

"Yosef, show us where you found some of this kind," Talon told his man.

"Yes, Lord." Yosef flicked the knife over, in a deft motion caught it by the blade, then threw it in one fluid, casual motion at a small wooden doorway to his left, which was half hidden by a leather curtain. It struck the wood with a sinister thud. The silence that followed was profound. Even the Welsh were silent. There was no need for anything else to be said. The Steward threw a terrified look in that direction, then a wet patch appeared on the lower portion of his tunic. He opened his mouth to say something, but Talon forestalled him with a raised hand.

"Say not a word, Steward. If you do, you might incriminate yourself, and that could mean a hanging. Just provide the Lord Conrad, myself, and my men with the good stuff from here on. The other men can continue to drink that swill you have provided. They don't seem to mind. My man," he indicated Yosef, "knows to the bottle how many there are, and we will be counting." Yosef smiled at the trembling steward, and his eyes widened in fear. He nodded frantically.

"Very well, then I shall leave you to your busy day. Thank you for your hospitality, Steward. We shall be on our way." Talon picked up the bottle on the table and then, as an afterthought said, "Oh, yes. I think I would like to take another bottle of wine with me, if that would not be inconvenient."

The Steward scuttled off and brought back not one but three bottles.

"Thank you, God bless you." Talon stood up gingerly and was helped with his crutches by Brandt, who grinned horribly at the terrified little man while thumbing the blade of the axe tucked into his belt. "God protect!" Talon's odd assortment of villainous louts chorused cheerfully as they exited the room.

"G... G... God protect, Lord!" the man stammered as he watched them leave.

"G... G... *Godde* p... p... protect!" Dewi mimicked, as they followed Talon along the stone corridor.

"Scared him silly, we did. Wet himself, even!" Caradog chortled. "Thank you, Lord. You have such a ve'ry persua'sive way about you," he snickered.

When they arrived back at Talon's chambers he had to rest, but he commanded them to gather around the bed.

"The Count came to see me today," he announced. "He was impressed enough by your performance the other day to want to enlist our help. You are going to assist me in training these people to fight in close quarters. It is very different from what they are used to, so pay attention. This is what we are going to do."

Chapter 26

The Assault

Here they come, those dogs of war.
Stand to your posts; fight bravely.
Defend yourselves, as there'll be more;
The foe comes hard and fiercely,

—Graham

The next morning Talon and his men made their way to the main courtyard in front of the city gates and waited while the Count harangued a line of assorted knights and other men. They numbered several score. The Count was seated on a huge horse and towered over the soldiers, who stared up at him. Gauging the mood, Talon guessed there was more resentment than enthusiasm in that crowd.

The Count noticed Talon and beckoned him over. "Bring this man a horse!" he bellowed. Talon was assisted to mount and edged his horse over alongside the Count.

"For those of you who do not know, Lord Talon de Gilles was at Hattin. He is a Templar and well skilled in the art of war. You will do as he tells you. If you do as you are told, you might survive this siege; but if you go against his wishes then you answer to me, and you will regret it because I shall hang you." He turned his horse away.

"Good luck and God help you, Talon. That is as motley a crew as ever I have had the misfortune to rule." He scowled at the men.

"Teach them to use those mangonels, too, if you would be so kind. No one seems to have a clue. I assume you do?" The Count jerked his thumb at three squat frames in the middle of the yard. They looked like smaller versions of the trebuchet, with a spoon-like arm into which one could place a large stone. Talon nodded and thanked the Count, then turned to face to the assembled men. The Count was right; they were a motley crew. Some were knights, some were squires, some were young and others old. Spearmen, crossbow men, swordsmen, all were ragged, and most looked back at him with sullen expressions.

He took his time, staring at them before addressing them, to the point where a few began to fidget. Some even gave him defiant looks, while others looked askance as though impatient for direction.

As always, he kept an ear open for any sounds that might indicate an attack. It was a sunny day, and the long banners were snapping in a fresh breeze coming off the sea.

"Has anyone here fought in a shield wall? Show your hands," he told the group. Two men immediately put their hands in the air. Both were big, blond men who could have been Brandt's cousins.

"They are yours, Brandt. Make them your assistants," he said over his shoulder. Then to the men, "Everyone will take part in a shield wall for today's practice."

One man, a knight from the Order of Hospitaliers by the look of his surcoat, stepped forward. "I am a knight! I *ride* to war!" he called out. His words were greeted with muttered agreement from many of the other knights, but one other man called out.

"This is Lord Talon de Gilles! You would do well to listen to him. I am with you, Lord," the soldier, a Templar, called out. "I was not at Hattin, may the Good Lord forgive me, but I can tell you all that Lord Talon fought at Montgisard as well as at Hattin! It was he who brought the Templars to the battle! I urge you to listen to him."

The entire group of men subsided, digesting this information.

Talon called out. "There is a time to ride and a time to fight on the ground. Today we fight on the ground, and you will learn from my man here. Brandt is your commander. Pay attention. You!" he pointed to the Templar. I remember you. Come here."

The knight walked over and stood squinting up at Talon. "Where have I seen you before?" Talon asked in a low tone.

"I was one of the knights with whom you talked in Jerusalem, Lord. They rest are all gone now. Rideford saw to that." His tone was bitter.

"You will take charge of the Templars who remain, how many of you? It doesn't look like many," Talon observed.

"We are a dozen, Lord. I was their leader when we rode here from Acre. I only wish that we had all perished at Hattin alongside our brothers."

"Perhaps the Lord has other work for you. What is your name?"

"Pierre de Carret, Lord."

"Well, now you have something solid to fight for. Know this, Sir Pierre, that Tyre is a very important and strategic port. That is *why* the Sultan is here. Our work is to frustrate his intentions. Do I make myself clear?"

Pierre nodded. "Yes, Lord. I am glad to be serving you."

"Send me the leader of the Hospitaliers, Pierre," Talon commanded, knowing that the next man would not be so easy to deal with. The very man who had questioned Talon came forward and stood in front of him, still defiant.

Talon dismounted with care, tossed the reins to Dewi, and then drew his sword out of its new, crudely made scabbard, and he brought it up to the on guard position.

Yosef made to step forward. "Lord! Let me deal with him!" he said quietly, his voice full of concern.

"Don't worry, Yosef. This I can deal with," Talon murmured back.

"Attack me!" he commanded the knight, who gave him an incredulous look and hesitated.

"But you are wounded. I do not fight a wounded man," he stated, sounding almost contemptuous.

Talon slipped forward and the blade of his strange sword flickered in the sunlight. A small bead of blood grew on the knight's cheek. "Draw your sword and fight!" Talon hissed. He heard a collective intake of breath from every man in the square.

The Hospitalier touched his cheek, stared at his bloody fingers and took a step back, fury beginning to form on his bearded features. He dragged his sword out of its sheath with a snarl, then raised it high. With a shout he committed himself to a downward blow, using all his strength as though he was determined to finish Talon regardless of consequences.

Despite his wound Talon could still move very quickly. He allowed the man to commit himself, tapped the descending blow aside and leaned back, then slammed the back of his blade, not the edge, into the man's knee, eliciting an involuntary yelp of pain. The man stumbled to his knees. Talon then thumped him hard on the top of the shoulders, which made the already confused man bow his head. His sword fell well away from his hand. He was about to reach for his weapon when Talon's blade touched his neck. "Know this, Knight of the Hospital. I am here to teach you, not the other way around. Do you submit?"

The knight hesitated, but he received another prod from Talon's blade and gave a reluctant nod of his shaggy head. Talon seized his arm to try and pull him upright. "Ugh," he grunted, as his leg threatened to give away. "You are a heavy man."

The knight stayed kneeling on the ground. "Forgive me, Lord. I mean no ill."

"Yes, I do forgive you, but you must hear me, and then we can make progress. We have walls to defend. You cannot ride along the walls on a horse, but we can defend them, and I need you and your men to help. Now go and join your men, and then become one with the rest of us."

"Hugh of Tiberius, show yourself!" Talon called out, once he had been helped back onto his mount.

"Here, Lord!" Hugh stepped forward, thumped his shield on the ground, and grinned. "I am right glad to see that *you* are here, Lord," he called out.

"I am glad to see you, too, Sir Hugh. I need your help to bring this bunch of misfits and hunch fronts up to some kind of standard," Talon called back. "You will be in charge of the spearmen. Today, however, you do as Brandt here tells you."

Sir Hugh nodded acceptance. "Very well, Lord Talon. We work with you. My word on it."

Next Talon sorted out the bowmen and handed them off to Dewi and Caradog, after which Brandt, with his two Saxon assistants, began to push and shove men into place, to form the lines necessary for shield walls. They ordered the men to put down their weapons and just keep their shields.

For the rest of the day, apart from a few brief intervals for meager portions of bread and water, the yard was filled with the yells of the combatants and crash of shield on shield as the two competing lines rushed at each other, then pushed and shoved back and forth across the stones, the advance going to those who possessed the most enthusiasm.

There were several boys in the group who had volunteered. Talon put them to work bringing water and, later, what little food they could scrounge from the kitchens. Curious citizens came by to watch; some brought with them shields and spears and were immediately pressed into service. Before long the lines were beginning to look more coherent, with one side consistently pushing the other back.

Brandt and his two Saxons went to the help of the weaker line. They joined the sweating, grunting men—no one had any breath left for shouts—and continued to push and shove. Brandt and his men demonstrated the craft of using the crush to advantage, rapping exposed ankles and knocking on heads that poked up once too often.

"These shields are pathetic little things, Lord. We need larger ones to be effective," a panting and sweating Brandt pointed out to Talon during a brief pause in the scuffles, who responded, "Then we need to have larger ones made. There is surely enough of wood and hides. I'll talk to the Count."

There was a lull in the activity when the third ship belonging to the Count made its way into the harbor. Naturally the city folk all went to greet it, but Talon refused to allow the men he was training to go.

"You can gawk all you like later, but it is nothing to be concerned about. Back into your lines. Brandt, get them ready," he barked. Brandt and his two burly Saxon aids roared out the commands, whereupon the tired men dragged themselves into line and the work began again.

Once the men were sufficiently practiced in forming and holding a purely defensive shield wall, Brandt found staves, long ones to use as mock spears, short ones to use as mock swords, and cudgels to use as practice axes. He demonstrated the technique, bashing one luckless man on the helmet. The man's eyes crossed and he nearly fell senseless to the ground, to the unkind snickers of amusement from others.

In short order, the men where practicing spear thrusts, sword strikes, and axe blows upon each other. Talon ordered his two archers to join the line, which they did reluctantly; but after a few actual blows were exchanged they fought with enthusiasm, roaring Welsh battle cries and shoving their shields against their opponents with the best of them. Yosef was off to one side with some of the knights, showing them how a real swordsman could perform.

Talon smiled to himself. This was working off the accumulated steam that had worried him before. It was strange, for despite the hard work it was not long before everyone appeared to be enjoying themselves. He was sure he heard laughter on occasion. Then he realized that the cunning Brandt had placed the Templars in one line and the Hospitaliers in the other!

They went at it with a will. Men slipped and fell, to be trampled on by their own and the men of the other line. Few enjoyed that experience, and thereafter people did their best to keep their footing. Nonetheless, there were bruises and cuts aplenty from staves and shield edges. The men were beginning to realize just how effective a shield wall could be, for offense as well as defense.

During one of the short breaks, Brandt walked up to Talon, puffing and sweating, but looking pleased.

"They are getting the hang of it," Talon observed.

"Its a bit like wrestling with a pig in the shit, Lord. After a short while you begin to notice that the pig is enjoying it," Brand responded with a glance back at the panting men.

Talon chuckled. "Sooo, you are used to wrestling with pigs eh?"

"My Lord....!" Brandt's tone was tinged with embarrassment, until he saw the grin on Talon's face.

"Keep them at it for a while longer," Talon told the Saxon. Brandt knuckled his forehead, and with a grin of his own turned away to bellow orders. The tired men re formed.

Brandt was about to show just how effective the shield wall was going to be. He ordered one of the double lines to block a street entrance. No one could get past it, no matter what they tried to do. Observing this, Talon silently thanked the Varangian Guardsmen in Constantinople for the lesson they had taught him during the disaster at the battle of Myriokephalon those many years ago. There, the only thing that had saved the Byzantine army from a complete rout by the Turks, was the dense shield wall the Emperor's personal guard of Varangians had formed.

There were of course some minor injuries, and a couple of the Genoese crossbow men limped over to Talon to protest.

"What is it?" he demanded. Ever since Hattin, he had not had much use for these mercenaries.

"It's those two people who work for you, Lord." One of them pointed towards the Welshmen, who were lounging against the walls with the Saxons, laughing about something. He heard Dewi say, "We should turn this into a sport. It's about cunning, you see, *Bach*, which we Welsh have in plenty. It's not your axe bashing that will win it for you!"

One of the Saxons muttered something indignant, spiced with the usual obscenities.

"What about them?" Talon turned back to the Genoese.

"They cheat, Lord. During the practice they... they...."

"They what?" Talon demanded, his patience wearing thin.

"They struck us in... in the *privates!*" The second one sounded very upset.

Talon had wondered why it was that, during the defense of the street, several of the 'attackers' had fallen to the ground with yelps of pain; but had put it down to normal accidents. Now he almost choked. He heard a low moan from somewhere behind him.

"It was not fair, Lord," the third Genoese shook his head. "They seize and hang on... and then—"

"Yes, yes, I see what you mean," Talon spluttered, then he attempted to assume a stern face. "Nothing is supposed to be fair in wartime, or had you forgotten that?" he snarled at them, trying desperately to keep from snorting with laughter. "But... I shall talk to them. *Now go!*"

He lowered his head and raised his hand to his face to hide his laughter as the three disgruntled Genoese shuffled off. He heard the odd sound behind him again and turned, to find Yosef banging his head against his horse's rump, weeping with mirth.

Eventually Talon called a halt, and everyone promptly collapsed to the stones, gasping and sweating from their exertions in the relentless heat of the day. He pronounced himself partially satisfied and told them all to return in the morning. Leaving their new students lying about amid the tumble of their shields and weaponry, Talon and his men made for his chambers.

When they arrived he faced them. "That was well done, particularly you, Brandt. Perhaps not quite so much *man-handling* in the line next time." He directed this at the unrepentant archers, who wore poker faces.

Talon sniffed the air. "Dear God, where does that stench come from? It smells as though someone died! Now, you stinking lot, put your weapons down. I have one more order for you. You will bathe in the pool, or you get neither food nor wine today."

His words were greeted with appalled looks, followed by actual fright. These warriors, who were afraid of very little, were terrified of bathing!

"Are my fierce and dauntless men such timid weaklings that they are afraid of water and some soap?" he taunted them. "Go and get cleaned up. You all smell like pigs in a midden. Ah yes, Brandt did mention pigs."

Brandt rolled his eyes as Talon continued. "Yosef will lead the way, just in case you others forget how to get there. I shall be right behind you. You too, Brandt! Who knows when any of us will be able to bathe again, so this is your chance!"

Brandt looked as though he was ready to jump out of a window rather than do as he was told. With what sounded almost like a whimper he hunched his large shoulders and joined the equally perturbed Welshmen, who also appeared to be searching for a way to escape.

Moving like a group of condemned prisoners heading for the scaffold, they trooped along the corridors after Yosef. The small procession made its way to the baths, with Talon hobbling along behind them.

"We will need to find them some clean clothes, Yosef!" he called ahead to his friend, who raised a hand in acknowledgment. "If you can keep them in the water for long enough, Lord, I can provide the clean clothes!" he offered.

"How long have you worn that tunic, Brand?" Talon asked, staring at the back of the filthy, patched, and mended tunic Brandt wore.

"About two years, Lord."

Talon had learned a few words while being around his warriors. "Fuck me!" he exclaimed, imitating the Saxon. "We'll need a hammer and chisel to get that off you!"

*****

The hard practice continued, and during this time Talon set the Italian merchants to work on the mangonels. The catapults were in sorry condition, so first the crews spent a day cleaning, replacing worn rope bindings, and greasing vital parts. The following day, while the knights and the shield wall combatants were taking a rest, Talon directed the crews to line up the catapults, roughly aimed at the causeway.

He hobbled up onto the battlements, accompanied by idlers and most of the trainees, to watch what the mangonels could do. He wished fervently that he had some of the Chinese powder that he had found so effective at home, but there was none of that to be had. They would have to make do with some rounded boulders and rocks scavenged from the base of the walls.

He himself felt some trepidation as he raised his arm and dropped it to signal the crews. All eyes were on the first mangonel, which jumped as the arm swung viciously upwards to thump noisily into its stop bar. For a terrible moment Talon thought the rock was coming straight at him, and everyone on the battlements instinctively ducked or lurched to the side. But the stone arced overhead with a soft whistle and with good clearance to plunge down into the sea to the left of the causeway, about half way along its length. A small column of water rose where it had landed. There were noisy cheers and some cheerful jeers from the observing idlers.

"We have to practice, but that was a good start," Talon remarked to Yosef, who was standing nearby. He gave instructions for the crews to fine tune the mangonels so that they could drop large rocks onto the surface of the causeway almost every time. A grizzled old Italian who had once been a soldier was put in charge and clearly enjoyed the role. Before long, the mangonels were as accurate as they were ever likely to be.

This activity was not lost on the Arab army. They responded with shots fired from their remaining trebuchets, now safely out of range of any further forays by the Christians, but their effectiveness against the walls was much reduced. More often than not, the rocks that they hurled at the city fell into the sea, merely wetting the jeering defenders on the battlements.

Greek Fire would be a huge deterrent to the average warrior running along the exposed causeway, so Talon asked the Italians to investigate supplies, and if none was to be found, to try to make something like it. He was gratified to hear that there was a warehouse almost full of barrels of the viscous, sticky material. He promptly put a party of men to work preparing medium-sized earthenware jars, with a couple of knowledgeable merchants to direct the process.

"Why do we not try one out, Lord?" an impatient Italian demanded.

"Surprise," was Talon's curt answer. "Be patient. They will draw close again before too long. Then we will use it."

He was not wrong. One morning a couple of days later, he and his now cleaner crew were preparing for shield wall practice when they heard shouts. They hurriedly donned hauberks and helmets, seized weapons, shields and bows, then rushed as fast as they could for the battlements, leaving Talon to limp along with the help of Brandt. Once there he found the Count already at the ramparts with his lieutenants.

"Ah, Lord Talon!" he called out with a cheerful wave of his arm. "Now we have a chance to see how effective the mangonels will be."

"What is going on, Lord?" Talon asked, as he glanced down at the feverishly working crews of the catapults.

"Your Sultan friend has grown tired of staring at us and has sent a large force. It is already nearing the causeway," the Count responded. He was clearly eager for a fight and strode ahead of the limping Talon towards the parapet nearest the gates. Hurrying as fast as he could despite the ache in his leg, Talon caught up with the Count. He was relieved to note that the crews of the mangonels seemed ready and that Giovanni, the old crew master, was coming up the stairs.

"God's Blessings, my Lords," he called up.

"Gods Blessings, Giovanni. Your men are ready?" Talon responded.

"Oh yes, Lord," the old man called back with some pride. "Whenever you say the word."

"Very well. Have the Greek fire made ready. I want to use it today."

Giovanni beamed. "Yes, my Lord. It is prepared."

"Good," Talon nodded and turned his attention back to the ramparts. His two archers were standing at the ready with their bows strung. They grinned at him. Talon was amused by how much more comfortable his men seemed after their forced bath. Fleas and lice were mostly gone, and they looked refreshed, despite the miserable diet they were all now forced to live upon.

The banners were fluttering defiantly in the sea wind, and the ramparts were becoming crowded with armed men waiting for the enemy to attempt to climb the walls. Talon could see dark clusters of men forming up beyond the causeway in preparation for an assault. The ruins of the burned trebuchet had still not been cleared away, and the rotting carcasses of horses lay on the road among the rocks that had struck them. It was already an obstacle course for the attackers, after which they would have to clamber over the rough rocks and slippery glacis before they could even place ladders against the walls. He didn't envy the Arabs at all.

"Prepare for the attack!" the Count bellowed. Trumpets sounded on the walls to warn the population that an attack was imminent, and bells began to peal out. Men nervously adjusted their straps and tested their blades. Brandt drew his axe and hefted it, a grin of anticipation on his bearded face. In the distance, they heard an answering call from the enemy trumpets signaling the beginning of the assault.

Talon stood a little off to the side of the Count, leaving him to observe the enemy through narrowed eyes. Clearly he was estimating the odds as he watched the enemy's movements. Soon men were swarming along the causeway, racing towards the city of Tyre, the prize they needed so urgently.

"Take the men on horses," Talon instructed his archers, who willingly lifted their bows.

The effectiveness of the bowmen was soon clear to everyone on the walls. They were downing horsemen one by one. There was an urgency to this attack, as though the Sultan might have decided to throw everything he had in a bid for success. The crowd of screaming men kept on coming. When they were almost in the range of the mangonels, Talon called down to Giovanni. "Ready?"

Giovanni nodded and raised his arm. "Wait...wait... Now!" Talon called. Giovanni dropped his arm and the men on the ramparts heard three loud thumps in rapid succession. Almost simultaneously, three earthenware jars, smoking from their openings, soared overhead and arced down towards the crowded causeway. The pots exploded onto the stonework and spattered their liquid contents everywhere.

The Greek Fire burned hotter than flaming oil, and it stuck to any clothing, or flesh, it touched. Screaming, yelling men ran in all directions, trying to get away from the hellish flames. Many jumped into the sea, while others cringed back, trying to escape the way they had come. But still more men were pushing them forward towards the walls. So still they came on, but with a great deal less enthusiasm than before.

The men carrying ladders had not been affected by the flames, and once they had clambered over the difficult ground they leaned these against the walls, struggling to hold them in place while other men climbed. The defenders managed to break most, or pole them off so that men clutching the ladders fell backwards, screaming, to the rocks below. Some determined soldiers actually made it over the ramparts, only to meet with a solid line of quickly raised shields. The shield wall men closed on their attackers remorselessly, putting what they had painstakingly practiced to work, pushing the interlopers back against the wall and stabbing them to death. Their bodies were then tossed over the walls to fall upon others below.

The defenders on the ramparts also had Greek Fire pots put together by the enterprising merchants, which were brought up by eager and excited boys. These were tossed over the walls to light up the rocks below and burn alive anyone so unfortunate as to be in the immediate area. The noise of the screams and shouts, combined with the regular thump of the mangonels and the clash of swords and shields, was deafening.

Gradually, as their casualties mounted and there was little progress, the enemy began to loose heart and reluctantly began to withdraw. Talon likened it to a tide of flashing steel that had washed up to the very tops of the walls only to recede, leaving behind the dead and wounded.

His respect for the Count grew as he observed Conrad and his men in the forefront of the fights for the battlements. He allowed the impatient Brandt to join the defense. The Saxon created havoc wherever he went with his bloody axe. Even Talon himself and Yosef were involved, as scuffles on the battlements surged back and forth. Talon was very glad that he had his little band of men about him on these occasions, because they dealt with any of the enemy rash enough to come near with protective ferocity. His leg wound was still a real liability.

The Arabs were harassed all the way along the causeway by the arrows of the Welsh archers and the Genoese mercenaries, leaving even more dead and wounded as they fled back along the narrow road. At the half way point their retreat was harried by rocks tumbling out of the sky from the mangonels. Gradually the noise of the retreating army faded, and on the battlements there was a quieter moment, broken only by the snap of the banners still flying defiantly and the groans of the wounded below the walls.

The Count called over to Talon. "We will need to collect arrows and spears and armor from below. Anything of value. Can your men take care of this?"

Talon nodded

He turned to Brandt, who had rejoined him bespattered with other people's blood. He had looked a lot cleaner before the battle; he wore a new tunic under his hauberk that Yosef had obtained somehow. Talon knew better than to ask from where. Brandt's beard was also trimmed, but he had insisted on keeping his long blond braids. Talon shook his head. The huge man was enjoying himself far too much.

"Brandt, we will want a defensive line to protect the others while they collect weapons. Take your men and as many knights of the Orders as you can muster and form a shield wall to block off the causeway."

Brandt grinned hugely and hurried off. To the watchers on the walls, it became apparent that volunteers far outnumbered the men needed. Finally Brandt and his chosen men slipped out of the gates and raced for the causeway, across which they formed a solid wall of shields: two shields high and three lines deep.

Talon noted with deep satisfaction that most of the men of the shield wall were from the two Orders, dedicated horsemen who would not usually fight on foot. Would miracles never cease, he wondered? With an eye on the distant end of the causeway, Talon told his archers to be ready for trouble. He didn't expect a second assault at this point, but it paid to be careful.

Meanwhile, men and boys who were not to be denied the opportunity to be useful were scrambling about beneath the walls collecting arrows, spears and other weaponry. Some were dispatching the wounded, or removing chainmail from the dead, as well as any other items of value they could plunder. The Count had ordered that there were to be only a few prisoners. Most were to be killed.

Talon glanced up; there was a shouted warning from men on the towers, who now pointed towards the end of the causeway. A large group of horsemen were racing down the causeway from the direction of the Arab army. Their obvious intent was to destroy the men on the ground and gain some form of victory at any cost.

"Watch out, Brandt!" Talon shouted. Many others yelled the warning from the wall. "Caradog and Dewi, do your work well," he instructed his two archers.

The horsemen were past the center of the causeway so quickly that the stones thrown from the mangonels landed behind them and splashed into the sea without doing any harm. The horsemen charged headlong with lowered lances against the dense line of shields. Fortunately, Brandt and his men were ready for them.

Had the horses been the heavy Destriers the Franks and the Orders used, it could have gone very badly for the men on the ground. As it was, the horses were the light cavalry so favored by the Arabs, and although it looked as though they might succeed to the tense men lining the walls, and the line did give a little, the men of the shield wall withstood the forceful charge.

Then Brandt and his Saxon companions began to use their long-handled axes with devastating effect, so that gradually the line straightened and the long spears could do their work. Try as they might, the horsemen could not get close enough with their mounts to do any real damage after that.

As soon as a man began to turn away, a spear would be thrust out from the wall to pierce the side of his animal, bringing it down screaming, and then the rider was butchered as he tried to get up. All the while, arrows were falling among them from above, taking a toll and making their situation intolerable. Still, there were casualties on Brandt's side as well.

While the fight on the causeway was in progress, the men who had been collecting discarded weapons and armor raced for the gates, their arms full of booty. Brandt, cognizant of the danger of reinforcements coming to the aid of the Arabs, shouted for an orderly retreat.

Brandt tossed his shield to another, then scooped up one of the wounded men, one of the Hospitaliers, and pointed to one of the dead nearby. His Saxon comrades seized the dead man by his arms and feet and chased after Brandt, who had thrown the wounded man over his shoulder like a sack of corn and was loping back towards the gates.

To Talon it was no surprise to see Brandt carry the man so easily; He himself had been carried without noticeable effort by the huge man; but the men on the battlements who witnessed it were clearly impressed.

"Dear Lord," one of them said, "but I am so very glad that those Saxons are on our side! Look at the giant. He makes it seem effortless, and the man still in his chainmail!"

"They work for the Lord Talon here," another commented in a low voice that yet carried. "They will not leave our wounded, nor our dead, to the tender mercies of the enemy. May the Good Lord bless them!"

Talon was pleased to hear the exchange. He had had begun to sense a change in attitude towards him recently, and this confirmed it. Previously, he had been only too aware of the surreptitious crossing of breasts when he passed and the signs to ward off evil made by the guards on the walls.

Many of the light cavalry were down in a struggling mass of horses and men, while those still mounted retreated far enough away to reconsider the situation. The men of the shield wall paced backwards until they were close enough to the gates to turn on a sharp order as a group and bolt for safety. When a number of reckless riders decided to give chase, they lost even more men to the deadly shooting of the Welsh archers.

The gates slammed shut while exuberant men cheered wildly down in the courtyard, and then the cheering began all along the battlements. Some defenders shouted abuse at the few remaining and chastened horsemen, who hastened away towards their own army, leaving their dead and wounded to their fate. The bells began to peal as news spread of the success of the defenders.

"You have done well, Lord Talon," the Count beamed at him. "Thanks to you, we have a fighting force to be reckoned with, even if some of them have terrible looking arses," the Count remarked with a grin, jerking his thumb at some men along the parapet. A number of the defenders had lifted their tunics and bared their backsides to the retreating enemy.

"That will give the 'Sultan' something to think about, I dare say. Thanks be to God, we survive to live another day!"

"He will soon have to leave, my Lord," Talon remarked.

"How so?" The Count frowned at him.

"His main objective is Jerusalem, and I am very sure he has not lost sight of that. He will want to take the holy city before it is reinforced from nearby castles. Therefore his time here is limited, even though he would dearly like to take us before he does leave. If he knew how few we were he might become more determined to finish this before he moves on."

The Count nodded somberly. "This is what you believe, Talon?"

"Very much so, Lord," Talon responded. "And if he succeeds in taking Jerusalem, he will not neglect Tyre for very long thereafter."

"Pity those lords and the King didn't listen to the likes of you and the Count of Tripoli when they should have," the Count said. His tone was bitter. "All of this could have been avoided. If he does leave, then I intend to cut that causeway with a large ditch. We'll see how he deals with that when he comes back, as you say he will.

"I agree, Lord. It should be cut," Talon said.

"I could wish for some allies to help us with this struggle," Conrad said, as he leaned against the parapet and stared out at the distant army. "No point in calling upon the Byzantines for help, I suppose?"

"I doubt it, Lord. There is little love lost between the Empire and the Latins since Manuel died. Besides, they have their hands full with the Bulgars in the North and the Turks, who are gaining ground every year. Andronikos made overtures to Salah Ed Din, and Isaac in Cyprus has also."

'You have a castle there, do you not?"

"Yes, Lord. And Isaac has tried to take that too, but with no success thus far," Talon told him with a grin.

The Count snorted with amusement, but then became thoughtful.

"That leaves the Normans of Sicily. But I know William; he is bent upon other schemes and will not help. His wife is Joan, daughter of Eleanor of Aquitaine, and Richard's sister. It would be nice if Richard could show some interest." Conrad sounded rueful.

"It is a question of time, Lord," Talon stated. "There is no time left for this kingdom. The best we can hope for is to retain Tyre. All else, I fear, is gone, or soon will be."

Conrad gave him a long hard look, but then nodded his head slowly in agreement.

"Then we are alone, for the time being at least. We shall have to see to it that we do not lose Tyre." His jaw set.

"I intend to send the Archbishop of Tyre to Europe to appeal for help. He isn't doing much good here, and his troupe of attendants are useless for anything besides eating our precious food. He has instructions to take the dire news and persuade those miserly kings to pay with men and coin for a new crusade."

Talon had already heard about this plan. The ship would sail into the European waters with black sails and images of the desecration of the true cross. His respect for the Count grew. This man was a politician as well as a fighter.

*****

Later in the afternoon, when Talon was resting on the bed —his leg was again playing him up—he called his men over.

They certainly smelled cleaner since their bath, Talon noted, and there was less scratching. The Welsh seemed even more attached to each other, and Brandt had gained confidence. Brandt had been petting the little dog, which still didn't have a name other than 'Dog', and he brought it over with him. It struggled free, to land on the bed, much to Brandt's chagrin and Yosef's horror.

"It's all right, leave it be," Talon said, then he addressed his men. "Today we gave the Sultan a bloody nose." He watched them beam with pleasure at his somewhat parsimonious compliment. "The drilling should continue with the shield wall, Brandt. Give Hugh of Tiberius a leadership role. He looks to me like a good man."

Brandt scowled but nodded reluctantly. Hugh was a scarred and experienced fighter who had served Raymond of Tripoli and had fought with them at Hattin, but he was a Norman, and everyone knew Brandt's opinion about them.

Talon continued, using a mollifying tone. "I have talked to the Count about larger shields and longer spears. He agreed, so we should see some before long. I think that the citizens and even the knights are beginning to realize their value. Today made that point very clear. I also expect the Sultan will lose interest before long. He has another objective in mind." He absently stroked the little dog as it pushed its nose into his hand.

"You two," he addressed the archers. "Even if you cannot find any other longbow men, I want you to keep those Genoese hard at it. They can still fill a role in the defense."

Dewi nodded. "They are a scummy lot, but as long as they are safe on the walls we can use them, Lord." He glanced at Brandt. "Our Saxon would not want them in his shield wall, of that me and Caradog are certain." Both men sniffed derisively.

Talon could only agree. The Genoese were a flighty crew who were confident enough high up on the ramparts, but wary of close quarter fighting.

They talked for some time about the training and shared their views on the way the siege was progressing. Eventually Talon dismissed the three men, who decided to go and raid the kitchens, leaving him alone with Yosef. He watched them leave, still arguing and teasing, but there was different note to their banter now.

"Yosef, we have no eyes in the enemy camp," Talon remarked casually.

As though he had been waiting for this, Yosef smiled. "We need to know what he plans next?"

Talon smiled back. "I would come with you, my friend, but... I think in this case I would be a liability. What do you think?"

"If he learned anything today it is that the city can easily repulse his army from across the causeway." Yosef said. "But we are not very many compared to his thirty thousand," he remarked, his tone thoughtful.

Talon nodded agreement. "Which is why we need to stay one step ahead of him. That leaves the sea, and getting across it somehow. It would be useful to know what is being planned in that regard. We should discuss how we can get you into the Sultan's camp and back in one piece."

———————————

Chapter 27

Assassins

Pain is a country of its own
where the roads are memories
stationed with regrets.
In this land lamentation rains...
one curses sunlight
and cowers from the moon.
— Stephen T. Vessels

Diocles, the one time Chief Minister to Isaac Komnenos, woke up and groaned. He rolled over onto his side, paused for a long moment, then he pushed himself slowly up the prison wall until he was finally standing but still leaning against it. He was cold and ached in every bone He clasped his hands over thin upper arms in a vain attempt to warm himself; the damp of the cell had penetrated the thin material of his tunic, making him shiver.

He groaned again, more with irritation this time, and scratched under his arms, then his belly, and then his legs. It seemed as though every flea that existed had decided to take up residence in his clothing and was busy sampling his wearied flesh. He stared down at the sodden, filthy straw on the floor, which had not been changed out for a very long time, the stink of which clogged his nostrils. He could not get used to it and felt like weeping because he wanted a bath so badly.

He noticed that someone had pushed his supper under the bars, and shuffled forward to pick up the wooden platter, only to contemplate the stale bread and mush on it with distaste. The guard who had pushed it into the cell was not someone he knew, and that disturbed him. Where were all these new men coming from? They seemed to be working only for Zenos.

It gave him cause to wonder whether anyone other than these men even knew he was down here! Perhaps there was a coup taking place and he would soon be joined by the Chief Steward. Surely his absence should have been noticed by now, and someone should be asking questions as to his whereabouts? The lady Tamura, for instance; would she not be perturbed by his absence?

He had of late paid her regular visits, which they had both seemingly enjoyed. He certainly had; she was a very beautiful woman and even he, an old man, was not immune to her charms. While the conversations had more often than not been an excuse to simply gaze upon her as they dissected the gossip bouncing off the walls of the palace, it had become just a little more than that, for him anyway, and he missed it.

Now, however, his prevalent fear was what they would do to him before they killed him. He had become resigned to the idea that his fate was sealed, but feared the ugliness of torture and execution. As he picked up the piece of bread his hand was shaking. He slid down the wall into a squatting position again and bit into the stale bread.

He looked around his cell. Its rough stone walls bore the marks of previous occupants who had scratched their names into the hard stone, or used food or even excrement to make their marks. This was a hopeless place where people came to spend their last hours on earth. He was doubtless doomed to be escorted from here to the executioner when the Emperor returned, which must happen soon, although he could not tell the duration of his imprisonment. The turnover of the sentries gave him some idea. It had to have been at least three or four days.

No one had come to see him in all that time, not even Zenos, which puzzled him, as Zenos had made it clear he planned to extract information from him at the earliest opportunity. Nor would the guards speak to him. Lately they had become tense and watchful, which puzzled him and made his feeling of isolation even more profound. He tried to compose himself, but it was hard. Wishing he had left the palace a long time ago when he'd had the chance, he sighed, then scratched some more. After a while, as happened more and more often these days, he dozed off.

He was rudely awakened by a fierce rattle of the door by one of the guards. "Wake up, old man! You have a visitor."

Zenos strode into the area in front of the several cells, one of which Diocles occupied, with an entourage of hard-looking armed men bearing torches that smoked and flickered. Leaving them to chat with the prison guards, he came and stood before the barred door of Diocles' cell. His face was tight and grim, his mouth turned down as he glared at his prisoner through the bars. Diocles might have been miserable and exhausted, but he had spent a lifetime reading faces, and what he saw did little to reassure him.

"So, you did manage to warn them!" Zenos hissed without preamble. "For that you will be executed as a traitor. But you know that, don't you? Would you like me to describe how you will be executed?" There was pure venom in his tone, which baffled Diocles almost as much as the words themselves.

"Warn whom?" he croaked, trying desperately to collect his wits and maintain his composure. It was hard under the circumstances. Zenos appeared to be very angry and his presence was intimidating.

The furious Chief Gatherer of Information almost shouted, "You know perfectly well what I am talking about! The castle, fool! You warned them, didn't you? I will personally enjoy taking you apart, old man, so that very little is left for the executioner."

Diocles felt some mixed emotions then. On the one hand he was relieved that the castle had been warned of something bad; on the other hand, here was Zenos threatening him with dire consequences for having done so. He wiped a shaking hand across his beard. "I really do not know of what you speak. I swear to God!" he exclaimed.

Zenos was so angry he shouted. "They were waiting for us when we arrived! They had already seen to the pirates, and somehow they took care of the assassins, so when we arrived they were waiting to greet us. Oh, they greeted us, all right!" He shook his head at the ugly memory. He had been scared out of his wits when the people on the castle walls sprung the trap, and he was still astonished that he had escaped with his life. More than half of his recruits from Beirut had died on the cursed mountain.

Diocles sighed, and for a brief moment he failed to keep his feelings of relief under control. Zenos, despite his rage, noticed and shouted, "You did warn them! I shall make you pay and pay! You will beg me to end your life before I am done!"

Mustering the remaining tatters of his courage and dignity, Diocles drew himself up. "I wish to plead my case before the Emperor. I have that right."

Zenos laughed. "You do not have that right! I will see to that. Besides, there is a fleet coming, and they are going to deal with him when he returns!" Zenos had not meant to let that slip out, but he was so angry at having lost his once in a lifetime opportunity that he didn't care any more what he said to Diocles. No one knew the old man was down here, and he was soon to disappear forever anyway. There and then, Zenos decided to execute Diocles in his cell and dispose of the body in a lime pit. He would have to make certain preparations, quietly, before he could carry out his plan. It wouldn't be as satisfying as denouncing him to the Emperor and overseeing public torture, followed by public execution, but he dared not allow the old man to speak before Emperor.

Diocles was stunned. "I beg pardon, but what did you just say?" he demanded.

"Nothing of interest to you, old man, nor is there anything you can do about it, so forget what I said and make your peace with God."

He whirled away and strode down the tunnel past the other subterranean chambers, which included the treasury, followed by the torchbearers. The two remaining guards were silent as their comrades' steps receded, and silence once more descended.

"Better make yourself comfortable, old man. He will be back before too long," one of them called over, not without sympathy.

"What happened out there to make him so angry?" Diocles rasped. "May I have a drink of water?"

One of them brought him over a leather cup full of bad tasting water and stood waiting while he gulped it. "You really don't know?" the guard asked him.

Diocles drew himself up again, trying to appear more formal. "No, how could I? I have been in here for the last... how many days? So no, I do not know. I have no idea what he is talking about. What has been going on?" he insisted.

The guards proceeded to tell him what they knew. One of them had accompanied Zenos in the attack. He was still shocked by the reception they had received and told Diocles in some detail what he remembered.

"They are wizards up there, and we should never have gone near them. I don't care for what reason. It was a disaster! As soon as I get paid I shall be leaving for Beirut and I never want to step on this pestilential island again," he added with some fervor.

Diocles wondered how the people up at the castle had been forewarned, but it would not have surprised him if they had used wizardry. The Lord Talon certainly possessed unusual powers. Diocles could guess accurately enough as to why the operation had taken place. He surmised the plot to take the castle revolved around the gold that was supposed to be hidden up there. It explained much, but what about the slip of the tongue by Zenos about a fleet?

What was that all about? How to reach the Emperor and get him to understand that it was he, Diocles, who was looking after his interests and not Zenos, who from the sound of it was indeed planning some sort of coup in the Emperor's absence. The information about the gold had to have come from the 'Ambassador', which meant that treason was afoot right here in the palace!

Having failed at the one enterprise, Zenos might just be mad enough to try and join the forces of Constantinople, which appeared to be in the wings waiting to strike, or even to try for the crown for himself! Whichever way it went, after what the guard had said Diocles doubted that he would survive the night. His mind raced as he pondered the situation. His life was not worth anything, so all he could do was to pass along what he knew to someone who could make a difference.

"May I ask a huge favor of you?" he called out to the guards.

"What is it?" one of them grunted. They were playing Bones to pass the time.

"Could one of you ask for the servant Siranos to come and see me and bring a blanket, as I am cold." He gave an exaggerated shiver, which wasn't all sham. "It cannot hurt, can it? He is just a eunuch and quite harmless. God will bless you for your kindness," he finished.

"A eunuch eh?" one of them snickered. "Yah, all right. I'll send a message for him to come here." He stood, hitched his trews up and adjusted his tunic and sword belt. He pointed with his chin at Diocles. "You don't go anywhere while I'm away. Keep an eye on that old man; he might try to escape," he joked to his companion, who laughed. "Go on, make sure you get back quickly," he said to the departing figure.

Nearly two hours later, they all heard a shuffling sound in the tunnel. The guards perked up and stood ready. Siranos emerged into the candlelight, looking scared. He carried a small bundle with him and a folded blanket.

Upon seeing the guards he stopped and stammered. "I, I have come as requested. I brought..."

"Let me see that!" One of the guards snatched the bundle away from him and opened it. There was only food, and this spilled out onto one of their benches: a small block of cheese, some fresh bread and onions, some olives and a strip of salted tuna.

"I think we have a feast before us!" the other guard said with a broken-toothed grin. "The condemned man's last meal! Here, take it and give it to him." He snatched up an oily olive and popped it into his mouth as he spoke. Siranos scrambled to gather up the other food and re-wrap it in the large cloth.

"Go on, get over there and give it to 'im!" The guard spat out the olive stone and pretended to lunge for Siranos, who shrank from him and sidled over to the barred door where Diocles stood. He tried to smile reassuringly at Siranos.

"It's all right, they are only playing with you, Siranos," he told the frightened youth, who thrust the bundle and blanket through the bars, before the guards changed their minds.

"Chief M... Minister!" he stuttered. "I am shocked to find you in this condition! What in God's name is going on?"

"I have been falsely accused," Diocles said loudly for the benefit of the guards, who might be listening. He scratched himself and apologized for doing so. "I am being devoured by these beasts," he said with a wan smile. "If they keep this up there won't be anything left of me to execute!"

His lame attempt at a joke elicited a whimper from Siranos.

"Stay calm, Siranos," Diocles sighed, trying to sound calm himself. "You have to make sure that the princess knows I am here and not in a grave just yet. Tell my servants, too. Can you do that for me?" He hadn't much hope that this would change anything, but it helped him to know Tamura was aware.

Siranos nodded his head vigorously. He was too afraid of the guards to even speak.

"Tell her to pass this along to... you know who. A fleet is coming to invade the island. We have to warn the Emperor!" Diocles then gave Siranos a quick summary of what he now knew about the disastrous events up at the castle.

The guards were beginning to fidget. They had not been given permission to allow Siranos to come in the first place, and he mustn't stay any longer. Zenos might come back at any time, and then there would be trouble.

"Time to leave, master Eunuch!" one of them called out mockingly. "Don't want the Chief coming back while you are here, or you will be in another one of those cells, I shouldn't doubt."

Siranos needed no further persuasion. He grasped the old man's hand in both of his and whispered, "Be of good faith. We will do all we can for you." He scurried away and out of sight along the tunnel, leaving Diocles feeling very alone, but with just a tiny glimmer of hope for the first time since he had been thrown into his cell. He knew, however, that time was not on his side. Zenos had condemned him to death, and more than likely would take care of him long before the Emperor returned from his foray to Larnaca.

*****

That same day, a ship nosed into the harbor of Famagusta. The official who came to check the ship and its cargo was rude and peremptory.

"What are you carrying?" he demanded, as soon as he had climbed clumsily aboard from the skiff that brought him to the ship.

"Olives and cheeses from Sardinia, with some hides and copper ingots," Rostam called down from the afterdeck.

"Are you selling the full cargo? I need weights," the short, hairy man demanded. He had brought some papers with him and flourished a quill, while an assistant, who had finally managed to struggle aboard with the help of some crewmen, opened the lid of tiny bottle of ink, which he held in front of the official.

"Stand still, for God's sake! I can't write with you hopping about all the time! Turn around and give me your back!"

His minion obliged, still holding the ink on high. The official dipped his quill and then looked expectantly up at Rostam, who recited from memory. "Four large barrels of salted tuna. Fourteen small barrels of olives in oil. Ten barrels of virgin oil." The list went on until he finished with "Twenty-four ingots of prime smelted copper."

"You had better not be lying about all this," the official threatened. Rostam gave him what he hoped was a look of disdain and said, "I do not have to lie to people like you. In fact, I can help you with the list." He touched a small leather bag at his belt with his fingers. The official's attitude immediately began to change. "Do you need gangs to help with the unloading?" he asked with more enthusiasm than before.

Rostam shook his head. "No, sir, not just yet. I need to visit the merchants and make my deals. After you have calculated the taxes, that is."

The official nodded and scribbled something on the parchment he held against the back of his minion, and then demanded an abacus. The minion reached into his tunic and produced a tiny abacus, which the customs official used for a couple of moments before finally writing again on his parchment. "This is the tax if you are selling all the cargo, as you stated." He waved the list at Rostam, who had by now descended the gangway and stood before him.

Rostam looked it over and his eyes widened with surprise. "This tax is outrageous!" he complained, staring back at the stumpy little man.

"It will be larger if you don't part with that." He indicated the small bag of gold that Rostam had taken from his belt. Rostam pretended to be deeply offended, but tossed the bag of coins at the expectant official with lots of muttering. "I hope I shall be left alone to get on with my business, now that we have concluded here?" he asked.

"Oh yes, indeed, indeed," the hairy little man smirked, weighing the pouch that chinked in his hand. "You may dock over there." He waved towards the inner harbor and a space along the stone quay. He and his minion collected their things and clambered back down to their skiff to be rowed away.

"Scummy little man. Wish someone had pushed him overboard," commented Junayd, as they watched him stamp pompously up the steps of the distant quay. "By now Dimitri should have seen the flag and have someone waiting on the quayside for us."

"I don't see anyone as yet." Rostam sounded doubtful.

'They will be there, Lord. Just wait until we are tied up," Junayd stated with confidence. "They won't be easily noticed, that's for sure."

The crew took to the sweeps and soon they were secured alongside the quayside, having tossed their hawsers to some disreputable looking men standing on shore. As the men completed their work, Rostam noticed something and laughed. "You were right, Junayd. See, those two men and a couple of others. The men tying us off!"

Junayd chuckled. "You have only just noticed, Lord? Yes, that's them. Dimitri sent Khuzaymah and Maymun, along with two others that I have spotted so far."

Rostam was chagrined at not having noticed beforehand. "I'll have to pay more attention," he muttered. Then, in a clearer voice, "What do we do now?"

"You and I leave the ship and follow those fellows at a distance, and they will take us to Dimitri, Lord."

Rostam posted guards on the side of the ship and told the crew he would be back once he had made contact with their merchants in the city, then stepped down the gangplank behind a fully armed Junayd. There were no greetings. Khuzaymah simply gestured to his men to leave and led the way into the crowded streets of Famagusta.

Within a few minutes they were deep in the maze of narrow alleyways. Some houses had dogs inside, which barked noisily at the passersby, but men ignored them, and finally they were standing at the entrance of a nondescript doorway made of wood with iron bars nailed to its surface. At a signal from Maymun, one of their escort gave a couple of knocks on the door. A tiny grill slid open, they were scrutinized, then it snapped shut. After a rattle of hasps from the inside, the door was half opened and they were beckoned to enter. Everyone slipped into the cool archway behind the door, and it was closed and bolted from within. Leading the way, Khuzaymah trotted off across a small courtyard towards a low tiled loggia on the other side of a small fountain. Dimitri almost ran out of the entrance with a shout of joy.

"I only received the message yesterday morning, and here you are! Welcome, welcome to our humble abode, Rostam!"

Rostam found himself wrapped in a bear-hug by Dimitri, who then held him by the upper arms and exclaimed, "My goodness, young man, but you have grown! You are a man! How long has it been since I saw you last?" He beamed.

"Just over a year now, Dimitri," Rostam grinned. He turned to observe Junayd and Dimitri's men embracing and talking at once, slapping each other on the back with pleasure. "They are glad to see one another again," Dimitri observed with a twinkle in his grey eyes. "Come, we have much to discuss." He put a hand on Rostam's shoulder and steered him towards the gloom of the loggia. "It's cool in here, and we have some good wine... I think you will know it!" he laughed. "Khuzaymah, did everything go the way it should?" he asked over his shoulder.

"Yes, Master, it went well. The customs man did his usual official thing and then they docked. We were there to greet them."

"Good. But, Rostam, where is the Master Reza? Where is Lord Talon? I was expecting to see one of them at least."

"There is much to tell, Dimitri. For the time being, Junayd and I were the only ones able to leave the castle. Reza was grievously wounded in Palestine and is recuperating in the castle." He paused. "We do not know where my father is, nor Yosef; and," he hesitated, "the news from that quarter is all bad. A note from Boethius in Paphos told us of the catastrophe in the Kingdom of Jerusalem." Rostam shook his head. "I suppose it will not be called by that name for much longer."

"Yes, I know the whole world over there is up in flames, but I do hear rumors that Tyre might still be holding out," Dimitri said, his tone grim. "There is still some hope that Talon is alive, my boy. Keep hoping, and we will keep praying. But you are here, so eat; then we can talk some more."

Later, when the roasted chicken, bread, olives, cheese and some sweet baklava had been consumed, and Rostam and Junayd had told Dimitri all that they knew about Reza's experiences at Tiberius, and the recent activities at the castle, there was a silence while everyone at the table digested the news.

Eventually, Dimitri leaned forward and looked across the table to meet Rostam's gaze.

"It is beginning to come together now, young Lord. Everything you have told us ties into what we are hearing here in the palace, although there is still something of a mystery surrounding the Ambassador Aeneas. What we have heard is that he is from Constantinople. Our informant, who works for the Princess Tamura, let us know that she thinks he is here to hunt down the gold that was stolen."

Rostam nodded. "Yes, it has to be all about the gold. We all agree on that, but there is more. You said that someone is in prison?"

"Yes. His name is Diocles, and he is—was—the Chief Minister for the Emperor. We have been told he is in prison, and once the Emperor comes back he will probably be executed for treason."

"Why? What has he done?" Rostam asked.

"He was caught sending a pigeon to the castle, which is why the warning was so incomplete, and so delayed. I didn't know about the plot until the princess informed me a day later, and by then it was already too late. We owe it to the old man to see if we can help in anyway."

"Who arrested him?" Junayd asked with a full mouth. He had returned to the remnants of the chicken carcass. Khuzaymah offered him some wine.

"A man called Zenos, the new Chief Information Gatherer. He is ambitious, and we think he was the instigator of the attack on you," Dimitri responded, and gulped some wine himself. "I hope you brought more of this with you," he said.

Rostam grinned. "Yes, we did. But you were saying about this Zenos?"

"After hearing about your news and putting it together with ours, I have come to the conclusion that it was he who brought the assassins from Lebanon into the game," Dimitri told him. "Khuzaymah and Maymun followed some suspicious people and saw them leave the palace the night before the attack. Khuzaymah, tell them what you observed."

"We watched one of them follow our spy from the palace, and he was good, very good indeed, so we were afraid he might kill our boy, but he merely searched him and then rejoined others at the palace."

"So now we had some nasty people from Lebanon, mercenaries from the same place, and the cousin of the pirates all joined in an alliance to try and take our castle. What does this Aeneas have to do with it all? Has he worked something out with this Zenos?" Rostam asked.

"More than likely," Junayd chimed in, "but the venture failed, which means something else. This is not over yet," he said, his tone was ominous.

"What do you mean?" Rostam asked with a frown, as he munched on a sweet cake dripping with honey.

"Master Reza and Lord Talon are of that kind. They, Reza in particular, are constantly warning and reminding us about their methods. The leader of the Assassins who lives in Lebanon will not take the failure lightly. I do not think we have heard the last of those people. We must be on our guard," Maymun stated with a glance at Khuzaymah, who nodded emphatically.

Everyone looked at one another in silence across the food-strewn table, thinking about this.

"Well, first things first," Dimitri stated. "It would be a show of faith if somehow we could get the old man out of prison and spirit him away from the palace. Any ideas, anyone?"

*****

While the group at Dimitri's villa were discussing options, another ship entered the harbor. When the custom's official came aboard he was informed that the only cargo it carried were messages for the Palace. After inspecting the sealed papers—and receiving a small bribe—the official departed and left them anchored in the main pool.

No one left the ship for the rest of the day, but its arrival had not gone unnoticed by one of Dimitri's spies, and he passed the information along to the villa.

Dimitri dispatched Maymun to check on the vessel, but was not particularly concerned. Ships and large boats came fairly regularly to the harbor, and not all of them carried cargo.

Maymun, however, found it strange that no one at all left the ship all day long. He decided to stay and keep an eye on the odd seeming behavior of the crew. He stayed watching right through the hot day and observed almost no activity at all, until late in the evening just before dusk, when a small boat was lowered into the water and some men carrying bows and swords climbed down to it and were rowed ashore.

Maymun sent an urgent message, via one of the beggar boys who infested the town, to Dimitri, warning him of what he had seen.

Dimitri pondered the information and sent the grateful urchin away with a small coin and a chunk of bread, then he said to his men, "We should follow these people and see where they go."

His unease was increased when it was reported that the youths made their way to the very house that Khuzaymah and Maymun had made note of when they shadowed the follower of Siranos. Dimitri and his companions were now aware that even more unwelcome visitors had arrived in the city, and these youths were similar to those who had attacked the castle less than a week ago.

"I will need to send a pigeon in the morning to let them know there is something going on," Dimitri told Rostam, who agreed. "I hope these men are not plotting another attempt on the castle."

"What puzzles me is that they did not go to visit anyone in the palace," Dimitri told the others, when they had gathered around the dinner table. "Not one of them has been near the place. That seems a little odd, considering that their predecessors were in and out of the palace not so long ago."

"Perhaps they are here for another reason?" Maymun offered. He shrugged. "What did you say, Junayd? That they don't like failure? If you ask me, they failed in a pretty spectacular manner the other day."

"You mean they have come back to settle a score?" Junayd asked.

*****

Later that evening, one of Dimitri's spies arrived breathless at the villa, demanding to see Dimitri at once. "Two of the men from the assassins' house went for a stroll not so long ago, Master," he told Dimitri and the others. "They eventually arrived at the villa of the Ambassador."

"Did they go inside and visit with him?" Rostam demanded.

"No, Lord. We watched while they walked around the place. I could swear that they were checking how to get inside. They did not go anywhere near the main entrance. They behaved just like, er, as I would, if I were about to get into a house and rob it." He looked uncomfortable, but his words caused the others to laugh.

"Sooo, in your seedy past you were a thief?" Junayd asked with a grin.

"Dimitri caught me, or rather, Khuzaymah and Maymun did, when I tried to get into this house to rob it, and they nearly killed me; but Dimitri spared my life and now I work for him, Sir," the thin, wiry man addressed Junayd respectfully.

"What do you think we should do, Dimitri?" Rostam deferred to the spy master.

"I have an uneasy feeling about this, Lord. But whatever they plan to do with that man is of little concern to us at this time. I believe we have a more pressing matter to deal with. Unless we get the old man out of prison, he is doomed. Zenos will see to that, and next to go will be the princess, which is even more serious because she is our main source of information in the palace. If they are killed we are blind! Zenos must be dealt with, Rostam," he insisted. "I see no other choice."

"Then we must waste no more time," Rostam stated. "Do we know where the old man is held?"

The one person who can tell us is Siranos," Dimitri said, "and I think he will be coming to the wine house tomorrow on one of his 'errands'. We will make arrangements with him then. We must be prepared to act swiftly on what he tells us."

————————

Chapter 28

Encounters of Every Kind

There is nothing wrong with wanting a woman,
And loving girls is hardly a sin—
But whether or not they are pretty or pure,
Arabia's daughters is what you should look for...
                                    —Todros Abulafia

The next evening, Rostam, Maymun and Khuzaymah went over the walls and into the gardens of the palace. There they waited for Siranos to find them, huddled in the bushes not far from the terrace that led into the palace. It had been decided that Junayd would go to the villa with some of the local men and try to intercept the assassins if they went prowling about. Junayd was concerned that, when they were done with whatever they were up to at the villa, they might head for the palace to help their companions. He intended to stop them.

The three young men observed a very nervous Siranos stroll into the darkness of the gardens, then stop and pretend to relieve himself. He nearly had a heart attack when they materialized just behind him.

"Oh my God!" he squeaked, as he wet himself in earnest. "You scared me to bits!"

"We certainly scared the piss out of you!" Khuzaymah commented unkindly.

"You are Siranos?" Rostam demanded in a harsh whisper.

"Yes, and you are the men from the Greek?" Siranos glared in the darkness at Khuzaymah.

"Take us to the prison; we fear there isn't much time," Rostam said.

Siranos obediently turned and led the way with care to the back of the kitchens, and after checking that there was no candlelight showing under the door, opened it very carefully.They slipped in behind him, and the door closed with a loud snap of its metal latch. The noise woke one of the scullery boys, who sleepily called out, "Who is there?"

The three intruders froze and disappeared into the deeper darkness of the kitchen, but Siranos called back in a soft voice, "It is all right, Gabby, it's just me, getting some food. Go back to sleep."

The boy needed no further reassurance or persuasion. Exhausted from his day's labors, he fell back asleep before his head hit the sacking.

Siranos peered around. He could see nothing of the three mysterious men he had brought here, and a cold feeling went down his back. But then one of them re-emerged from the shadows, to be joined by the other two in utter silence. Forcing his fears down, he beckoned them to follow him. They were, after all, here to help the kind old man who had helped his mistress deflect the worst of the Emperor's excesses and cruelties. Bolstering his confidence with these thoughts, he lead them along darkened corridors and down a flight of steps to the dungeons. It looked like the pit of Hades, it was so dark, but Siranos knew the way and padded down the steps, heading for a glimmer of light that showed in the distance.

He led them silently along a cold, dark tunnel towards a lighted chamber, stopping before they came to the corner of the area where candles burned. The distinct sound of snoring came to their ears. "The two guards are there," Siranos whispered to Rostam, who was right next to him. Rostam nodded and peered around the corner to note the two men lying on straw pallets in front of the cells. Both guards were fast asleep. Then he spotted a narrow archway at the other end of the arched chamber. He assumed it lead to another corridor. More importantly, he could see a ring of keys hanging on a large nail in the wall above one of the sleepers.

Rostam beckoned Siranos closer. "Which cell is he in?" he whispered.

Siranos pointed to the one at the end of a row of four. "That one."

Rostam beckoned to the other two, pointed out the sleepers, and then the far end where Diocles was kept.

"I would like to take him out of his cell without killing them," he whispered. "Can you make sure they don't wake up at the wrong time?"

Both men nodded and slipped past. "You stay here; we will bring him out," Rostam told Siranos.

Moving silently, he glided over to carefully lift the ring of keys and, holding them gingerly, went to the cell where Diocles was held. He could see what looked like a bundle of clothing on the floor, which emitted soft snores. Opening the door took a little time; he had to try several keys before the lock turned. All the while he expected the occupant of the cell to wake up and make enough noise to alert the guards, but no one stirred. Finally, the lock turned with a grating sound and he was able to push the iron-barred door open. It groaned on its hinges and he tensed, but it was still not enough to wake the sleepers.

Rostam nodded to his two companions, still standing over the guards with pommels positioned for a swift strike to knock unconscious either guard who stirred. He slid into the cell and nudged the bundle; at the same time he put his hand over the old man's mouth. Diocles struggled awake, kicking weakly at the straw beneath his feet with a plaintive moan, but Rostam whispered into his ear, "Do not struggle. We are here to take you away." Diocles subsided, but he was breathing hard and shaking with fright. Rostam hauled him to his feet and whispered again, "Do not make a sound. You are to come with us to the castle."

At this Diocles breathed more easily and settled his clothing, trying hard to regain his dignity and composure. "You are from the castle?" he enquired.

"Yes. Questions later. Come."

They walked silently past the snoring guards and were well on their way along the tunnels when Khuzaymah stopped and held his finger to his lips. They all heard the unwelcome sound of approaching steps and voices. Diocles and Siranos recognized one voice immediately. "It is Zenos!" Siranos hissed in terror, and Diocles said with absolute certainty, "He is come to murder me!"

Desperately looking around for an escape route, Rostam felt a tug on his sleeve. Siranos beckoned urgently. "This way! Hurry!" The group chased after him like silent ghosts; even Diocles managed as they followed Siranos along a short, dark tunnel, then up a narrow flight of steps. Diocles realized where this led and nodded to himself. This route would do nicely, if they were going to leave by the gardens and the main halls.

Without warning, the keen-eared Maymun snatched Siranos from behind by his tunic and dragged him backwards. Stifling an exclamation of surprise, Siranos stumbled back into a recess in the tunnel where the others, including Diocles, huddled. This recess opened into yet another corridor, which Diocles knew was where the Emperor's treasury was hidden. There was a glow of light back where the guards were, but their immediate concern was what Khuzaymah had heard or seen. They all froze against the curve of the walls and waited.

The wraiths that glided past in the darkness were silent, except for the occasional, almost imperceptible scraping of a bare foot sliding on stone. In the darkness it was very hard to see them; all the crouching fugitives could see were four phantoms drift by towards the dim light at the end of the tunnel from where they had just come.

Khuzaymah whispered into Rostam's ear, "They are the assassins, Lord. They have come back and we must leave as quickly as possible."

Rostam was thankful that Khuzaymah had sensed danger. He had heard much about these ghostly people, for Reza had trained him thoroughly, but this was the first time he had actually seen the people his uncle talked about, and run the risk of a confrontation.

Then the shouting started, and they froze yet again.

*****

Far back down the tunnel, Zenos and his four mercenaries came upon the sleeping guards and kicked them awake, shouting at them. Zenos stalked to the door of the cell and pushed it open.

"Where is he?" Zenos roared at the two sleepy and utterly bewildered men, who shook their heads, aghast at what they were seeing—or rather, not seeing. The cell was empty. "Lord," one guard cried, "we did not hear nor see anyth—" he didn't finish. Zenos took two strides across the chamber and back-handed him across the face. "Of course you didn't see anything, you stupid, stupid fools! You were asleep!" he yelled, and was about to repeat the blow when he became aware that his men were staring past him. Then they all took a step back, reaching for their weapons.

Zenos whirled about to see four youths of the kind he was now all too familiar with, crouched at the entrance to the chamber. Their dark clothes and half covered faces allowed them to blend with the shadows thrown up by the only candle in the room. One of them held a bow, drawn with an arrow on the string. Zenos was not a brave man, and he felt a trickle of real fear creep down his back as he stared at these sinister figures. For a moment Zenos and the guards stood frozen; the sense of menace emanating from the youths was palpable.

The bowstring twanged and an arrow thudded hard into the chest of the very man Zenos had been about to strike. He fell with a grunt of surprise, knocked backwards to crash against the wall and lie still.

Realizing that there was to be no mercy from these people, and knowing exactly why they were here, Zenos grabbed one of his men by the sleeve and jerked him in front of himself, at the same time he screamed at his other men. "Kill them! Kill them!" Drawing his sword, he and two of his men turned to flee down the other corridor, which was just behind them. As they did, Zenos heard a choking sound and knew with terrifying certainty that the arrow intended for him had struck the man he had ducked behind.

He hurled himself into the gloom of the corridor, past the occasional torch in its sconce that flickered and barely lit the length of the corridors and but threw shadows. He took a left which he knew would lead him to the steps up to the main halls, rather than to the kitchens. He knew most of the tunnels and corridors of the labyrinth under the palace, but not all. There was a risk that he himself could get lost. His heart was pounding as he sought desperately to evade the assassins who he knew were after him. If he could make it to the upper level he could call upon his other mercenaries to protect him.

He and his escort were scurrying along when the flickering light of a distant torch on the wall ahead allowed him to make out that some other people were also in a hurry. In an instant Zenos recognized the smaller shape of Diocles being almost carried by two taller men, while a third, slighter man at the rear of the group turned and faced the oncoming men.

Forgetting his own plight he shouted. "Get them! That's him! Get the old man if it is the last thing you do!" The young man turned like a whip to face them. "Get out of our way!" Zenos bawled.

Rostam called out to the men ahead of him, "Go! Take the old man out of here as fast as you can!"

"But..." Khuzaymah called back, uncertain. "It is an order, Khuzaymah! Do it!" Rostam shouted.

Khuzaymah and Maymun frog-marched Diocles away from the oncoming confrontation as fast as they could.

Rostam's sword was out and waving menacingly at the fast approaching men. Before Zenos could do more than hesitate, his man wailed, "Behind us! Those ghosts are right behind us!" Shadows emerged from the darkness of the tunnel behind them. Zenos whirled to face their pursuers. He rightly deemed the four assassins behind them to be far more dangerous than a single boy head, who had been running away.

Rostam was uncertain whether to attack Zenos's men, follow after his own companions, or simply watch what was about to transpire. The decision was made for him. Siranos must have doubled back, for he grabbed Rostam's elbow and began dragging him along yet another dark corridor.

"Come, Lord, hurry! We must hurry! Your friends can take care of Diocles, but we *must* go!" he whispered urgently. Rostam allowed himself to be pulled away, and the two of them ran off. Rostam had the presence of mind to take one of the torches off its mount and stamp it out, they then disappeared, swallowed by darkness. Zenos flicked a glance back to where Rostam had been, and shivered. These people were like phantoms! Here one moment and gone the next. "Hold them off! I must catch the old man no matter what!" he ordered his thoroughly frightened accomplices, then muttering, "He knows far too much to live," he fled, leaving his luckless guards to deal with the menace.

Rostam blindly followed the eunuch, who seemed to know his way through the maze below the palace, even in darkness. He shrugged mentally. At least the old man was out of immediate danger.

Siranos had, in fact, no idea as to where they should go. By now the palace was in an uproar. The shouting in the cellars had woken the kitchen staff, and then the guards, who were running down the kitchen steps, carrying torches and swords at the ready. They now outnumbered the assassins, who had dispatched the guards, but Zenos had vanished.

*****

Khuzaymah and Maymun obeyed Rostam's orders, albeit reluctantly. "This old man had better be worth it!" Maymun muttered as they came to the gardens. As they hurried across the deserted grounds—all the guards seem to have been summoned elsewhere—he had an idea. Had Lord Talon not done this once before? And had he not created the necessary diversion that allowed him to escape? He himself had been with Talon at the time. "Take him, and hurry through the gateway," he instructed Khuzaymah. "Be ready to shut the door when I come through!"

"Why? What are you going to do?" his companion huffed. Helping an old and weakened man to hurry along corridors and up stairs was harder work than he would have guessed.

"The leopards! I'm letting them out. You'd better hurry. They are quick once they realize they are free."

By now candles flickered in windows, sentries shouted to one another and lit torches, while sleepy women and eunuchs peered curiously out of the upper stories. Maymun turned and ran towards the cage where the animals were kept and peered inside.

A low growl reverberated from the back of the enclosure as he tested the padlock. It was a good solid one, and took some time to open with the point of his blade. All the while the leopard's interest in him increased. The fearsome animal began to saunter towards him. Maymun finally opened the door, then backed away, his sword at the ready. Then he turned and fled. One beast came out of the cage with a bound and a growl, paused, and swerved its head to track the running shadow that was Maymun. Instinctively it registered a fleeing creature, and its eyes narrowed. It crouched, gathering its legs, then leapt after its prey.

Maymun didn't dare to look back; he just ran for his life towards the door, which Khuzaymah had unbolted and held open. Maymun threw himself through the opening to the garden beyond, rolling as he landed. He heard the door crash against its frame, and Khuzaymah thrust the metal bolt into place. Almost simultaneously, there was a tremendous thump and a chilling snarl of anger and frustration as the animal struck the unyielding wood, which shook with the force of the impact. They heard the leopard clawing at the wood on the other side.

"Dear God, but I hope that door holds," Khuzaymah gasped. "Come quickly, we are not out of danger yet." He seized the breathless Diocles by the arm and dragged him forward.

"We must get over the walls before anyone finds a way around those cats," Maymun gasped, picking himself up off the grass.

They reached the walls without encountering any guards and slipped up the wooden steps onto the parapet, roughly at the point where they had arrived. Khuzaymah gave a soft owl hoot and stood back. An arrow with a rope attached flew overhead and landed on the grass behind them.

"We are going to lower you to the ground, old man. You will be met by others who will take you to safety," he informed Diocles, who nodded mutely. He was exhausted and frightened, but he trusted these men. "God protect you and bless you," he whispered. "Are you going back for the boy?"

"Yes," came the short answer. With the rope biting into his chest, Diocles was lowered carefully from the parapet into the darkness below. As soon as the rope was jerked the two men tossed the end back over the wall, ran lightly down the steps inside of the walls, and vanished into the shadows of some bushes.

"We cannot go back the way we came," Maymun whispered. "I do not wish to slake the hunger of a great cat, and I have no idea where to look for an unguarded entrance, but we *must* find the young Master."

"He is resourceful, my friend. I would not be too worried, except for all those *Batinis* from Lebanon," Khuzaymah whispered back. They were silent as a group of soldiers hurried by and raced up the stone steps to the parapet.

"No one here, Sir!" someone called out.

"What about on the other side?" someone else shouted back.

Men peered out over the battlements. "All quiet here," they called.

*****

The assassins were desperate to find Zenos. He was their target; the Master had demanded that he should die, but he was now protected by a formidable number of his men, many of whom had descended below, alerted by cries and shouts, to deal with the intruders. A sinister and deadly game of hide and seek began in the tunnels and corridors underneath the palace. While the assassins did not know their way around and were badly out-numbered, they were very good indeed at hiding in dark shadows and ambushing anyone who came by, and this they began to accomplish with terrifying efficiency.

Before long there were dead mercenaries lying in several places. However frightening this might have been, the mercenaries themselves were hard bitten warriors, and they began to wise up to this tactic. Their leaders enjoined them to move about in larger groups instead of twos and threes, holding torches on high and calling to each other repeatedly.

The tunnels echoed to the clash of steel and the screams of fighting and dying men, and the nervous shouts of the groups of mercenaries as they began the hunt in earnest. Zenos, once he felt safe enough to get out of the tunnels without encountering any of the phantoms, raced up the steps and out onto the terraces leading to the back gardens, calling for men who came rushing towards him.

"Escort me to the house of the Ambassador!" he barked at them, and headed for the doors opening out onto the gardens. He didn't want to be seen leaving via the palace main entrance, but leave he must.

A guard who opened the doors for him stopped abruptly and recoiled. "Lord! Not that way!"

There was a leopard on the lawn, and it was staring at them, its tail lashing from side to side. The other leopard had just turned away from the garden doorway, which was shut. There was no way they could get past the animals without having to kill them, and Zenos didn't relish the prospect of explaining this to the Emperor. He knew with a chilling certainty that the old man had been taken that way. Someone had deliberately opened their cage and used the deadly cats to delay their pursuers. He cursed and swore, then signaled his nervous men back into the building, where they slammed the doors shut before the animals could gain entry. They had heard unnerving tales of the time, a year past, when the leopards had somehow found entry and run rampant all through the palace.

*****

Rostam and Siranos scurried along several corridors, then raced up yet another flight of steps to what Rostam judged to be the second floor of the palace. Even though his eyes were used to the darkness, he could not make out where he was in relation to the landmarks outside. He began to be nervous, but just as he was about to stop and demand some answers, Siranos halted in front of a recessed doorway and knocked gently. The door opened, and without any ceremony Siranos hauled Rostam into a chamber, where he halted in some confusion. This was a distinctly feminine place, with a distinct aroma of perfume; he was no expert, but his startled senses told him it was a very pleasant scent.

The girl who had opened the door squeaked with alarm and drew back hurriedly, while Siranos closed the door quietly but firmly behind them. Then he spun around and held a finger to his lips. "Don't make a sound, Martina!" he begged. "He is not dangerous."

"He certainly looks dangerous!" A female voice came from a large bed that stood against the right-hand wall. Rostam turned slowly and stared. The young woman sitting up in the bed continued. "Martina, light another few candles so that we can take a good look at this intruder before I call the guards."

Siranos hastened to the bedside. "Mistress Tamura! He is one of the people from the castle who have come to save Diocles. We rescued the minister, but all sorts of guards and mercenaries showed up in the dungeon and we fled. We sent the minister to safety, but this man was trapped behind, and that is why he is here," he babbled, plucking at the bed covers in his agitation.

By this time Martina had lit another candle, and she proceeded with a shaking hand to light two more. Rostam remained riveted to the floor and stared around, a trifle less warily. As the candles were lit he could make out Tamura's features more clearly, and he was impressed. He was used to beautiful women; his mother was to his mind the most beautiful woman in the world, and Auntie Jannat came a close second; but this woman was very beautiful. Her wide-eyed inspection of him began to make him feel slightly uncomfortable.

Tamura didn't look in the least bit frightened, merely interested, and she raised her hand to calm Siranos. "The last time something like this happened it was a leopard. Do you bite?" she asked the stranger, pleasantly enough. "Siranos, I think you had better take a deep breath and start at the beginning. Before that, though, tell me, who are you?" She addressed this question directly to Rostam, who gulped.

"Well, do you have a tongue?" she demanded.

Rostam shook his head. "N...no, er, yes, my Lady. I am called Rostam, and I am the son of Lord Talon!" he blurted out.

A small sigh escaped Tamura's lips. "The son of *Lord* Talon of the castle!" she murmured. "So you came. The minister safe now?" she asked.

"He is with my men, my Lady, and I must join them as soon as possible," he replied.

"Siranos!" she said sharply. "Why did you bring him here?"

He darted a look at Rostam. "We became separated. My lady, the palace is crawling with Zenos's guards hunting for the Chief Minister, and soldiers hunting down the... er, the assassins who came to kill Zenos. At least, I think they came to do that," he stuttered.

"Small loss to anyone if they are here for that purpose," she commented. "I know there is something going on; the uproar woke me and Martina. Assassins? What are you talking about, Siri?"

"It is a long story, my Lady, and I am truly sorry about this intrusion. I did not know of any other place that might be safe at this time!" He wailed and wrung his hands.

"It's all right. Stop fretting, you silly boy. I don't think you did anything wrong," she said soothingly, but her gaze never left Rostam. "He is very young to be doing this kind of thing," she purred. Tamura was beginning to sound as though she might have something on her mind other than brawling soldiers and roaming assassins.

Rostam felt a different kind of tension build in the room and felt even more awkward. The beautiful lady patted the side of the bed and motioned him to come closer. "I need to see what kind of person you are," she said. "Now tell me all about what has been going on in my palace. Siranos, Martina, go and make some tea; no, bring some wine. I think I would prefer to have wine tonight."

The two servants gave each other a look and retreated to the back quarters to carry out her command, while Rostam, who was not usually hesitant, placed his bow on a low table, sheathed his sword and took the few strides to the side of the bed, where he sat in the place she indicated. It gave under his weight, and he was very close to her. It felt like one of the softest beds he had ever encountered. At home he slept, as did the other trainees, on hard pallets. He gave Tamura a tentative smile, wondering what would happen next.

Tamura's eyes devoured him. "You are so young! And so very handsome," she murmured. "Now...." she didn't finish. The quiet of the room was disrupted by a loud banging on the door and a shout from outside.

"Open up!"

Her eyes flew wide open. Siranos rushed into the room and snatched up Rostam's bow and threw it to Martina, then frantically waved to Tamura, who without hesitation lifted the bed clothes and commanded, "Get in! and do not move a muscle." Rostam was just as alarmed and dived into the space she had made; he was immediately covered. His world went black and a light hand patted the bed clothes around him. A cushion landed on his back. "Not a word, and do not move," she hissed. He froze.

Siranos had meanwhile gone to the door. Upon a signal from Tamura he opened it to reveal Zenos standing at the entrance. Behind him were half a dozen well armed men. Siranos whimpered. Zenos, with a dismissive glance at him, called out, "My lady, with your permission, I am going to place guards outside your door. It is for your protection." His tone was differential and polite.

"Pray tell me, what is the alarm all about, Chief of Information?" she called. "You will understand if I do not get up. I am already in bed and not suitably dressed for company."

"I, I quite understand, my Lady. I simply came to provide protection for you. I shall now go about my other duties. There are assassins in the palace and my men are hunting them down. Do not fear; these guards are here to prevent anyone from entering to your chambers." He could not resist stepping forward and glancing in her direction. He was rewarded with a vision of Tamura on the bed. In the light of several candles her pale, oval face was framed by a halo of gleaming golden hair. The silk bed covers, which reflected the light of the candles, were drawn up to her chin, and she was surrounded by mounds of pillows and rumpled bed clothes.

She gave a squeak of indignation at the sight of him. "Zenos! What are you doing?" He hurriedly withdrew. "Sincere apologies, my Lady," he smirked, then said, "I shall report later, my Lady. I wish you a peaceful and safe night."

Siranos shut the door, bolted it, and whirled about. "Oh my God! What do we do now?" he all but wailed, pointing to the recumbent and motionless mound next to her. But Tamura was reacting to the fact that, lying as he was, Rostam's hand had inadvertently come to rest on her lower thigh. He might have been utterly motionless, but the hand was warm and her blood was beginning to heat up. She wriggled down lower and the hand move higher up her naked thigh. Then the fingers twitched on her inflamed skin and began to move of their own accord.

"You may go now, Siranos and Martina. Bring... bring the wine later, when I call," she commanded, barely loud enough for them to hear. Siranos looked shocked and disapproving; Martina, who had been appraising the young and well muscled boy herself, arched an eyebrow but said nothing. As soon as they had disappeared, Tamura reached down and moved Rostam's hand even further up. He needed little persuasion after that.

"Get out of your clothes!" she husked, throwing the bed clothes aside. Rostam obliged, rolling out of the bed and doing as he was told. He tore off his jacket and shirt, then unbuckled his sword belt and threw it onto a cushion, after which he tore off his trews. Tamura watched him with a predatory gleam in her eyes as he stripped naked in front of her.

"Oh my," she whispered to herself. Then, without a word spoken by either of them, he went into her open arms.

———

Chapter 29

The Emperor Returns

The Name, is Renowned;
The Title, Royal:
So Renowned, is the Name;
So Royal, is the Title:
It makes, even
Rhetorick, to be Silent:
Impudence, to be Asham'd:
and Treason, to be Amaz'd.

—Anthony Sadler

That same night, after a brief conference with his men, Dimitri had decided that he wanted to accompany Junayd and his men on a mission to the villa where the Ambassador was housed. "It might be useful for me to know the inside of the place sometime," he told Junayd, who nodded, albeit somewhat reluctantly. This reconnaissance called for silence, and Dimitri was not so skilled in that quarter. However, Junayd would not deny his friend, who, after all, was serving Lord Talon very well.

They had watched as Rostam and his men scaled the palace walls, then left them to their own devices and hastened across town to the villa, where they hid in the darkest shadows, waiting and watching. At this time of night it was very quiet.

After several hour of fruitless waiting, when Junayd was beginning to wonder what might be happening in the palace, he heard approaching steps. He gripped Dimitri by the arm and leaned over to whisper, "Some one coming."

Dimitri, who had been yawning, eased himself deeper into the shadows and froze as, did the other three watchers dotted about the street.

Making no attempt to be quiet, two men came hurrying along the street from the direction of the palace. Junayd whispered to Dimitri, "Who are they?"

Dimitri peered out from his concealment to study the men. 'My God! One of them is Zenos, the new Gatherer of Information for the Emperor. Wonder what he is doing here at this hour?" Both men appeared to be anxious, frequently looking over their shoulders, and both had their swords drawn. They ran up the step of the Ambassador's villa and banged on the door; when it opened they disappeared inside. The door slammed shut and silence fell.

"Who is the other one?"

"A mercenary, by his armor and bearing. Can't tell otherwise," Dimitri responded.

"I would like to know what brings that man here at this time of night," Junayd whispered back. He resisted the temptation to get into the villa and find out what he could, but the urge to investigate grow stronger as time passed and nothing happened. The night sounds came back into focus; dogs barked in the distance, a cat yowled and an owl hooted. An owl?

Junayd started. Another owl hooted, closer this time. Could it possibly be something else or... someone! Reza and Talon had on occasion used owl hoots, but it was impossible for them to be here. The hair on the back of his neck rose.

He gripped Dimitri's arm again. Dimitri touched his hand, acknowledging that he, too, had heard. Junayd hoped that their men had the good sense to stay well out of the way.

Then they saw a shadow leave the darkness of a street entrance about a hundred paces to their left. Junayd was profoundly glad that none of his men had been anywhere near where the shadows had come from. There was no doubt in his mind that these people would have sensed a presence nearby and would have investigated. The first shadow was joined by another dark figure, which turned and pointed to the walls of the villa.

As Junayd and Dimitri and his spies watched, two lithe figures climbed the wall of the villa, using the recesses in the masonry. In a remarkably short space of time they were at the top and had vanished as though they had never been there.

"Assassins!" Dimitri breathed. He sounded both awed and scared. Junayd thought furiously. The assassins had gained entry; how would this affect his own mission? It was clearly too late for him to try and enter the villa unobserved; he quietly cursed his hesitation, but also considered what might have transpired had he been inside when the assassins arrived. It could have been much worse.

"We must wait and see what happens, and take them when they come out. We don't play games," Junayd warned. "We take them down. They cannot be allowed to go to the palace; it would complicate things," he whispered in Dimitri's ear. Dimitri nodded and watched as Junayd took his bow off his shoulder and held it ready with an arrow knocked in the string.

*****

Without ceremony, Zenos brushed past the servant who opened the door of the villa. Once inside, he breathed easier. "I want to see the Ambassador!" he demanded of the surprised servant who had let him in. Uninvited, he snatched up a bottle and poured himself a large cup of wine. He was gulping it down when Aeneas came into the living area, looking rumpled and grumpy.

"Zenos, what on earth are you doing here at this late hour?" he demanded without preamble.

"All hell is going on at the palace, and there have been numerous attempts on my life!" Zenos replied in a tone which he tried to keep normal, but his voice shook, and Aeneas was not slow to pick up on this.

"You sound very disturbed. Have some more wine to settle you down and tell me what is going on." He waved to the hovering servants. "Bring sweetmeats and light refreshments," he ordered. "Here, sit down, Zenos, and calm yourself," he said to the distraught man. "What is the problem?"

Zenos sat and breathed deeply. "They came tonight. Dozens of them!" he rasped, exaggerating the numbers, and took another large gulp from the cup in his shaking hand.

"Who are you talking about?" Aeneas demanded, looking puzzled.

"The Assassins, of course!" Zenos snapped. The reaction from Aquila and Macrobius, standing by the door, was instantaneous. They paled and looked at one another with genuine fear in their eyes. "Assassins, you say?" Aeneas repeated stupidly.

"Yes! Yes! How many times must I repeat myself!" Zenos almost shouted. He finished the wine and held it up for more. Aeneas obliged, filling it from a jug he took off the table. His hand also shook now.

"You never mentioned these people before," Aeneas accused. "What are they here for?"

"They came to kill me, you fool!" Zenos said, and his tone was resigned. "I think we killed them all—I used the palace guards—but I came here just to make sure none of them survived to do me in while I was in bed." He looked at Aeneas. "We failed at the castle! We failed, do you hear me?" he almost shouted. The silence that greeted this remark was profound.

"You...you failed?" Aeneas stammered stupidly.

"Yes," Zenos replied slowly. "They had been warned; they were waiting for us." He shook his head at the memory. "They destroyed us, and we gained nothing."

It was Aeneas's turn to shake his head as he stared disaster in the face. "When? When did all this happen? You did not tell me any of this!" he said accusingly. "The castle, you went there without telling me anything? Nothing?" He sounded incredulous and his face had gone pale. "You worthless... *useless* people!" He shouted in his frustration and anger, then, "What am I to do now?" he asked the world at large in a plaintive tone.

Zenos took a swig of wine, which dribbled down his chin. As though he had not heard Aeneas he said, "They came for revenge, but we got them. Curse them, but we got them before they could get to me." He gave a shaky laugh and stared up at the pallid features of Aeneas. "I kept the details of the attack to myself because I could not trust you!" he snarled. "What difference does it make now, anyway? All the same, I want to stay here for the night, just in case. I shall go back to the palace in the morning."

Aeneas was still dealing with the shock of disappointment, but he nodded reluctantly. "Very well. Aquila and Macrobius are two of the best. They will be on guard for the rest of the night outside your door and mine." He glanced a the two men, who nodded their heads reluctantly as they contemplated the sleepless night ahead.

"I think we all need a good night's rest. The villa is well guarded, so have no fear, my friend. Macrobius will show you to your bedchamber. I bid you goodnight," Aeneas said, and turned away to hide his expression. His anger and frustration threatening to over whelm his common sense. He still needed Zenos.

His guest tossed back the last of the wine in his goblet, then heaved himself up.

"God save us from provincial idiots!" Aeneas muttered as he watched Zenos's departing back.

*****

Junayd, Dimitri and their men were rewarded for their patience two hours later. A nudge from Junayd and Dimitri, who was very sleepy by this time, jerked awake.

"Make ready, they are coming," Junayd whispered and began to move; he had his bow ready. Dimitri and his men slipped out of their hiding places and followed him as he moved from dark shadow to dark recess, bringing them ever closer to the wall.

The two figures who had appeared at the top of the wall were now making their way silently back down. The twang of Junayd's bowstring made both assassins jerk, the one with surprise, the other with the shock of the arrow penetrating his back. Junayd had aimed true; his victim gave a croak of agony and fell the remaining distance to land in a crumpled heap on the ground.

The other assassin recovered very quickly, almost too fast for Dimitri and his men. He dropped to the ground and, ignoring his dying companion, would have sped away had not Dimitri and his two men surrounded him, slashing at the assassin as he rose from the crouch.

Thus it was that the second assassin went down with a choking scream from four men hacking and stabbing at him. Once he was down, Junayd went over to check the other man. Blood was trickling out of his open mouth; he, too, was very dead.

"Find a place to hide the bodies for at least a day," Junayd suggested to Dimitri. "I will meet you back at the palace. You need to hurry, as Rostam might need help. I still have work to do up there." He pointed at the top of the wall.

"Are you going in there now?" Dimitri asked. "Shouldn't I come?"

"No. Stay and deal with these two, Dimitri. I am going to find out what mischief they were up to in the villa. They didn't just go there for a conversation," Junayd responded.

He slung his bow over his shoulder and went up the wall in much the same manner as the two dead assassins had. Dimitri watched in awe as he gained footholds and fingertip holds that did not appear to exist. Dimitri shook his head. The assassins scared him, but Reza's men were no less frightening. He was very glad Junayd was on his side.

Only when his dangerous friend had vanished over the wall did he and his men pick up the two corpses and carry them off to a midden, where they buried them under heaps of dung. Later they would collect the bodies and take them out to sea. Dimitri had gained influence in many places in this town by now, and that included fishermen who could take a catch out to sea just as easily as to bring one in.

*****

Junayd gained access to the villa with little difficulty. The guards walking the perimeter moved slowly, and they were sleepy. He slipped into the servants' quarters and then along the corridor that connected this part of the house to the main building. At the main house he heard a scraping sound and froze. It came from the other side of the living room area, where he supposed the sleeping chambers might be located.

He glided silently as a ghost until he was closer to the odd sound. Then he smelled it, the metallic and sickly sweet smell of blood. He peered cautiously into the gloom and saw something bulky on the tiles ahead of him. Approaching and stooping over it, he could make it out to be the body of a man whose throat had been cut. The floor was puddled with his blood. Very carefully Junayd stepped over the corpse; ten paces away yet another body was lying on the floor. But this one moved, or rather, jerked about in feeble motions, which caused the scraping sound he had heard earlier.

He knelt next to the dying man and examined him. The man's throat had been cut, but not completely, which was a little surprising; assassins were usually very efficient at killing. This man was slowly bleeding to death. He opened his eyes. "Help... me," he croaked, and flapped a hand vaguely at Junayd. But moments later his eyes rolled up into the back of his head and he jerked in his death throes.

Junayd wasted no time in useless efforts to save a dead man. Instead, he looked into the room beyond and saw a bundle on the bed. The bed covers were thrown back; the room was stuffy and smelled of old clothes. Junayd sent a sharp glance around the room to ensure he was alone and noticed nothing menacing, but there was something very interesting next to the head of the sleeping man. It was a knife buried in the pillow within two hand-spans of the man's face. Junayd crossed over to read the one word on the paper that had been impaled by the knife.

"*Leave.*"

Junayd made his way out of the room without disturbing the sleeper, sent a cautious glance down the corridor, then checked the other room. The dark mound of the occupant was very still on the bed, and protruding from his chest was another knife. There was no message. The knife and killing sent the message plainly enough.

He left the villa then, watchful, returning the way he had gained entry, and made his way through the silent streets of the still sleeping town towards the palace. There was much to ponder, but it was clear that the post of the Gatherer of Information was once again vacant.

*****

Many hours later, Rostam stirred. A light snuffle beside him made him turn his head, and there, next to him was Tamura, fast asleep. She was the first woman he had been with, and he was still in a state of total awe. But instinctively he was listening to the sounds beyond the chamber, and he knew it was time to leave. He felt a pain on the skin of his back, and remembered how she had raked him with her nails as she climaxed, grinding her pelvis into his and biting his shoulder till he growled with the pain. She had told him later that she had wanted to scream out loud but had dared not. That had precipitated another frenzied round of love making. He realized that what he had done had been utterly reckless, but he would not have changed anything, not even if his life hung in the balance.

His life! Oh God! What on earth was he still doing here? He had to get out of the palace! Capture meant torture and death. He eased his way out of the bed without disturbing the sleeping woman, who lay curled up in a ball alongside him. Even so, he wanted to take her in his arms and make love to her yet again. But it was time to leave. He realized that there would be sentries at the door, but there was a window. Rostam slipped into his clothes and quietly buckled on his belt and sword, then made sure he had his knife within easy reach. He tip-toed to the servant's quarters where the two servants slept the sleep of the innocent, and retrieved his bow and the arrows without waking them.

Reza had trained him well. The window opened out onto a ledge, which ran the length of the floor. It was still dark, but there were indications that dawn was not far off, so he moved quickly and silently until he could descend onto a balcony. He looked down at the inviting grass of the garden below and was just about to drop the fifteen or so feet to the ground when he saw a movement in the bushes next to the small doorway that had been his objective. A leopard's head emerged, and it stared right up at him.

Rostam froze. Dear God! he thought. His mind whirled. This was the first time in his life he had encountered a great cat, and he instinctively went cold. He looked around for another route, and realized that the only way to the battlements left open to him was along the roof. Swinging himself up a wooden pillar, he eased his way over and up onto the tiles, and finally gained the rounded ridge of the roof. He rose to a crouch and made his way along the tiled surface towards the beckoning parapet and ultimate safety. It was damp with dew and treacherous under his feet, so he proceeded with caution.

He glanced down in the direction of the cat to find there were now two of the beasts. Their baleful yellow eyes followed him with interest, as though they were waiting for him to slip and fall. Gritting his teeth, he moved along the ridge of the roof as silently as he could, but then a new hazard presented itself.

A figure rose from the darkness of one of the corner pieces of the parapet and stared at him. Rostam froze once more, but then the figure beckoned to him. He wondered if Maymun or Khuzaymah had returned to find him; the man was dressed much as he was, and had his face covered. Rostam waved to the figure, acknowledging its presence, then refocused on the ridge and gaining access to the parapet where the figure stood waiting.

Still unable to see who it was, Rostam became more wary. The man seemed more slight of build than either Maymun or Khuzaymah. He slowly drew his knife and held it close to his side as he negotiated the last few paces of the ridge work.

The figure on the parapet must also have felt that something was amiss, because he stepped back a pace and called over in a harsh whisper, "Is that you, Mahmud? Where have you been? I have been waiting for an hour!" Then the figure went still. 'You are not Mahmud! Who are you?" he hissed, drawing a knife and holding it out in front of him.

By this time Rostam realized that the other was one of the assassins who had been sent to deal with the minister. He had to get past him, but the man had other ideas.

"*You* will die anyway. I shall avenge my comrades who died in those accursed tunnels!" he lunged, and his long knife flashed so closely to Rostam's belly that he had to arch his torso to make sure it didn't gut him. His own knife snapped forward aimed at his attacker's eyes, but the assassin was fast. He danced back with a hiss of breath and went into a fighting crouch, his blade flickering in the poor light. Rostam parried another lunge and made one of his own; it came close but his opponent easily evaded it. Rostam was very careful not to commit too far. He realized he was up against an experienced fighter. This man would take advantage of any tiny mistake he made, of that he was very sure.

Time was also the enemy; while they fought it out, any one of the sentries posted on the battlements might notice the two dark figures, dancing about and waving knives at one another, and sound the alarm. Somehow he had to finish this as speedily as he could. His opponent obviously felt the same way, and after a clever feint he stepped in for a deep lunge at Rostam's midriff. With a hard downward strike Rostam slashed his forearm, causing the man to grunt with pain and pull back. But he was not done. With another grunt he attacked ferociously, lunging and slashing, forcing Rostam back until the gap he had just crossed from the building roof was right behind him. He took a backward pace and skipped onto the narrow tiled ridge, shuffling back the way he had come.

His opponent followed as though to deny him any respite, but Rostam knew he had one advantage. The man's knife arm was hurt and bleeding copiously; spots of blood were even landing on him as the man weaved his knife about with bewildering speed. But then he flicked the knife into his left hand and continued to come forward. Rostam met him, this time knife to knife, which made a harsh, rasping sound. Remembering his training, Rostam forced the knife out with his own and spun slightly away, then kicked hard, using the edge of his right foot to strike the assassin's knee cap, then landing in a crouch to regain his balance. His reward was a gasp of pain, and the man fell to one knee. Rostam barely managed to retain his own precarious footing on the slippery ridge. He glanced briefly downwards, and sure enough the leopards were keeping pace with their potential breakfast. It was time to put some of his other training into effect.

Rostam struck again with the same foot, but this time at his opponent's head. The edge of his foot landed hard and knocked the assassin off the ridge to tumble down the tiles and land on his belly. He slid towards the edge, taking some tiles with him. He scrabbled frantically for a hold, but it was too late. He went over the edge to fall with a scream to land with a thump on the ground below.

Ignoring the screams and growls that followed as the leopards indulged in an unexpected feast, the scent of blood having had already whet their appetites, Rostam raced for the parapet once more. He slipped over the edge of the wall out of sight of the now alerted sentries, who came running along the wall to investigate the screams. It was a simple matter to drop to the ground below, although it was a long way down. He rolled and regained his feet just like a cat, only to find dark figures coming out of the shadows all around him. There was no escape from these sinister looking people, who had appeared as though from nowhere.

His heart racing, Rostam drew his sword and held it *en garde* as the figures converged on him. Then he heard a voice that was very familiar. "It's Rostam! Where in God's name have you been, Lord Rostam?" Junayd did not sound as though he was very pleased. "We have looked all over for you!"

*****

Junayd was understandably annoyed with Rostam.

Khuzaymah and Maymun, looking harassed and worried, had finally reappeared in the dark hours before dawn, after conveying the old man to the only place they thought safe enough: aboard the ship in the harbor. They had returned to find the palace in an uproar and soldiers everywhere. Anxious to find Rostam, they had made a vain attempt to return to the cellars, but there had been men at all the entrances, and a deadly hue and cry could be heard from below.

Reluctantly, they had slipped away from all the fighting and mayhem in the palace itself, keeping an eye open for any of their 'cousins', as Maymun called them. They'd joined Junayd to wait for any sign of Rostam. When that worthy had finally appeared at the back entrance, they had surrounded him with a view to finishing him off, should he prove to be one of the assassins who might have evaded the soldiers.

Now all three gathered round him.

"Whatever happened to you?" Maymun demanded.

"Whose blood is this?" Khuzaymah asked, alarmed.

Much to Rostam's embarrassment, Junayd's sharp nose picked up on something else. "You smell different, Lord," he remarked in a low tone to Rostam, after he ascertained that the boy was all in one piece.

"Yes, um, er, listen, Junayd. I am very sorry about the delay. I, er, I got lost, and the slave hid me until it was safe to get out. Also," he added with a look at his two companions, "the leopards were running loose in the garden, so that path was denied to me." That shut them up, and he added, "While I was making my escape across the roof, I ran into one of the assassins and we had a fight."

498

"I will assume that he lost the fight," Junayd commented, his tone dry.

"Those, um, those cats got him in the end," Rostam said, hoping that there would be no more questions about smells and such like.

"You do kind of smell funny, Lord," Maymun said. His face was deadpan. "Did you fall in with the leopards? They don't normally smell like that, as far as I know."

"I have smelled that perfume before... somewhere. Oh, yes, *indeed*," Dimitri said with a snort of laughter.

"Hmm, you are right, Maymun. He does smell odd. Not bad, mind you, but not how he smelled before he went into the palace, from what I recall," Khuzaymah said. He twitched his nose to emphasize his point.

"Listen, you two..." Rostam began, but Junayd, who had a shrewd idea as to what may have occurred, interrupted.

"We have the old man on the ship. We all need to go there at once, and I will tell you what I found at the villa," he said. "Come. *Lord* Rostam can tell us all later what he was doing for a couple of hours while we all risked our lives searching for him and waited for him out here in the cold."

Maymun and Khuzaymah chuckled, and Rostam grinned ruefully in the darkness. His companions were not going to let him off.

"Dimitri," Junayd continued, "you should come with us to speak to the old man, but it would be best for you stay back in the shadows and not show your face at all. The old man knows that you exist, but he should not know who you are."

They jogged off through the still, quiet streets to arrive at the harbor, which was deserted at this hour, so it took little time to answer the challenge call from the alert guards on the ship and step aboard.

With Junayd leading the way, they entered the main cabin, where they found Diocles seated on a bunk with his hands clasped together between his knees, looking dazed and very nervous. He didn't know, even at this time, whether he had escaped the clutches of Zenos only to be abducted by people planning a coup of their own. Yet he sensed that, although these men did not want to be identified, they meant him no harm. The youth, his face covered closely, resembled the one who had rescued him, and greeted him politely enough.

"We hope that you are not feeling too indisposed," the young man said.

Diocles waved one of his bony hands in the air and replied, "I think I am in your debt for taking me out of the dungeons. Somewhat of an irony, wasn't it? I have sent people there myself before. I am very grateful to you for having taken me out of there. God bless you."

The first man to have entered the cabin leaned forward and said, "We felt it would not be a good thing to leave you captive, but there is other news that you should consider."

Diocles shut his eyes. He feared more bad news. Nevertheless, he said, "What is it? Please tell me."

"Firstly, we know the lady is safe," Junayd said with a sideways glance at Rostam. Old he might have been, but Diocles still had his faculties about him. His nose twitched at a familiar scent in the air.

"Ah," he said. "What with all the noise and fighting, she was a concern. It is good to know she is safe. Is there something else you wish to tell me?"

The first man then said, "I am here to tell you that the man who is called the Gatherer of Information is dead."

Diocles gasped, and even the youth seemed surprised at the news. "Where, how... how did this happen?" Diocles stammered. "Did you..?"

"No, we did not. But I have seen his body and I can tell you he is very dead. The same people who came to the palace also went to the house of the Ambassador from Constantinople."

"How do you know all these things?" Diocles demanded, surprise and shock in his voice.

A bulky man standing against the wall chimed in. "It is enough that we *do* know these things; and be glad, old man. If we had not intervened, you might not be alive now."

Diocles nodded his head. "Don't think I am ungrateful," he replied, "but it comes as a shock. Did they kill the Ambassador, too?"

Junayd shook his head. "No, but they left a message. I think we will see his ship depart with the dawn."

The youth spoke up. "A knife?"

The first man nodded. "The bodyguards were slaughtered, but he still lives—if he doesn't die of a heart attack when he sees what has happened." His tone was very dry.

"We will leave in the morning, and you will come with us to be our guest for a while until things settle down, then we will find a safe place for you to live," the youth said.

The man by the wall, whose face and form were indiscernible in the shadows and blocked from Diocles' view by the four other men, interjected. "I have another idea; that is, if we can all agree upon it," he said.

They all looked at him expectantly.

"As I see it, we have proof that this Zenos, your chief enemy, is now dead." He addressed the Chief Minister. "The assassins have been eliminated, as well as many of the mercenaries, the men who were protecting Zenos. If I am not mistaken, those who survived the attack on the castle will want to leave, and in a hurry. Especially when they discover that Zenos is dead."

"Go on," Diocles encouraged the man. He continued slowly. "That means that there will be no one in the palace to dispute your position any more, Chief Minister. Very few of the Emperor's staff even knew you had been taken prisoner. Zenos knew that he could not move against you without strong proof, for you are respected. That means that you might be free to return and resume your duties."

A long silence ensued as the people in the room considered this notion.

"Well, Chief Minister, what do you think?" the youth demanded. Diocles gave a thoughtful nod. "Perhaps you are right," he said. "But how do I get back in? And how will I know if there are not some mercenaries who will hold a grudge because of the killing of Zenos?"

The first man spoke up, casting a look at the youth for confirmation—a show of respect that Diocles noted. "We could provide you with two bodyguards," he said.

The youth nodded emphatically, and the older man in the shadows spoke up. "Our people will look out for you in that regard, but if we are going to do this we must hurry. Dawn is almost upon us."

"Very well," the young man stated. So, clearly, for all that he was the youngest, he was in charge, Diocles decided. "I agree we can give it a chance. When does the Emperor return, Chief Minister?"

"He is due to return tomorrow, if he abides by his original plan, although that is far from a certainty," Diocles stated.

"So we have a little time for you to calm the palace down and take control?"

Diocles smiled for the first time. "This Lord Talon of yours is certainly surrounded by enterprising people. But what shall I tell the Emperor?"

Tell him the truth," the bulky man advised. "Always better in the long run; and besides, when the people in the villa wake up there will be no hiding what happened. The Gatherer of Information was murdered for his treachery. It is my guess that he crossed the Old Man of the Mountain, Rashid Ed Din."

"Perhaps you are right," Diocles said, "but know this, he told me something else that concerns all of us."

The cabin went still as they all paid attention. "Zenos in his rage spoke out of turn and said that an invasion by the Emperor of Byzantium is immanent." He could not have riveted their attention more if he had lit a Greek Fire bomb and tossed it in amongst them.

There was a hiss of breath from more than one person, then silence, finally broken by the young man. "We must alert the castle immediately. But are you sure you heard him correctly, Chief Minister?" he demanded.

"As sure as I can be, given that the man was raging at me and didn't care what he said because I was going to die anyway," Diocles affirmed.

"Dear God, but this could be very bad," the shadowed man muttered.

"Not... not if I can make it known to the Emperor in the right manner," Diocles told them. "Leave that to me for the time being. If I cannot manage, I will notify you by the usual methods."

"You should go, Minister. Please do keep us informed as to how this matter is resolved!" the first man urged. "Go with God, Minister." He looked over at the two men who stood silently, their faces concealed. "You two will know how to get him in, not forgetting the leopards. Stay with him for as long as you deem there is a need."

Both men touched their foreheads in acknowledgment, after which they escorted Diocles off the ship. The three men disappeared into the gloom of the narrow streets just as the first streaks of dawn began to light the city and its inhabitants began to stir.

Rostam and Junayd spent the next hour talking to Dimitri about what they had heard, but came to no conclusions as to how to deal with the pending threat. They did, however, agree that they needed to leave Famagusta very soon.

Dimitri departed, promising to keep them informed, that was if his spy, the boy Siranos, had survived the latest shambles at the palace. They bade one anther an emotional farewell. As he embraced Rostam, Dimitri muttered in his ear.

"You are a very bad boy, Lord. But... I hope it was worth it!" He laughed and turned away to embrace Junayd. "My friend, I thank you for your help from the bottom of my heart. God protect you, Junayd. God protect you both, and give my respects and sentiments to their Ladyships in the castle, along with my respects to Master Reza. I hope very much that Lord Talon comes home soon. He will be in my prayers every day."

The ship was made ready, Rostam assumed his captain's duties, and the ship was cast off. Men from Dimitri's gang were there to assist, and soon they were moving slowly away from the quayside.

It was then that Rostam and Junayd noticed activity on the other quay. A figure they recognized as the Ambassador was gesticulating and shouting at people around him. He abruptly strode down some steps to a small boat, and this was rowed out to the ship that had brought him to the port in the first place. In short order, this ship had also weighed anchor and was unfurling its sails. Rostam's ship slid past to lead the way out of the main harbor of Famagusta.

"It seems that he took the hint," Junayd said with a grin at Rostam. "Appears to be traveling light, too."

"You are going to tell me what you found inside the house, are you not?" Rostam demanded eagerly. "I want to know the details."

"Hmm, yes, but one story deserves another. If you see what I mean, Lord. But perhaps you should spare me the finer details." Junayd gave the young man an enquiring smile, and Rostam had the grace to color. He looked out at the entrance of the harbor.

"Hey! Take care that you don't put us on those rocks!" he snapped at the steersmen, who hurried to obey and right the vessel down the exact middle of the channel.

Rostam turned back to his friend, who appeared to be intent upon the other ship's activities. "All right, then. I'm sorry I made everyone worry. But, well, it all happened like this...." he began.

*****

As dawn came to Famagusta, Tamura stirred and opened her eyes. Hearing a small sound she peered over the edge of the bed covers to find Martina tidying up and regarding her with inquisitive eyes. "How is my mistress today?" the girl enquired with an enigmatic look.

"I am very well, thank you, Martina; and you can take that look off your face before I have you flogged," Tamura said, but her tone was furred. She stretched and yawned, then realized that something was amiss. She looked around the bed, and then the chamber.

"Where is he?" she demanded.

"Vanished, my Lady. Like a ghost!" Martina responded with a wide-eyed look. "Took his bow and left."

"Surely he didn't leave without you knowing? What about the guards?" Tamura asked with a frown.

"We never heard a thing, my Lady. Siranos made a discreet enquiry of the guards, asking if there had been any further disturbance anywhere in the palace. He has gone to find out what has happened since the disturbances of last night," Martina told her. The girl was clearly dying to know more about Tamura's adventures of the previous night. Delicacy forbade her from asking, but Tamura gave her a smile that told her much.

"I am exhausted!" she exclaimed with another luxurious stretch. She had enjoyed the night immensely. She tossed her maid a bone. "He had such energy! Goodness me, yes!" she sighed at the memories.

Martina laughed with delight and envy. She had gathered that, from the noisy rattling of the bed to the point where Siranos had been seriously worried. "It is going to fall apart and the noise will bring the guards knocking on the door!" he'd moaned. "Then we are all doomed!"

Martina had told him to hush and had continued eavesdropping shamelessly, then she had rounded on him and planted a kiss on his lips. "I want you to... you know!" She'd growled, with desperation in her voice. They had done their best in the servants' quarters while the main event was taking place on the other side of the wall.

"More enthusiasm than skill?" she ventured, with a grin to her mistress, who smiled like a cat which has just consumed all the cream. "I could swear that he had never been with a woman before, but oh my, yes! Such enthusiasm!"

Martina gasped, and then laughed with delight. Only a day or so earlier her mistress had complained about the increased attentions of the Emperor. "He is like a rutting pig! I shall have to bribe one of the other ladies with a jewel or a favor, to go in my place!" she commented sourly. "I am worn out down there!"

But Martina could tell that her mistress appeared to have enjoyed the night, which made a change. Then Martina said pointedly, " The Emperor comes back tomorrow, my Lady. We must prepare for his arrival."

Tamura gave a sigh of resignation. "I know," she said shortly; then, "I wonder if I will ever see him again?" Her tone was wistful.

"God's will, my Lady. You never know," Martina reassured her with an understanding smile.

*****

There had been little enough sleep in the palace of the Emperor of Cyprus what with all the uproar, but the senior servants had rallied and put people to work cleaning up the bodies, some on the ground floor of the palace, and even more in the cellars. Those wretched leopards had escaped again; the lock appeared to have been forced. There was a half devoured body on the lawn of the garden, which the great cats wanted to take with them as they were driven, at spear point, back to their cage.

"If I had my way I'd kill them now," muttered the chief huntsman, whose responsibility they were. "They have done this twice now, and it won't be long before they attack again, perhaps even the Emperor himself."

"Why, you sound almost hopeful!" exclaimed one of his men.

"Shut up, you. That's treasonous talk and I won't have it!" he growled.

The man who was ostensibly in charge, Zenos the Gatherer of Information, was generally a late riser; so it was not until the sun was well up in the sky that people began to wonder about his absence. However, the Chief Minister appeared, as though from nowhere. He had been absent for several days, but now here he was. He looked a little tired, a little thinner, and was inclined to scratch himself, but otherwise he seemed well enough. He offered no explanation for his absence and no one dared to ask. He dined alone in the small chamber that opened onto the gardens, on his usual meal of ripe figs and bread with olives and goat's cheese, seemingly unconcerned about the mayhem that had transpired during the previous night.

One thing, at least, had changed about the minister. There were two very dangerous looking men hovering about his person at all times. Despite his recent absence he was well informed, and he took charge of the situation. He ordered the remaining soldiers who were loyal to the Emperor down to the tunnels and corridors under the palace to check once more that no one unwelcome people were still lurking there, after he had verified that he personally knew all of them. They were a detestable crowd of men, but they were the Emperor's detestable crowd, so he could trust them at least to do this. Having been assured that no enemy remained below, either of Zenos's mercenaries or the terrible assassins, he ordered the servants to clean the palace from the basement to the top, so that throughout the day the building was a hive of activity and few had time to dwell upon the peculiarities of the preceding hours.

Diocles was bracing himself for news from the Ambassador's villa. It came not long after he breakfasted. A breathless servant from the villa was brought before him, to fall on his knees and sob out the whole gruesome story. No one registered the fact that Diocles appeared quite unmoved by the tragic news.

"Where is the Ambassador?" he demanded.

The crying servant shook his head. "No one knows, Lord," he sobbed, "but there is talk of his ship leaving the harbor at first light. I don't know if this is true, Lord."

Diocles pretended not to have known this, and gave the impression to all that he was very angry.

"So the Ambassador murdered our Gatherer of Information and his servants, and then fled like the craven traitor he is! There is no doubt that he would have tried for our Emperor as well, had he been here," he said loudly for all to hear. He hoped that this would register with anyone who might be inclined to pass information directly to the Emperor. No one could be trusted these days.

Diocles spotted Siranos in the audience; good. The Lady Tamura would soon know that he was restored to his post of Chief Minister. He sent men, with strict orders to keep quiet about what they found, to the villa to investigate. Gradually the palace came back under control, and preparations continued for the return of His Majesty, Isaac Komnenos.

"I wonder where the old fox has been?" one of the older eunuchs asked of his companion of many years in an undertone. "D'you think he has a woman hidden away somewhere? He looks as though he is wrung out!" They snickered together and made themselves scarce. There was work to be done, and they didn't want any part of it.

After a discreet but very busy interval, Diocles made his way up to the women's quarters to reassure the ladies and their personal maids and eunuchs that he was back and firmly in charge. He deflected the rumor that Zenos had been gruesomely murdered by simply stating that it was too early to say just what had occurred, but he, Diocles, was doing his best to ensure that everything was put back to normal.

Eventually he found himself at the entrance to Tamura's chambers and tapped gently on the door, which opened as though Siranos had been standing right behind it waiting for him. The eunuch smiled a genuine smile of welcome and bowed very low, while managing at the same time to announce him. "My lady, The Chief Minister is here to see you."

Lady Tamura glided across the floor of the apartment and gave her hand to him with a smile to melt his heart. "I am so very glad to see you, Chief Minister. We have been very worried about your... health." Her eyes told him of her relief to see him. Instead of drawing her hand away after he had gone through the motions of kissing it, she held onto his hand and led the way to the low table, which was laden with his favorite sweetmeats and fruit; clearly it had been prepared with a view to his expected visit.

"You must tell me *everything* that has been happening to you. Is the news good, my Lord?" she asked with a slightly nervous smile.

He smiled back. Tamura seemed genuinely pleased to see him. For the first time in a long while Diocles felt that he had someone who cared for him in his life. Having no family of his own, it meant a great deal.

"My Lady, I will be happy to tell you everything I know," he responded. He seated himself, and Martina bustled up with a cup of his favorite wine. "We have a little time before the Emperor comes back. Did any of the disturbances of last night affect you, my Lady?" he asked solicitously. There was a mischievous glint in his eye, which Tamura didn't fail to notice.

She gave him a look from under her pretty brows and said, "I was not troubled by any *disturbances*, Chief Minister, and certainly I did not feel any sense of danger."

The slight curve at the corner of her mouth told him all he needed to know, and it amused him immensely. So he *had* detected her perfume when the young man from the castle had arrived on the ship. He smiled again; it was almost as though he had a slightly wayward daughter of whom he was very fond. Their conversation re-focused on the previous night's events, and he told her of the impending invasion.

Tamura was initially very alarmed, but Diocles hastened to reassure her, explaining what he intended to tell Isaac, and the actions he had already taken to thwart the invasion. She frowned at the thought of bolstering the reputation of the dead Gatherer of Information, but finally agreed it was all for the good.

*****

Isaac Komnenos, the self-styled Emperor of Cyprus, arrived in the middle of the afternoon the following day. He enjoyed the pomp and ceremony which, after much practice supervised by Diocles himself, had improved greatly from the first dismal attempts made by the ruffian mercenaries. The blare of the trumpets, the shouted commands and the lines of men at attention always put Isaac in a good mood. One day, he decided, he was going to have a real parade, just like those that the Emperor of Byzantium held every year on his birthday.

He made his way slowly toward the palace, followed by the commandant who had accompanied him to the other cities of his empire. They were greeted at the steps to the main entrance by the Chief Minister in all his finery, who looked impeccable and appropriately subservient as he led the bowing and scraping of the courtiers. The Emperor mounted the steps and turned to survey the populace.

There was the usual crowd of onlookers, except that perhaps there were fewer of the peasants to attend his arrival. Isaac was not popular. There were still those who were bold enough to shout insults from the back of the crowd, which annoyed him no end. He liked large crowds of cheering followers and had once raised the notion of sprinkling paid cheerers among them, to the horror of his Chief Minister, who had disagreed tactfully.

"My liege, it would cost money we cannot spare, and hirelings in the crowd could lead to arguments and dissent. I shudder to think that one of your hirelings would cause injury and perhaps even death on our streets. Or worse, what if they brag to others that they were paid, and peasants clamor to be paid for cheering you?"

He had almost rolled his eyes at the suggestion, but the Emperor had been watching him with his own slightly protuberant brown eyes, so he'd had to maintain an impassive face despite his feelings.

It was during the meal later that day that the Emperor looked around and remarked, "I notice that you are accompanied." He indicated the two men with his chin. " Why is that? You don't normally have an escort."

"They are, in fact, for your protection, my Liege," Diocles said smoothly. "I found two of the best, most capable men to guard your august personage."

"They certainly look dangerous to me. I hope they are trustworthy," the Emperor said, but then his shallow mind twitched elsewhere.

"Where is my Chief Information Gatherer? Why was he not present to welcome me? Is he still in Paphos?"

"Ah. Forgive me, my Liege. I have been waiting to tell you of this. It is such tragic news, and I wanted to chose the right moment."

"What is it?" Isaac snapped, beginning to look bothered.

"Ahem. The was doing his duty when, as far as we can make out, he uncovered a heinous plot against yourself, indeed against the country, my Liege."

Isaac started and glared at him. "What are you babbling about? Go on, spit it out!"

"My Lord, remember the 'Ambassador' who came to visit us?"

"Of course I do. Where is he, by the way?"

"My Lord, he has departed, fled like the cowardly dog that he is, after seeing to it that your Chief Gatherer of Information was, ah, dealt with. Zenos must have confronted him with the knowledge that the Emperor of Byzantine was going to send a fleet to invade Cyprus!"

Isaac gasped and stopped eating; he even stopped chewing. His face went dark and he stuttered. "G-God help us, what are you saying, man? That we are to be invaded?"

Diocles nodded his head, looking very sad. The already deep lines of age and worry on his features appeared to deepen even more.

"Zenos, God bless him and grant his soul peace, managed to get a message back to me before he left for the villa, where he expected to extract a confession and arrest the man.

"Yesterday, when we had heard nothing, I became suspicious. I sent men to the villa. They found it abandoned and the 'Ambassador' gone. His ship was seen to sail with the dawn yesterday. I am very grieved to say that Zenos and his two soldiers were found murdered, just left lying there!" Diocles choked as though deeply affected and even managed to make his eyes wet with grief as he shook his head. He dragged out a piece of cloth from his tunic to dry his eyes. "He died a hero, my Lord!" He lifted his eyes upwards with a pious expression on his face, as though appealing to the very heavens. "He died trying to protect us all, my Lord!"

But Isaac was barely listening. Everything he had accomplished, the capture of this ripe fig of an island and holding it against all odds, was now threatened. Simply because a spy had come to undermine his rule, and that upstart of an 'Emperor', Angelos, wanted to steal what was rightfully his!

"The filthy swine!" he muttered.

"Beg pardon, my Liege?" inquired Diocles, as though not fully understanding.

"How do we stop this, this invasion?" Isaac demanded in a louder tone. He looked more insulted than fearful.

"Erm, I have already taken steps to counter the invasion, my Liege," Diocles replied. "I pray I have not overstepped my authority, Lord, but I sent two fast boats with a message for King William the Norman, warning him of this act of perfidy. If the wind holds, they should arrive in Sicily within a matter of days. I reminded him that you were a most loyal ally, but that we are vulnerable to an act of this magnitude and treachery. I begged for his help in your Royal name."

Isaac nodded his approval and relaxed a little. "When did you send the messengers?" he demanded.

"Yesterday, the moment I knew, Your Majesty."

"It will be at least a couple of weeks before we know anything," Isaac remarked, counting on his fingers and looking distracted.

"Yes, Lord, but your presence will be of *immense* value to the loyal citizens of the island. If they see you traveling about unperturbed and showing kindness to all, they will draw courage from your presence and remain steadfast. Now more than ever they need the illuminating leadership of their emperor." Diocles knew how to ooze flattery as well as any of his eunuchs.

Isaac preened. "I agree with you. I shall show myself to be the leader they know me to be and give them courage."

"What, may I ask, should I do about the late Chief Gatherer of Information, Lord?" Diocles asked politely.

"He shall have a state funeral, of course, with all the honors due a hero of the empire," Isaac pronounced. "I only wish I could get my hands on that bald bastard spy from Constantinople!" he said savagely. His fingers twitched as he spoke. "I thought he was a mere abacus flicker. Who would have thought he was an assassin?"

Chapter 30

Spies

If you can talk with crowds and keep your virtue,
Or walk with Kings—nor lose the common touch;
If neither foes nor loving friends can hurt you,
If all men count with you, but none too much;
If you can fill the unforgiving minute
With sixty seconds' worth of distance run,
Yours is the Earth and everything that's in it,
And—which is more—you'll be a Man, my son!
—Rudyard Kipling

The boat moved like a dark ghost over the calm sea as Brandt and the Welsh archers rowed it quietly towards the beach. This was a small falukah they had found within the boundaries of the city harbor; fishermen all along the eastern seaboard used boats very similar to this one. They were now several leagues south of the city of Tyre, and well away from the bulk of Salah Ed Din's army. They had sailed just after dark, and an overcast sky helped conceal them. The Welsh had brought their bows just in case the landing, or the departure, went badly.

They approached the rocky outcropping and the low surf, which they could hear rather than see. Everyone scrutinized the dark coast line with great care. On a low-voiced command from Talon, the rowers back-paddled and brought the boat to a stop, to rock gently in the water. The archers reached for their bows and made ready. No one wanted to hear a challenge. The night was very quiet; the only sound was the hiss of small waves breaking. Beyond the beach was a low sand bank covered with boulders and rocks. Just behind the coast were sharply defined, rocky cliffs, thought to be an effective defense, which would not present a problem for one such as Yosef.

Talon strained his eyes to see into the dark, searching for any movement, then whispered to the rowers to start again. The boat moved slowly towards an even darker mass of rocks that Talon had seen just to the right. Here he could put Yosef on shore without getting him wet, and more importantly, without leaving a trail of footprints as he walked inland.

Yosef stood in the front of the boat, watching for an opening. He was clad only in a thick cloth tunic carrying only his sword and the bow slung over his shoulder. He whispered instructions to guide them into a narrow channel where the water surged gently in and out. He checked the bow on his back, tapped his quiver to ensure it was secured to his belt and then with a wave he was gone; leaping off the boat, which rocked from his passing. They saw his dark figure skipping over the wet rocks, to vanish into the darkness beyond as though he had never been there.

Talon whispered for the rowers to back the small boat out to sea. They pulled away, then rowed in place, struggling to hold their position against the surging tide while everyone strained their ears, listening for anything untoward. All they could hear was the hiss and crash of the surf, nothing of any suspicious nature to alarm them.

Finally, Talon growled an order and the rowers settled into a steady rhythm, and before long they were a good half league out at sea, where Talon thought it safe enough to raise the sail. The light wind bellied the long, triangular lateen and the boat began to move faster through the sea in a northerly direction, heading for the safety of Tyre. The men relaxed as their small craft sped over the water. Talon murmured a small prayer for Yosef. He and his companions would be returning the following night, and every other night for several days if Yosef did not show up on the first. The only signal for a pick up would be the light from a very small lantern that Yosef would place in a prominent position near the cliff and the small beach.

*****

Yosef skipped across the rocks with care and in almost total silence, like a shadow passing with the wind. Soon he had left the rocks behind, along with the sound of the sea. He easily scaled the low cliffs to crouch in the absolute silence of the scrub oaks and dense bushes at the top. He wanted to find a good place to stay until daylight, when he could examine the army of the Sultan.

Dawn came with a dim light growing slowly in the grey east. Rain clouds had moved in, covering the entire sky. A wind began to pick up and sough through the upper branches of the trees. Yosef glanced up, thinking that while rain was good, as it would cover his movements, it might make his return to the boat more hazardous.

He put that thought firmly aside and concentrated on reaching the road, which ran parallel to the coastline. His route lay to the north, and while the road was really no more than a deeply rutted track, it was the main highway to the interior, well traveled by men, horses and wagons.

While he stood in the cover of the trees not far from the road, he noticed some early risers plodding along the dusty track, then he saw a small detachment of riders cantering along the way. He retreated further back.

Once the cavalry patrol had passed, he approached the road with the view to using it, but then he became aware of another, larger body of men coming from the north. That was the direction of the army. Were they leaving? He glanced to the south and took a sharp intake of breath. There, not two leagues away, anchored in a small bay, were several ships. He paused, still well out of sight of the road, and counted the vessels.

Their presence changed everything, and gave his mission sudden, added urgency. What was the Sultan planning? Yosef faded back into the cover of the trees and made sure he would not be visible from the road. As the east brightened and sunrise briefly stained the clouds apricot and lavender, he could see a large body of spearmen and archers on the move. Without doubt they came from the host laying siege to Tyre. The armed men made directly for the harbor at the east end of the bay.

Yosef decided to investigate further. Turning south parallel to the road, which he no longer dared use, and wary of patrols that might be scouring the woods and coast, he moved with the utmost caution until he was lying in some shrubs overlooking the bay from the north. From here he had a clear view of the ships and could observe the activity surrounding them without detection.

By the time the sun was high in the sky, the area of the bay and the five large ships were bustling with activity. Many small boats were plying the space between the vessels and the shore. Most boats that left the shore were packed with armed men, and Yosef could see more soldiers lining the banks around the bay, waiting their turn to be ferried out to the ships.

It didn't take him long to realize that the vessels were to be used for an attack from the sea. They were equipped small mangonels, as well as frameworks that looked like copper tanks. At first he could not figure out what these were, then he realized that these were Greek Fire cauldrons!

The Sultan was preparing a force to be reckoned with, and surprise would be the key unless Yosef could get back this very night with a warning. He glanced up at the grey clouds gathering above and wondered. He was quite sure that Talon would be at the beach to greet him, no matter the weather, so he laid low and watched while he waited for dusk and his return to the pick up point. The activity carried on all day well into the late afternoon, as the army prepared to take to the sea. From his perch, Yosef estimated numbers of men and observed what manner of weapons they took with them aboard the ships.

A light rain began to fall as the sun set, and Yosef set out for the cliffs. The wind picked up and the sea became agitated, with small white crests. This worried Yosef, for the jagged rocks of the rendezvous could make matchwood of the boat if Talon misjudged the landing.

Yosef knew exactly where he had been dropped off. It remained for Talon to find it again in the dark and rain; no easy task. Yosef was hunkered under the scant cover of the stunted trees, when his ears pricked up. He had heard a sound that was alien to his surroundings. Voices!

Men were walking along the cliff edge, and soon they would be walking right past his new hiding place! Yosef eased an arrow out of his quiver. Then he pulled back even deeper into the shadows. This might be just a few men who had decided to take a walk, or it could be worse. A patrol in this area was the last thing he needed.

Yosef hoped not to have to use his bow, especially in the rain. Furtively he took the string out of his pouch and strung the bow, then eased a couple more arrows out of the quiver by his side.

The men who approached his hiding place were grumbling about the wet; the rain had increased considerably with the oncoming night.

"I want to make a fire," one of them said. "I am cold and wet and tired."

"We are supposed to be looking for infidel ships, not sitting around a fire warming our asses!" another stated. "Mind you, there is not much chance of that in this weather, God be praised."

"The Christians are bottled up in the city, and it's very unlikely that they will be sailing about in the dark, either. Suit yourselves," growled the former speaker. "I've had enough of being miserable. We can sit it out up here by the trees on the edge of the cliff until dawn and then go back, but I want to warm up."

"All right, but make sure it isn't visible from the bay," the leader said.

The first speaker set about looking for some dry kindling. The other two stood and talked while staring out to sea. The fire maker blundered about in the gloom under the trees. He came very close to the crouching Yosef, who caught the smell of onions on the man's breath, but Yosef had learned from Talon and Reza how to make himself utterly inconspicuous day or night, and this he achieved. The man poked around and finally went off with a small bundle of twigs and branches, totally unaware of how close he had come to having his throat slit.

Before very long, the three men had laid aside their spears and shields and were sitting cross-legged around a small, discreet fire that would only be visible from the sea. They began to relax and paid little attention to their surroundings, which allowed Yosef to glide by and ease himself down the cliff and onto the rocks directly below their camp.

Glancing up, he cursed silently as he noticed the glow of the fire above. It was like a beacon. Talon, if he could make it in this ever worsening weather, would home in on the fire like a moth to a flame, and there would be little Yosef could do about it, other than to be ready on the rocks when they landed. He crept along the sharp, black rocks in the pouring rain, keeping the fire in line with the landing site, then wedged himself into a crevice which allowed him some relief from the chill wind, and waited. He shivered. He was soaked to the skin.

*****

The visibility was poor when Talon and his very wet crew arrived in the general area of their rendezvous. He peered intently at the darker outline of the coast, searching for any sign of a signal from Yosef, praying that his companion was alive and well. They were hugging the coastline, but were acutely aware of the danger of coming too close and becoming snagged on some rocky outcrop. The surf on the shore was not the quiet wash it had been the night before, but a booming sound that warned them of the peril they risked should they make a mistake. The choppy waves were tossing their small boat about like a cork, and they were also shipping water.

"There!" Talon pointed towards the cliff's edge. "I see a light. Lower the sail, lads; we will have to row the rest of the way," he said in a hoarse voice.

The sail came down. Brandt and Caradog took up oars and bent their backs to the task. Dewi went forward with his bow, armed and ready for problems should they arise. Both he and Talon were peering intently at the dark, looming coastline. Caradog passed back several urgent whispers of warning from Dewi as they came too close to spume-covered rocks. Although it was painful for him to stand, Talon steered them, standing up in the thwarts of the boat, observing the black dangers slip by, then snapping his eyes forward again.

He was perplexed as to why there was a fire on the cliff. Yosef had carried a candle and tiny lantern with him. It would have been very dim and difficult to see from the sea, but a fire! What was the boy thinking?

They were now in the lee of the cliffs, and the rocks were uncomfortably close. The boom of the surf drowned out almost every other sound now as Dewi and Talon desperately

521

searched for the channel. Then Dewi called back in a low tone, "There is someone on the rocks ahead, Lord. I think it is him!"

Yosef didn't wait for the boat to touch shore. He jumped, and landed slightly off balance just next to Dewi, who reached out and seized him by his soaking cloak to steady him. "You right there, *Bach*?" Dewi enquired, barely able to see.

"We must leave! Now!" Yosef insisted, his tone urgent. "There are sentries up there!"

They all heard him, and both oarsmen immediately back-rowed hard, while Talon sought space enough to turn. They backed out of the tiny inlet and then negotiated the surf, the bows of the boat lifting high before plunging down the other side, the rowers pulling with all their strength to get them beyond the danger. After some harrowing rising and falling, with the big waves boiling by level with the thwarts, they settled into slightly calmer waters and were able to row off into the darkness.

No one said a word while this maneuver was carried out; the sea was demanding all their attention. Still maintaining silence, they arrived about a half league off shore, and on a sharp order from Talon the sail was raised. The small falukah scurried northwards with its soaked passengers. Everyone breathed a thankful sigh of relief.

Talon gripped his companion by the arm and said, "I am very glad you are safe, but did you really need a fire to tell us where you were, Yosef?" His tone implied a certain disapproval.

Yosef chuckled. "No, Lord. I didn't make the fire. Some sentries, sent to watch out for people just like you, lit it and were warming themselves as you came in. It's a good thing you saw the fire, though, after all, isn't it?" he laughed.

The others joined in with the relief all felt. Despite the cold and wet, they were glad to be bringing one of their own safely home.

"So did you find out anything of value?"

"Yes, I am fairly sure I did, Lord. The Sultan is preparing ships to attack from the sea." He went on to tell them all he had seen, and why he considered an attack imminent.

Talon was silent while he digested this information. He glanced up at the sky. If this weather persisted, it was unlikely that the Sultan would be able to get his troop-laden ships out of the shelter of the bay and out to sea the next day. They therefore had a chance in Tyre to prepare a welcome for the enemy.

"You did very well, Yosef. Let's get home and find a good fire." He was also pleased that Yosef had not left any evidence of his visit behind. Bodies were always an inconvenience, but three dead men around a fire on the cliffs would have shouted to the enemy that they had been compromised.

*****

Count Conrad was wakened from a deep slumber by loud voices at the entrance of his chambers. He sat up and tossed the blankets aside, burying the maid who had been his bed companion under the covers while he surged to his feet. A disheveled attendant came into the room, carrying a large candle, which threw shadows about the chamber walls. Conrad could hear the wind moaning outside, and rain was pelting against the shutters, rattling the dried wood.

"What in hell is going on?" the Count roared, rubbing his eyes.

"My Lord, you have a visitor! It is Lord Talon, and he says it is most urgent," his attendant said anxiously. He moved the candle to light others on the main table in the middle of the room.

"Blast and damnation! It must be well after midnight!" the Count protested. "Oh, very well, let him in." Behind his bluster the Count knew that Talon would not have come to wake him unless it was serious.

Talon hobbled into the room, and it became immediately apparent that he had been out of doors. His wet cloak dripped water all over the floor, and he was soaked to the skin, as was the shadowy companion at his side. Both looked bedraggled, but this did not detract from the determination in Talon's eyes, nor the purposeful stance of Yosef. The man's dark eyes missed nothing, the Count thought ruefully as he noticed Yosef's eyes slip towards the bed, registering another person.

"Where on earth have you come from, Talon? You look as though you took a dunking in the harbor."

"God's greetings, Lord. You are nearly right," Talon said, and offered a grin, swiping his dripping, lank hair aside. "I would not have troubled you, but this is too important to leave for morning."

"Get mulled wine for these men. Can't you see they are wet to the bone!" the Count called to his sleepy and aimlessly milling attendants.

"What is going on, Talon?" he asked, dispensing with rank. He reached for a couple of dry blankets lying on the dresser nearby and tossed them to the two wet men. Talon and Yosef shed their sodden cloaks and wrapped the blankets around their shoulders. The Count cast a surreptitious look at the bed, but the girl was motionless under the pile of covers. He gave a mental shrug.

"Last night, we put my man here ashore to try and find out what might be going on in the enemy camp, Lord," Talon told him.

Conrad gaped. "How in God's name did you manage that?" he jerked out.

"By boat, to the south of here," Talon replied shortly. "It is a good thing we did, because he made an interesting discovery. He can tell you in his own words. He speaks enough French."

Mulled wine arrived, and Conrad indicated that Talon and his man should sit. He took a seat across the table from them and listened with an incredulous look on his face. When Yosef finished, he took a deep swig from his cup and put it down slowly, a thoughtful look on his face.

"You are a man of many talents, Talon, and your man here is to be commended for his bravery in this venture. It is worthy of a knighthood. By God, yes it is! Now, tell me the details and numbers. We must be prepared. Do you think they will come with the dawn?" he demanded.

Yosef shook his head. "No, my Lord. I am sure they intended to do so, but this weather has thwarted that timing. They cannot sail tonight unless it clears up in a matter of hours, which is very unlikely."

"I agree with Yosef, Lord. We have some time now, but we will have to use it well. You have three ships in the harbor, they could be used...." Talon's voice trailed off.

"Three against five. Poor odds, methinks, but they are all we have. Hmmm, his ships will have to come close to our walls, and it is from there that we will strike at them. Our own ships can be used to block off the harbor entrance." Conrad banged his fist down onto the table. "Wake the garrison, but do not, I repeat do *not* sound any alarms. I shall hang anyone who rings a bell, priest or otherwise, *and* any impetuous trumpeters who are stupid enough to disobey me." He took another swig of wine. "We will be the ones to surprise the Sultan, by God! Not the other way around."

As several attendants scurried off, he turned back to Talon and Yosef. "You have done the city a great service tonight. We shall meet again in a few hours, when you have rested. I have need of your council, Lord Talon. Meanwhile, go and get dry; you are dripping all over my floor!" He laughed and rubbed his hands together. "I do so like surprises, especially when I am delivering them. Ha ha!"

*****

Talon and Yosef left the room while a voluble discussion was going on between the Count and his knights. It was Yosef who reached out and gripped Talon by the arm as they moved down the darkened stone passageway. "Someone was listening, Lord," he whispered.

Talon immediately stopped and listened himself. He became aware of a faint patter as feet ran off into the darkness. "Go, but be careful. Find out who it was," he instructed. "I shall wake the others. If the Sultan has spies here we might have a problem."

Yosef sped off, silent as a phantom, while Talon hobbled as fast as he could to his own chambers, which were not too far away. He woke his exhausted men and told them of his concern. At that moment, Yosef arrived breathless.

"I think it was a spy, Lord. He disappeared in the direction of the walls facing the causeway." He sounded chagrined at having missed catching whomsoever it might have been. Talon shrugged inwardly. Everyone was spying on everyone else! He should have known the Sultan would have someone working for him within the city.

"Come!" Talon barked. "We cannot let this get out. It is the perfect time for a spy to get over the walls. The rain and storm will mask his activity. He cannot just jump; he needs either help or a rope. Go, Yosef, and take the Welsh with you. Bows, men!" he called out.

The three vanished like eager hounds while Talon, frustrated by his leg, let Brandt help him along as fast as they could go. "Damn this leg!" he muttered, but he was sobered by the knowledge that if he had not had a good physician and the care from Yosef, he might not even have it. "Come, Brandt, we must hurry!" The big Saxon grunted agreement and helped him with the steps.

They arrived on the parapet in the darkness to find a small group of men clustered around the archers. Someone brought a torch just as Talon and Brandt arrived.

"You were right, Lord," Yosef said to Talon as he arrived. "Here is the rope still in place."

Talon muttered a curse. "Have you seen anyone cross the causeway?" he demanded. He turned to the sentries, although he knew the answer. Their garments were almost completely dry; they had not been patrolling the wind- and rain-swept parapets. They shook their heads. "What is happening, Lord?" one enquired.

"A spy is trying to escape and reach the Arab army," Brandt growled.

"There is one way to find out if anyone is still down there, Lord," Dewi said. "We toss torches down and flush him out."

"Several at once. If he is down below he will have to make a run for it," Caradog said.

"Good idea. Do it." Talon said. "Have your bows ready. Can you take a man down in this rain and darkness?" he enquired.

"*Dieu, Dieu, Bachan!*" Dewi said with a sniff. "How do you think we managed to steal so many cattle from the Saxons, Lord?"

Stifling a snort of amusement, Talon leaned over the parapet. Other sentries arrived, carrying torches. "Throw them down, there and there," Talon indicated.

The pitch torches flickered wildly and sizzled in the wind and rain, but they were well alight and, when tossed down, they illuminated the rocks below. Everyone on the battlements peered down. Initially they saw nothing, but then the sharp-eyed Caradog called out, "There! I see something!" He pointed to their left.

Sure enough, there was movement below. The spy may have noticed the activity on the battlements and intended to lie quiet until the hue and cry had died down, but now with the alarm well and truly raised he had no choice but to run the gauntlet. He leapt to his feet and began to sprint over the rocks towards the causeway.

"Wait for it, *Bach*," Dewi cautioned his fellow archer. "Let him get to the flat, and then we have him."

Caradog and he raised their bows and waited for the few moments it took for the desperately running man to gain the causeway, where he begin to sprint even faster as he felt the flat, even stones beneath his feet.

"Now!" Dewi called, and two bow strings twanged and two arrows sped off into the darkness. The dimly seen figure staggered, then sprawled face down on the stones and did not move again. The range had been in excess of seventy paces!

Yosef, who was no mean archer himself, nodded his head to Talon. "That was incredible," he remarked, with something akin to awe in his voice.

"Brandt, I want to know who it was. Bring the body back. Yosef, go with him and cover his back. We will do the same from here." Talon doubted it would be necessary, but preferred to err on the side of caution. His two men departed, leaving Talon and his archers scanning the causeway for any danger. "Good shooting," he commended them.

Talon gazed across the causeway towards the Arab lines. At least they had been able to stop one spy. He would have to alert the Count about the fact, of course, if he didn't already know by now.

They may have prevented the Sultan from learning that they knew of his plans to attack from the sea, assuming Tyre was indeed his target. But even if the rain delayed the Sultan's ships, it was just a matter of time, and he was stuck here until his own people in Cyprus came to collect him.

Whatever their successes this night, Tyre was still under siege, and there was no way out. Not for anyone.

*****

The next day, when the rain was beginning to ease and visibility was improving, a sharp-eyed sentry sighted a ship out to sea. The alarm was called out and men rushed to the walls. The Greek Fire cauldrons were started, and two mangonels, which had been hauled with great effort from the causeway side, were loaded with rocks, ready to be discharged.

Men stood to and stared over the water. Sure enough, a two-masted ship was beating its way through the choppy whitecaps, spray flying high as it made its way towards the city. The shape of the sails alarmed everyone, for it seemed to be a precursor to the Sultan's fleet, which by now everyone expected. There was surprise, too, that the enemy was prepared to fight in this kind of sea. The weather was inclement and would certainly make any attack on the seaward walls very hard to manage. Then, as the ship approached, Yosef and Talon both recognized it.

"It's one of ours, Lord!" Yosef gasped, his rough voice filled with emotion and excitement. It had never fully recovered since his wounding in China. "They have finally come, Lord!"

Talon reached out and gripped Yosef's upper arm hard. "Hold everything!" He bellowed to the men on the walls. He turned to the Count, who was standing on the damp battlements nearby, also watching. "It is one of my ships, Lord! I would know them anywhere, and it is flying my banner."

They watched with delight as the ship approached, trying to tell who captained it. Finally they decided it must be Henry. It was his ship, although they could not see his stocky frame on the afterdeck. They enjoyed hearing the gasps of surprise as watchers observed how skillfully the ship slid between the island and the city walls, then performed a nimble pirouette to negotiate the narrow entrance to the harbor.

"We have to greet them," Talon said, and snatched up his crutches. With the help of Brandt, he made his awkward way towards the harbor, closely followed by the Welshmen. Yosef had skipped ahead in his eagerness to meet the ship.

The vessel was already tying up when they arrived on the quay, and to their utter surprise it was not Henry, nor even Guy who greeted them, but Rostam who yelled excitedly from the deck and waved when he saw them coming along the stone wharf. The men on board cheered; they all seemed relieved to see Talon and Yosef.

Rostam gave a sharp order and men hauled the ship close to the wharf, then he jumped nimbly off the side of the ship, closely followed by Junayd. Both were yelling greetings as they rushed towards Talon. He stopped and waited, his heart pounding in his chest, too overcome with relief and joy at seeing them to say anything. Rostam opened his arms and embraced his father with fervor, as Junayd and Yosef did the same. Eventually Rostam released Talon, who held onto him, tears in his eyes and a look of amazement on his features. "You came, you came back for us!" he exclaimed, and embraced his son again.

Rostam gazed at his father with a huge grin on his face. "Of course we came back, Father! It just took longer than we thought."

Talon frowned, wondering why.

Junayd interrupted them to embrace Talon, and Yosef did the same for Rostam, then they took stock of one another. At this moment Rostam became aware of the crutches and noticed Talon was favoring his right leg. His father looked gaunt, as did Yosef.

"What happened to you, Father?" Rostam asked, his voice full of concern.

"A little accident, but we are doing well, my son. More importantly, how is your mother? And Reza, Jannat, Max, everyone? It is truly good to see you! We have been stuck here, waiting and wondering," Talon replied.

"I was just getting used to a diet of roasted rat," Yosef chortled, his excitement bubbling over.

After the laughter had died down Rostam spoke up. "There is much to tell, Father. Reza is well on the way to re-covering, but for a while it was touch and go. Mother has been worried sick about you, too, and says you are to come home at once!" he said with a laugh. Now he had time to ob-serve the others. He studied the huge man hovering protec-tively next to Talon; it was the Saxon he had seen once before during the sea battle. He wondered what he was doing with his father. There were also two short yet strong looking men, carrying what looked like long, shaped staves. He guessed they were bows.

Talon noticed his glance and said, "Brandt you have met before. Dewi and Caradog are from Wales. This is my son," he told them, with pride in his voice. "It appears that now he is a ship's captain, as well as a navigator." Talon waved at his new found retainers. "These men are part of our group, and I owe them much," Talon told Junayd and his son.

Junayd glanced at Yosef, who nodded agreement. "You have to see their archery to believe it!" he said. "As for the Saxon, he is a very useful man to have in a fight. Now we are friends," he added, with a smile at the huge man. "This is Ju-nayd, Brandt. His is my companion of many years."

Brandt looked Junayd over from under his heavy blond brows. He could see little difference between the two men. Lithe, dark, and very dangerous, he decided.

"It is good to know you are a friend," he said solemnly. "These two," he jerked his thumb at the Welshmen, "have hoodwinked Lord Talon into believing they are useful to have around. No doubt, when he realizes his mistake, he will want them thrown overboard, and I shall take great pleasure in doing that."

"Ignore that Saxon lump over there," Caradog stated with a sniff and a disdainful look at Brandt. "Jealous he is of our skills, see!"

Junayd and Rostam looked to Yosef for clarification.

"They always behave like this. Talon assures me they are friends. I really wonder about that at times. But they are very good fighters, and very trustworthy," he told them in Arabic.

"That *is* what counts in the end," Talon laughed, having overheard him.

Chapter 31

Homecoming

Home: I'd thought I'd held the place
through firestorm and sneak attack;
while all the time I'd fought to lose
any hope of coming back.
                    —*Jacob Polly*

They were slowly moving along the quay toward the ship, keeping pace with Talon, who was thumping along on his crutches when they all heard a shout from behind them.

"Lord Talon, please wait!"

"What now?" sighed Talon irritably, turning carefully to watch a servant of the Count running towards them, leading a horse. He came up to them, puffing with the exertion, and stopped before Talon to make a bow.

"Lord Conrad asks that you attend him on the eastern parapet, my Lord. He sent the horse to assist you." The servant presented the reins of the animal to a puzzled looking Talon, who handed off his crutches to Brandt.

"Must be important," he muttered. "Help me up, someone." Dewi made a cup with his hands and Talon scrambled onto the horse's back. "Do you want to come along, Rostam, Junayd?" he asked.

Junayd indicated the ship. "We have a guest on board, Lord. One of us should stay."

"Ah, yes. I'd forgotten about him; you brought him with you, eh? Interesting. Yosef can keep you company then, and tell you all about our adventures. Rostam, come with me and we'll find out what the Count wants. Might as well introduce you to him."

It was not far to the battlements, but the horse made a big difference to Talon, who had not relished the prospect of another long, limping walk. Accompanied by his archers, Brandt and Rostam, he arrived on the eastern battlements to find a large crowd of officers and knights peering off towards the shoreline. They made way respectfully for Talon, who came up to the Count and gave a short bow. "Good morning, Lord. I am here. What is it that you want of me?"

The Count smiled at him, glanced curiously at Rostam, then said, "Ah, Lord Talon. What do you make of that?" He gestured at the distant Arab army, which seemed to be unusually active. "D'you think they are getting ready for a fight?" he asked.

Talon stared across the causeway for a long time in silence, and then said carefully, "If I am not mistaken... that army is on the move, Sire." He paused to stare harder. "Look! They are picking up their sticks and leaving, Lord. I am sure of it!"

"You are sure, Talon?" the Count demanded.

"I am very sure, Lord. He is going to Jerusalem." Talon's tone was bitter. He shook his head with real anger. The siege might be lifted, but now it was the turn of Jerusalem, and the Sultan would have his way at any cost. He would also be back.

But those distant and future concerns made little difference to the men on the parapet. For a while, at least, they were free of the constraint of a siege. Men around them began to talk excitedly. "They are leaving!" was called out, and then the cry took hold and the men in the courtyard began to cheer. Before long everyone was shouting with joy, and finally the bells began to peal out. One after the other, the six chapels and churches rang their bells, and the crowd cheered.

The Count was pleased, but also sobered by the implications. "So, now he is heading for Jerusalem," he mused. "And there is nothing I can do about it!" He banged his clenched fist onto the parapet in frustration.

"'The Kingdom was lost at Hattin, Lord. Not here," Talon pointed out.

"But lost it is. That is what you are saying, Talon. Is it not?" The Count's tone was one of bleak bitterness. "Dear Lord God, but I wish we could save it somehow."

"If it is any comfort to you, Lord, I doubt we would have lost it had you been present at those crucial times," Talon said. His tone, too, was bitter with regret.

"Small comfort that is now, eh?" the Count stated, glaring at the departing army. "Well, God protect those poor souls in Jerusalem, but our duty here is clear. We remain and defend Tyre." He turned away from his glum contemplation of the activity on the other end of the causeway and looked at Rostam.

"Who is this?" he demanded.

"Lord Conrad, this is my son, Rostam," Talon declared, drawing his son forward by the arm. Rostam bowed politely to the Count and said, "My Lord, I am honored,"

"He is young," the Count stated, without taking his eyes off Rostam. "I could not help but notice that you brought that ship in very smartly," he smiled. "Where did you learn to captain a vessel?"

"I helped my father sail back from China, Lord."

Conrad's eyes opened wide with surprise. "Ah, I keep hearing strange things about you, Lord Talon, but there is even more to you and your family than I had imagined. You have a remarkable father here," he told Rostam. "I shall be very sorry to see him leave." He glanced at the activity going on to the east, then said, "I suppose you want to go home now, Lord Talon?" His tone was dour.

Talon nodded, his face grim. "Yes, Lord, I do. But I shall be helping you in the process."

"What do you mean?" The Count almost had to shout. It was a difficult to talk now, over the clanging of bells and the excited shouting going on all around them.

"Those ships were not coming here, Lord. They will be going to somewhere like Acre, or even Jaffa. I'd like to pay them a visit before I return home, with your permission."

The Count barked out a laugh. "You are not serious, Talon?" he said. "Your man said there were five of them, and you have but one ship, from where I am standing."

Talon put a hand on his son's shoulder. "Yes, Lord, but we have a little something that could surprise them." Talon knew he was taking a risk, because the Arab ships would have Greek Fire. However, that deadly stuff took time to prepare, and if they were taken by surprise he might be able to pull off an attack, then make off before they could arm their weapons.

Count Conrad gave a bellow of laughter at that. "Very well, and the good Lord go with you, Lord Talon. I admire your courage."

"You should know that the Sultan will be back, Lord. And next time he will stay, because whether or not he succeeds in taking Jerusalem, and I fear he will, he will want to deny the Crusaders an accessible port for all time. I shall send a ship from time to time with livestock and food for your people. Even if I have to steal it from the Emperor of Cyprus himself. You have my word."

Conrad chuckled. "I have heard nothing to make me think that Emperor is anything but a rogue. Steal what you can. And yes, I know the Sultan will be back, and before he comes there is much to be done. The first thing I need to do is to cut that causeway in two, then re-enforce the walls. Send me what you can, Lord Talon. I trust you to keep to your word." He grinned. "I shall bid you God speed and not keep you, or you might miss those ships you want to deal with. I think you are quite mad, by the way! Ha ha! Surprise is all, though, is it not?" He laughed again, and then without warning he embraced the surprised Talon. "I hope we meet again before too long," he said quietly.

"I, too, Lord. I shall see you again, God willing. May God protect you and this city. No one else is as capable," Talon said, and turned away. He would miss the brusque but cheerful leadership of this remarkable man.

*****

As they made their way through the celebrating crowds, with Brandt pushing people aside to let Talon ride through, Rostam looked up at his father. "He really admires you, Father," he commented. "It is clear from the way he talks to you."

"The feeling is mutual, Rostam. He stopped the city from being given away, and if I am not mistaken will continue to hold it against all odds. God protect him and his people."

It took only a short while for the archers and Brandt to collect all their belongings from the chambers they had occupied for those long weeks. Rostam and Junayd helped Talon onto the ship, and told him the events that had taken place at the castle. Soon his newfound companions were seen hurrying along the quayside, carrying their belongings and those of Talon and Yosef. Talon was of two minds about allowing the puppy on board, but one look at the stubborn jut of Brandt's jaw convinced him that it might be better to accept the fact that the Saxon was not going to be parted from his pet.

When everyone was aboard, the crew went to work and cast off. Talon watched critically as Rostam took charge. The boy knew what he was about. A few well timed orders, swift actions on the part of the crew, and they were clear of the city, passing the small islands scattered about to the north.

Once they were well on their way out to sea and moving southwest, the ship rising and falling in the ocean swell, Talon called a meeting on the upper deck. Junayd brought a chair from the main cabin for him, and Talon sat down. He sighed; his leg was mending, but too slowly for him. He was deep in thought for a few minutes, oblivious of his companions, who waited in respectful silence for him to speak.

Finally, he looked up from his reflections and said, "Everyone pay attention. We have some work to do before we go home, but first I want to talk to that pirate. Bring him up here, Junayd."

Makhid was brought up onto the deck, his chains clinking with every step. He looked very angry. "Why do you keep me in chains all the time?" he bellowed, shaking his arms angrily. Then he saw Talon and clinked his way over towards him. Yosef and Junayd forced him to his knees before the seated Talon, who eyed him up and down before speaking.

"After what I have been hearing I have every right to hang you from my masthead," he stated. "Your cousin's treachery is reason enough. The attack on my castle and my people? What do you have to say? And stop complaining about the chains. They will stay on as long as I want them to," he said.

"I gave my word not to try to escape, and I kept it," Makhid replied. His tone was sullen, but he also looked uncomfortable. "There is bad blood between myself and my cousin. I cannot speak for him. He has never been one to be trusted, and I dare say he was working with others when he tried for your castle."

Rostam and Junayd had told Talon that this was what they thought, too, so he nodded and said, "We are going to Acre. Behave until we get there, and then we will talk again. Meanwhile, you wear the chains for a little longer. Take him below." Junayd and another man hustled the protesting pirate below decks, and then Junayd returned to hear what else Talon had to say.

"We are going to pay a visit to a small harbor just over the horizon in that direction." Talon pointed east. "There are five ships which might already be on the move, but I would like to at least try to lessen their numbers a little before we go home. Do we all agree?"

Seeing the grins and hearing the excited murmurs, he continued. "Rostam, I will need you to stay in command of the ship, so who else is capable of working the Scorpions?"

Rostam didn't hesitate. "Junayd, of course, and Yosef is quite skilled, Father. I am confident that they can manage."

"Even the explosives?" Talon asked.

"Yes, Lord. Master Reza has spent a lot of time with us," Junayd told him.

"Good. Then here is what we are going to do. Rostam, please set a course just south of Tyre. Yosef, you stay with him long enough to show him what we are looking for, then help Junayd man the Scorpions. You were, after all, the one who saw the ships in that bay. God, but I hope they are still there," he added fervently.

"Dewi and Caradog, string your bows and be ready to use them. You will be assigned forward at first, to make sure no one takes a shot at our men while they work," he commanded, "but be ready to come back here in a hurry. Brandt, you stay with me. Incidentally, is there any food? My ribs are sticking to my backbone. We've been faring very poorly of late."

Junayd laughed and gave orders for a meal to be brought. Cold lamb, bread, olives, smoked fish and cheese appeared in short order. Talon helped himself with a sigh of relief, then motioned the others to take what they needed. Brandt seized a leg of chicken and a wing, surreptitiously slipping meat into his tunic. Dewi and Caradog reduced the brass tray of food to a few crumbs, watched in awe by the steersmen, then went forward, still stuffing their faces with cheese and fish.

"You'd think they had not eaten in a month!" Rostam laughed.

"In fact, we have not eaten well for about six weeks now," Talon replied. "But feast or famine, those two never change. I am truly concerned that we will not be able to survive their appetites."

Brandt, who was standing nearby, snorted his agreement.

"Are they as good as Yosef says they are?" Junayd asked with a skeptical glance at his friend.

"I would guess that they could kill a rabbit at well over one hundred paces," Talon said, but added when he saw their surprised expressions, "The down side to that is that they would have eaten it before anyone else got close."

Yosef nodded his head in emphatic agreement. "By God, I have never seen anything like their shooting—or their eating!" he grinned.

Everyone grew tense as they scanned the waters ahead for the expected fleet. Talon had hoped to find it still anchored in the bay. In this regard they were disappointed. As they rounded one of the promontories they could see that all the ships were under sail and slowly tacking towards the open waters.

"This changes things just a little, Rostam. You are going to have to go about very quickly once we have shot our Scorpions. We will only have one chance at one ship, and it is going to be a narrow opportunity."

"I hear you, Father," Rostam responded. He began to call out orders, which were relayed to the crew. Talon remarked how well the men responded to the young man's orders. There was genuine respect there, he noted. Before long they were speeding towards their objective with both sails as tight as drums and a brisk wind on their larboard quarter. Salt spray was thrown high into the air as the bows ploughed into the choppy waves.

Yosef wanted to stay near Talon. "I can protect you with my shield, Lord," he tsaid. But Brandt stepped forward and growled. "You go with them," he jerked his head at the bows. They need you there, Yosef. I will stay here and protect him, do not worry."

Yosef looked at Talon askance, but his Lord nodded and smiled. "Go forward, Yosef. I think it is important that you help Junayd. I am well protected here with Brandt."

"They are taking a chance with the weather," Talon observed to Rostam as their ship raced to intercept the enemy before they could get to the open sea. "The Sultan must be in a hurry to get to Jerusalem. We might have to tack smartly out of the bay, after we are done. I want to get at least one of them!" Talon thumped the arm of his chair.

Rostam observed his father's tight features. "That may not be necessary, Father. If we don't have to go into the bay too far, it will be easier to get back out, and they are coming towards us." Rostam pointed to the leading ship, which was just approaching the narrow entrance to the bay.

"Go straight for that one, Rostam," Talon commanded. His son nodded agreement and called a course over to the steersmen. Their galley heeled a little to larboard, then settled onto its new course, their bow pointing straight at the side of the leading ship.

Talon motioned Brandt over. "Our galley is not unlike their ships, so their lookout might take us for one of their own. I'd like to get in as close as possible. As Lord Conrad is fond of saying, surprise can make all the difference. Cover your head, Brandt. You'd be a giveaway with your light hair."

Brandt nodded and went below, to re-appear with a cloak and a hood that covered his head. Then he came and stood just a few paces in front of the seated Talon, holding his large shield at the ready. At a low spoken suggestion from Talon, several other men carrying shields were detailed off by Rostam to stand by the steersmen. Talon knew all too well how a well aimed arrow could disrupt these men and leave a ship floundering. By this time their galley was within half a league of the enemy ships. These were large, lumbering vessels that Talon estimated had been captured in Acre when that city was taken. Now they were being put to good use by the Sultan to transport a sizable part of his army. The ships were ideal for transporting troops and horses, but not as nimble as his own ship. He felt more confident that they could outmaneuver them when the time came.

Everyone on the galley was quiet now. Junayd and Yosef were crouched over their Scorpions, the two Welsh archers hidden just behind them. Dewi and Caradog had never encountered these smoldering menaces; they stared wide-eyed at the contraptions which Talon's companions so confidently prepared for their deadly work.

The tension on the ship became even more intense as they approached the lead vessel. Now they could see men standing on the decks, watching them; some even waved, mistaking them for an ally come to escort them. But as the course of the galley continued without change and without any acknowledging signal, signs of alarm became evident. Men could now be seen running about, while others pointed and gesticulated towards the silent ship bearing down on them.

"Ready the Scorpions!" Rostam yelled. Junayd and Yosef waved. They were ready; a thin tendril of smoke that drifted up from their positions was blown forward by the wind to disperse over the bows. They were now within sixty long paces of the transporter. They could see the crowded decks, even some horses, and hear shouts of alarm from men who thought they were going to be rammed.

"Break out the banner!" Talon called, and the two men on the top of the mast released his banner to the wind. It streamed straight out, clear for all to see, and the crew cheered. There was further consternation on the other ship as they realized that they had been tricked, but it was far too late for them to do anything about it.

Talon and Rostam were both fidgeting with impatience. They had left it to their men to decide when to release their missiles, but they were cutting it very fine. If Junayd and Yosef delayed too long there was a risk of collision; if they loosed their spears too soon they might not strike in the right place. Then everyone heard the first loud twang of a giant bowstring, and a long, dark object streaked out from the larboard bow.

The distance was a mere forty paces, and closing. The spear hammered into the wood just below the anchor stone, and for a moment while everyone held their breath it just stayed there, smoking. Some of the people on the other ship were even staring down at the long spear jutting out of the bows when it exploded. There was a flash and a huge bang, and the shock wave washed over the people on Talon's galley. The front of the transporter seemed to disintegrate in a storm of splinters and chunks of railing which flew high into the air. Then, as Rostam had the steersman begin their turn away from their victim, the other Scorpion string twanged, jerking the machine in its mounts, and another arrow streaked across the narrowing distance between the ships. This one disappeared into the smoke and chaos, and it must have struck lower, for when it exploded the sea around the area boiled briefly.

Not even waiting to see the results, Rostam was already howling orders at the crew, who leapt into action. The rowers thrust their oars out and hauled on them for all they were worth. The galley seemed to come to a stop in a flurry of foam and mad activity; the sails were hauled round and the vessel heeled. Briefly the sails flapped angrily, then went taut again, and their galley began to pick up speed. Now they were almost parallel to the stricken transporter, which had also slowed almost to a stop.

"Archers!" Talon called, and Dewi and Caradog came running to stand on the larboard side and begin their game of death. The officers and crew of the stricken vessel were so shocked by what had happened that they were slow to react and thus made easy targets; Talon had told the two men to shoot anyone who looked as though he was a leader. Junayd and Yosef, not to be left out, soon joined them. No one on the other ship dared to show themselves after the first few volleys of arrows downed their comrades.

"Good work!" Talon called to his men, who laughed and continued to contribute to the chaos and panic on the enemy ship. But soon the stricken vessel was far behind, and the archers finally stopped their deadly work.

"That was like shooting fish in a bar'rel, *Bach*!" Dewi exclaimed happily. They could all see that the transporter was sinking; the remnants of the shattered bows were dipping into the choppy seas and not rising as they normally should. It was not long before the entire ship was wallowing deeper in the water. The frantic activity on board was focused on getting boats launched and abandoning the vessel.

"Father, it looks as though they will sink across the entrance of the bay!" Rostam exclaimed.

Talon agreed. "I hope so. That will delay the other ships for a while." The other ships were still under sail and approaching the stricken transporter. There was no more that he could do now; it was time to leave. The screams of the dying and wounded receded as the galley picked up speed and made for the open sea.

"I have kept my word to the Count," Talon told his son. "There is one more thing I would like very much to accomplish, and then we go home. Set sail for Acre."

*****

From the deck of the third vessel, His Excellency the Sultan Salah Ed Din peered forward at the sinking ship, which was partially obscured by smoke. "Who was the owner of that galley?" he demanded of his brother, Al-Adil, who was also staring in fascination at the destruction before them. "I am sure I know that banner. Was it Lord Talon de Gilles?"

"You are not mistaken, Brother," Al-Adil ground out between clenched teeth. "It was indeed his banner, of that I am sure. God curse the son of a dog!"

"We will be delayed because of this, and I am not pleased. Perhaps the *next* time you have him within your power you will insist upon having his parole *before* you begin any other negotiations?" the Sultan's tone was cutting.

"The next time, I shall immediately execute the slippery dog and not even bother to get his parole," Al-Adil muttered to himself.

*****

The galley hove to within sight of the walls of Acre, and waited. The Christian banners, which had been a familiar sight in the past, no longer fluttered from the battlements; they had been replaced by the banners of the various Arab nobles who had taken up residence. Dominating the lesser ones was a single enormous banner with the crescent and the sword emblazoned upon a green background.

Talon ordered that Makhid be brought up on deck and relieved of his chains. "Provide him with the best clothes in the cabin, and help him with his toilette," Talon ordered. "Would you like a shave?" he asked the bemused pirate solicitously.

"What are you going to do to me?" the prisoner demanded aggressively. "Clean me up, then hang me in front of those walls?"

Talon struggled to a standing position, supporting himself with a hand on Brandt's shoulder, and glared back. "Don't think it has not crossed my mind!" he snapped. "I have every right to do so after the treachery displayed by your cousin. But I shall not. I made a half-promise to your cousin Prince Al-Adil that I might release you, and I intend to keep my word," he told the surprised man. "A boat will be coming out soon to investigate our business, and you will be free to go."

Just at that moment, they heard a call from the masthead. "Sail coming out of the city!"

Sure enough, a small dhow with a single lateen sail came speeding towards them, and rounded smartly once it was parallel with them. "Who are you and what is your business?" someone shouted.

"We have a passenger for you," Junayd shouted back. "Send a boat over." Within minutes, a small dingy was bobbing over the agitated waves to pull alongside.

Just as he moved to descend to the main deck and over the side, Makhid was stopped by a hand on his arm.

"Remember, I still have your son. Find the monk. If he is not in Acre, then send back a message to that effect. If he lives and is still there, send him to me. I trust your word, Makhid. Give my best regards to Al-Adil and tell him I kept *my* word. Safe journey, and God's blessing. I think you will need it with your other cousin. *Salaam.*"

Makhid frowned. "Have no fear, Lord Talon. I keep my word. I entrust my son to you, and I shall do my best to find the monk. *Salaam.*" He went over the side and was soon seen boarding the other vessel, which set sail, and they watched it speed towards Acre.

"What now, Father?" Rostam asked.

"We wait, and while we wait you will tell me all about what has been going on at home. And for the love of God, feed those two archers or they will eat the dog, and then there will be blood all over the place!" Talon patted his son on the arm with a smile. "I promise I shall tell you all about our adventures in return, but I am eager to hear your side of things. Is your mother well?"

A good four hours later, when a disappointed Talon was ready to depart because the light was changing and Rostam was looking apprehensively at the sky, the lookout shouted down that a sail had emerged from the harbor. Once again, the dhow came speeding towards them and drew close.

"Ahoy there! We have a passenger for you. Send a boat over."

Talon breathed a sigh of relief. He peered over and could just make out the features of a ragged figure seated in the middle. He smiled and said to Rostam, "Go and help him, son. He is going to need it, by the look of him, to come aboard. His name is Brother Martin, and he is a good man. He helped us with our troubles in Acre."

*****

Two days later, they came within sight of land, and Talon could just make out the castle high on the mountain ridge. "There she flies, Yosef!" he called out. He felt a surge of excitement and relief at seeing his home emerge from the light haze over the sea. They watched as a thin line of smoke reached into the sky to emit a small bright flash. "They have seen us. We are home."

Yosef came to stand next to him, barely able to contain his excitement, and they watched together as Rostam negotiated the harbor entrance and nosed the galley into the quiet waters.

There was a large crowd to greet them on the quayside, and to his delight there was Rav'an, his beautiful Rav'an, standing quite still and watching him. Pressed against her legs were the two hounds, held in check by Dar'an, who was grinning like a porpoise. Then his eyes picked out Jannat, and to his surprise and relief there was Reza beside her, standing straight but he looking a lot thinner.

The shouts of greeting drowned out any words, so he waited impatiently until their ship was tied up. Then, with Brandt's help, he was able to negotiate the narrow gangway and limp across the short intervening space to stand in front of his family.

He saw the shock in their faces, but he smiled to reassure them. His heart was beating very hard now, to the point where he thought it must burst from his chest as his gaze locked with that of Rav'an. He noticed that Jannat was crying. Without waiting, she rushed up to him and embraced him, her tears wetting the side of his neck. "There, there, Sister. I am here and well; don't weep so," he chided her gently, as he held her hard to his chest. Then he released her back to Reza, whose eyes were also wet.

"Welcome back, Brother. We have missed you." Reza grinned and embraced him carefully.

"Are you better now, Brother?" Talon asked, his voice thick with held in emotion, holding him out by the arms. "You look thin."

"Never better Brother, and so do you. Who would not be better with these lovely ladies to take care of me?" Reza laughed shakily and gripped his arms hard, emotion making his mouth tremble.

Dar'an was next, with the excited, writhing, squealing hounds getting in the way of their embrace. "I am glad to see you, Lord. You have been missed," he said, and dashed tears away from his eyes. Talon smiled at him with deep affection.

"Rostam has told me of your good work, Dar'an. I thank you from my heart."

Talon turned then to the waiting Rav'an and held his arms open to her. She dashed away her own tears and walked into his embrace. They held each other hard for a very long moment, oblivious of the murmurs of the crowd around them. She was trying desperately not to cry, but her eyes were very wet when they finally parted. The crowd cheered wildly, even more so when he kissed her on the lips in front of everyone.

Oblivious of the gawking villagers and crewmen and the excited chatter around them, they looked at one another. She nodded silently, tears running down her cheeks. It was as though she was responding to the words he thought but could not say here, but would be spoken later when they were alone.

"For ever and ever my Princess!" he said with a crooked smile. At this point she gave a delighted laugh through her tears. "You remembered, my Prince!"

"Always, my Princess. It is good to be home at last. I have missed you so very much," he told her with another grin, and, holding her tight around her waist, he turned and waved at the cheering crowd.

"Is Max well, and Theodora? Our children?"

"They are all well and await you at the castle. Welcome home, my Talon."

The End

Author's Note

The year 1187 was a catastrophe for the Christian world, although the Byzantine church, having experienced similar disasters in the past, might have shrugged and blamed the Latin church and its Crusaders for the debacle which heralded the final and irretrievable loss of Jerusalem to the Moslems. There was little love lost between the two orders of Christianity.

Talon and his family have grown with the times; but he, like so many others, had no control over the events that took place in this particular year. It was a challenge to weave his story alongside the larger than life names of people like the Sultan, Salah Ed Din, aided very effectively in his mission by General Muzaffar ad Din-Gökburi a very capable general. Salah Ed Din dominated events and therefor their consequences, and eventually realized his life's ambition by taking back Jerusalem for the Arab world. His place in history as one of its great leaders was assured after Hattin.

History has not been kind to the others, nor should it be; but we can neither ignore them nor undo what they did. These men, Raynald Châtillon, Gérard de Rideford and Guy de Lusignan, by their mind-numbing arrogance and willful ignorance of the country wherein they held sway, threw away every opportunity provided to them and lost the entire Kingdom of Jerusalem to the Arabs. Perhaps lessons can be learned from their stories but it is doubtful.

One name that I felt I could weave Talon alongside, because they were both native to this conflicted land, was Count Raymond of Tripoli. He was a *pullani*, like Talon, born to the land as a Lord, rare in that he truly understood and respected the peoples amongst whom he lived, a man who is historically in the half-shadows because he was really on neither side. Raymond, who knew the Arab world as well as his own, was focused on his own survival. For that he was largely reviled by those few who did record the times from the Latin perspective, including the Bishop of Tyre, who favored Lusignan and his ilk. Raymond was more kindly regarded by the Arab chroniclers of his time, and he is generally thought of as being respected and liked by Salah Ed Din.

I attempted to describe what might have transpired between Salah Ed Din and Raymond. He was desperate to survive and protect Tripoli, despite the foolishness of the people in Jerusalem. However the end result was that an army of Salah Ed Din did indeed cross his lands, thus technically breaking the fragile truce, and that led to the battle of the *Springs of Cresson,* which was the disastrous forerunner to the conclusive, and equally disastrous battle of the *Horns of Hattin.* The lead up to these conflicts and the siege of Tyre needed only some small tweaks, because it is well recorded that Rideford, the Grand Master of the Templars, most certainly did destroy his own Order and that of the Hospitaliers, and later betray them even further as a prisoner. They did eventually recover but never in the Holy Land.

It was as though the devil was seated on Rideford's shoulder helping him lead the disastrous charges, reaping the souls of the dead, and then making sure that he survived to repeat the crimes. The battles are described as closely as I could research them, but of course our hero could not be killed in the conflict, so he too survived.

It was too tempting to bring into play the shenanigans at the palace of Cyprus, so forgive the license. Isaac and his minions went on through life as though the titanic events in

Palestine were not even taking place, such were the limitations upon communications at that time. The invasion of Cyprus by the Byzantines never did occur, although it had certainly been planned. The fleet that was sent from Constantinople was intercepted by another fleet from Sicily. The Byzantine ships were destroyed by the Norman King William.

One must not forget the irrepressible and courageous character of Count Conrad de Montferrat who held Tyre throughout, even when Salah Ed Din came back to try again after taking Jerusalem. The Arabs called the Count *al-Markis: "He was a devil incarnate in his ability to govern and defend a town, and a man of extraordinary courage."* They admired him greatly. He held the city until Richard the Lion-heart arrived in 1192.

But that is another story.

People are often surprised at the seemingly endless violence and bloodshed which took place in the Middle Ages. It was indeed a very bloody era, both in Europe and in the region, then known as the Crusader states. It is simply impossible to disguise the fact that life was so very cheap in those days.

Why did Gérard de Rideford hate the Count of Tripoli so much, to the point of blindness to any good advice? The Count had promised Rideford a ward, Cecile Dorel, in marriage, and then changed his mind and married her off to a wealthy merchant for a huge sum of money. Rideford, having lost the chance of a fortune, took a vow of poverty and joined the Templars, but his hate continued to fester to the point of madness.

And no, I shall not apologize for the Welsh archers, nor the foul-mouthed Saxon. They just showed up and that's that! People like them do appear unexpectedly from time to time, you know.

James Boschert

About The Author

James Boschert

James Boschert grew up in the then colony of Malaya in the early fifties. He learned first-hand about terrorism while there as the Communist insurgency was in full swing. His school was burnt down and the family, while traveling, narrowly survived an ambush, saved by a Gurkha patrol, which drove off the insurgents.

He went on to join the British army at the age of fifteen, serving in remote places like Borneo, Malaya and Oman. Later he spent five years in Iran before the revolution, where he played polo with the Iranian Army, developed a passion for the remote Assassin castles found in the high mountains to the North, and learned to understand and speak the Farsi language.

Escaping Iran during the revolution, he went on to become an engineer and now lives in Arizona on a small ranch with his family and animals.

IF YOU ENJOYED THIS BOOK

Please write a review.
This is important to the author and helps to get
the word out to others.

Visit

PENMORE PRESS
www.penmorepress.com

All Penmore Press books are available directly through our website, amazon.com, Barnes and Noble and Nook, Sony Reader, Apple iTunes, Kobo books and via leading book-shops across the United States, Canada, the UK, Australia and Europe.

OTHER TALON BOOKS BY JAMES BOSCHERT

ASSASSINS OF ALAMUT
BY
JAMES BOSCHERT

An Epic Novel of Persia and Palestine in the Time of the Crusades

Knight Assassin
The second book of Talon
by
James Boschert

Assassination
in
Al Qahira
James Boschert

GREEK FIRE
BY
JAMES BOSCHERT

A Falcon Flies
by
James Boschert
The fifth book of Talon

The Dragon's Breath

by

James Boschert

Talon stared wide-eyed at the devices, awed that they could make such an overwhelming, head-splitting noise. His ears rang and his eyes were burning from the drifting smoke that carried with it an evil stink. "That will show the bastards," Hsü told him with one of his rare smiles. "The General calls his weapons 'the Dragon's breath.' They certainly stink like it."

Talon, an assassin turned knight turned merchant, is restless. Enticed by tales of lucrative trade, he sets sail for the coasts of Africa and India. Traveling with him are his wife and son, eager to share in this new adventure, as well as Reza, his trusted comrade in arms. Treasures beckon at the ports, but Talon and Reza quickly learn that dangers attend every opportunity, and the chance rescue of a Chinese lord named Hsü changes their destination—and their fates.

Hsü introduces Talon to the intricacies of trading in China and the sophisticated wonders of Guangzhou, China's richest city. Here the companions discover wealth beyond their imagining. But Hsü is drawn into a political competition for the position of governor, and his opponents target everyone associated with him, including the foreign merchants he has welcomed into his home. When Hsü is sent on a dangerous mission to deliver the annual Tribute to the Mongols, no one is safe, not even the women and children of the household. As Talon and Reza are drawn into supporting Hsü's bid for power, their fighting skills are put to the test against new weapons and unfamiliar fighting styles. It will take their combined skills to navigate the treacherous waters of intrigue and violence if they hope to return to home.

PENMORE PRESS
www.penmorepress.com

Historical fiction and nonfiction
Paperback available for order on line
and as Ebook with all major distributers

Assassins of Kantara

by

James Boschert

After returning the heads of assassins to the Master of Hashashini, Talon flees with his family and closest companions to the Kingdom of Jerusalem to escape retribution. But death and disaster follow them, dashing hopes of finding a safe haven. Talon and Max travel to Cyprus only to discover that it is ruled by a psychopathic tyrant. The self-styled emperor Isaac Komnenos captured the island earlier in the year with the help of mercenaries and is plundering his kingdom into destitution. When Talon swindles Komnenos out of a prominent castle fortress, he quickly earns the emperor's enmity and the population's support.

With old and new enemies determined to eliminate him, Talon must bring to bear the martial arts skills he learned in China, his training as an assassin, and his skills as a leader. At stake is his survival—and that of his newfound followers.

PENMORE PRESS
www.penmorepress.com

Penmore Press

Challenging, Intriguing, Adventurous, Historical and Imaginative

www.penmorepress.com